Vamos Caminando
A Peruvian Catechism

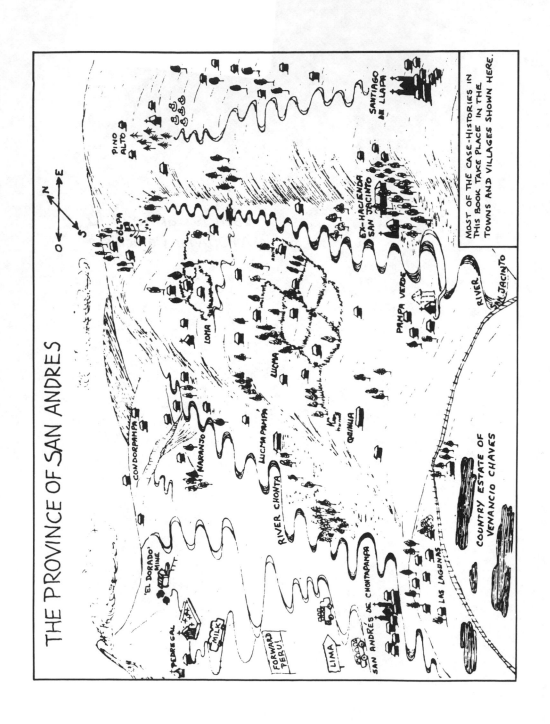

THE PROVINCE OF SAN ANDRES

MOST OF THE CASE-HISTORIES IN THIS BOOK TAKE PLACE IN THE TOWNS AND VILLAGES SHOWN HERE.

Vamos Caminando
A Peruvian Catechism

Pastoral Team of Bambamarca

SCM PRESS LTD

Translated by John Medcalf from the Spanish
Vamos Caminando
published by Centro de Estudios y Publicaciones,
Lima, Peru 1977

334 01744 0

First published in English 1985
by SCM Press Ltd
26–30 Tottenham Road, London N1

Typeset at The Spartan Press Ltd, Lymington, Hants
and printed in Great Britain by
The Camelot Press Ltd, Southampton

Contents

Introduction
by John Medcalf

Hilaire Belloc's quip that 'The Faith is Europe; Europe is the Faith' sounds oddly antediluvian in this penultimate decade of the twentieth century. The majority of the world's Christians now live in the three continents known collectively as the Third World, that vast and variegated underbelly of the planet where sixty-five per cent of our fellow human beings enjoy less than fifteen per cent of the wealth and resources of the earth.

The Northern Andes of Peru, scenario of this book, contain in fairly typical form most of the characteristics of a third-world country: an increasing impoverishment, land tenure problems, migration on a large scale to the cities, the maleficent presence of multinational companies, the inefficiency caused by over-centralization of government, a rapid breakdown of basic health and educational services over the past decade, and an alarming increase in the malnutrition of the majority of the population.

Against this background of Andean deprivation the Good News of the Risen Christ is being proclaimed with vigour, and the present book, written by the Pastoral Team of Bambamarca in the northern part of the diocese of Cajamarca, is a powerful testimony to the capacity of the post-conciliar Catholic Church in Latin America to adapt to the cultic and cultural needs of the Amerindian population. Inevitably, European and North American readers will recognize the pervading influence of Liberation Theology, which can be said to have received its birth certificate in Peru with the publication in 1971 of the pioneer work of Gustavo Gutierrez (*A Theology of Liberation*). Yet in spite of repeated references in this book to 'liberation', 'freedom' and 'deliverance', it would be more accurate to speak simply in terms of a 'gospel' theology, in which ortho-praxis is seen as no less important than ortho-doxy.

In this translation I have tried to preserve the unsophisticated imagery of the original Spanish; lack of sophistication and urbanity do not, of course, indicate shallowness or an inferior culture: quite the contrary. Several words, terms or phrases have been difficult to translate, precisely because our European culture has become so urbane. The protagonists of the book are known as 'campesinos' in the original Spanish version; after much deliberation I decided against the word 'peasant' as a translation of this word, and decided in favour of 'farm-worker'. I also decided not to inflict on English-speaking readers the local currency unit (its galloping inflation rate of over a hundred per cent per annum would have rendered all costs and prices meaningless), but to use the US dollar, which is in any case the normal point of monetary reference throughout Latin America. Other similar changes have been made for the sake of a clearer understanding of the text.

The structure of the book is simple. Fifteen units or sections are divided into one hundred and seventy chapters. Each chapter, or double page, is intended as complete lesson material for a small group of Christians, usually for use at their weekly meetings in their mountain homes, villages or churches. A fictitious mountain province called San Andres is the backcloth to all the case-histories, though all of these are inspired by real-life situations. Although the principal authors of the text (Manolo Sevillano, Miguel Garnett and Rudi Eichenlaub) disclaim the title 'catechism' for this book, there is nevertheless a sufficiently complete treatment of the major tenets of Christian belief to permit certain comparisons with the Dutch, German and other catechisms produced in Europe in the years following the Second Vatican Council; however, a greater appreciation of local cultural influences and a recognition of their importance in the growth of faith is present in the Peruvian work.

Even the casual reader of this Andean catechism will recognize the influence of European thinkers like Darwin, Marx and Freud, in addition to the more indigenous cultural background. It must be remembered in this connection that it is Latin America that is the closest of the three third-world continents to the European heritage of thought and culture; the blood of the conquistadores runs freely in a great part of the mestizo population. This unique blend of indigenous and European ('Latin') blood has produced a highly particularized cultural environment which has, in its turn, moulded the forms of Christianity and given the world a harvest of saints, scholars and (especially in Central America) martyrs.

May we Christians of the 'old world' have the courage to recognize in the simple, direct Good News from the Andes, the voice of God's Spirit speaking through the new 'anawim', the poor of Yahweh. Beneath their straw sombreros and multi-coloured ponchos a cry of the heart has been discerned by all of us who have had the great privilege of living and working in Peru: 'Vamos Caminando!' 'Let Us Go Forward!'

We are Farm-workers

'The Andes are pregnant with hope. No longer are they inhabited by a race characterized by submission and resignation. New gusts of wind are blowing through mountain villages and homesteads. The "New Indians" have appeared . . .

The distinctive feature of the "New Indian" is not so much his newly acquired knowledge as his new-found spirit. He waits. He has an aim in life. There is his secret and his strength. Everything else in him is secondary.'

(José Carlos Mariátegui, 1895–1930, Peruvian essayist and founder of the first Trades Union Confederation)

The farm-worker

Talking points

▷ Who are you? What do you do?

▷ What is your life like?

▷ Where did you come from?

▷ Where are you going?

▷ Do you live alone?

I'm a poor 'campesino'
and this is my song:
that I wear a patched poncho
and here I belong,
and that is what life is about!

Work with your spade,
Work without rest,
Only hard struggle
can change worst to best.

The family

Talking points

▷ The woman in this drawing is worried? Why?

▷ What is a woman's life like?

▷ How do children in the Andes live?

▷ What happens when somebody falls ill in your family?

▷ Where do you live?

The farm

Talking points

▷ What is your farm like?

▷ Large or small?

▷ Does it produce enough to feed your family?

▷ If not, what do you do to feed them?

▷ For whom do you work?

▷ Can small farms go it alone?

The community

Talking points

▷ Describe your village.

▷ Who are the village authorities?

▷ How do they behave?

▷ Do the villagers perform any community tasks?

▷ How many times a year is your village church opened?

▷ Can you stay in your village without ever leaving it?

The town

Talking points

▷ Why do you go to town?

▷ Sometimes you like going to town. Why?

▷ Other times you dislike the town. Why?

▷ Why do you pay for a Mass for the dead?

▷ When you go to market, how much do you get for your produce?

▷ Do they pay you a just price?

▷ Why do townspeople work?

▷ To get richer and richer?

▷ Is God pleased that there are rich and poor?

and so . . .

If your work doesn't benefit you and your family . . .

If other farm-workers take advantage of you . . .

If the townspeople become rich at your expense . . .

If they tell you that it's God's holy will that you put up with the hardships and injustices of this life . . .

What can we do?

What should we do?

The mayor of San Andres de Chonta-pampa once tried to impose an unjust and unlawful tax on all the farm-workers.

In every community there were meetings to discuss the new tax, and everybody was against it.

One Sunday we said: 'Let's have a bigger meeting, with one person from every community.'

A Central Committee was formed.

Then we said: 'Let's have a protest meeting in the town itself!'

And so on the agreed day people came into town from all the villages and communities. Only very young children and really old people stayed behind to look after the animals and guard the maize crop.

The main square was packed tight with thousands of farm-workers from all parts. The mayor had gone into hiding somewhere, and there were very few police on duty. The townspeople had closed their shops and shuttered their windows, because they were afraid. During the meeting lots of people spoke, including two women. Anyone who wished to speak was allowed to do so.

It was a marvellous gathering of farm-workers from all over the province. There was no violence and no drunkenness, and because of what we did the mayor agreed to forget all about the unjust tax.

Talking points

▷ Do farm-workers suffer from injustice in your area?

▷ What can you do about it?

▷ Why is it usually so difficult for farm-workers to organize themselves?

▷ How can we overcome these difficulties?

▷ Some people say that farm-workers can't do anything to improve their lot unless they join up with the town-workers.

▷ What do *you* think?

We can be sure of one thing: God doesn't want us to be exploited or to live in dire poverty. The Bible, the Word of God, makes this very clear.

When the Hebrew slaves were being exploited by the Egyptians, God didn't take a siesta. He called Moses and told him that the people must be set free. Moses put all his trust in God and organized the Hebrew people. And the people finally won their struggle.

The Lord works vindication and justice for all who are oppressed. He made known his ways to Moses. (Ps. 103.6f.)

But you, Israel, my servant,
Jacob, whom I have chosen,
the offspring of Abraham, my friend.
Fear not, for I am with you,
be not dismayed, for I am your God;
I will strengthen you, I will help you,
I will uphold you with my victorious right
*   hand.* (Isa. 41.8–10)

We shall change our fate
if we stand together.
We shall starve to death
if we stand alone.
Like eucalyptus trees
we must grow together,
like Andean peaks,
we are proud of our might.

Let's walk with the Lord

Lord, you show the poor the way,
look on us and have mercy,
for we are poor,
and no one gives us help.

Show us your ways, Lord,
to free your people. (after Ps. 25)

UNIT 2

Our Family Life

Pity the farm-worker's child
Who must forget that he is a child
To do a man's work in the fields.

(popular saying)

The path of life

Juan Chuquimango and his wife Gumer-cinda, from the village of Condorpampa, are walking slowly homewards. It's a difficult and tiring journey, as always.

'All that mud!'

'But we'll be home in a jiffy!'

'Come on!'

'There always seems more uphill than downhill.'

'Well, if we don't do it, we'll never reach home.'

Talking points

▷ Why do farm-workers have to travel so much?

▷ Can you live without ever travelling?

▷ Has travelling anything to be said in its favour?

The whole of life is a path

Talking points

▷ Where does the path of life begin? Where does it end? Sometimes we feel that our life is useless and pointless. Life is short, and full of suffering, like a path that is muddy and mostly uphill.

Perhaps we sympathize with these words in the Bible:

Has not man a hard service upon earth,
and are not his days like the days of a
*   hireling?*
Like a slave who longs for the shadow,
and like a hireling who looks for his
*   wages?* *(Job 7.1f.)*

▷ So, why go on?

Because we know that the path of life has a lot of beautiful things as well.
These make it worth while.
When the path of life becomes hard we can meet God. Jesus has said:

'I am the Way, the Truth and the Life.'
(John 14.6)

▷ Which good things and which bad things do you find in *your* life?

▷ Who accompanies you along the path of life?

Let's walk with the Lord

To our church at last arriving,
Long the journey, hard the striving,
But you teach us to be free,
And your path we now can see.
O Father, Son, Spirit,
We give you our hearts.

Blessed is the man who walks not in the counsel of the wicked, but his delight is in the law of the Lord. He is like a tree planted by streams of water, that yields its fruit in its season. For the Lord knows the way of the righteous, but the way of the wicked will perish. *(after Ps. 1.1–6)*

Our home

The Chuquimango family are together in the kitchen. The two older sons have just returned from a journey. While Gumercinda, the mother, cooks over the open wood fire, the younger children warm themselves and the men talk.

'How did the trip go, my boy?' asks Juan.

'Pretty good on the whole, Dad. We've brought back mangos and bananas.'

'Nothing happened during the journey?'

'Not to us, but Jaime Longa was scared out of his wits by Cunshe, who pretended to be a ghost just when we were going round the last mountain in darkness. We killed ourselves with laughing!'

'And I expect Jaime crept off pretty quickly.'

'He certainly did, looking like a ghost himself.'

All the family laughs, and they continue to share jokes and stories. Then Gumercinda serves the stew.

Talking points

▷ Do you like to sit by your fire in the kitchen and chat?

▷ What do you think the woman in the drawing is thinking about?

▷ Is the kitchen fire the only thing in life that makes you feel warm and protected?

▷ Who are the people who give you love and happiness?

When we're walking over the bleak uplands and it's raining, or a strong Andean gale is blowing, we say, 'I wonder how soon I'll be in the warmth of my home?' There is a lot of suffering for us along the path of life, but we are greatly helped and encouraged by the love of our wife and of our children. We say, 'I wonder how much longer before I'm with my family?'

But it's God who gives the greatest warmth to our lives. A warmth that not only gives us joy, but that urges us to go forward as well. The prophet Jeremiah felt the same thing when everybody had been making fun of him and he felt very discouraged:

'There is in my heart as it were a burning fire shut up in my bones, and I am weary with holding it in, and I cannot.'

(Jer. 20.9)

▷ Is our family always known for its warmth and hospitality?

▷ Have you ever felt the presence of God inside you? Describe how it was.

Dear kitchen fire,
Dear flame that gives warmth,
You are just like our God,
Who draws us with love.

Let's walk with the Lord

Lord,
You are my light
You lighten my darkness
You fill me with strength,
You make straight my path.   *(Ps. 18)*

The long-suffering farm-worker's wife

Juan Malaver is a bad-tempered sort of fellow. He beats his wife and children at the slightest provocation.

One day a big sparrow-hawk swooped down and carried off one of his chickens. Juan gave a belting to his eight-year-old daughter Filomena for not looking after the chickens properly.

When his wife Ana tried to defend Filomena, Juan began to beat his wife as well:

'You stupid woman! Why do you always interfere?'

'Don't beat Filomena.'

'Shut up, you ignorant slut!'

'I tell you Filomena is not to blame.'

'She's bone idle and I'll teach her a lesson.'

'No, Juan, don't do it!'

'Stop your whimpering, woman. I'm the one who decides things round here, not you. Get out of my way!'

Talking points

▷ Do you know cases like this?

▷ Why do some men treat their wives badly?

▷ Have you ever treated your wife in the way Juan treats Ana?

▷ Why did you do it?

▷ How are the children affected by these sorts of goings-on?

God wants a husband and wife to be united.

This is what the Bible says:

My soul takes pleasure in three things, and they are beautiful in the sight of the Lord and of men: agreement between brothers, friendship between neighbours, and a wife and husband who live in harmony. (Sirach 25.1)

There can only be agreement and union if the husband recognizes that his wife is not inferior to him.

But Juan Malaver says:

'Men are much more important than women. We men are the ones who have to make the decisions and take control of things. Women don't know anything. A good woman is one who works and doesn't interfere.'

▷ What do you think of Juan Malaver's attitude?

▷ What do you think women can do to improve things in the community?

▷ What can we all do so that husbands don't ill-treat their wives?

I can't read or write
(only boys go to school),
So he calls me a fool
And treats me like dirt.
I'm a farm-worker's wife,
It's a difficult life
If only our men understood!

Let's walk with the Lord

Look, O Lord, and behold, for I am despised. (Lam. 1.11)

Women are not inferior!

This is what Ana says:
It's hard luck being a woman!
We work all day cooking and washing,
We have to feed the animals,
give birth to children,
look after everything in the home,
with none of the freedom
enjoyed by our menfolk . . .

Talking points

▷ What does a woman do in the house?

▷ (*for women*) How do you feel about your life and your chores?

▷ (*for men*) Have you ever shown gratitude for what your wife does?

▷ Should women work outside the home?

▷ What can we do to bring about more equality between men and women?

Mary, the mother of Jesus, was also from a small community.
She was a humble woman, but her husband, Joseph, didn't ill-treat her.

Let's see what the gospel tells us:

The angel Gabriel was sent from God to a city of Galilee named Nazareth, to a virgin betrothed to a man whose name was Joseph, of the house of David; and the virgin's name was Mary. And he came to her and said, 'Hail, O favoured one, the Lord is with you!' But she was greatly troubled at the saying, and considered in her mind what sort of greeting this might be. And when the angel departed from her,

Mary arose and went with haste into the hill country of Judah, to the house of her cousin Elizabeth.   *(Luke 1.26–29, 39)*

It was there that Mary sang this song:

I sing with great joy
to the Lord my Saviour.
He has looked on me, a poor woman,
who suffered from oppression.

They all say to me,
'God support you',
for he is good,
and he always has mercy on the poor.

Let's walk with the Lord

O daughter, you are blessed by the Most High God above all women on earth. May God grant this to be a perpetual honour for you and may he visit you with blessings, because you did not spare your own life when our nation was brought low.
(Judith 13.18–20)

19

Our children suffer greatly!

In Condorpampa, Elvira Montenegro is talking with her neighbour, Lucha Campos.

'Oh Lord, I've got to finish this weaving and my head is aching and my back is killing me. I'm soon going to have my eighth baby, and life just seems to be all work and nothing to show for it . . . And if I don't work there's not enough for us to eat.'

Lucha Campos adds:

'How right you are; we women always seem to be pregnant and we can never rest from the chores of the house.'

Talking points

▷ Do you know families like this?

▷ Is it God's will that women should always be pregnant?

▷ Who are responsible for this situation?

▷ Do the children suffer as a result? Why?

In the northern Andes the conditions of life are so bad that we cannot have all the children we would perhaps like to have. Many of our children die through malnutrition or lack of medical attention. Sometimes we just cannot afford to buy medicine or clothes for our babies. Those babies that survive often lack strength or are anaemic. Often we cannot afford to send them to school.

This is the situation in most of the farm-working families. In these conditions how many children should we have?

The Peruvian bishops have said: 'It is the personal decision of wife and husband together as to how many children they can afford to have and to educate. This decision cannot be the result of a mere whim or of merely selfish motives, but must come from a love that grows and matures and takes into account the good of present and future children, as well as the good of society.'

The bishops are telling us that we must not act like the animals in this matter; we must not bear children in a haphazard way without thought for the future. We are men and women who must act responsibly, and we must not bring into the world a lot of children who are going to die shortly afterwards because we cannot look after them.

▷ We should have another child only if we are able to give it health, education and the chance of being happy in the service of society. Discuss what this means.

▷ The problem is difficult and complicated. Do you think we can resolve it without resolving also the problem of our extreme poverty and the fact that we are being exploited?

If everyone's united
then we'll change our world,
our children now are hungry
our banners are unfurled
to proclaim God's justice
and his daily bread for all.

Let's walk with the Lord

Lord, you said, 'It is not good that the man should be alone; let us make a helper for him like himself.' And now, O Lord, I am not taking this sister of mine because of lust, but with sincerity. (Tobit 8.6f.)

Looking after our children's interests

In the village of Loma, Hugo Cruzado is very pleased with himself because his son Felipe is soon going to go away to Lima to school.

Proudly he tells his neighbour Marcial Luna:

'I want my Felipe to have a professional career and a good salary so that later on he'll be able to help me. It means a lot of sacrifice for us at the moment, but I know it will be worth while.'

Marcial doesn't reply, because he's not really convinced that Hugo is right in what he's doing. Felipe has always struck Marcial as being rather spoiled by his parents.

Later on he says:

'Your boy may well earn a good salary when he's grown up, but what sort of a *man* is he going to be?'

Talking points

▷ Is Hugo right to be proud of his son?

▷ Why is his neighbour Marcial doubtful about whether Hugo is right in sending his son to Lima?

▷ What do you understand by 'a good education'?

▷ What can we do so that our children can live in conditions that are more human?

It is right for parents to make efforts to educate their children and make provision for their future. But this can only be done by helping them not to turn their backs on the farm-working class to which they belong. They must learn too the lesson of solidarity with their brothers, and not betray them. This is the education that begins with manual farm-work, so that children learn to love their native soil and learn to be responsible human beings.

While the town children often lead a lazy and privileged life, the children of the farm-workers earn their food by the sweat of their brow.

To help these children
is our duty indeed
so that they follow the path
of love, not greed.

We feel great joy
that they share Christ's light,
for one day they'll inherit
our suffering and our fight.

Let's walk with the Lord

O Lord, I pray, let the man of God whom you sent come again to us, and teach us what we are to do with the boy that will be born. (Judg. 13.1–25)

How hard is life!

Emilio Vasquez says: 'What a lot of suffering there is in this life . . . We suffer when we work and when we travel. We suffer when food is scarce. We suffer when our children and old people and our animals are ill. How hard is the life of a farm-worker.'

And while he works, Emilio sings this folk song:

Hard is the life of an Andean peasant
who lives high above the warm plains
and the vales.
Whatever the weather, hail, rain or sun-
shine,
the harvest is meagre, and often it fails
to give us the food and the nourishment
needed
to keep up our strength and keep illness
at bay.
O God of the heavens, please lessen the
sorrow
of your poor children who suffer and cry;
Give us the chance of a better tomorrow,
bless us with good things before we must
die.

Talking points

▷ Have you suffered like Emilio?

▷ Why is there suffering?

▷ What is the attitude of the man in the photo?

▷ Should we do anything more than just put up with our bad fortune or resign ourselves
to 'God's will'?

To be able to 'put up with things' is not wrong or bad. But we must not give in when bad luck and misfortune come our way.

Sometimes we're inclined to blame others for our misfortunes. If the baby falls ill, we say he's the victim of an 'evil eye'; if there's a blight of potatoes, we say that God is punishing us; if somebody dies in a mining accident, we say 'his time had come'.

Knowing the causes of suffering often helps us to be able to do something about them, by working together. But when we know we can do nothing to remedy a difficult situation, we can recall how the Son of God came to share our sufferings.

Jesus frees us from *useless* suffering, and helps us to derive real benefits from our pains. This isn't easy to understand: but it is true! For this reason a Christian should never despair.

We shall overcome
We shall overcome
We shall overcome some day.
O, deep in my heart
I do believe that
We shall overcome some day.

We must stand united
We must stand united
We must stand united some day.
O, deep in my heart
I do believe that
We must stand united some day.

Let's walk with the Lord

Come to me, all who labour and are heavy laden, and I will give you rest. Take my yoke upon you, and learn from me; for I am gentle and lowly in heart, and you will find rest for your souls. For my yoke is easy and my burden is light. (Matt. 11.28–30)

UNIT 3

We Work the Land . . . but Who Benefits?

'Ain't a Christian worth more than an animal? We're worse off than dogs . . . I've still got something to eat, thanks be to God, but those poor villagers from Huaira with their cryin' and beggin' and never findin' nothing 'cos there's nothing to find while the drought's still on . . . I tell you, sir, it's our sweat and our work and our lives that has made the likes of you what you are today; everything you eat and what your animals eat as well, is thanks to us poor farm-workers . . . '

(*The Starving Dogs*, by Peruvian novelist Ciro Alegria)

God has put the world into our hands

In the village of Naranjo, Alejo and Maria Salvatierra have just finished building their new house, and so are feeling very pleased with themselves.

'Well, Maria, at last we have a roof over us.'

'Yes, Alejo, we've made ourselves a fine house.'

'But we'll have to improve it every year, Maria. There are still lots of things missing, and when we have a little money saved we'll . . . '

'Yes, Alejo, especially a separate kitchen for me to cook in. But all this isn't the most urgent . . . '

'Well, what is?'

'To look after our children well, and to give a big welcome to anyone who comes to our house.'

'You're right, Maria. The first thing is to be a good family. The new house is only a beginning.'

Talking points

▷   What's the point of having a good house?

▷   What improvements would you make to your house?

▷   What improvements could you make to your family life?

The world is the house that God has put into our hands:

O Lord, our governor, how mighty is your name all over the earth! When I consider the heaven, the moon and the stars which you have made, I think, 'What is man that you are mindful of him?' You have given him rule over the work of your hands.
              (after Ps. 8.2–7)

But St Paul reminds us that our world suffers:

The whole world cries out and suffers like a woman giving birth.   *(Rom. 8.22)*

In other words, it's like waiting for the overdue child to be born.
    So our world is like a house that needs finishing off; or like a child waiting to be born.

▷   What improvements can we make to our lives as farm-workers?

▷   Do our small improvements help the rest of the people in Peru?

We should not forget that selfishness has been the cause of a lot of God's creation going wrong. We must try to put right this damage.

Our world is growing more and more
each day: because you're here;
One day we'll make a better world
for all: because you're here.

Love is not possible
if you don't give your heart;
justice is not possible
if we don't love one another.

Let's walk with the Lord

The Lord rules over all.
Bless the Lord, you who hear his word,
Bless the Lord, you who do his will.
Let all creation bless the Lord.
I will bless the Lord with all my soul.
           (after Ps. 103.19–22)

Our mother earth

Ciro Alegria, a writer from our Northern Andes, understands well the sufferings of farm-workers. In his book *The Starving Dogs* he describes the close union between men and the land.

'The acts of sowing, tilling and harvesting renew for the farm-workers, year after year, the joy of living. They are simple people whose lives are formed by a multitude of furrows. And that is everything. Life is good when it is productive.'

Talking points

▷ Do you like your farm-work? Why?

▷ Do you feel happy when you see your harvest approaching?

▷ Do you try to improve your land? How?

The people of Israel were also a farming people who loved their land very much. This was why they imagined Paradise to be a fertile garden. And this is how they described the world's beginning:

When the Lord God made the earth and the heavens, no plant of the field was yet in the earth and no herb of the field had yet sprung up – for the Lord God had not caused it to rain upon the earth, and there was no man to till the ground.

Then the Lord God formed man of dust from the ground, and breathed into his nostrils the breath of life; and man became a living being.

And the Lord God planted a garden in Eden, in the East; and there he put the man whom he had formed. And out of the ground the Lord God made to grow every tree that is pleasant to the sight and good for food.

And the Lord God took the man and put him in the garden of Eden to till it and keep it. (after Gen. 2.4–15)

In this wonderful description the writer shows us how closely united God is with man and man with the earth. God gives man his own breath when he makes him, and he makes him in his own likeness. When he makes a good job of cultivating the land he becomes more human – and more happy!

Working, working
we spend each day
opening with our hands
the furrows of clay.

The sun, the soil, the water
are weapons mightier than guns.
The harvest is bright with promise
for the future of our sons.

Let's walk with the Lord

The earth has yielded its increase;
God, our God, has blessed us,
God has blessed us;
let all the ends of the earth fear him.
(Ps. 67.7f.)

Working on the land

Alejo Salvatierra
from Naranjo says:

'What a lot of pain
and suffering there is
in hard work...
opening up furrows,
sowing seed,
weeding, watering,
harvesting. It all
seems endless.'

Maria, Alejo's wife, says:

'I have to look for
water, gather firewood
for cooking, milk the
cow, feed the babies,
make the clothes for all
the family, cook, wash
and look after the
animals. If I don't do all
this, nothing goes well in
the family.'

Talking points

▷ Is it true that country people work hard?

▷ Does our work always bring good results?

▷ Why do things sometimes turn out badly, in spite of our hard work?

We must remember that some of the reasons why things turn out badly are outside our control. But there is a lot we can do to change things for the better.

▷ Should we apply 'scientific methods' to our farm-work?

▷ Are we really using all the 'natural' techniques that we could?

▷ For example, are we getting the best out of our animal manure?

The Bible tell us that farm-work is certainly hard work:

God said to Adam, 'Cursed is the ground because of you; in toil you shall eat of it all the days of your life; thorns and thistles it shall bring forth to you; and you shall eat the plants of the field. In the sweat of your face you shall eat bread till you return to the ground, for out of it you were taken.'
(Gen. 3.17–19)

Men don't pay attention to God. So the land is under a kind of curse. God has given us intelligence, with which to tame and control our world. But what happens? We use our intelligence for evil ends. People from rich countries don't think of the suffering of farm- workers in Peru. They prefer to use their technical power for useless objects or for making weapons of war . . .

▷ Are we also to blame for sometimes making our lives unnecessarily difficult? Give an example.

The maize fields are bad,
the potato crop worse!
It's the fault of us all:
We deserve the Lord's curse!

With the strength God gives us,
everything can be better,
we need to be less selfish
and learn to work together!

Let's walk with the Lord

Restore our fortunes, O Lord, as the drought gives place to rain. May those who sow in tears, reap with shouts of joy!
(after Ps. 126.4)

Why are we hungry?

Ambrosia Huaman says:

'I don't know what to do. I've a lot of children and not enough food to feed them. This year's harvest has been a disaster. I've nothing to sell in the town market in exchange for food. My man Emilio earns very little, although he's always making sombreros in his spare time. There's just nothing to eat!'

Talking points

▷ Why are people hungry in the Andes?

▷ Sometimes we eat great amounts and then feel hungry shortly afterwards. Why?

▷ Have you noticed that the population increases but the land doesn't? Why does all this happen?

▷ What can we do about it all?

Not just in our village, not just in the Andes is there hunger. If we divide all the world's people into three parts, only one part is *not* hungry: the other two parts are hungry or are badly fed. Some people in the first part eat far too much.

Hear this word, you cows of Bashan, who are in the mountain of Samaria, who oppress the poor, who crush the needy, who say to their husbands, 'Bring that we may drink!'
The Lord God has sworn by his holiness that, behold, the days are coming upon you, when they shall take you away as captives, leaving your city in ruins.
(Amos 4.1f.)

This is the way Amos, the farm-worker prophet, speaks to rich women: 'Cows of Bashan!' Bashan was a region full of lush pasture lands.

A few very rich people lived at the expense of the majority who were poor; they lived in luxury and were surrounded by waste. This is what the prophet Isaiah says to them:

Is not this the fast that I choose,
to loose the bonds of wickedness,
to undo the thongs of the yoke,
to let the oppressed go free, and to break every yoke?
Is it not to share your bread with the hungry,
and bring the homeless poor into your house;
when you see the naked to cover him,
and not to hide yourself from your flesh.
(Isa. 58.6f.)

Peasant farmer of the Andes
Who devours all your harvest?
Join hands with the city workers
and the future will be yours.

The wholesalers are rich
and know how to entice:
You sell them your crops
at an unjust price.

Let's walk with the Lord

Lord, my feet almost stumbled,
because I was so envious,
when I saw the prosperity of the wicked.
If I had wanted to say, 'Should I speak like them?'
I would have been untrue to the generation of your children.
(after Ps. 73.2–15)

35

Life has its hard knocks

Marcial Luna from the village of Loma tells us this:

'One day we were working in the field, getting the oxen ready for yoking. There wasn't a cloud in the sky, when suddenly a piece of the sun seemed to be disappearing. The dogs went to the house, the chickens found shelter, and there was an intense coldness.

Then my father said: "Sons, today we mustn't be working; we must say prayers instead."

We began to pray the Rosary together for a few minutes, but then the sun appeared once again and it was like it had been before. But our father said:

"Sons, let loose the oxen and let us go into the house to pray. Something strange is going to happen!"'

Talking points

▷ Is the father right about 'something strange'?

▷ Why does an eclipse of the sun occur?

▷ Other things in nature cause us problems, such as frosts, droughts, avalanches, earthquakes. Why do they occur?

▷ Does praying or paying for a Mass help the people who live in the house shown in the photo?

▷ What else could they do apart from praying?

Nowadays a child who goes to school can tell us why an eclipse takes place. It occurs when the moon passes in front of the sun and covers it up.

Perhaps there are other things like this that haven't been explained to you, and therefore you don't know the reason for them.

We must always look for the real explanation of things so that we can defend ourselves from any harm.

For example, those farm-workers who know where diseases come from can cure their animals when they are sick.

God has given us the earth to live in it and control it.

Let's remember what the Bible tells us:

And God made the beasts of the earth and saw that it was good. Then God said,

'Let us make man in our own image, after our likeness; and let them have dominion over the fish of the sea, and over the birds of the air, and over the cattle, and over all the earth, and over every creeping thing that creeps upon the earth.'

So God created man in his own image, in the image of God he created him; male and female he created them. And God blessed them, and God said to them, 'Be fruitful and multiply, and fill the earth and subdue it, and have dominion over the fish and the birds and over every living thing that moves on the earth. (Gen. 1.25–28)

We must come together, brothers,
we must talk about the cost
and the way to fight diseases
and protect our fields from frost.

With the strength God gives us
everything can be better
let us apply our intelligence
and learn to work together.

Let's walk with the Lord

God of our fathers, by your wisdom you have formed me, to have dominion over the creatures you have made. Give me wisdom. She will guide me wisely in my actions, and guard me with her might.
(after Wisd. 9.1–11)

The harvest is ours!

Venancio Chavez has a large estate in the village of Las Lagunas. To make it more profitable he rents it out to a poor neighbour, Benigno Rojas, according to local custom: Venancio loans the land and the seed, and Benigno must do all the work.

But the harvest turns out to be very mediocre, and Venancio wants to keep the entire harvest.

'I have a right to all the harvest because I have to recover the price of the seed; anyway, you have worked badly and don't deserve anything.'

'But you don't understand, Don Venancio. If you take everything, my family and I will have nothing at all to eat. It wasn't my fault that the harvest was bad: that was because of the frost.'

'That's your problem. I must get back the price of the seed: that was the agreement.'

'But it's unfair. I've worked and sweated, so I have a right to something.'

'I bought the seed, and I can't afford to lose money!'

Talking points

▷ Which of the two men is right in this quarrel?

▷ Do you know other cases similar to this?

In our country we are used to seeing the rich get steadily richer and the poor get poorer. Why does this happen?

It is part of what we call the capitalist system, which is so unjust that one day it will have to disappear. Here is what the Peruvian bishops have said:

'It is our duty to affirm that the real right of possession springs from work. This new way of viewing society provides us with a model superior to that of capitalism. In the capitalist system it is only money that has worth, while human work is a commodity that can be bought and sold.' (*Justice in the World*)

There is nothing new in this. It is similar to what the prophet Isaiah said centuries before the coming of Christ:

They shall build houses and inhabit them;
they shall plant vineyards and eat their
*   fruit.*
They shall not build and another inhabit;
they shall not plant and another eat.
My chosen shall long enjoy the work of
*   their hands.*   *(Isa. 65.21f.)*

Let's suppose we receive the fruit of our work. Then we shall have to concern ourselves with the needs of the whole community . . . especially the sick and the old.

It was like this in the days of the Inca empire, when a part of the land was reserved and cultivated especially for the elders of the community.

It's not at all proper or right
to spend our lives sweating and working
so that others can take all the profit
and spend their lives sleeping and shirk-
    ing.

It wasn't like this at the start:
the land was meant for all
and its fruits were chiefly for
those who had done all the labour and
    toil.

Let's walk with the Lord

Faithfulness will spring up from the
*   ground,*
and righteousness will look down from the
*   sky.*
Yes, the Lord will give what is good,
and our land will yield its increase.
*   (after Ps. 85.12f.)*

The smallholding

In many parts of Peru the large feudal estates have been broken up. Thousands of families now own what had once belonged to one man.

Each smallholding is now divided from its neighbour by fences of stones, cacti, or whatever.

The fence has now become something sacred, and you can be in trouble with the law if you disturb it. But the farm-worker needs more land if he is to support himself and his family.

The Agrarian Reform did something to break up big country estates. But it didn't help the owners of patches of land ·too small for survival.

Talking points

▷ Is your patch of land too small?

▷ Why are there so many smallholdings?

▷ What happens when land is scarce?

▷ How do you plan to divide your land among your children?

▷ What solutions can there be for these problems?

In the village of Lucma a group of people are talking about the same problem:

'If we don't do something, it's going to get much worse,' says Eladio Chumpitaz.

'Fifty years ago there were six houses in Lucma, and now there are a hundred. What's going to happen to our children?' says Walter Oyarce.

'But there's a problem,' says another. 'Years ago the big landowners threw out the peasant farmers on to the infertile smallholdings, keeping just a few back to work as slaves on their estates. Now these same rich men are owners of factories in Lima, bought with the compensation paid to them by the Agrarian Reform. If we go to live in the shanty towns of Lima, we'll be suffering the old slavery all over again.'

'They say that in the time of the Incas there was enough to eat for everybody, and now every year sees more hungry people.'

▷ What do you think of all this?

Let's walk with the Lord

I tell those present
and I tell them again:
that the land belongs to us workers
and we'll not plough it up in vain.

The fences must come down, my boy,
the fences must come down;
for the land is all of ours, my boy,
the land is all of ours.

Woe to those who devise wickedness
and work evil upon their beds!
When the morning dawns, they perform it,
because it is in the power of their hand.
They covet fields and seize them;
and houses and take them away;
they oppress a man and his house,
a man and his inheritance.
They will not be able to escape,
for a time of disaster will come upon them.
(Micah 2.1–3)

Community ownership?

In the village of Las Lagunas a group of neighbours have reflected over a passage in the Acts of the Apostles where the first Christians put all their possessions into a common pool and shared according to each one's need.

The villagers of Las Lagunas decide to do the same ... twelve families unite their land, eat the same food, and so on.

But soon there are problems. Some families had had more land than others, and when harvest time comes they expect more than the others. When the others object, they withdraw from the community.

They had never felt really united, and even when they had joined their lands together there was never quite enough for everybody to eat sufficient.

By the end of a year the experiment had failed completely.

Talking points

▷ Why do you think the plan failed?

▷ Was it a good idea in the first place?

▷ Is it worth looking for this kind of solution to our problems?

There have been other sorts of experiments. Later on in the book we'll be looking at the case of the San Andres Co-operative, where the members earn according to their work and their need.

The first Christians made an attempt to live and work in common. Let's see what the Acts of the Apostles says about them:

And all who believed were together and had all things in common; and they sold their possessions and goods and distributed them to all, as any had need.

(Acts 2.44f.)

But we also know that a few years later there was a great famine among those same Christians, and that Christians from other parts had to come to their help.

They had tremendous faith and goodwill. Why, then, did they fail?

Let's walk with the Lord

Words and intentions
cannot be enough
to unite our New People.

We must give our lives
tracing out new paths
to unite our New People.

risking together
hands and hearts linked
to unite our New People.

Lord, fill us with your love, that we may rejoice and be glad all our days. Make us glad as many days as you have afflicted us, and as many years as we have seen evil. May we and our children see your works and your glory.

Let the favour of the Lord our God be upon us.
Lord, bless our work,
yes, bless it.

(after Ps. 90.14–17)

4   Our Community

The yellow wheat waved gently at twilight; one ear
of corn apparently identical to the next, and the
entire field an exquisite sight.
'One man is similar to the next, and together they too
represent an exquisite beauty; but men have head
and heart,' thought Rosendo, 'and therefore there are
differences, whereas the life of the ear of corn comes
only from its roots.'

(*Broad and Alien is the World*,
by Peruvian novelist Ciro Alegria)

Relations helping each other

Pancracio Quispe from Pedregal village is in a difficult situation. He has a mentally handicapped boy; last year the boy was playing with a box of matches, and set fire to the whole house. Soon everything was in ashes. The family had to live in a makeshift hut for a long time.

Then the rainy season came, and they were still unable to build again.

Meanwhile Ludmila (Pancracio's wife) went down with pneumonia and eventually died because there was no money for medicine.

At the moment Pancracio has to look after his five children and is often at his wits' end. The rest of his family are too poor to help with money.

But there is an aunt, Teresa, who has taken pity and visits him often. Pancracio says that it is these visits by Aunt Teresa that give him the strength to struggle on.

Talking points

▷ Do you know any family in as difficult a situation as the one just described? Tell us about it.

▷ Can relations do more than Teresa did?

▷ Do relations always help each other in the Andes?

▷ If Pancracio had had any better-off relations, do you think things would have been easier for him?

We all know cases of farm-workers who have gone to live in Lima, but they still remember to help their relations in the mountains. In the Bible we have the example of Ruth, who refused to abandon her mother-in-law Naomi, even when Naomi implored her to return to her home and marry again.

Ruth replied: 'Do not force me to leave you and go away from you. Your people will be my people and your God will be my God. Where you die I shall die and there will I be buried. May the Lord do to me what he wills; only death shall part me from you.'
(Ruth 1.16)

When a poor man shares the nothing that
   he has,
When a thirsty man offers us water to
   drink,
When a weak man gives strength to his
   brother,
God himself is walking on that road.

Let's walk with the Lord

Behold how good and pleasant it is when brothers dwell in unity. For there the Lord gives blessings: life for evermore.
(after Ps. 133.1–3)

. . . and neighbours who take advantage

Artemio Becerra is the owner of the village shop in Colpa, and he's thinking of organizing a carnival fiesta for the whole village.

He says to his wife Clothilde:

'We must put on a really good fiesta this year so that the neighbours can have a good time.'

'What a good idea, Artemio.'

'There's enough suffering in this life as it is, and we've got a right to enjoy ourselves occasionally.'

'You're right. And at the same time we can sell more goods in the shop.'

'Without a doubt.'

Talking points

▷ When do you get together for a fiesta with your friends and relations?

▷ Why do you celebrate these occasions?

▷ What do you think of the motives of the Becerra couple for organizing a fiesta?

▷ How do you think the Becerra fiesta will turn out?

In the Bible we read:

It is God's gift to man that every one should eat and drink and take pleasure in all his toil. *(Eccles. 3.13)*

▷ How can we enjoy ourselves in a reasonable way?

▷ What are the advantages of village fiestas?

The Becerra couple have organized a fiesta for selfish motives: to bring more customers to their village shop. But Jesus tells us how to organize a fiesta so that everybody can enjoy themselves and not just a few:

When you give a dinner or a banquet, do not invite your friends or your brothers or your kinsmen or rich neighbours, lest they also invite you in return, and you be repaid. But when you give a feast, invite the poor, the maimed, the lame, the blind, and you will be blessed, because they cannot repay you. You will be repaid at the resurrection of the just. *(Luke 14.12–14)*

Come, come, come to the fiesta,
come to dance and come to sing,
Though we're poor it doesn't matter:
share your food,
share everything.

Let's denounce the cruel oppression:
let no one be king and no one slave;
sharing our lives and hearts and fortune
is the most Christian way to behave.

Let's walk with the Lord

I will praise the Lord; the Lord lifts up those who are bowed down; he gives the oppressed their rights and he gives bread to the hungry. *(after Pss. 146; 147)*

You gave me lodging

Sometimes we farm-workers have to make long journeys over the mountains, and even stay overnight with strangers.

This has happened to Pancho Escobar, on his way to Condorpampa. Imagine his contentment at hearing Juan Chuquimango's words of welcome!

'Come right in and rest yourself.'
'Thank you.'
'You are very welcome to share the little we have. Feel completely as if you were in your own home!'

Talking points

▷ Have you ever been given lodging after a lonely journey?

▷ How did you feel?

▷ Do you open your house to strangers?

Our faith is great, but it's nearly always expressed in the little things of life.

If we give a warm welcome to a fellow human being who needs lodging and food, then we are expressing our faith as well as our love of neighbour.

To give lodging to a stranger is to welcome Jesus himself.

On the day of the last judgment, Jesus will say:

'Come, O blessed of my Father, inherit the kingdom prepared for you from the foundation of the world; for I was hungry and you gave me food; I was thirsty and you gave me drink; I was a stranger and you welcomed me.'

Then the righteous will answer him,
'Lord, when did we see you hungry and feed you, or thirsty and give you drink? And when did we see you a stranger and welcome you?'

And the Lord will answer them, 'Truly, I say to you, as you did it to one of the least of these my brothers, you did it to me!
(from Matt. 25.34–40)

When we open our house to a stranger we are helping someone in need. But we are also receiving something. It was this way with Zacchaeus who gave a welcome to Jesus one day, and Jesus said to him, 'Today salvation has come to this house.'
(Luke 19.9)

This is the way it is with us. The visitor brings us Jesus. And he always brings us something that we can learn or share.

Welcome and bless you
Your journey is done,
our poor home is your home,
you and I are as one.

Jesus inspires us
a new world to make,
so throw off the darkness:
farm-workers awake!

Let's walk with the Lord

Lord, if I have found favour in your sight, do not pass by your servant, but dwell in my house. I will bring something to eat that you may refresh yourself, and after that you may pass on – since you have come to your servant. *(after Gen. 18.3–5)*

The country school

Roberta Villanueva is the village teacher in Quinua, and she talks about her bad working conditions.

'Everything is just hopeless. The school building is falling down and the desks in the classroom are broken. The villagers are not united. The local authorities are not interested and would rather see the school fall down before they do anything to help.

The villagers themselves are apathetic in spite of the fact that I am trying to teach their children. The few books that existed before were the property of the former teacher and now I am accused of having stolen them.

When I want to travel to the town at weekends there is never a horse free to take me.

The people here just don't understand that I was brought up in Lima, and this cold mountain air makes things even more difficult for me.'

Talking points

▷   What is really wrong with this school?

▷   Is the teacher right to blame the local authorities and the villagers?

▷   Do you have similar problems in your village?

▷   What can be done to make country schools better?

Not all Andean schools have the difficulties described by Roberta Villanueva. For example, in Lucma things are different, as Walter Oyarce (one of the village authorities) relates:

'With our teacher, Nelly Vargas, things are going quite well. We have decorated the classroom recently, and they sent us some posters for the walls from the Ministry of Education in Lima.

Nelly Vargas is a punctual and conscientious teacher, and the girls have been taught by her how to weave, while the boys are learning about vegetable gardening. Sometimes she has to go to meetings in the town, but she always tells us adults what she has learned there.

Once a month she calls a PTA meeting and gives an account of how the school is getting on. She has recently put a first aid box in the classroom.

But then, she is one of us: she was born in the Andes, and so she understands our ways.'

Although Walter Oyarce paints a rosy picture of the school at Lucma, we discovered a few problems.

For instance, by no means all the village children attend the school. The girls especially are mostly absentees. Also, the children of the better-off families are being sent to Lima to study there.

▷   Why do these problems exist in Lucma?

The people are tired of theory
and of bureaucratic speeches,
we have our own folk-wisdom
and we don't need Lima leeches.

But we need your solidarity,
in the struggle for our liberty,
And if you're honest and sincere,
you'll win a ready ear.

Let's walk with the Lord

I will again make instruction shine forth like the dawn, and I will make it shine afar; I will again pour our teaching like prophecy, and leave it to future generations. Observe that I have not laboured for myself alone, but for all who seek instruction.
(Sirach 24, 32–34)

How should we learn?

Florencio Rojas from the village of Quinua is annoyed with his wife Maria. He wants to send the youngest children to the high pastureland to look after the sheep, while Maria wants them to go to school.

'Let them go with the sheep!'

'But Florencio, the children ought to go to school.'

'Shut up, woman; you don't know anything. I want them to pasture the sheep.'

'But if the children don't go to school they'll never better themselves, and they'll be no different from us.'

'I need my children to help me with the work. Schools aren't for poor folks like us; anyway, they'll learn more useful things by working than from all that book stuff.'

'But that's why we stay poor: because we never studied. We must make an effort so that our children can do better in life than us.'

Talking points

Both Florencio and Maria have made some good points.

▷ Can we learn from working, as Florencio says?

▷ Is there such a thing as 'the school of life'?

▷ Is Maria right when she says, 'we are poor because we never studied'?

▷ What is the purpose of a school?

Schools have a lot of faults, and we ought to ask a lot of questions about the school system. We ought to unite in our efforts to bring about the kind of education that we and our children need to make us better at our agricultural work, as well as happier in our daily lives.

We must not expect that the school-teacher will have all the answers to our problems. We parents above all are the real educators of our children, and we must help them to learn from the school of life.

St Paul has some words to say about this:

Fathers, do not provoke your children to anger, but bring them up in the discipline and instruction of the Lord. (Eph. 6.4)

St Paul is telling us that everyone has received a responsibility from God to help to make a different and better society. We have to ensure that our children are able to fulfil their great mission:

So that we may no longer be like children, tossed to and fro and carried about with every wind of doctrine, by the cunning of men, by their craftiness in deceitful wiles. (Eph. 4.14)

I'm not a fuddy-duddy
with a tightly-closed mind
my heart I keep open
God and life help me find
the secret of happiness
when work is just 'grind'.
O Jesus Christ, my master,
help me to want to learn!'

Let's walk with the Lord

*O Lord, my heart is not lifted up,
my eyes are not raised too high;
I do not occupy myself with things
too great and too marvellous for me.
I am like a small child
in the arms of its mother.
My people, look to the Lord,
now and always.*
(after Ps. 131.1–3)

A bribe for the Justice of the Peace

Almanzor Alvarado and Concepcion caruajulca are quarrelling about a fence. Almanzor changed the position of the cactus fence during the night, and so has increased the size of his smallholding. Concepcion has complained to Clodomiro Paisig, the Justice of the Peace in Pampa Verde, but Almanzor has already given the Justice a chicken so that he will be on his side.

'I demand justice, sir,' says Concepcion.

'Now calm down, Concepcion Caruajulca. I don't want you shouting around here. I must find out the truth.'

'The truth is that . . . '

'Shut up, and don't interrupt!'

'But . . . '

'I see you are a born trouble-maker. Almanzor Alvarado must be the innocent party in this dispute.'

'Impossible!'

'Stop shouting! My conscience is clear, and if you want to carry on quarrelling go and do it outside.'

'But I . . . '

'Enough! you've caused enough problems already. If I hear another word I'll send you to the police station.'

Talking points

▷ Do you know of cases like this?

▷ How do authorities (like Justices of the Peace) get their jobs?

▷ What can we do when we know that a Justice of the Peace is corrupt?

▷ Is it sufficient to change one authority for another?

▷ Bribing authorities is a sure way to corrupt them. What can we do to stop this practice?

Samuel was an important Justice of the Peace for the people of Israel. When he was an old man he said:

'I have walked before you from my youth until this day. Here I am; testify against me before the Lord and before his anointed. Whose ox have I taken? Or whose ass have I taken? Or whom have I defrauded? Whom have I oppressed? Or from whose hand have I taken a bribe to blind my eyes with it? Testify against me and I will restore it to you.' They said, 'You have not defrauded us or oppressed us or taken anything from any man's hand.' (I Sam. 12.2–4)

The Bible praises honest authorities and speaks harshly against those who are corrupt:

Woe to those who acquit the guilty for a bribe, and deprive the innocent of his right. Therefore as the tongue of fire devours the stubble, and as dry grass sinks down in the flame, so their root will be as rottenness, and their blossom go up like dust.
(Isa. 5.23f.)

In this world of knaves,
the knave lives off the fool,
and the fool lives off his work,
while the Devil laughs up his sleeve.

Why should the guilty go free
and the innocent rot in jail?
The robber of a loaf is imprisoned
while the millionaire drug-pusher gets
  bail!

Let's walk with the Lord

You speak unjust judgments.
The mighty act with evil intent.
Lord, break the teeth of these lions!
Let them vanish like water that runs away,
like grass let them be trodden down and
  wither.
And then people will say, 'Truly there is a
God who judges on earth.'
(after Ps. 58.2–12)

The fiesta

Some of the villagers of Pampa Verde have met to plan the approaching patronal feast day, or fiesta.

'All right, neighbours,' says Arnulfo Perez. Let's elect those in charge of music and the fireworks.'

'Excuse me, Arnulfo. Don't you think that this year we ought not to spend so much money on the fiesta, and celebrate it in a different way?'

'What do you mean?'

'Well, instead of paying for a professional band to play for us, we could organize a competition for amateur musicians from our own region.'

'And the fireworks?'

'We should stop paying out good money on such stupid entertainments. I feel sure that a theatre group or a puppet show would be better for everybody.'

'If we don't have a firework display the fiesta will be a flop, and we'll be blamed by visitors from the other villages.'

'Well, I think it's time we changed our ideas. Do you think God is pleased to see us just getting drunk and wasting our money on the day of our Patron Saint?'

'There has to be drink at a fiesta!'

'But then we finish up in front of the Justice of the Peace. Is that your idea of honouring our Patron Saint?'

'It's our traditional way of doing things.'

'But if traditions harm the people they should be changed!'

Talking points

▷ Is it possible to change traditions?

▷ What do you think of the changes suggested?

▷ How do you celebrate *your* village fiesta?

▷ What are the good effects as well as the bad effects of a village fiesta?

▷ What does God think about fiestas?

Let's see what the prophet Amos says:

God says: 'I hate, I despise your feasts, and I take no delight in your festivals. Take away from me the noise of your songs; to the melody of your instruments I will not listen. But let justice roll down like waters, and righteousness like an everflowing stream.' *(Amos 5.21–24)*

At the time of Amos there were many fiestas in honour of God, but God was displeased because there was no justice for the poor.

▷ You sometimes hear people saying, 'The patron saint wants it done this way, otherwise he'll punish us for being disobedient.' What do you think of this?

Let's walk with the Lord

Father, we praise you
as we gather together,
united at Mass
to pray for good weather,

We shall walk with you
along life's way,
struggling for justice,
day by day.

*Praise the Lord with good music,
sing to our God because it pleases him.
The Lord restores his people,
he brings together those without land.
He heals the brokenhearted,
and binds up their wounds.
Great is our God, and abundant in power.
He stretches out his hand to the poor,
and casts the wicked to the ground.*
(after Ps. 147.1–6)

Religious statues

Today is the feast day of St John in the village of Pampa Verde. The statue is raised up on a wooden stretcher next to the High Altar.

In front of the statue a lot of devotees are praying and conversing. A lot of candles have been lit and it is very warm as a result. Another group of farm-workers enters to replace the first; they, too, light candles and put offerings of money and coloured ribbons beside the saint.

LUCY JOCHAMOWITZ

One villager puts a question to Arnulfo Perez, the sacristan of the church:

'Where is the priest?'

'Why, do you want to speak with him?'

'I want to pay for a Mass. I do it every year, but last year the priest wasn't here and I couldn't do it; as a result all my potato harvest was blighted.'

'I'll see if the priest has arrived; but you'll have to put your offering in the plate first.'

'Yes, of course, I always pay St John, especially this year because I want him to punish my neighbour for damaging my fences.'

Talking points

▷ Do you think the potatoes were blighted because a farm-worker didn't pay for a Mass?

▷ Have you ever seen persons making profit out of devotion to a saint?

▷ What other abuses do you know of, related to statues of saints?

▷ What benefits come to those who pray at a saint's shrine during the village fiesta?

▷ Does God want us to approach him in the manner of the man in the picture?

A religious statue can remind us of God, who wants to be present among us, and who can make use of statues for this purpose. Obviously, if we go to the statue with a bad intention (such as asking a punishment for our neighbour) God will not hear our prayer. We cannot use God for our own caprices and bad purposes, or to become financially better off. But if we pray before a statue in good faith, then we can meet God and he will hear us. Above all, he who has a good and true faith is:

He who does no evil to his friend, nor takes up a reproach against his neighbour, who walks blamelessly and does what is right, and speaks the truth from his heart. Who does not go back on his word even if it is to his disadvantage and does not lend his money at interest and does not take a bribe against the innocent. (after Ps. 15.3–5)

Come, my brothers, to the fiesta,
to the fiesta of Saint John;
all the harvest is safely gathered,
rain has fallen, sun has shone.

Our Saint John lights up our way
inviting us to bear our load
along a straight and narrow path
to our sure and last abode.

Let's walk with the Lord

Lord, you do not want sacrifice or offerings, but you have shown me your will. Therefore I have said, 'Here am I. It is written in scripture that I should fulfil your will, and I bear your law in my heart.'
(after Ps. 40.7–9)

Taking unfair advantage of others

Leoncio Benavides and Segundo Aguilar are conversing while they are working for the wealthy landowner Venancio Chavez.

'I don't like working as a hired farmhand for a rich man.'

'Why not, Leoncio?'

'Because he pays badly and his food is terrible.'

'Poor people are always taken for a ride by the rich; it used to be the Spanish conquistadores, now it's anyone who is better off than you.'

'I'm an enemy of any sort of exploitation.'

'So you should be. But I've a question for you.'

'What?'

'Don't you exploit anybody?'

'Of course I don't!'

'How much do you charge when you hire out your mule?'

'Ah well, that's different . . . we have to make an extra penny when we can . . .'

'That's what I mean. Although you're poor, even you exploit somebody when you get the chance.'

Talking points

▷ Do you know cases of exploitation like this?

▷ What about the marketing of cheese, milk, etc.?

▷ Have you ever been exploited by others?

▷ In your region, who are those who come off worst?

▷ Who is most likely to exploit the girl in the photograph?

Agustin Goicochea is walking past the house of Emilio Vasquez in Pino Alto. Emilio is squatting at the door making a straw sombrero.

'That's a nice sombrero you're making; I'll give you three dollars for it.'

'I can't sell it, I'm afraid. Abelardo Julca paid me two dollars in advance, and I needed the money urgently. So I can't sell it to you at any price.'

'And that Abelardo Julca will re-sell it for at least five dollars.'

'That's probably true, but then that's life: the poor get poorer while the rich get richer.'

You shall not oppress a hired servant who is poor and needy, whether he is one of your brethren or one of the sojourners who are in your land within your towns; you shall give him his hire the day he earns it, before the sun goes down (for he is poor, and sets his heart upon it); lest he cry against you to the Lord and it be sin in you.
(Deut. 24.14f.)

A new commandment
from Christ our brother
as he loves us
to love each other

The sign of all Christians
is their love for one another.
He who says he loves God,
but exploits, is a liar.

Let's walk with the Lord

Lord, have compassion on me.
My enemies wish evil upon me.
Even my friend whom I trusted has
*   betrayed me.*
Happy is he who thinks of the poor and
*   needy.*
You will protect him.   (after Ps. 41)

We can't go it alone

Pedro Ruiz has his smallholding in Loma. He is fond of saying, 'I don't need anybody else. I can work and get on by myself; it's better like that because you're not beholden to anybody.'

Talking points

▷ Is what Pedro says true?

▷ How do you feel when you work alone?

Pedro wants to be on his own so as not to have any problems.

And if he doesn't want to have any problems that means that he doesn't help anybody. That is selfishness. The teachings of Jesus are completely against selfishness. We have to forget ourselves and think of others!

'He who finds his life will lose it, and he who loses his life for my sake will find it.'
(Matt. 10.39)

▷ What do these words of Jesus mean?

If you are just concerned with yourself, and don't want to share with anybody, then you lose the friendship and help of others. Instead of having a life full of happiness, your life becomes narrow and bitter. How can a man who lives in that way enjoy eternal life with God? If your heart is closed to others, then it is also closed to God.

Strength comes from unity

Life is sad
and work makes moan
but bitterer far
is to live alone.

Alone I work,
alone I walk,
alone I live and
alone I talk!

Let's walk with the Lord

And above all, have a good deal of love, which binds together all things in perfect harmony. And let the peace of Christ rule in your hearts, because God has united you in that like a body. And whatever you do, do all in the name of the Lord Jesus.

(after Col. 3.14–17)

Community work

In Pedregal, the village elder Fulgencio Chuquilin is pleased because a lot of people have turned up to build a cemetery chapel.

'There we are, because there are a lot of us we shall soon finish the chapel. Our village will be the best in the valley, because we are the only one with a cemetery chapel.'

There is a lot of enthusiasm and good spirits. The building work advances quickly. However, not everybody is contented.

Vicente Maluquish says,

'They force us to work, and I wanted to weed my potato patch today. And in any case, why did we need a cemetery chapel when the village church is only a few yards away?'

Talking points

▷ Why are the people so enthusiastic with this community work?

▷ Is Vicente right in making certain criticisms?

▷ What communal activities have you done in your village?

▷ Which jobs should have priority?

▷ Should anyone from outside the community assist or intervene?

When a community activity is finished, everybody is pleased at having made some contribution. The community is all the better for this. But this isn't sufficient. So that everybody in the community can make real progress, it is necessary that there be no selfish interests involved. Everybody must share the work and the reward. Then what the Psalmist says will come true:

Behold how good and pleasant it is when brothers dwell in unity! (Ps. 133.1)

Jesus says: 'Where two or three are gathered together in my name, there am I in their midst.' (Matt. 18.20)

▷ Why can some community activities be useless?

▷ Who can advise or direct a community in their joint activities?

With the hands of everybody
we'll make a mighty chain:
a great and mighty people
where equality will reign!

Hand in hand
we'll walk together
destroying for ever
the landlord's fetters!

Let's walk with the Lord

Let the favour of the Lord our God be upon us, and establish the work of our hands. (Ps. 90.17)

There are good and bad authorities

In two neighbouring villages the elders are planning community work.

In Pedregal, Fulgencio Chuquilin says:

'I'm going to make my people sweat it out; I've got an order signed by the police chief to make them work three days next week. If they don't work well, they'll finish up in jail! You've got to show a firm hand in this village; the people are very rebellious and disobedient.'

Meanwhile, in Pampa Verde, Teodosio Cruzado says to his neighbour:

'Miguel, can you join us tomorrow to work on the new bridge? Concepcion Cauajulca has to go to town and we'll be a man short.'

'All right, then, Teodosio. I like work-

ing with you because I know that you work hard yourself and set a good example to the other villagers.'

Talking points

▷ Why can Teodosio use persuasion instead of compulsion?

▷ What sort of leaders or authorities do we need in our communities?

Jesus chose disciples to continue his work. They didn't always act in the best way, so Jesus corrected their attitude:

A dispute also arose among them, which of them was to be regarded as the greatest. And Jesus said to them, 'Those in author-ity are called benefactors. But not so with you; rather let the greatest among you become as the youngest, and the leader as one who serves. For which is the greater, one who sits at table or one who serves? Is it not the one who sits at table? But I am among you as one who serves.'
(Luke 22.24–27)

It's not easy to pursue,
what is right, what is true.
It's not easy to fight on
when the others lose their heart.

How quickly we forget
our neighbour's sorrow
How blind we are to see
beyond tomorrow.

Let's walk with the Lord

Do nothing from selfishness or conceit, but in humility count others better than yourselves. Have this mind among yourselves, which was also in Christ Jesus.
(Phil. 2.3–5)

Lima and the Other Cities Exploit Us: What Can We Do?

'And who remembers the grand finale of the fisher-men's strike, Solano? Why, it's a national joke! Braschi and I roared with laughter . . . The workers got a rise of thirty cents per ton of anchovy, and a few days later we "devalued" the national currency. So now the fishermen are earning thirty per cent less than before the strike.

'There's no escape, my lad! In Peru, as in all other countries I know, it is just a small number of us who give the orders and rule the roost.'

(*The Two Foxes*, by the Peruvian novelist and anthropologist José María Arguedas)

What are state employees for?

On Tuesday, Teofilo Chuquimango walks down from Condorpampa to the town of San Andres de Chontapampa. He is bringing his wife Clemencia to see the doctor.

'Come along, Clemencia.'

'I can't go any faster, Teofilo, my whole body is aching.'

They arrive at the town Health Centre and are told to wait. Hours pass, and there is still no sign of a doctor. Would he have gone to a remote village to visit the sick? No. Impossible. Doctors never leave the Health Centre. So where is he?

In fact, Dr Vargas is snoring in bed. He got very drunk last night and wasn't home till five o'clock. He was telling his friends at the party of the good times when he was a doctor in Lima, before he had to come up to this godforsaken hole in the Andes where, according to him, it is impossible to work.

Talking points

▷ How do doctors and other state employees treat the farm-worker?

▷ Relate cases that you know of.

▷ Why do they act in this way?

▷ How should a *good* state employee behave?

▷ How do you recognize a bad state employee?

If someone has a responsibility given him, it is not just so that he can earn a salary. An employee of the state must discharge his duties to the best of his ability.

It is what society and God demand of him, and it is what he promised to do when he accepted the position he has.

The Lord said:

'Who is the faithful steward whom his master will set over his household, to give them their portion of food at the proper time? Blessed is that servant whom his master when he comes will find so doing. Truly I tell you, he will set him over all his possessions. But if that servant says to himself, "My master is delayed in coming", and begins to beat the menservants and the maidservants, and to eat and drink and get drunk, the master of that servant will come on a day when he does not expect him and at an hour he does not know and will punish him severely.

Everyone to whom much is given, of him much will be required; and of him to whom men commit much they will demand the more.' (after Luke 12.42–48)

▷ Do we just have to put up with bad officials, or is there something we could and should do?

▷ Give examples of positive action.

Words and intentions
cannot be enough
to create a New People.

We must give our lives
tracing out new paths
to make our New People.

Risking together,
hands and hearts linked
to form our New People.

Let's walk with the Lord

Woe to you who trample on the weak and take away their grain. You oppress simple people, take bribes and sit in judgment on the poor. Therefore he who is prudent will keep silent in such a time, for it is an evil time. (after Amos 5.10–13)

What's the price of documents?

Nicolas Cubas, from the village of Quinua, wants his daughter to marry Heriberto Oyarce as soon as possible, because Leoncia is pregnant. Nicolas wants his daughter to do things properly by having a civil wedding as well as a church wedding. But Leoncia hasn't a birth certificate.

Nicolas says:

'Leoncia, I insist that you get all your documents.'

'But, Dad, the lawyer in town wants to charge us nearly fifty dollars.'

'Don't you worry, my girl. The mayor is an old friend of mine; I'll give him a couple of chickens and a rabbit and he'll sort it all out.'

And Nicolas was right; the mayor did sort it out.

Talking points

▷ What do you think of Nicolas' attitude?

▷ If you need a document, what do *you* do?

▷ 'Authorities often accept gifts.' Are they the only ones guilty of doing so?

In the village of Lucma there are several couples who want civil weddings. But nobody has the fifty or sixty dollars necessary. So the village elder Walter Oyarce goes on an official visit to the town mayor to ask him to go to their village for a combined ceremony.

'Your worship, we want you to come to Lucma to officiate at civil weddings.'

'Quite impossible, my good man. I'm very busy with affairs of the town. Why can't the couple concerned come to this Town Hall?'

'Because it all costs so much money, sir. We can pay you ten dollars per couple, and there are ten couples. You'll receive a hundred dollars for just one ceremony.'

'Oh all right, then. In view of your determination and for the public good I'll go.'

And he did!

▷ What do you think of Walter's initiative?

▷ Do town authorities only go to the mountain villages when they are well paid?

▷ Give other examples of farm-workers uniting to obtain help and attention from the town authorities.

When we all unite
and claim our due,
the landlords will tremble
throughout Peru.

Sooner or later the people
will have their glorious hour,
whether you like it or not,
the people will soon have the power!

Let's walk with the Lord

This is what the Lord says against those who mislead the people: 'They say "All is well" when they have something to eat, but declare war against him who puts nothing into their mouth. But as for me, I am filled with power, with the Spirit of the Lord, and with justice and might.'
(after Micah 3.5–8)

The secondary school

As it is

In the Head Teacher's office in the Chontapampa Secondary School, the Head is talking with Santos Llamoctanta, a farmworker with a son at the school.

'I am sorry to have had to call you in like this, Don Santos Llamoctanta, but it was the only way.'

'Yes, sir.'

'This year you have not paid the quota for your son's sports clothes.'

'No, sir.'

'But why not? Your son ought to be proud to wear the same sports clothes that boys wear in Lima. Apart from that, I bought them at a very favourable price.'

'I'm sorry, Head Teacher, I am a poor farm-worker. I just don't undersand why I should have to pay for elegant Lima-style uniforms. That sort of thing will make my son become a spoilt brat!'

Talking points

▷ Why do you want your children to go to secondary school?

▷ What difficulties do you find if they wish to study?

▷ When your children leave school, how can they use what they have learned?

▷ How could secondary-school learning be improved so as to be more useful for the sons and daughters of farm-workers?

As it could be

What is happening in the Chontapampa Secondary School? The sons of the farm-workers are learning to despise their rural way of life, to regard everything that comes from Lima as superior, and to 'get on' at the expense of others.

What do you think of this kind of education?

You must have heard of the Education Reform Law. It has a lot of good ideas, especially for those parents who are not well off: it encourages dialogue between teacher and pupils, it encourages initia tives instead of stifling them, and so on.

In the new and future society we all dream of, there won't be all these ugly and exaggerated differences between Peruvians.

At present some of us have to work manually and never get the chance to study or time to read, while others go around in suits and ties all the time, and sit in offices without ever getting their hands dirty.

We lose a lot by never stretching our minds, and *they* certainly lose a lot by never exercising their bodies.

Talking points

▷ When will a day come when we shall all exercise our minds and our bodies, sharing menial tasks and mental labour?

▷ What are the good and positive things about rural life that should be taught in the Chontapampa Secondary School?

▷ What are the bad and negative things in rural life against which we need to struggle?

▷ How can we farm-workers collaborate in the construction of a more just society?

Let's walk with the Lord

Give us a heart big for love,
give us a heart strong and just.
New people struggling in hope
workers with aspect uncouth
New people casting off chains
pilgrims in search of the truth.

'My people, I raised up prophets among your sons, and consecrated some of your young people for my cause. But you made the prophets dumb,' says the Lord. '"Say no more!", you said to them.'

(after Amos 2.11f.)

We're off to town today!

One Sunday a group of farm-workers are going down to the weekly market in the town of Chontapampa. In spite of the rain and mud they have put on their best clothes and are chatting away merrily.

'That's a nice fat pig you have there, Pedro.'

'Well, I'm asking twenty dollars for him.'

'Hope you get it, then.'

'So do I. My wife wants to buy a new stewing pot with the proceeds.'

'And how's your kid?'

'Still a bit weak after the accident, but thanks be to God he's getting better every day.'

'Thanks be to God then.'

'Move that daft mule up there!'

And so they converse as they make their way to the market, happy to forget their problems, or at least to share them with their neighbours.

Talking points

▷ What do you like most about market day?

▷ Who do you meet up with in the market?

▷ Is it necessary to go to town now and again?

▷ Why?

We've never had it so bad!

Delfin Posito says:

'Let's call a spade a spade. We farm-workers in the Andes have never had it so bad. The prices of all the simple tools are going up continually, and what can we do without a pick and a spade? The same happens with fertilizers and insecticides and especially with the price of seeds. Yet when we try to put up the prices of our maize and potatoes in the Sunday market, the local authorities won't let us. They say our prices are 'controlled'. And when there is a potato glut they don't mind when the prices go down – the prices are only controlled to stop us getting more, not less. How on earth are we going to get enough money to replace our tools and fertilizers? It's high time we got organized and stopped being kicked around by everyone.'

Talking points

▷ Have you ever felt as Delfin does?

▷ What are the causes of the situation?

▷ What can a farm-worker do so as not to lose the fruit of his work?

Money is their god

Venancio Chavez is pleased with himself. He has just opened a large new shop in Chontapampa.

'Now I'm going to be all right. After all, it's money that counts in this life, and I want to have enough of it not to be ordered around.'

At that moment a farm-worker comes into the shop and asks:

'Do you buy potatoes, Don Venancio?'

'How much do you want for them?'

'Five dollars.'

'I'll give you three.'

Three dollars seems very little to the farm-worker, but he has to accept because he needs to buy things for his family.

When the potato sale is concluded, he asks Don Venancio to serve him rice, sugar, salt and a few other things.

'That will be four dollars altogether.'

'But I haven't quite got it; can you let me have a dollar's credit?'

'Well, money doesn't grow on trees, you know. I'll have to charge you interest. Five per cent per month and ten per cent for the first month. OK?'

The farm-worker has to accept, and finishes up with yet another debt to pay.

No one can serve two masters. You cannot serve God and mammon.   *(Luke 16.13)*

Talking points

▷ Do you know persons who have made a god out of money?

▷ How would things be if there were no money at all, as in the days of the Incas?

▷ What do you think of the slogan, 'Let everyone work according to his capacity and earn according to his needs'?

▷ Why is there so much injustice?

In 1972 a lot of Christians from all over Latin America met together to discuss questions like these. At the end of their meeting they said:

'Injustice is not the result of misfortune, the will of God or laziness.

Rather, it is because of the fact that a very few persons own most of the land and the industries (that is, the means of production). These persons organize society as they wish it to be, and to suit their interests. They are few, but powerful, and they form the capitalist class.

On the other hand, there are lots of us who are farm workers, manual workers, employees. We work for the capitalists. They keep the profit we make for them. We receive a wage or salary, which is often not enough to feed our families on. Although we are the majority, we are not free. We form the working class.'

▷ What can we farm-workers do to change things?

Peasant farmer of the Andes
who devours all your harvest?
Join hands with the city workers
and the future will be yours.

The wholesalers are rich
and know how to entice:
they buy up our crops
at an unjust price.

Let's walk with the Lord

Hear this word, you who trample down the poor and bring the poor of the land to grief, saying, 'We will falsify the measures, raise the prices and sell the poor for money.' Yahweh has sworn, 'I can never forget all your actions. The day will come when I shall turn your feasts into mourning. That will be the end, a day full of bitterness for you.' (after Amos 8.4–10)

There'll be pie in the sky by and by

Glicerio Longa is annoyed. He has just been forced to sell his potatoes at a very low price in the market. He meets up with Alberto Gomez, a cousin, and he starts to complain.

'They're all a lot of robbers in this town; I'm going to have a drink or two to drown my sorrows.'

'Glicerio, it's obvious that you are a sinful man. Drinking alcohol is very sinful. You ought to join our evangelical religion and then you'd learn to put your trust in God.'

'What! And wait around for God to give me pie in the sky when I'm dead? That's what the Catholic priests used to tell us in the old days.'

'God rewards those who are patient and accept their fate. Some men have been born to be poor, others have been born to be rich: that is called destiny.'

'And do you think that is God's will?'

'Poverty is a test from God. He'll reward us one day.'

Talking points

▷ After doing business in the market, lots of men get drunk like the one in the photograph. Why?

▷ Does getting drunk solve anything?

▷ What do you think of what Alberto Gomez says?

▷ Why do some people want us farm-workers to believe that there always must be rich and poor?

The rich don't want to give up their riches. Therefore the poor remain poor.

The rich will use any means they can to maintain and justify their position – even religion.

▷ Have you ever played football on a sloping field?

▷ What happens to the team that has to play uphill?

The rich are like those who play downhill. Their wealth permits them to play like that always. It is a lie to say that God wants people to be poor and suffer because that is his will.

How much longer are we going to play uphill?

How long, O Lord, how long?
How long until the poor are free?
They tell us we must never raise our voices
They tell us that the poor are really blessed,
and meanwhile those with riches take advantage
and use their wealth to feather their own nest.

How long, O lord, how long?
How long until the poor are free?

Let's walk with the Lord

Woe to those who oppress the poor and rob them of their possessions. When the land is redistributed in the assembly of the people there will be nothing for them. 'Say not so,' they say. 'Misfortune will not reach us. We know how Yahweh will act; his words are always full of kindness.'

'But,' says Yahweh, 'you are the enemy of my people. War would be better for my people than peace on your side. Arise and go, for this is no place to rest!'

(after Micah 2.1–10)

They want to keep the peace!

The parish priest of Chontapampa has decided to convert the old parish house into a centre for the pastoral team. This means that farm-workers can use the house for training courses, and that the rural catechists will have somewhere to stay the night when they have to come to town. But the townspeople are highly displeased with this arrangement.

'Now the farm-workers are taking over the parish. We'll have to stop them at all costs. If the priest doesn't need the house then we can use it as a town youth centre.'

The night before the inauguration of the centre a group of townspeople take over the house by force, throwing out two rural catechists, Oscar Campos and Jesus Flores. The following day these same townspeople, headed by the mayor, petition the police to intervene so as to prevent what they call a 'Peasants' Revolt'. As a result the police do not permit the inauguration of the centre.

Several farm-workers are hurt in a scuffle, and Guzman Perez and many others spend the night in the town jail for disturbance of the peace.

'Thanks to the police force,' says the mayor, 'order has been maintained. These new-fangled Catholics from the villages must not rise above their station.' One of the policemen is feeling very unhappy, because his parents are farm-workers. But he knows he must obey orders.

Talking points

▷ Why do you think the townspeople of Chontapampa were so keen to prevent the inauguration of the pastoral centre?

▷ What do you think of the attitude of the police?

▷ Who are the real disturbers of the peace in this incident?

Blessed are those who are persecuted for a good cause, for theirs is the kingdom of heaven. And happy are those who are calumniated and persecuted and have all kinds of evil said of them for my sake.
(after Matt. 5.10f.)

The case of Chontapampa is based on something that really happened in the Diocese of Riobamba, Ecuador. The Bishop, Leonidas Proano, commented afterwards:

'The pastoral work that is going ahead in this diocese is based on the living word of God, a word that frees us from all oppression, injustice and all attacks on human dignity. The farm-workers have begun to defend themselves, are discovering that they have a right to respect from others. This is what is displeasing the townspeople of Riobamba, who until now have grown rich at the expense of the farm-workers.'

Your people want to *see*, Lord,
and they don't let us, Ayayay!
Your people want to *speak* Lord,
and they don't let us, Ayayay!
Your people want to *walk*, Lord,
and they don't let us, Ayayay!
Your people want to *live*, Lord,
and they don't let us, Ayayay!

Let's walk with the Lord

Hear the word of Yahweh, king of the people. Thus says Yahweh to you and your servants: 'Do justice and righteousness, and deliver from the hand of the oppressor him who has been robbed. And do not wrong or violence to the alien, the fatherless, and the widow, nor shed innocent blood in this place.' *(Jer. 22.2f.)*

The arrival of the bus from Lima

The town of Chontapampa sleeps peacefully at the foot of the Picacho mountain. It is five o'clock in the afternoon and the streets are nearly deserted. Then suddenly a klaxon hoots in the distance: it is the daily bus arriving from Lima, a journey of sixteen hours. Doors and windows start to open, heads pop out, the streets become alive with people.

'The bus is coming!'

'My son ought to be on it!'

'I'm expecting a parcel from my daughter.'

'I wonder what the newspapers will have to say?'

'Perhaps there'll be a letter for us today.'

The bus has already reached the outskirts of the town. Boys are running behind it. People stand waiting at the corners of the streets. The arrival of the bus is the most joyful event in the day: it brings contact with the outside world.

Talking points

▷ Why is the arrival of the bus the reason for joy?

▷ Do you know people who migrated to Lima?

▷ How did they get on in the capital city?

▷ Have you ever read a newspaper?

▷ Have you ever seen news of the Andes in a newspaper?

▷ What sort of news impressed you most?

We who live in the mountains live isolated from other parts, and we like to know what is going on elsewhere. For this reason the arrival of the daily bus arouses our curiosity and pleases us. Sometimes, even though we don't recognize the fact, we expect good news from Lima, because we know things are centralized there, and that the government is there also. Perhaps one day we shan't be so dependent on Lima for the answers to all our problems. Then we shall have more sensible solutions.

My New People awake
with the new day
ready like pilgrims to march
along the way.

My New People arise
with the sun's light
to struggle for freedom and life
with all their might.

Let's walk with the Lord

How beautiful upon the mountains are the feet of him who brings good tidings, who publishes peace, who brings good tidings of good. (Isa. 52.7)

Those who migrate to Lima

Chontapampa, main square, seven o'clock on a Monday morning. A group of farm-workers are standing near the lorries being loaded up with merchandise for the journey to Lima. Among those waiting is eighteen-year-old Feliberto Carranza, a youth with golden dreams for the future.

'Lima is the city! There's everything there a man could ever want. I'll soon have a job and be able to buy a good radio/cassette player like the one belonging to Segundo Arribasplata. Fancy anyone wanting to waste his youth up here in the mountains!'

The lorry-driver looks at Feliberto and smiles. He knows Lima only too well. He knows how much the mountain people suffer when they arrive in that monster of a city, he knows all about the lack of jobs, the lack of any organization to receive migrants. He knows that relations in the shanty towns will put up with somebody like Feliberto for a few weeks at the most, but their patience will wear thin if he cannot find a job after that. He knows that it's tough being without money in a place like Lima.

'I knows Lima, Mister. I've seen with me own eyes wee kiddies eatin' pig food, and glad to get it. I can still smell the stink of

that there shanty town built on a rubbish heap, where black vultures fight for food and sometimes pick up live babies instead. I knows Lima, Mister. I said to myself, "This isn't a right place for a Christian to live in; it's more like hell than earth," so I comes running back to my Andes mountains and I'm not in the least ashamed of what I did by coming back.'

(*Todas Las Sangres*, novel by Peruvian writer José María Arguedas)

Talking points

▷ Who are those who migrate?

▷ Why do they go?

▷ What do they expect to find?

▷ What do you know about Lima?

▷ Why are so many migrants disillusioned?

The situation in the Andes is certainly bad. There is not enough for everybody to live on. For this reason many people have to go to Lima. But the Andean farm-worker who goes to Lima feels lost among the thousands, millions of people who live there. He is not trained for office or factory work, and so cannot usually get a job. The factory owners are pleased when there are a lot of migrants looking for jobs, because then they can keep wages low and conditions inhuman.

▷ And what happens to the thousands of *girls* who go annually to Lima in search of work?

Reinaldo has had to go to Lima. He has been lucky enough to get a job because he is physically very strong. Soon he'll sell his plot of land in the mountains and take his wife and children with him to a shanty town in Lima.

But his neighbour Tomas has not been so lucky. He has returned, sadly, because he could not find work anywhere. He has returned penniless and heavily in debt.

Such is the capitalist society in which we live.

Let's walk with the Lord

'On that day I will raise up the fallen huts of my people and I will restore them as in former days. I will bring home the exiles of my people. They will again build up the abandoned cities and dwell in them, they will make gardens and eat their fruits. And they will no more be taken out of the land that I have given them,' says Yahweh, your God. (after Amos 9.11–15)

The roads from Lima
are varied and many;
they are thronged with travellers
without e'er a penny.
     (popular rhyme)

Those who return for the fiesta

The city of Chontapampa is full of people who have come for the patronal fiesta in honour of San Andres (St Andrew the Apostle). There are a fair number of visitors from Lima, easily recognized in their tight-fitting suits and ties, accompanied by wives wearing the latest creations and blinking self-consciously with false eyelashes.

In the hotel bar belonging to the Galvez brothers the Lima visitors recall their younger days before they migrated from the Andes to the capital.

'I hope there are good bulls for the fiesta bullfights. A fiesta without bulls isn't worth coming to.'

'How right you are, cousin. Everything must remain as it has always been in the past. This is my first visit for fifteen years, and I want to see everything just as I knew it as a boy. Tradition and culture must be respected and handed on intact, without changes.'

'Have you seen the elegant new library constructed with the funds we sent from Lima?'

But the owner of the hotel interrupts the conversation:

'Gentlemen, have you not realized that the library has a flat roof, as in Lima? But here in the mountains it rains, unlike Lima and the desert coastlands! Within a few months when the rainy season begins the building will be ruined!'

Talking points

▷ Why do some people like to come back to their home town for the annual fiesta?

▷ What interests them when they come back?

▷ What do you think of the library incident?

▷ Have you ever seen Andean houses constructed in the Lima style?

▷ What do you think of them?

▷ How could the Lima migrants give real help to their town of origin?

Some of those who return for the fiesta are well off. But the majority are poor, and live in shanty towns, and have to save up a lot of money to return for the fiesta.

It is a normal and good thing for people to want to return home for the yearly fiesta, but unfortunately they often try to impose false and alien ideas on us.

In Lima the 'consumer society' has affected most of the inhabitants; they believe that you are more if you have more, an idea that is completely anti-Christian.

Brother, let me tell you this:
that my town has the worst fiesta,
men get so tight on local liquor,
they're only fit for a five-hour siesta.
Call that a fiesta?

Brother, let me tell you this:
that my town lacks both school and
    clinic,
yet money is burned on fireworks and
    whisky –
it's a sight to make even God turn cynic.
Call that a fiesta?

Let's walk with the Lord

I hate and abhor your feasts; your festivals do not please me. My will is that justice should prevail everywhere. You are poor in that, you rich, you important ones in the city. You do not suffer in the misery of my people. (after Amos 5.21–6.7)

The Andes: a worsening situation

Eladio Burga has urgent reasons for travelling to Lima, and goes to the bus station to buy his ticket.

'Good morning. Can I have a ticket for tomorrow's bus to Lima?'

'No, I'm sorry, there's no bus tomorrow.'

'But tomorrow is Thursday; there's always a bus on Thursdays.'

'Well, it's developed engine trouble, so there'll be no bus till Saturday.'

'Saturday! That's terrible. I have to get to Lima as quickly as I can.'

'Then you'll have to travel in a lorry, won't you.'

'My God, the situation up here in the Andes gets worse every day. Two years ago the fare to Lima was half what it is today, and there were buses every day. Nowadays there are three a week if we're lucky, and we're packed in like animals.'

Talking points

▷ In your region, does the transport function better or worse than a few years ago?

▷ Have you seen anything else that has deteriorated recently?

▷ Why is there a worsening situation?

▷ What can we do, faced with this situation?

The Bishop of Cajamarca, on many occasions, has denounced the way the central government has abandoned the mountainous regions to their own resources, without giving any real support. Here are a few extracted paragraphs from a pastoral letter written by him on 1 December 1975.

'I have recently returned to Cajamarca after an absence, through illness, of nearly two years. My first impression on my return has been amazement at the total state of abandonment throughout the region.

There are no longer any projects for highways or simple roads.

The agrarian reform has not affected the problems of smallholdings and their farm-worker owners. Instead of sending us more teachers for our rural schools, we have more secretaries and office-workers.

Another serious deficiency is that all the planning for the region is done not here in Cajamarca, but in Lima.

We only know that there is any state activity at all because we see a few Land Rovers passing by with slogans painted on them, and new offices opened in the towns without the people knowing what goes on inside them. Afterwards both the Land Rovers and the offices disappear, without leaving a trace behind them.

When large, foreign-subsidized projects are planned, like the Tinajones Dam, all the benefit goes to the coastlands and their people. Yet this water, which has its source in our mountains, could be used also to irrigate the farmlands of the Andean population.

In this way the Andes region becomes daily more dependent, with no iminent solution in sight'

(But the Bishop speaks later of the

'hopes' of the region, especially because of the qualities of character of its inhabitants, and of forestry projects being undertaken.)

'There is grave urgency for the central government to undertake energetic and conscientious action to stop the decline of the entire Andean region, and that these actions be effectively carried out, and not as before being the means of a few people filling their pockets.'

God help us and save us
for the times we live in,
if the harvest ain't better,
then we'll soon be in heaven.

The bosses in Lima
are the cause of our woe,
but if we stand together
we can ruin their show!

Let's walk with the Lord

O God, why have you forsaken us for ever? Remember your people which you founded of old. Do not forget us completely. We are as weak as doves. Do not allow the oppressed to be trampled under. The poor and the weak will praise your name. O God, arise and support your cause! (after Ps. 74)

The parish has changed

After the fiesta of San Andres, one of the better-off visitors from Lima walks round to the parish one morning. In the parish office he discovers a young farm-worker writing out a marriage certificate behind a desk.

'Good morning, sir.'

'Good morning, young man. I want to talk with the parish priest.'

'Father has gone out to the villages now that the fiesta is over. Can I help you at all?'

'I wish to donate to the church an altar frontal in honour of St Andrew. Surely the sacristan at least must be around.'

'Well, things have changed around here in the last few years. Now there is a pastoral committee running the parish.'

'And which of the townspeople presides over this pastoral committee?'

'I'm afraid that up to now none of the townspeople have wanted to join the committee, so all of us members are farm-workers.'

'How strange! In the old days the parish priest did everything, and farm-workers had no responsibilities at all.'

'That's right. The priest was more on the side of the townspeople and those who had money. But nowadays the parish is made up of those of us who want to search together for some kind of solution to our problems.'

Talking points

▷ What is your parish like at the moment?

▷ What changes have you noticed in the church since you were young?

In the old days the church was much more concerned about celebrating novenas, vespers, anniversary Masses for the dead, and so forth. The priests tended to preach more about the after life than this life.

▷ What do you think about this change?

▷ What should a priest do in a parish like yours?

The church must be concerned about the problems of the area of its responsibility if it is to be faithful to the words of Jesus:

I was hungry and you gave me food; I was thirsty and you gave me drink.
(Matt. 25.35)

And in order to be able to do all this, Christians of all shapes and sizes must take an active part in the work:

For as in one body we have many members, and all the members do not have the same function, so we, though many, are one body in Christ, and individually members one of another. *(Rom. 12.4f.)*

Let's walk with the Lord

They've petitioned me to sell you
a God that is easy to buy:
a mere insurance agent
or a bearded man in the sky.

And the only God I can give you
is a God who knew suffering and pain:
who invites you to freedom from bondage
and who gave you both body and brain.

You are a stronghold to the poor, a help to the needy in distress. You will bring the voice of the proud to silence; as heat disappears in the shade of a cloud so will the song of the tyrants be ended. God, the Lord, will grant his people honour. On this day they will say, 'Here is our God. Now we are content because he has freed us. The hand of the Lord rests on this work.'
(after Isa. 25.1–12)

Is the Co-op the solution?

In the city of Santiago de Llapa there is a Credit Co-operative. At the AGM there are only a few members to hear the annual balance, but most of them are contented enough. The president explains to them:

'Gentlemen, I assure you that everything is on a very good footing. We now have a capital sum of nearly forty thousand dollars, and we are in a position to make more loans this year. Are there any questions?'

'Yes, Mr President. I understand that a Co-operative should educate its members. There are very few members at this AGM and I would like to ask how you are spending the money earmarked for the Education Fund.'

'Very good question. This year we have donated a hundred dollars to the town creche.'

'But what sort of education is that, Mr President?'

'It is a charitable work. We are helping the future generation.'

'That may be so. But that is not helping

or educating the members of the Co-op. It seems to me that most of the members of this Co-op are just using it like a bank, and are members just for their own individual gain.'

Talking points

▷   Are there any Co-operatives in your region? What kind of Co-operatives?

▷   What are the economic problems of your region?

▷   How do Co-operatives help to improve the economic situation?

▷   What is wrong with the Co-op in Santiago de Llapa?

▷   Does a Co-op help its members to overcome their individualism and selfishness?

Those who work in the Co-op of San Andres de Chontapampa are talking about the situation:

'Do you guys realize that those who benefit most from the Co-op are those who have most capital to start with? At the same time, we who do most of the hard work earn very little.'

'What can we do? It's always been like that.'

'There must be some way of improving things.'

'How?'

'Well, for example, the capital could be used to create new jobs. Those who have invested their money won't lose out at all, but most of the future profit would go to those who do most of the work.'

'Seems like a good idea.'

'And besides that, we could take into account the particular needs of the members. For instance, a man with a big family has more priority than an unmarried man.'

Talking points

▷ Is it possible to put this sort of thing into practice?

▷ Is it just that those who have more capital should have a greater benefit than those who do most of the work?

▷ Will a greater number of Co-ops resolve all the problems of all the farm-workers of your region?

If everyone's hungry
then we'll change our world;
our children now are hungry,
our banners are unfurled,
to proclaim God's justice
and his daily bread for all.

Let's walk with the Lord

Lord, in distress we sought you; we cried to you in our torment like a woman with child when she is near her time, who writhes and cries out in her pangs. So were we because of you, O Lord. We were with child, we writhed, and when we brought forth it was no more than wind. We brought our land no deliverance.
(Isa. 26.16–18)

Towards a more just society

In Chontapampa a group of farm-workers have started a small business, run on a community basis. There is already a strong foundation of equality among the members. After a short time they decide to buy their own lorry, so as to be able to save transport costs and thus be able to sell goods at a cheaper price to their fellow farm-workers. To begin with everything goes like a dream, but then certain problems arise:

'The other lorry owners of the city don't like our competition,' says a member. 'They are doing everything they can to make difficulties for us.'

'And that's not the end of the story. The increase in the price of petrol has hit us very badly, especially because our lorry is a small one. Perhaps we'll have to transport our merchandise in the big Volvo lorries belonging to Venancio Chavez. They are diesel lorries and can operate more cheaply.'

'It's always the same story: the big fish swallow up the shrimps!'

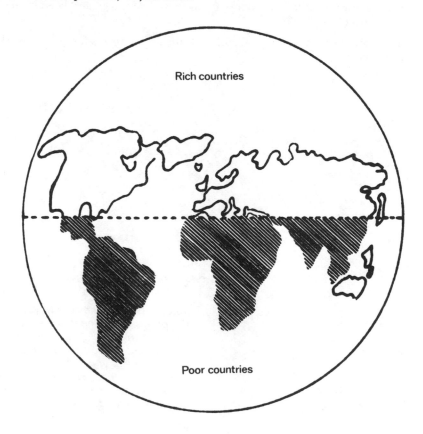

Rich countries

Poor countries

Talking points

▷ Have you known a similar problem in your region?

▷ Is it possible for the poor of the world to resolve their difficulties?

▷ What do you think when you look at this map of the world?

As the farm-worker said above, 'the big fish swallow up the shrimps'. Venancio Chavez swallows up the small farm-workers' community business. This happens in a small region of the Andes. But precisely the same thing happens on a much bigger scale. The rich countries of the world swallow up the poorer ones. This is part of the capitalist system.

The rich countries have a vested interest in men like Venancio Chavez and they will give him every support, because he is part of their system. But they won't be at all interested in supporting a group of poor farm-workers who struggle against exploitation.

God does not hold with this situation:

I will deal harshly with you for your sins, for they sell the innocent for money and the poor for a pair of sandals. They trample under the poor and cause difficulties for the humble. *(after Amos 2.6f.)*

And the bishops of Peru tell us:

'The experience of the farm-worker is contrary to the system of capitalism, because capitalism favours individualism, profiteering and the exploitation of one man by another.

For this reason a different sort of society must be created, a society that is more just, in which men are equal and where we can all help the weaker members. To achieve this society, we must all educate ourselves in a social and communitarian way of life.

It is thus understandable that Christians today recognize in the socialist movement a certain number of aspirations that they bear within themselves in the name of their faith.'

▷ What does this mean for us farm-workers?

Those of us who were slaves
have broken the fetters that bound us
we have lifted our hearts in joy
for the grace of the Lord has crowned us.

To make a world that is new
the Lord has his whip in his hand,
he drives out the changers of money,
and the meek shall inherit the land.

Let's walk with the Lord

See, I will make you a new earth. I will make my people a joy. They will no longer build houses for others to live in; they will no longer sow for others to reap. My elect will live on what their hands have wrought, achieved by their own hands.
(after Isa. 65.17–22)

Nothing is gained without struggle

In the days when San Jacinto was an enormous country estate belonging to one family, the farm-workers once tried to form a trade union to protect their interests. For this reason the police were always persecuting them.

Confronted with continuous friction, the farm-workers acted in the way described now by Agapito Nunez:

'We soon realized that the more united we were, and of course the more we were in numbers, the more difficult it was for

the police to do anything. Faced with so many determined men and women, what could they do? And another important thing: we made a resolution not to tell the police the names of our union leaders. When the police commander asked, "Who are your leaders, or representatives? Let them step forward," we replied, "All of us are leaders." And when he said to the women, "Who are your leaders and delegates?" "All of us! All of us!" "Well, who brought you here?" "Nobody, we all came together."'

Throughout history, and in different parts of the Andes, farm-workers have banded together to defend their rights against their oppressors.

Centuries ago they had perfected an organization which was able to look after all the minute details of rural life and work.

But sometimes outsiders have tried to impose alien types of organization on the population, and these attempts have always ended in failure, because they are imposed from outside, are not a natural growth and development from the farm-workers themselves.

A farm-worker from the neighbouring country of Colombia said this recently with regard to certain government 'reforms':

'The Agrarian Reform affects principally the agricultural worker himself, yet nobody has ever asked him what he wants or expects.'

Talking points

▷ Most of us know nothing of the farm-workers' struggles of the past. Why?

▷ Some people say that all those struggles led only to failure. Why can they say that?

▷ Relate any united action undertaken by farm-workers in your zone.

▷ Do you know of any organization that tries to support this sort of action?

▷ Do you know of any organization that is trying to put obstacles in your path?

▷ Is Peru the only country where farm-workers have labour problems?

Let the bosses see their errors
otherwise they're bent for hell
let us not relax our struggle
lest they toll our funeral knell!

Let's walk with the Lord

In the Lord I feel full of power,
and now I can face my enemies.
No one is so holy as you.
The power of the strong is broken;
we, the weak, become strong.
You guide the steps of your people.
                    (after I Sam. 2.1–10)

UNIT 6

The Poor on the March: Achieve-ments and Failures

'Young man, it is the dependence that must be destroyed; there is no complete salvation for the soul in the underdeveloped countries.'

(*The Two Foxes*, by the Peruvian novelist and anthropologist José María Arguedas)

A square meal, or a better deal?

In the village of Condorpampa live Oscar Campos and his brothers. Oscar has a way of life his brothers find difficult to understand.

'Oscar, what's wrong with you? Your field is an absolute shambles. Your wife and kids aren't getting enough to eat. Why don't you spend a bit more time cultivating your field, like we do? You've got a fairly good little plot of land, as things go, and your family could get along all right if you applied yourself to it full time. But instead of that you seem to spend half your time going to those training courses organized by the parish. They won't help you to get a square meal.'

'Look, mates, I go along to the training courses because I've got an urge to learn more. I want my kids, and all of you as well, to have a better life than what you've all got at the moment. I've got to understand more about why there is so much injustice, and then help to unite the farm-workers so that we can get a better deal.'

'You must be mad. Who do you think you are to change the world?'

'I'm nobody at all, that's true. But I feel a push inside me to do what I can. I know that my family are suffering at the present time, but I'm sure I'm doing the right thing by them. If we all stayed at home all the time, nothing would ever change. Things would just carry on in the same way. By the way, the brothers of Jesus called *him* mad, so I'm in good company.'

Talking points

▷ Do you know persons like Oscar, with a bee in their bonnet to improve the world?

▷ Is it always the case that our family suffers if we give time to educating ourselves?

▷ If Oscar's brothers were to help him in his task of self-education, do you think that the situation of his family would be better?

▷ Where does the 'push' come from that inspires Oscar to want to change the world?

The first time that God called a man to change a situation was when he called Abraham:

Because Abraham trusted in God, he obeyed when God called him and went to the land that God was to give him as a gift. He left his homeland without knowing where he was going. Because he trusted God, Abraham lived in the land which God had promised him as a stranger. He waited for the city on a firm foundation, which God himself had planned and built. He died without having received God's promise. But because he had trust, he saw it from the distance and in faith he looked forward to it with joy. So he recognized that he was a 'sojourner and an alien' on the earth. (after Heb. 11.8–13)

▷ God and the world will always need people like Oscar and Abraham, people ready to leave a lot of things behind them so as to find something new. Are you one of these people?

▷ What can you do?

Lord, my friend
you have taken my hand
you take me with you
towards the promised land.

You are the Way I follow
You are the Truth I believe
You are the Life that fills me
with love, joy and peace.

Let's walk with the Lord

Then I said, 'Ah Lord God, behold, I do not know how to speak, for I am too young.' And Yahweh said to me. Do not say, '"I am too young", for wherever I send you you shall go, and whatever I command you you shall say. Do not fear for them, for I am with you to save you,' says Yahweh.
(Jer. 1.6–8)

No family can go it alone

Anaximandro Marin, from the village of Pedregal, is migrating to Lima. Before going, he pays a farewell visit to his cousin Pancracio Quispe.

'Why are you going, Anaximandro?'
'To earn a living for me and my wife.'
'Can't you live off your smallholding?'
'No, it's too small. I'm still young and I've got to find something better.'

'And you think things will be better in Lima?'
'I hope so. My brother Walter has written to tell me to join him there.'
'In that case I wish you luck. In my case, even though I managed to get a fairly good job in Lima, I couldn't get used to the lack of freedom. I just felt all the time that everybody was taking advantage of me and exploiting me.'

Talking points

▷ Why is Anaximandro going to Lima?

▷ How many persons will have a better life if Anaximandro gets a good job?

▷ Even if Anaximandro does resolve the problems of his own family, what are the problems that he leaves unresolved by his migration?

When Jacob, Joseph's father, learned that there was grain in Egypt, he said to his sons, 'Why do you look at one another? I have heard that there is grain in Egypt; go down and buy grain for us there, that we may live, and not die.'

So ten of Joseph's brothers went down to buy grain in Egypt. Joseph was the governor over the land; he it was who sold to all the people of the land. When his brothers came before him, they bowed themselves before him with their faces to the ground. *(Gen. 42.1–3, 6)*

Joseph was alienated from his brothers because of what had happened in the past. They didn't recognize Joseph, though he did recognize them, and so played a kind of joke on them. In the end he revealed himself to them.

When Pharaoh learned of this he said to Joseph: 'Say to your brothers, "Return to your land and bring your father and your family. All come to me and I will give you the best of the land of Egypt!"'

(Gen.45.17f.)

Joseph resolved the problem of all his family, but what happened afterwards? The famine increased more and more, and the whole country suffered a lot. Gradually even Joseph's family began to suffer with the rest of the people, and then something worse happened.

And when the money was all spent, the whole people came to Joseph and said, 'Give us food.' And Joseph replied, 'Hand over your cattle and then I will give you food in exchange.' So they brought their cattle to Joseph and he gave them grain. The next year they returned to him: 'Buy us and our fields for bread. We will be slaves of Pharaoh and serve him with our fields.' Joseph bought up all the farmland and the people said to him: 'You are good to us, you have saved our lives. We will be slaves to Pharaoh.' *(after Gen. 47.15–25)*

And this was how all the people (and afterwards Joseph's family as well) became the slaves of Pharaoh.

Talking points

▷ What does this history teach us?

▷ The clay model of the shoe-shine boy was made by Casimiro, a farm-worker from Frutillo village. What do you think he wants to teach us with these two figures?

When hunger gnaws our bellies
then to Lima we shall go,
but unless the Lord goes with us
our journey will bring us woe!

Pray for your peasants, Mary,
for heavy is the cross,
Pray that we follow Jesus
accounting all else as loss.

Let's walk with the Lord

Hear what Yahweh says:
'The ox knows its master but my people does not know me, it has no insight. Now its land is devastated. Invaders have plundered the fields before their eyes. All is empty and abandoned, since the aliens went through.' *(after Isa. 1.2–7)*

Oppression hits us all

The farm-worker has always had to work hard. In pre-Inca times there was a lot of exploitation, and the Incas themselves were hard task-masters towards those of our ancestors who lived a long way from the imperial city of Cusco.

Afterwards very many died in the mines and feudal estates administered by the Spanish conquistadores. And the situation didn't change with the Independence from Spain one hundred and fifty years ago. Whenever the farm-worker protested against his condition, he was punished severely.

We meet this same situation in the Bible when we read how the Israelites were treated in the land of Egypt:

The king of Egypt said: 'Behold, the people of Israel are too many and too mighty for us. Let us deal shrewdly with them, lest they multiply and, if war befall us, they join our enemies, and fight against us.' Therefore they set taskmasters over them to afflict them with heavy burdens.

(Ex. 1.9–11)

When Israel was in Egypt's land,
let my people go,
oppressed so hard they could not stand,
let my people go.

Go down, Moses, way down in Egypt's land,
tell old Pharaoh to let my people go. . . '

Pharaoh commanded the taskmasters:

'You shall no longer give the people straw to make bricks as before; let them go and gather straw for themselves. But the number of bricks which they made hitherto you shall lay upon them, you shall by no means lessen it; for they are idle; therefore they cry, 'Let us go and offer sacrifice to our God!' Let heavier work be put upon the men that they may labour at it and pay no regard to lying words.'

Then the foremen of the people of Israel came and cried to Pharaoh, 'Why do you deal thus with your servants?' But he said, 'You are idle, you are idle. Go now and work; for no straw shall be given you, yet you shall deliver the same number of bricks!' (Ex. 5.6–9, 15–18)

Talking points

▷ Relate abuses committed against farm-workers in your region.

▷ Who always wins on these occasions?

▷ Why do prices of necessary items of food increase so rapidly?

▷ Is it God's will that farm-workers should always be exploited by others?

Let's walk with the Lord

The Egyptians treated us ill, they oppressed us and forced us to become slaves. Then we cried to Yahweh, the God of our fathers, and Yahweh heard our voice, saw our misery, our tribulation and oppression. (Deut. 26.6f.)

Who will bring us freedom?

No, God does not want people to be exploited. He made that quite clear in the case of the Israelites:

'I have seen the affliction of my people in Egypt and I have heard their cry because of their taskmasters: yes, I know their suffering. I have come down to free them from the power of the Egyptians. And I have also seen the tribulation with which the Egyptians torment them.' (Ex. 3.7–9)

Talking points

▷ Some people say, 'There's nothing *we* can do; only a miracle of God can bring us freedom. The rich are very strong, and we are very weak.'

▷ What do you think of this opinion?

▷ What do you think is the opinion of the man in the drawing on this page?

Normally God does not perform miracles. He wants our collaboration, and so he often gives a special 'call' to certain representatives. Look what happened in the case of Moses, the leader of the Israelites.

'Come, I will send you to Pharaoh that you may bring forth my people, the sons of Israel, out of Egypt.' But Moses said to God, 'Who am I that I should go to Pharaoh and bring the Israelites out of Egypt?' And God said to him, 'I will be with you.'

(Ex. 3.10–12)

Talking points

▷ In your community, who claim to champion the rights of the farm-workers?

▷ Do they really champion and defend your rights, or are they looking after their own self-interest?

▷ What happened to the state employees who used to work with you?

▷ Do you know where they live now and what they do for a living?

▷ Did those persons really identify themselves with the people of your region?

The Bible helps us to understand what should be the qualities of a good leader. In the case of Moses, who had been brought up and educated in the palace of the king of Egypt, it says:

He grew up without knowing the affliction of his people. But one day, when he had grown up, he went out to his people and saw their forced labour. And he saw an Egyptian beating a Hebrew, one of his brothers. He looked this way and that and, seeing no one, he killed the Egyptian and hid him in the sand. (Ex. 2.11f.)

Because of this, Moses has to flee from Egypt and from Pharaoh's anger. He went to live in the desert, as a poor shepherd. While Moses was in the desert God called him to return to Egypt to be the leader of the Israelite people and to lead them out of their slavery.

At first Moses did not want to accept. But in the end he obeyed the call of God, and returned to join his people and eventually to lead them to freedom.

Let us praise the Lord, the God of Israel!
He has come to the help of his people and
has set them free.
He has provided for us a mighty saviour,
a descendant of his servant David.
He promised through his holy prophets
long ago
that he would save us from our enemies
from the power of all those who hate us.

Let's walk with the Lord

Moses said to God: 'If I come to the people of Israel and say to them, "The God of your fathers has sent me to you", and they ask me, "What is his name?", how shall I answer them?'

Then God said to Moses: 'I am who I am.' And he continued, 'Thus you shall say to the Israelites, "I am has sent me to you."'

(Ex. 3.13f.)

It's time to do something

Feudal landlords, foremen, rats and cockroaches

'In some places, like Las Lagunas for example, the treatment given to farm-workers is still inhuman. There are feudal landlords with immense farms, and plantations who pay foremen a good salary just to force the workers to work hard. These landlords don't even know all their land, while the foreman doesn't share the manual work with the hired workers. He just gets rich at their expense. Some foremen even try to have their own 'farmhands' at their beck and call.

I saw terrible sights in the living quarters given to the workers. They are given very little space, and they cook, sleep and live in the same dormitory. Worse, they even have chickens and other domestic animals in the same dormitory. Rats and cockroaches continually molest the inhabitants and often prevent them from sleeping. This must be the reason why so many of the men were ill.

I said to the hired farm-workers, 'Why don't you clean up this place and fumigate the mattresses, so as to prevent more illnesses?' But they replied, 'That's the job of the bosses.' So I said, 'Let's talk with the foreman; perhaps he won't like us complaining, but there are a lot of us, and if we stick together . . . '

One day I managed to have a word with the foreman of our plantation, and I put some questions to him: 'Why are you always effing and blinding at the workers? Why don't you share in the manual work so as to give an example? The time of big bosses has come to an end, or should have done.' I told him about the history of the Incas, when even the princesses wove wool and did other menial tasks. We had a couple of stormy sessions together, but in the end we became friends.

Later they told me that the foreman had spoken with the boss, and they had both come to an agreement that conditions for the farm-workers must improve.

The following day, and ever after, the foreman worked with us, and was much less severe with us.

As a Christian I feel obliged to do something. The Bible tells us that 'the poor man deserves respect'.

(An article written by Raymundo Silva for the parish magazine *Despertar*)

Seeing the situation in which his fellow Israelites were living, Moses spoke to them of God's revelation to him:

Moses said to the people of Israel, 'God will free all from oppression and slavery.'
(after Ex. 6.2–9)

God said to Moses:

'Tell Pharaoh to allow the sons of Israel to depart from the land. But I will harden the heart of the Pharaoh and he will not listen to you. But with my power I will lead my people out of the land of Egypt.'
(after Ex. 7.1–5)

Talking points

▷ How does God present himself to the Israelites and to Moses?

▷ What does God ask of us in the situation in which we live?

Love is not a question
of looking up to heaven.
Love is being active
mass-transforming leaven.

Love is blood-stained wool
making up a skein
of exquisite happiness
and excruciating pain.

Let's walk with the Lord

*I heard the voice of the Lord, and he said,
'Whom shall I send and who will go for us?'
And I replied,
'Here am I, send me.'*
(Isa.6.8)

Beginnings are always difficult

Eladio Chumpitaz relates the following:

'Ever since we can remember we and our forefathers have been slaves of a feudal landlord. He had complete control over our lives, taking away the harvest we had worked to produce, obliging us to do the most menial tasks for him without any kind of payment. The midday meal he gave us consisted of a plate of watery soup and a few potatoes, served up in dirty tin plates.

In 1969 we formed a committee, and decided not to perform the menial tasks. Even though the Agrarian Reform of that time supported our action, at least in theory, we were imprisoned, humiliated publicly, ill-treated, and some of the farm-workers were killed by the landlord and his henchmen. In all this affair the local authorities acted as passive or active accomplices to the crimes.

Today we realize that we must trust in our united strength in order to make any progress for the farm-workers of the Andes. We have already decided to take possession of the entire estate, and we are prepared to use violence as a last resort, should it prove necessary.'

Talking points

▷ How do the powerful landowners react when we farm-workers begin to defend our rights?

▷ Can justice be obtained for the poor by the normal, legal channels?

▷ Do the experiences of Eladio have any echo in your own region?

Let us read together the experiences of other farm-workers:

1. Moses begins to bring the Israelites together: he speaks of the need they have to free themselves, and that God is on their side:

But they did not listen to Moses because of their broken spirit and their cruel bondage. (Ex. 6.9)

2. Moses confides completely in his brother Aaron, who is a good public speaker, while Moses himself is more a man of action:

They went together to Egypt and assembled the people around them. The people believed. They understood that Yahweh saw their suffering and came to visit them. (Ex. 4.29, 31)

3. Moses forms a commission to go to Pharaoh and request permission for the Israelites to leave Egypt:

Free my people. Let us go! (Ex. 5.1)

4. Pharaoh punishes them by making them work even harder than before. (see Ex. 5.4–21)

5. There begins a long struggle between Pharaoh and the Israelites. (see Ex. 7–11)

6. Only when Pharaoh witnesses the death of the firstborn does he finally consent to Israel's departure:

Arise and go from my people. Otherwise we are all dead men. (after Ex. 12.31–33)

▷ What is the Bible teaching us with the facts of this history?

Most people don't like hardship

The farm-workers of what had been until recently the feudal estate of San Jacinto are holding an assembly. The estate is now functioning on an experimental communal basis. There is much more equality now than before, but there are many problems as well. One of the experiments has been to pool the stock of seed potatoes, but because of the selfishness of a few there are not enough to go round.

Everyone is complaining about the community leaders.

'We were better off under the landlord!'

'Seed potatoes were never lacking in the old days.'

'I'd rather have a landlord and a full belly than have to sweat all day working and get nothing out of it. Call this freedom!'

Talking points

▷ Is it true that we farm-workers were better off under the feudal landlord?

▷ Do we always appreciate how wonderful it is to be free?

▷ Why is it that some people are more interested in having more possessions than in living like free people?

Talking points

▷ Why do you think the man in the drawing is being accused by his fellow?

▷ Do you ever get disillusioned with the community work in your village?

▷ If people become 'rebellious' and don't want to collaborate, what is the solution?

▷ Must we apply force and violence?

The Israelites reacted the same way as the farm-workers of San Jacinto. On several occasions they opposed Moses:

And the whole community of the people of Israel murmured against Moses and Aaron in the wilderness. They said to them: 'Would that we had died by the hand of the Lord in the land of Egypt, when we sat by the fleshpots and ate bread to the full; for you have brought us out into this wilderness to kill this whole assembly with hunger.' (Ex. 16.2f.)

The Bible tells us that the same thing happened to many of the great prophets and leaders. A moment comes when they get very discouraged and can't go on. For example in the case of the prophet Elijah:

Elijah was afraid and fled to save his life. He wanted to die, and said: 'It is enough, Yahweh, take away my life.' An angel said to him: 'Arise and eat, otherwise the journey will be too long for you.' In the power of that food he travelled forty days and forty nights to the mountain of God.
There Yahweh said to him: 'Go, return on your way.' And Yahweh told Elijah what he had to do for his people.
(after I Kings. 19.1–18)

Talking points

▷ What are the difficulties we are likely to face when on our way to God and in our efforts to make a better world?

▷ If we listen to those who discourage us we'll never arrive. How should we react to these people?

Let's walk with the Lord

Why do you say, my people, 'Yahweh does not see me, my way is hidden from the Lord?' Do you not know? Yahweh is an eternal God who created the whole world. He gives power to those who are faint and increases strength to those who are weak. Young people will grow weary and faint. But those who hope on Yahweh will gain new power, they shall get wings like eagles. They will go and run and not become faint. (Isa. 40.27–31)

The people start to criticize
Let my people go!
Fleshpots yes! and freedom no!
Let my people go!
Go down, Moses, way down in Egypt's
    land,
Tell old Pharaoh to let my people go.

117

God walks with us

Eladio Chumpitaz has been in prison for several months. He was sent there for being one of the most determined leaders of the fledgling trade union in the estate of San Jacinto.

But now he is returning to his village of Lucma. He has no idea whether he will find his family still there or whether his rustic hut will have been destroyed by the local police during his absence. His wife had been a tower of strength to him while they were struggling to put the trade union on a firm basis.

Eladio walks through the valley just as the sun sets over the mountain-tops.

'How I hope my dear wife is at home, and that nothing has happened to her,' he says to himself, looking anxiously towards his village.

My God, how marvellous! There is smoke coming from his home, but it is the smoke of a meal being cooked. His wife must be there!

Talking points

▷ Have you ever felt that sense of great joy felt by Eladio, when you've returned home and seen the smoke of the kitchen rising to join the clouds?

▷ Why is the smoke a sign that somebody is at home?

Eladio received great strength during his months in prison from thinking of his wife. In this way he was able to put up with a lot of hardship. And now the sight of the kitchen smoking reminds him once again of her presence. Something very similar happens between us and God. He too gives us strength and encouragement in our struggles.

God took the first initiative in the freedom of the Israelites:

'That is why I have come down to free my people from the power of the Egyptians.'
(Ex. 3.8)

And then he accompanied the people along the path to the promised land:

Yahweh went before the people to show them the way, by night in a pillar of fire to light them and by day in a pillar of cloud to show them the way. The pillar of cloud did not depart by day nor the pillar of fire by night from in front of the people.'
(Ex. 13.21f.)

And God said to Moses:

'I will come in your midst in a thick cloud, so that the people hear when I speak to you, and believe you for ever.'
(Ex. 19.1f.)

▷ Nowadays we don't see God appearing as a column of fire and cloud. But are we as convinced as were the Israelites that God really *is* walking with us all the time?

▷ What signs or indications do we have that God is walking with us?

My people are a walking people
moving forwards towards the land
where abundant milk and honey
will reward that pilgrim band.

I am with them as their manna
I am with them as their bread,
as a fiery pillar I'll lead them
through the wilderness ahead.

Let's walk with the Lord

Moses said to Yahweh:
'You said to me, "Bring up this people," but you have not let me know whom you will send with me. You said, "I am your friend." In that case show me the way, for this is your people.'
Yahweh replied, 'I myself will go with you to bring you to freedom.'
Moses replied, 'If you do not go with us, then do not bring us away from here. How shall it be known that I have found favour in your sight, I and your people? Is it not in your going with us, so that we are distinct from all the other peoples on earth.'
(after Ex. 33.12–16)

119

Don't be deceived!

One Sunday, Hugo Fernandez from Santiago de Llapa meets up with his cousin Artemio Cotrino in the city.

'Hullo there, Artemio! How are you? Still getting into trouble for worrying about other people's business?'

'What do you mean, cousin?'

'You know, all that stuff about uniting the farm-workers and things like that.'

'Well, I'm sticking up for the underdog, if that's what you mean.'

'If I were you I'd forget all about it. After all, what have you got out of it? Nothing. In fact quite the opposite: you look poorer than ever to me. As for me, since I came to live in the city and stopped poking my nose into other people's business I've never looked back once.'

'Yes, I can see you're better off, and you've put on weight as well.'

'That's right. My little shop is going very well, and I'll soon be able to buy a lorry. That's the way to get on, Artemio, and that's the only way this country is going to get on its feet, by hard work and . . . '

Talking points

▷ What do you think of Hugo's opinions about life?

▷ Do you know persons who think like him?

▷ Do you think his way of thinking will ever lead to freedom for the poor?

▷ What else in his life acts as a deterrent to our perseverance in doing our duty?

▷ Look at the photo! (The men are carrying an enormous quantity of 'aguardiente', or strong liquor, to a fiesta.)

Some persons get very enthusiastic about an ideal, like Artemio. But then they get tired; especially when they meet up with types like Hugo who are 'doing well' in life.

And so they become convinced that doing well is the only important thing, and 'the only way this country is going to get on its feet . . . ' But they deceive themselves and others, because only a few individuals are going to 'get on their feet', and they'll do it at the expense of the others.

Besides, economic progress is by no means everything, as the prophet Amos reminds us:

You fools, the rich and eminent in the city.

A year of violence is in store for you. You recline on extravagant beds, eat well, drink wine from large cups, use the most subtle perfumes, but do not care about the downfall of my people. (Amos 6.1–6)

When the Israelites were going through the wilderness, on one occasion Moses was delayed, and the people said to Aaron, 'Make us a god who will lead us onward.' So Aaron made them a golden calf out of the trinkets and ornaments they'd brought with them from Egypt, and the people had a big fiesta.

And so God said to Moses on the mountain, 'Go down, for your people has sinned. They have quickly turned aside from the way which I had shown them.'

(after Ex. 32.1–8)

▷ A lot of people want to convince us that economic progress is the answer to everything. Who are they?

▷ Do you see any comparison between the golden calf and this economic progress which is proposed as a total solution?

Tempting whispers pursue us
tormenting us on the road
inviting us to rest a while
and forget our heavy load.

Shifty eyes regard us,
eyes that are full of betrayal,
but we must stay our course, m'lad,
and resist the temptation to fail.

Let's walk with the Lord

A voice on the bare heights is heard, the weeping and pleading of Israel's sons because they have perverted their way and forgotten their God. 'Here we are,' they say, 'we are returning to you. The feasts which we held are no good to us at all. Only the Lord is the salvation of our people. The false god has swallowed up all that we possessed. We have sinned against our God, we have not hearkened to his voice.'
(after Jer. 3.21–25)

Some fall by the wayside

Eladio Chumpitaz tells us the following:

'I was one of the most active in leading the farm-workers against the exploitation of the landlord. This is what happened at the end of the struggle. We finished up by rising as one man against the landlord. Some of us were armed with sticks, others with rifles, and we went together to the large house where the landlord lived in order to throw him out. We had come to this because we could no longer stomach his terrible cruelty against us. Everyone went armed with something, though the more cowardly carried nothing.

Now that it is all over, the land is divided among us, but very unequally: some have up to twenty-five hectares, while others have barely half a hectare. Those who have more land have become little landlords themselves, and are no longer interested in defending the rights of the poor, and have even become friends of the rich and of the town authorities.'

Talking points

▷ What do you think of what happened to the farm-workers of San Jacinto?

▷ Why do some leaders turn into exploiters afterwards?

▷ What is the position today in the ex-feudal estates? Do the farm-workers have the same amount of land to farm?

▷ Why do you think the estates were split up into unequal lots?

▷ What do you think the two men in the drawing are talking about?

When the Israelites arrived in the Promised Land, new problems arose. Many of them forgot their struggle to be free from the Egyptians and they became attached to the gods and the customs of the land where they now lived. Even the leaders of the people were led astray by greed.

This was the trap that Gideon and his family fell into when they deserted Yahweh (Judg. 8.22–27). Gideon had been one of the most determined fighters among the Israelites when they had to fight off the new enemies. God had said to him:

'Go, and with your strength you will save Israel from the Midianites. I am the one who is sending you.' *(Judg. 6.14)*

Gideon began well, but afterwards he tried to extort money from the people. When he had enriched himself sufficiently he made an idol and constructed a sanctuary to put it in, and in this way he made himself even richer, by the offerings of the people to the idol. He lived luxuriously and with a lot of women; quarrels and fights broke out in his own family, and among the rest of the Israelites. His son Abimelech was so ambitious that he killed seventy of his relations to make himself king. And the Bible tells us this about the people of Shechem:

They laid an ambush on the tops of the hills and robbed anyone who came that way. *(Judg. 9.25)*

▷ If some persons become too powerful it is because others help them to become so. Do you know any case similar to this?

▷ What should we do to ensure that we and others do not fall into the same trap?

Let's walk with the Lord

Every one of us is sinful
and our faults we do confess,
we have strayed far from our Master,
and our lives are now a mess.

But if you give us peace and pardon
if you help us start again,
then our path we can recover,
and our lives are not in vain.

There is no righteousness among us, salvation does not come to us, for we have sinned greatly before you. We have not practised justice as we should. Righteousness stands afar off and truth has fallen in the public squares, and honesty cannot enter. No one keeps his word any longer, and they persecute those who keep far from evil. *(after Isa. 59.9–15)*

Free and independent?

In the history of Peru we see the story of the feudal estates on a bigger scale. When Peru was a Spanish colony it was really like a huge feudal estate, the landlord being the king of Spain, the administrator (or foreman) being the viceroy in Lima. In the year 1821 General José de San Martin declared the country a free and independent republic like the other countries of the continent.

Let us see what José Carlos Mariátegui says about this change in the power structure and what it meant for the farm-workers and masses of poor:

'The new criollo landlords have become more tyrannical than their Spanish predecessors. The "Indian" under the republic has continued his life as if nothing had changed. All the indigenous revolts and uprisings were drowned in a sea of blood. The just petitions of the Andean population have always been met with a violent response from the Army. The silence of the mountain plateaux has kept the secret of their deaths.

The republic has also given us the bureaucracy of Lima – all the hundreds of offices and thousands of functionaries. Almost everything is centralized in Lima, and the majority of the people in Lima are entirely ignorant about the rest of their country.'

124

Talking points

▷   Has the situation changed in a hundred and fifty years of so-called independence?

▷   What are the continuing errors we have inherited from the past?

In their efforts to become independent, the people of Israel felt the need to organize themselves like the other countries that surrounded them:

They assembled and said to Samuel, the last judge: 'Appoint a king to govern us, as kings rule in the other countries.'

This request displeased Samuel. So he spoke to God and God said to Samuel: 'Give your people what they ask of you; they have not rejected you, but they have rejected me.'

Samuel told the people what God had said to him, and said: 'These will be the ways of the king who will reign over you: he will take your sons and make them serve him in war. They will have to work his land and give him the harvest. He will take away their fields, vineyards and the best olive groves, to give them to his chiefs. He will take from you a tenth part of your flocks and produce, and you will become his slaves. On that day they will lament over the king whom they have chosen.'

The people said: 'No, we will have a king, and we will be like the other people.'
(after I Sam. 8.4–20)

The Israelites eventually had a succession of kings, most of whom built great edifices in Jerusalem the capital, and lived in great luxury, forgetting the needs of the mass of the people.

Walking forward in the truth
walking onwards to the sun
knowing that the lies will cease
when your kingdom comes at last.
With the long-expected light,
total freedom will be ours.

Let's walk with the Lord

Then they remembered former times. 'Where is he who has put his holy spirit in their midst? Why, Yahweh, do you allow us to lose your way? Come, for the love of your servants. Why can a tyrant gain power over your people? We have become like those over whom you have never ruled.'
(after Isa. 63.11–19)

A religion that brings no freedom

In the former feudal estate of San Jacinto you can still see to the left of the ex-landlord's large house the chapel that had been built at the order of the previous owners.

Agapito Nunez remembers how it was in the days of Don Pedro, the last of the great landlords:

'Every Sunday he made us go to chapel to say prayers, and three times a year the priest would come to say Mass. It was all very pretty: the priest put on very special vestments, gaily coloured, and I recall as a child staring at the white host, and feeling that God was there. But as I grew older I began to wonder whether God was really in the midst of all that luxury surrounded by the terrible exploitation suffered by the farm-workers, or whether perhaps he hadn't gone to another place.'

Talking points

▷ Do you have experiences similar to that of Agapito? Tell us about them.

▷ Some farm-workers are nostalgic for the ornaments and ceremonies of the past. Why do you think that is?

▷ What is the ceremony pictured in the photograph?

▷ Can God be present where there is luxury and exploitation?

Not only in the Andean estates, but also in the cities, there are large church buildings. The Spanish conquistadores always built cathedrals next to government palaces.

It is a good thing when men want to build a church to honour God in an important place. But there is also the danger that the building will be used to further vested interests.

When the Israelites were progressing through the desert they were accompanied by a cloud that represented the presence of God.

Then, when they had established themselves in the Promised Land, they constructed the great temple of Jerusalem. The cloud entered the temple.

And later on God showed his displeasure at the luxurious life-style of the rich and the injustices committed by them, and he withdrew his presence.

The prophet Ezekiel tells us that the cloud went to a distant land where a group of Israelites lived in simplicity and poverty:

The glory of God rose from the city. And the spirit lifted me up and brought me to the exiles in a distant land. And I told the exiles all that Yahweh had shown me.
(Ezek. 11.23–25)

▷ It isn't always easy for us to know what is wrong and evil. For this reason we need men and women to remind us. What do we call these people?

How long, O Lord, how long?
How long until the poor are free?
They tell us we must never raise our
  voices,
They tell us that the poor are really
  blessed,
And meanwhile those with riches take
  advantage
And use their wealth to feather their own
  nest.
How long, O Lord, how long?
How long until the poor are really free?

Let's walk with the Lord

Listen, what does the mass of your sacrifices mean to me? I have had enough of sacrificial offerings? Why do you keep making them? Cease to bring me vain offerings. I will no longer tolerate feasts and sacrifices; I hate them with all my soul; I am weary of bearing them. However much you pray, I will not hear. Your hands are full of blood. (after Isa. 1.11–15)

Voices of protest

What we are going to think about now is something that happened a very long time ago, about eight centuries before Jesus Christ.

The country of Israel was very rich. But the riches were in the hands of very few people, and the number of poor people was increasing dramatically. Those who had wealth and power made a mockery of the rights of the poor and humble. Meanwhile the worship of God continued, supported by the rich; the priests were on the side of the *status quo*, and were keeping very quiet about the injustice and exploitation. Until God called Amos, a poor shepherd, to be his prophet and announce his truth.

This is how Amos spoke:

Hear these words, you fools, who trample righteousness underfoot, who oppress the weak and rob them of their grain. You grind good men down, take bribes and prevent the poor from getting what is their right. But let justice roll down like waters, and righteousness like an ever-flowing stream. (after Amos 5.7–24)

And the shepherd Amos had quarrels with civil authorities as well as with priests.

▷ We are living in times similar to those of Amos. Could you point out some of the similarities?

▷ Are there nowadays any shepherds or farm-workers whom you know, who raise their voices to protest against injustice?

Amos said: 'I am not a professional speaker. I'm a simple shepherd and God told me to speak out on his behalf.'
(Amos 7.14)

Amos knew the reality of the society he lived in, and the causes of the evil situation. He always defended the interests of the most humble and was no friend of the rich.

Today many people speak of the need for 'revolution' and of 'the rights of the farm-worker', and so on. Sometimes they are just toying with fashionable words and phrases. Compare them with Amos to see if they are genuine or not.

▷ And we – what are *we* doing?

I sing of your eternal love,
I am happy to be your witness, O Lord.
Your word is a fire that burns in my
    mouth
my lips are now flames and ashes are my
    voice.
I am frightened to proclaim you
but you say to me:
Fear not, I am with you always!

You send me to sing with all my voice
I don't know how to sing out your mes-
    sage of love;
Many people ask me: What is your job?
I tell them: witness of the Lord!

Let's walk with the Lord

You were angry when we sinned. For a long time we did not obey you. We fall like leaves and our sins blow us away like the wind. No one calls on your name and tries to follow you. You have turned your face from us and left us to the power of our guilt. Yet you, Yahweh, are our father. We are your people, Do not be angry with us too much. All that made us happy is now in ruins. Can you still keep to yourself when you see this? (after Isa. 64.4–11)

In a world of exploitation

We have seen what happened to the people of Israel after they had set out on their path of liberation. What happened afterwards? Well, the Israelites fell under the sway of foreigners once again and became slaves for the second time in their history.

There were powerful nations that wanted to extend their power and become richer. It was very easy for them to capture Israel. Why? Because many of the rulers of Israel were selfish and also because the ordinary people were very passive.

When Jesus Christ was born, the situation was more or less like this:

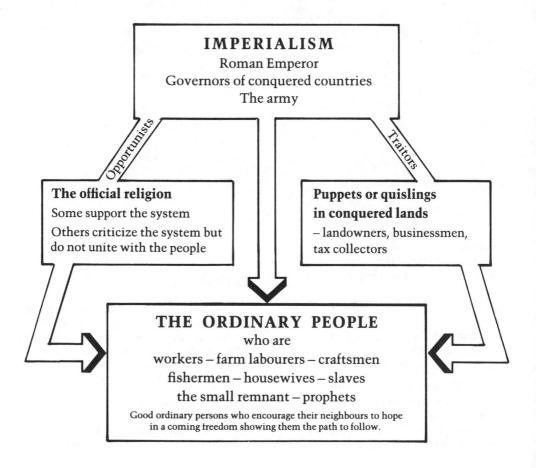

IMPERIALISM
Roman Emperor
Governors of conquered countries
The army

Opportunists

Traitors

The official religion
Some support the system
Others criticize the system but do not unite with the people

Puppets or quislings in conquered lands
– landowners, businessmen, tax collectors

THE ORDINARY PEOPLE
who are
workers – farm labourers – craftsmen
fishermen – housewives – slaves
the small remnant – prophets
Good ordinary persons who encourage their neighbours to hope
in a coming freedom showing them the path to follow.

Talking points

▷ Where does the Petromax paraffin lamp in your house (or your neighbour's) come from? Is it made in another country?

▷ The Petromax has increased tremendously in price recently. Who decides on these price-rises?

▷ No, it is not the owner of the shop in town, but somebody in the country where the Petromax was made. That person knows little or nothing about the farm-workers of Peru who use his product.

▷ Not only the Petromax, but many other products come to us from other countries, usually rich countries that wish to become richer at our expense.

▷ Let's look at the diagram on the opposite page.

▷ Does our situation resemble that of Israel's?

▷ What is 'imperialism' like today?

▷ Are there people who call themselves religious (or Christian) and who support a system of exploitation?

▷ Who are the sorts of persons today who collaborate with Imperialism, even when they live in Latin America?

▷ How do ordinary people live today?

▷ Who would be the equivalent today of slaves?

▷ Are there today good ordinary people who encourage their neighbours to hope in a coming freedom, showing them the path to follow? Who are they? How do they act?

Your people want to *see*, Lord
and they won't let us, Ayayay!
Your people want to *speak*, Lord
and they won't let us, Ayayay!
Your people want to *walk*, Lord,
and they won't let us, Ayayay!
Your people want to *live*, Lord,
and they won't let us, Ayayay!

Let's walk with the Lord

Woe to those who heap up goods at the expense of others. How long will it last? They will suddenly rise up and demand justice from you. You shall not escape their hands. For you have plundered a multitude of people, and all the other peoples will plunder you because of the blood that has been shed, because of the devastation of the land, the city and all its inhabitants. Woe to those who make dishonest gains.
(Hab. 2.6–9)

Forward, even though we are few!

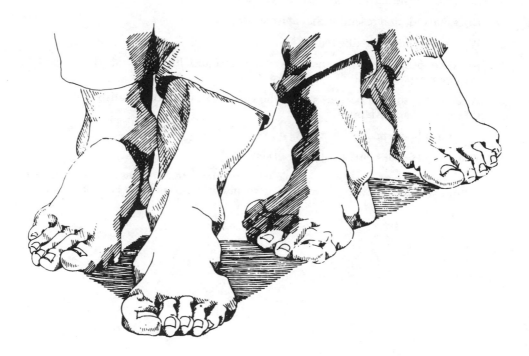

In the village of Loma, Jesus Flores realizes that all is not well. The elected village elders are either downright lazy or corrupted by the desire for bribes.

Jesus Flores is one of the Christian leaders of Loma, and so he is able to make his view known to many people.

'We should not turn a blind eye to what is happening. Let us collect signatures asking for their removal from office, and then we'll elect different elders.'

At the beginning the people were enthusiastic. But once Jesus had begun going from house to house collecting signatures many of them refused to sign and turned their backs on him; in fact they were afraid of reprisals.

Jesus is not discouraged by the cowardice of the people, but goes ahead with his denunciation. Unfortunately for him, however, the police have been bribed by the elders, and Jesus is thrown into jail.

Talking points

▷ Relate similar cases where somebody wants to help their community but the people don't understand or sympathize with what he is trying to do.

▷ What can you do when the people don't want to stand up and be counted?

▷ In the cases discussed, what did *you* do?

▷ What happened to the prophets of the Old Testament?

Amos was accused of meddling in politics, and was deported.

Jeremiah was laughed at by everybody and felt himself deserted by God; they threw him into a well full of mud, and ran off.

Elijah was abandoned by everybody and had to flee.

Ezekiel was thrown out of his country.

It seems as if the prophets were failures, but in the face of suffering they hoped against all hope. They were certain that God would never desert men and women who placed their trust in him.

Let us protect the fire
that gives light and heat
round which, in hope and faith,
the people meet.

Let us protect the fire
that makes us one,
that it may bring us close
to God's own son.

Let's walk with the Lord

For I will leave in the midst of you a people humble and lowly. Their hope shall rest on Yahweh. This small remnant of Israel will do evil to no one, nor will it speak lies. My people, let cries of joy be heard. Yahweh has withdrawn the judgment that lay upon you. He has cast out your enemies. Do not fear, my people, do not lose courage. Yahweh, your God, is in the midst of you. He is a mighty saviour. He heaps up joy upon you and makes you new through his love. (after Zeph. 3.12–17)

133

The Lord has Come to Free Us

He came back yellow-faced, without shoes,
even without sombrero.
He came back as poor as he had gone,
but in his eyes there was God . . .

What God? How do you know?
God is hope, God is joy. God is enthusiasm.
He had left ill, dispirited, hunchbacked.
He came back, strong as a condor.

(*Todas las Sangres*, by the Peruvian novelist
and anthropologist José María Arguedas)

In a despairing world there is a new hope

The situation in the Andes gets steadily worse. Our economic position deteriorates rapidly. Many of our best leaders have to migrate to Lima or to the jungle, where they are caught up in new forms of exploitation. The ancient forms of organization in the rural communities are weak.

All this is reflected in the damage being done to our natural environment. There used to be beautiful woodlands in Colpa. Now there are only sawn trunks.

But look! There are new shoots on the old eucalyptus trunk.

The farm-workers' communities and organizations are beginning to show signs of new life. Soon they will be strong.

When the Jews found themselves powerless and under the domination of the Roman conquerors, as if God had deserted his people, then this prophecy of Isaiah was fulfilled:

There shall come forth a shoot from the stump of Jesse, and a branch will grow out of his roots. And the Spirit of the Lord shall rest upon him, the spirit of wisdom and understanding, the spirit of counsel and might, the spirit of knowledge and the fear of the Lord.

He shall not judge by what his eyes see, or decide by what his ears hear; but with righteousness he shall judge the poor, and decide with equity for the meek of the earth; and he shall smite the earth with the rod of his mouth, and with the breath of his lips he shall slay the wicked. Righteousness shall be the girdle of his waist, and faithfulness the girdle of his loins.

(Isa. 11.1–5)

Talking points

▷ What hopes do we have?

In the last few years the large feudal estates have been broken up.

New forestry projects are giving new life to the dry hillsides, preventing soil erosion.

In many places the farm-workers are more conscious of their strength and their importance.

But the greatest hope of all is that in the small remnant of men and women who continue the struggle, Christ is present.

The risen Christ is living among us!

▷ How does Christ show himself present in our world?

Let's walk with the Lord

Arise, shine, for your light has come. There is darkness upon the earth, but the light of the Lord shines over you, the glory of his presence is clear to you. Your days of sadness will pass. There will only be good men among the people, and they will possess my land for ever. They will be the new shoot which Yahweh has made to grow. For just as the seed germinates in the ground and grows, so the Lord makes our happiness and righteousness grow.

(after Isa. 60.1–21)

My New People is awaking
with the day, with the sun,
confident that I am with them
and their final victory's won.

The risen Christ is among us

Oscar Campos lives in Condorpampa, the last village in the province. All his life he has been a hard worker, and has always been concerned with the welfare of his community.

But he always felt that something was missing; this was because he had always worked on his own before, whereas now he is a member of a group of Catholics who meet every week.

'Before, I was always alone in my efforts to improve things, although we did build ourselves a school in those days, but now I believe that a man needs something else, if he is really going to be a man.'

'And what is that something else, Oscar?'

'For me it means discovering that Christ is walking with us along the path of life. I remember the great joy I felt when I was first aware of his presence. The priest had come to the village to speak with us, and we explained to him our efforts to resolve our difficulties, and our isolation. It was then that he told us that however often men and women let us down and desert us, Christ can never let us down. He is with us always. And now when we meet every week we try to deepen our sense and understanding of his presence.'

On the same day, the day of the resurrection, two disciples were going very sadly towards the village of Emmaus, for they did not know that Jesus was risen.

While they were discussing what had happened together, Jesus came and joined them on the journey. But they did not recognize him. They seemed to be struck with blindness.

'What are you talking about in such agitation, then?'

They stopped in amazement and told him about the actions and words of the man from Nazareth and how the priests had condemned him to death.

'And we had hoped that he was the man who would free Israel.'

Then Jesus said to them:

'How can you be so slow in understanding! Did not Jesus have to suffer all this to enter into his glory?'

And Jesus told them the words of Holy Scripture which related to him.

When they came near to the village to which they were going Jesus made as if to go on, but they restrained him and said, 'Stay with us, it is almost evening, and soon it will be dark.'

Jesus remained with them. And while he was sitting with them at table he took bread, gave thanks to God, broke it and gave it to them. Then their eyes were opened and they recognized him. But he had already vanished.

They said to one another,

'Did not our hearts burn within us when he talked with us on the way and explained the scriptures to us?'

(after Luke 24.13–32)

Talking points

▷ When do we recognize Christ present among us?

▷ What does a meal remind us of?

For this lightless world
Christ is born.
To banish earth's darkness
Christ is born.
To transform our world
Christ is born every day.

To bring us peace,
for this world which bleeds.

Let's walk with the Lord

Thus says the Lord: 'The people has survived the sword, and now they are on the way to liberation. My people, I have not ceased to love you. I am building you up again. You will again plant and sow on the mountains. Those who rise up early will cry, "It is already day, go out, where God our Lord is." Give praise and thanks, tell it about that the Lord has freed all who remain of his people.'

(after Jer. 31.2–8)

God becomes man in Mary

So that man could be God
God became man
God the Father sent his Son
to become man on the earth.

Talking points

▷ Are there some persons who are more ready than most to experience and learn something new? Describe those persons.

By means of the angel Gabriel, God the Father announced to Mary, a young girl of Nazareth, that she was to be the mother of his Son!

'Rejoice, Mary, for God has chosen you for great things. You will conceive and bring a son into the world. You shall call his name Jesus.'
  Mary was confused and frightened, but she accepted the will of God and said: 'I will be utterly devoted to God. It shall be as you have said.'
  Then the angel left her.
                              (after Luke 1.28–38)

God chooses Mary, a poor and simple woman, so that his Son can be born on earth. He does not choose a princess or a person of importance.

Mary is the small remnant of Israel, like the tender shoot that burgeons on the damaged eucalyptus tree.

That is why the Virgin Mary inspires so much trust for us poor, and why we can pour out to her our pains and worries.

To think of Mary, to have recourse to her, means opening our hearts to hope and joy. The plan of God – our liberation – begins its course.

Mary invites us
to walk with God

Let us walk together;
he is our salvation,
Let us sing with gladness,
He is liberation.

Humbly we adore him;
He is our Creator,
Gratefully we thank him;
He is liberator.

Let's walk with Mary

'Rejoice, Mary! God loves you and helps you. The Lord is with you. He has chosen you from all women, you and your child.'
                              (after Luke 1.42)

Holy Mary, Mother of God,
Pray for us sinners,
Now and in the hour of our death.
Amen.

Mary and Joseph: a committed couple

In the village of Lucmapampa there were once two young persons who were madly in love.

'We want to get married – and soon!' they said to their parents.

'Joseph is earning quite a bit with his doors and windows,' the girl said to her mother.

'Wait for a year, my girl, at least until the next rainy season has come and gone.'

They waited, the rains came – and went, the girl continued pasturing her sheep on the high mountain plateau, dreaming of her lover, waiting . . .

'Joseph, my boy, what happened to your girl? I swear to you that she's pregnant! Who on earth can have touched her? You've been in the yard, she's been up with the sheep. She's deceived you, and all the village is laughing at you behind your back!'

Joseph is near to breaking point.

He shuts down his timber yard; he has no desire to do work of any sort.

'My God, is it true? (And it was) . . . My loving girl taken in by a stranger. Well, she can't be to blame, she is as innocent and pure as a baby.'

That night Joseph wept (even the most 'macho' types weep and cry sometimes) and he fell asleep in his workshop, between the half-finished doors and chairs of the eucalyptus wood, and he dreamed.

He dreamed that there are some mysteries in life that we never manage to understand; that his darling girl was as clean as the snow that crowns the highest peaks, pure as the ice found in the early mornings, and that life involves a lot of guts and sheer putting up with things and hoping against all hope and . . .

At the end of the dream the great Spirit God, Creator of the Mountains, appeared to him and spoke to him in a soft voice like a warm breeze:

'Don't be afraid, Joseph. Take Mary as your wife, because the child she expects is the work of the Holy Spirit. And she will give birth to a son whom you will name Jesus, because he will save his people from their sins.' (Matt. 1.20f.)

Joseph and Mary were very much in love, more than any other couple in history. For this reason their love could be completely at the service of God, of his plans for the liberation of the people.

In our time there are also many examples of men and women who have placed their great love for each other at the service of the people. For example, two Christians from Bolivia, Cecy and Francisco (Francisco died in 1970 as a guerrilla fighter). A short while before he died he wrote these lines to Cecy:

'Here in the camp it is winter time, and today I will spend some time studying the Gospels and praying the Psalms . . . I am keeping very well, my darling, but I miss you very, very much. But by being here I am more fully with you because we are fulfilling the dream of our life. I am conscious of your presence at my side. Yesterday we renewed our pledges in front of a portrait of Che Guevara . . . and for me it was a twofold pledge of love, to you and to the Revolution; when all is said and done, it is the same love.

We are now beginning to go forward. Whatever happens, I believe that something good will come out of all this that will affect for ever the history of this country. I would be sad to leave you alone, but if necessary I shall do it. I shall stay here to the end, an end which is victory or death.'

Talking point

▷ How can there be such men and women? Surely the Spirit of God is with them.

Love is patient, love acts kindly,
is not jealous, is not proud;
love refuses to remember sins long past.
If our struggle is inspired with love,
victory is sure.

Let's walk with the Lord

Set up waymarks for yourself;
make yourself guideposts;
how long will you waver without a destina-
    tion?
See, Yahweh has created a new thing on
    the earth:
a woman protects a man.
                                    (after Jer. 31.21f.)

'I sing to the Lord for he is great'

Mary went hurriedly to a small town in the mountains of Judah. Her cousin Elizabeth, already an elderly woman, lived there. The angel had told her that Elizabeth would bear a son; indeed she was already in her sixth month. (The son was to be called John the Baptist.)

When Elizabeth heard her greeting, she was delighted. The spirit of God filled her, and she said to Mary.

'God has chosen you from among all women, you and your child. Who am I that the mother of my Lord should visit me? You may rejoice, because you have believed that the message which God gave you is being fulfilled.'

Then Mary sang this Indian festival song:

I sing full of joy to the Lord,
my saviour.
He looks on a poor farm girl,
exploited and suffering.

Now they will all say to me,
'God has helped you.'
He is good and will always
give help to the poor.

Now we know he is great;
he has sent the haughty away.
He raises up the oppressed,
and brings the powerful down.

To the hungry bread he gives,
and the rich he treads underfoot,
as he promised,
God always fights on the side of the
people.

Refrain:
While we struggle let us sing
Of the Lord's great victory
All the poor must be united
so that we may not be conquered.
                    (after Luke 1.39–55)

In the southern Andes, in the church of Yanaoca, there is a portrait of the Virgin Mary with open arms. Beneath the cloak of the Virgin are the portraits of Tupac Amaru II and Micaela Bastidas.

The story runs that the picture was painted twice: before and after the deaths of our heroes.

After their deaths the Spaniard Areche ordered their portraits to be painted out. But after his death the Indians painted them in again.

Talking points

▷ Why did the Indians paint Tupac Amaru and Micaela Bastidas beneath the Virgin's cloak?

Tupac Amaru II, descended from the Inca nobility, headed an uprising against the Spaniards nearly two hundred years ago, because of the abuses and injustices of the colonial system. Micaela, his wife, helped actively in the organization of the rebellion, 'for the just claims of my people that have reached heaven, in the name of Almighty God'. The uprising almost succeeded, and was certainly the seed of revolt which was harvested by Bolivar and San Martin some thirty years later. But Tupac Amaru and Micaela suffered cruel torture and death in the ancient imperial capital of the Incas, Cusco.

▷ On whose side was God? With the Spanish invaders or with Tupac Amaru and his people?

▷ What do we learn from Mary's song, the Magnificat?

The Virgin Mary belongs to the poor

At the time when the Spaniards were conquering our American continent, the Virgin Mary appeared to a poor Indian boy called Juan Diego. It happened near Mexico City in the year 1531. The bishop was living in a huge palace, surrounded by the conquistadores, who had thrown the Indians out of their beautiful city.

One day Juan Diego left the poor adobe hut where he lived, and as he was walking towards the city centre the Virgin appeared to him on the way.

'Dear Juan Diego, where are you going?'

'Dear lady, I am going to your house in Tlatilolco, where the priests teach us Christian doctrine.'

'I am the mother of the true God. I want you to go to Mexico City to see the bishop. You will tell him to build a large church, which will become my dwelling place. There I will show my love. There I will listen to your sorrows and complaints and I will cure your pains and griefs.'

The following day Juan Diego met the Virgin once again.

'Dearest lady, I am sorry to have to tell you this, but I am very sad, my mother, they didn't believe me because I am very small and young, and the bishop didn't trust me. I beg you to send a more important messenger than me.'

'My son, it must be you, the smallest one, who must bear the message. Return tomorrow.'

Juan Diego returned to the bishop the following day.

'The lady wants you to make her a church on the plain next to Tepeyacac hill.'

The bishop was still sceptical.

'Bring me a sign and a proof.'

The Virgin gave Juan Diego some roses and said to him:

'Dear Juan, you are my trusty ambassador. Go to the bishop. My love goes with you.'

The small Indian boy went off hurriedly, very happy.

'Now everybody will have to believe that my lady, the Queen of Heaven, wants a shrine in Tepeyacac, so that she can show her love for the people.'

With the roses in his poncho he came before the bishop: 'My dearest mother sends you these roses as a sign and proof of her love.'

And as the roses began to fall to the ground, the portrait of Mary you see on the opposite page began to appear on the poncho of Juan Diego.

This is the story told by the simple farm-workers of Mexico about the origin of the picture and the shrine of Our Lady of Guadelupe, the Virgin of the Poor.

Talking points

▷ Does this story agree with what we know of Mary from the Gospels? What do the Gospels tell us about Mary?

▷ Why didn't Mary go directly to the bishop?

▷ Why didn't she want to have her shrine among the houses of the rich?

▷ In our towns and cities there are also churches containing portraits of the Virgin Mary. Do these churches help or impede the liberation of the poor? Relate what you have seen and heard.

'You will go ahead preparing his way'

In Loma village the Catholic group are having their weekly meeting. Jesus Flores, Artemio Cotrina and Juana Mego are trying to convince Tomas and Valico, who have become discouraged lately:

'These meetings have been a waste of time,' says Tomas.

'Yes,' continues Valico, 'because we are getting poorer every day. We sweat away at work, and for what? We go to town and the shopkeepers put their prices up when they see us coming. Life is all go, and all suffering, especially for us farm-workers.'

'There's nothing we can do. We've tried all sorts of things, all in vain. I'm fed up with talking about unity, and about getting together. Perhaps we'd do better each to go our separate way . . . '

'It would be better if we had a real famine for a couple of years, then the people really would get together and rise up against the system. A lot of us would die, but perhaps something would change in the end.'

'I agree,' says Artemio, 'that the situation is very bad. But we should not give in to discouragement. What we must do is to continue meeting together so as to learn better what is going on, and why these things happen, and how they are making out in other rural parts. If we were more united we could change the situation.'

'Well,' says Juana, 'I think we've made some progress, at least where we women are concerned, just by having these meetings and letting us women say what we think. In the old days we were only allowed to cook and clean, and never allowed to speak in public. I've learned a lot about how the Virgin Mary must have lived, and knowing that helps me.'

'We Christians must never lose hope,' says Jesus Flores. 'We know that there is a way. We have a great responsibility. I propose that we learn a new song and that afterwards we discuss what it means for our lives. It is the song of Zechariah, father of John the Baptist:

I sing to the God of the people,
who has come to set us free.
He has sent us a mighty saviour
descended from David's tree.

He was promised by prophets and sages,
throughout our long history,
we know that he'll save and protect us
from all those who hate you and me.

And you, holy child, are a prophet,
the last of a very long line,
you will make a way straight for the
saviour,
and your light in the darkness will shine.
(after Luke 1.68–79)

Talking points

▷ What do you think of the arguments of Tomas and Valico? Do you know anyone like them?

▷ Zechariah says in his song, 'the Lord has visited and freed his people.' How can this be so when we know that we are still so enslaved, as are lots of other people?

▷ Can we apply to ourselves the words, 'You will make a way straight for the saviour?'

▷ What do we have to do if we wish to prepare his way?

Let's walk with the Lord

My messenger is already on the way. He is preparing the way for me. Then the Lord whom you expect will suddenly come. The guardian angel of my covenant, to whom you look, is already on the way.

(Mal. 3.1)

Unit 8 uses numbers instead of names, so as to facilitate its use for group theatre or liturgical theatre. The key is as follows:

1. Narrator
2. Joseph
3. Mary
4. Man in the street
5. Woman in the street
6. Shepherd I/Villager
7. Shepherd II/Villager
8. Shepherd III/Villager
9. Jesus
10. A mother
11. Bishop
12. Teacher
13. Doctor
14. Neighbour I (female)
15. Neighbour II (female)

Jesus Shares our Life of Poverty

'Holy Child . . . you walked barefooted over stones and thorns, you knew the weight of back-breaking loads, you knew what it was to be hungry, thirsty, poor . . . Your father made doors, ladles, ploughs, just as we do, and our holy mother Mary used to cook and take food to her man in the fields, just like our women . . .'

(*New Stories from the Andes*, by Enrique Lopez Albujar)

Joseph and Mary rebuffed

1. In those days, President Juan Velasco issued a decree that everybody in Peru should have a valid birth certificate. This was ordered while Richard Nixon was President of the United States and while Leonid Brezhnev governed the Soviet Union. Everybody had to return to their places of birth, at least those (the major ity) who were without valid documents. Most of the Peruvian farm-workers were without documents, and they wished to put right their situation, taking advantages of the facilities offered by the decree.

And so it was that José Blanco left his village of Lucmapampa and went to the city of Chontapampa in the region of Cajamarca. He was accompanied by his young wife Maria Silva, who was pregnant. When they arrived at the city of Chontapampa nobody wanted to give them lodging.

And so José said to Maria:

2. 'We'll have to stay the night, Maria, because it's after five o'clock and the Town Hall is already shut. We can get our documents tomorrow.

3. 'José, I think I'm going to need a midwife to help me, and we don't know anybody in this town.'

1. José approaches a well-dressed man in the street.

2. 'Sir, for the love of God, my wife is ill and needs somewhere to rest tonight. We have money and . . . '

4. 'No I don't, I certainly don't. This town is full of Indians and beggars as it is. Why don't you sleep in the park?'

2. 'Because we are Peruvians like you and we are also human beings.'

4. 'And I bet you're also revolutionaries; one of these days we're going to put you all in your rightful place!'

1. A large woman approaches, her arms full of parcels and packages.

2. 'Excuse me, madam, would you by any chance . . . '

5. 'My goodness me, I nearly dropped all my Christmas presents; help me carry these things to my house round the corner, my boy, but go careful with that new radio/cassette player, they cost so much and they are so delicate, it's so difficult getting the right present for everybody these days: they all seem to have everything already, and things have gone up in price so much, and the ser vants are beginning to want more money (as if we didn't give them their food and their clothes and their beds); they'll be forming trade unions next, and wanting to go to night-school and have free days . . . Oh well, here we are at last; one moment I'll see if I have a loose coin for you in my handbag . . . '

2. 'Madam, my wife is going to have our first child, and we need a room to stay the night; would you . . . '

5. 'It's the same old story! All you farm-workers ever think of is producing babies, and then afterwards you expect us towns people to give you handouts. No, I don't have rooms for the night and even if I had I . . . '

1. By which time José has turned his back and walked away.

At that time Caesar Augustus ordained that a census should be made of all the inhabitants of the Roman empire for taxation purposes. It was the first time that something of this kind had happened. At that time Quirinius was governor of the province of Syria. So all the inhabitants went to their ancestral homes to be enrolled. Joseph also made the journey. From Nazareth in Galilee he went to Bethlehem, which is in Judaea. That is the place from which King David came. He had to go there because he was a direct descendant of David's. Mary, his wife, accompanied him. She was expecting a child and they had found nowhere to stay.

(after Luke 2.1–7)

Let's walk with the Lord

For consider your call, brothers; not many of you were wise according to worldly standards, not many were powerful; not many were of noble birth; but God chose what is foolish in the world to shame the wise, God chose what is weak in the world to shame the strong, God chose what is low and despised in the world, even things that are not, to bring to nothing things that are, so that no human being might boast in the presence of God.

(I Cor. 1.26–29)

Jesus born in a corral

1. José returned to Maria.

3. 'Did you find anything, José?'

2. 'Not yet, Maria, but we mustn't lose hope. In the cities there are not just rich people; there are also working people who are poor like us. They know what suffering is like, and so they'll help us, I know.'

3. 'Look, José, here is a small corral with a few animals inside. Why don't we just stop here?'

2. 'But Maria, our child can't be born in a corral! That's impossible; he'll catch some illness and we haven't got money for medicine, and you . . . '

3. 'José, I'm a woman. I know as much about suffering and hardship as you or any man. There's no shame in poverty, except when it comes from sin . . . Let's go inside; here's some clean straw where I can lie down. Lend me your poncho, José, and see if you can find a midwife, please.'

Talking points

▷ In what conditions are the children of the rich born?

▷ In what conditions are the children of the farm-workers born?

▷ Why do you think God wanted Jesus to be born in a corral for animals?

Quite a few years before Jesus was born, the conditions of the poor in Israel were also very bad. So God sent them a prophet to encourage them. He told them that the situation would have to get worse before it got better:

It too shall be a remnant for our God, says Yahweh. Then I will encamp at my house as a guard against the robbers. No oppressor shall again overrun them, from now on I will care for you.

Rejoice and sing, my people, for your king comes to you, righteous and victorious. He rides on an ass; humble is he. He does away with the chariots and the war horses. He commands his peace to all peoples.

The oppressed return to you in hope. My people, today I declare to you and promise fulfilment: I will restore to you double; I will brandish your sons and wield them like a warrior's sword.

On that day God, the Lord, will save his people like a shepherd. The sons of my people will shine on their land like glittering jewels. It will be great and strong! How glorious it will be. (after Zech. 9.7–17)

While they were staying in Bethlehem the time came for Mary to give birth. She brought a son into the world, wrapped him in swaddling clothes and laid him in a manger. (Luke 2.6f.)

154

In the arms of a maiden
a child was sleeping,
while in the world
the poor are weeping.

I would like, dearest child,
to warm your heart
and tell you my hopes
before I depart.

If the world should forget you
I never will,
stay with me always,
loving and still.

Let's walk with the Lord

And Yahweh said to Ahaz,
  'Ask a sign from Yahweh your God!'
  Ahaz replied,
  'I will not ask a sign and I will not tempt Yahweh.'
  'Hear, O king, you who should be seeking the liberation of the people and striving to go the way that Yahweh shows you. Is it not enough to weary men? Will you weary your God also? The Lord himself will give you a sign: See, the young girl will give birth and bear a son and call his name Emmanuel, that is, God with us. He will feed on buttermilk and honey like a poor man.'   *(after Isa. 7.10–15)*

Good news for shepherds

There were shepherds out in the field near Bethlehem, watching over their flocks by night. Suddenly an angel of God came to them and they were sore afraid. But the angel said,

'Fear not, I bring good news to you which will delight all mankind. Today a liberator is born for you, sent by God, the Lord. See for yourselves: you will find the child wrapped in swaddling clothes and lying on straw in a manger.'

Suddenly with the angel there was a great host of other angels, who praised God:

'Glory to God in heaven! His peace rests on all those on earth who allow him to love them.'

Then the shepherds said to one another, 'Let us go to Bethlehem.' They set off immediately, and found the child lying on straw in the manger.

(after Luke 2.8–16)

1. Once the baby was born some shepherds from the mountains arrived.

2. 'You are very welcome, brothers. My name is José Blanco from the village of Lucmapampa, and this is my wife Maria, and this is our new baby – born just last night. Please forgive these poor surroundings.'

6. 'The present, Don Narciso, the present!'

7. 'We've brought just a little maize-flour, for you to eat . . . '

2. 'Many thanks to you, friends.'

8. 'And here is a ball of wool, spun by my own wife; perhaps you'll be able to weave his first poncho with it.'

3. 'May God reward you, friend.'

6. 'I'm afraid I haven't got anything except this bottle of home-made spirits. I hope you won't be offended, but you

156

know how cold it gets out in those mountain fields, and after all surely God wouldn't have given it to us if he . . . ah well, you know what I mean; here's to your health' (passes bottle round in Peruvian fashion).

2. 'Friends, we have suffered all our life, just as our fathers and grandfathers did before us. Life has always been all go and all suffering. The townspeople have always devoured us like the condor devouring the young chickens and lambs, without pity or feelings.

But things are changing, brothers. Soon we shall become human beings with dignity. The sky will be the limit. We shall have teachers and schools and doctors and medical centres and . . . just like the townspeople.

We must unite ourselves with the workers of the towns; they too are many in number like us, and they too know what suffering is. If we unite we can win, as long as we don't get disheartened.

Last night our first boy was born. He is new-born, and is a great hope for all of us. He'll be on the side of the downtrodden and the poor when he grows up: of that I'm sure, because he is a present from God himself, and God loves justice.

Very soon a time of justice will arrive for us all, when the poor will be free at last, when the terraces of the Andes mountains will be cultivated with love once again. The baby is a sign of our future happiness.'

Baby Jesus
what can I give you?
Roses and daisies
I will leave you.

Baby Jesus,
all I have
is a new-baked loaf
and all my love.

Baby Jesus,
nothing I bring,
except my voice
and a song to sing.

Old folk are needed too

Joseph and Mary gave the child the name Jesus, which means 'God frees'. They brought the child to the temple in Jerusalem to dedicate him there.

At that time, there lived in Jerusalem a man named Simeon. He was pious, prayed to God and awaited the liberation of his people. The Spirit of God was with Simeon and had made him certain that he would not die before he had seen the liberator promised by God.

Simeon went into the temple. When Jesus' parents brought the child there, he took the child in his arms, praised God and said, 'Lord, you have kept your promise. Now I have seen the liberator whom you have prepared for all peoples. He is the light which will shine over all.'

Joseph and Mary were afraid. Simeon said to Mary,

'God has destined this child to make many people fall and many rise. He will be a sign to which many will object and in so doing betray their innnermost thoughts. But anxiety will pierce you like a sword.'

In Jerusalem there lived a prophetess called Anna. She was very old and never left the temple. She served God day and night with fasting and prayer. Now she too came, thanked God and told of the child to all those who looked for the liberation of the people.

(after Luke 2.21–38)

1. José and Maria choose a name for their child.

3. 'Our boy must be called Jesus.'

2. 'That is a beautiful name, José.'

1. And so José and Maria took the child to the church in the city to have him baptized . . . It was a Sunday and there were a lot of farm-workers there for the eleven o'clock Mass. Among them was Don Salatiel, father of Eladio Chumpitaz. He was a very dedicated man, who prayed a lot and waited anxiously for the day when the farm-workers would be free.

He was convinced that he would not die before seeing the beginning of a real change in the lives of his fellow workers.

Don Narciso had told him what José Blanco had told him in the corral, and so when he saw José and Maria enter the church he stood before the child and prayed in these words:

6. 'Thank you, God, for being true to your word. A child like this has to be the hope of all of us who are poor, and of the whole world. Soon there will be a sun to light up all the darkness in this corrupt and unjust world.'

1. And he said to Maria:

6. 'The authorities are going to cause a lot of trouble for us farm-workers in the future and this child will have to struggle hard; you too will suffer a lot, but then you are a woman of the people: you know what suffering and hard work are. You are a great woman.

1. There was also in the church that morning Sister Ana, who was known affectionately as 'Granny' by the prisoners she visited daily and all the other people who knew and loved her for her many good works and deep faith. When she saw the child she started to lavish praises and prayers on him and his parents.

10. 'Very soon we shall be free! We must make our final efforts – the Lord is on his way!'

Afterwards everybody sang this song:

Welcome and bless you,
your journey is done,
our poor home is your home,
you and I are as one.

Jesus inspires us
a new world to make,
so throw off the darkness,
farm-workers awake!

Lift up your heads, boys
and lift up your hearts,
the poor are uniting
from all different parts.

The Light is among us,
for now and for ever
the sadness of slavery
will return to us never!

Talking points

▷   Is it true what Don Salatiel says about women?

▷   Those of us who wish to help our fellow farm-workers, should we be men and
    women of prayer, or men and women of action?

Three professional persons

Astrologers from the East came to Jerusalem and asked, 'Where shall we find the newborn child who is to be king of the Jews? We have seen the rise of his star and have come to worship him.'

When King Herod heard that, he was very disturbed and asked the teachers of the law where the king promised by God was to be born. They told him:

'In the city of Bethlehem in Judaea. For this is what the prophet wrote: 'You, Bethlehem, are by no means the most insignificant city, for out of you will come the man who will lead my people.'

Thereupon the astrologers went to Bethlehem and found the child with its mother Mary. They knelt before the child and worshipped him. Then they spread out the treasures which they had brought as presents: gold, frankincense and myrrh.

(after Matt. 2.1–11)

1. One day three strangers arrived in Chontapampa. Anybody could see at once that they were important people. The mayor visited their hotel and offered to show them the latest projects of the Town Council. But the visitors were not interested. They said,

11. 'We haven't come here as tourists but rather to know how the farm-workers are living or surviving in these difficult times. We have heard that something new is beginning here. Can you direct us to the leaders of the farm-workers?'

1. The teacher of Lucmapampa, Santisteban, heard of this request and went to speak with the visitors. He told them of the child of José Blanco and Maria Silva, and what the poor people were saying about him. So then the visitors went to visit the child.

11. 'Good afternoon, Don José, good afternoon, Doña Maria. I am a bishop from Lima. I am very happy indeed about your son, and I offer you both my congratulations. I also wish to offer you a small gift, for you and for all the farm-workers of the region. It is a book, and it contains what we Latin American bishops propose must be done to improve and change radically the conditions in which you all live. Perhaps you have already heard of Father Bartolome de las Casas, a Spanish bishop who lived about three hundred years ago, and who devoted all his life to the defence of your ancestors from the greed of the conquistadores. Well, we wish to continue in his tradition.'

12. 'My friends, I also come from Lima, and I am a professor from the university there. I too wish to be of service to the poor and oppressed of the land, and therefore I always try to meet workers of the towns and countryside and learn what they are thinking and doing. I was not sure what to bring you, but finally I decided on a small book of poems. They were written by a young university student from Lima, called Javier Heraud. He always dreamed of a Peru where there would be justice for all Peruvians; he joined the guerrillas and was killed at the age of only twenty-one years. But he left behind a lot of beautiful poetry and he is already recognized in our universities as one of the finest poets in the Spanish language. Listen to some of his words:

Because my fatherland is beautiful,
like a sword in the air,
and because she can become yet more
  beautiful,
I speak and I defend her with my life . . .

Ours is the sky,
ours is the daily bread,
for we have sown and reaped
the corn and the earth
and the corn and the earth
are ours,
and for ever belong to us
the sea
the mountains and the birds.

13. 'I am a medical doctor. I used to have a very comfortable life and earned a lot of money. My wife and I were always going to parties in the better suburbs of Lima. But then one day a friend of mine took me to a poor shanty town where I saw the horror of abject poverty. I came to know many wonderful persons in those pestilential streets, and so eventually I decided to work in the Andes mountains, from where so many of them had migrated. And now my wife and I are completely changed persons. We want to do everything we can to help those whose lives are handicapped by malnutrition and unemployment. I want to offer you both the solemn pledge of my dedication (as well as that of my wife) to the poor of the Andes.

1. José and Maria are very moved by what they have heard.

2. 'I don't know how to thank you for your visit and your gifts, friends. It has been a wonderful surprise for us. Some people come to gape at our poverty, others come to make high-sounding political promises that are never fulfilled afterwards. How wonderful it would be if you professional persons were always united with us poor. Then we should certainly change the world we live in. God has given us all different talents, as well as different degrees of intelligence, and they must not be used selfishly and greedily, but for everybody.'

Talking points

▷ Sometimes professional people come to help us from Lima or from foreign countries. Do they really help the farm-workers?

▷ What attitudes must professional persons have if they really want to help us?

Finally a Samaritan, an alien, came along. When he saw the man who had been attacked by robbers he took pity on him. He went up to him and treated his wounds.

Jesus asked the teacher of the law, 'Which of the three do you think acted as a neighbour towards the victim?'

The teacher of the law replied, 'The one who helped him.'

Jesus retorted, 'Go and do likewise.'

(after Luke 10.29–37)

161

A dangerous child

When Herod saw that the astrologers had avoided him he became very angry. Thus it came about what the prophet Jeremiah had prophesied:

'Weeping and wailing was heard: Rachel weeping for her children and will not be comforted, for they are all dead.'

(after Matt. 2.16–18)

1. José Blanco and Maria Silva returned to Lucmapampa, and life became fairly normal again, with lots of hard work for them both; but they were very happy now.

One day, when the child was beginning to walk a few steps, Maria came running home:

3. 'José, José, the neighbour's baby has just died, and they say it's whooping cough, and that there's an epidemic and a lot of children could die because it's catching. José, our boy could die . . .'

2. 'All right, Maria, calm down a little, and let's visit the neighbour and try to console her.'

1. Many neighbours have arrived for the 'wake' in honour of the dead child; some of them pray the rosary, others make comments.

6. 'Whooping cough is a killer of an illness; I don't know what we can do.'

14. 'Why can't they send up the vaccine from town? They knew some days ago.'

7. 'It seems they don't care too much down there. I even heard one of them say that we farm-workers have a lot of children and so a few deaths won't matter. They think it's dangerous to have too many Indians, as they call us.'

15. 'How terrible of them.'

2. 'The blame is really on those leaders of the rich countries of the world. Do you remember, Esteban, what we learned

about in the parish training weekend? They are frightened there are going to be too many poor people in the world, because they think we will rise up one day and take the power away from them!'

8. 'And I remember hearing what one of those politicians from a rich land had said: "Our country is hardly growing at all," he said, "but the poor countries are growing very quickly. They'll be able to beat us in a war, if we're not careful. Even if they share out more equally the wealth of all the world, we'll not be very well off afterwards."'

2. 'And the same person said: "We must make great campaigns so that they don't have so many children; if we spend money on making them have fewer children it will work out cheaper than buying bombs to kill them when they are grown

up." And the bishops of Bolivia have protested because when the farm-workers there went to medical centres to be treated for something like 'flu, they were given something that stopped them ever having babies again.'

3. 'And besides that, the rich countries take away a lot of our herbs and plants, and then put them into special containers that look good and sell them back to us as expensive medicine. They are also to blame for our children dying.'

Talking points

▷ What can we do faced with the fact that the rich countries don't want us to have a lot of children?

▷ It's not a good thing to have too many children. The best thing would be for us to have the children we can feed and clothe, and help to become defenders of their fellow farm-workers when they grow up. How can we do that?

Love is patient, love acts kindly,
is not jealous, is not proud;
love refuses to remember sins long past.
If our struggle is inspired with love,
victory is sure.

Let's walk with the Lord

Rachel, my people, weep no more; for your work shall be rewarded, your sons shall be free.

Are you not my people, my favourite son? You can be proud; I am always thinking of you.

I want you to go the good way. If I punish you, to improve you, I am always grieved within myself, and my heart goes out to you in pity.

Set up waymarks for yourself, consider the way you have to go. Come home! Come home! How long will you waver, my son, when you have to come home.

Yahweh has created a new thing in your land: a woman returns to her man.

(after Jer. 31.16–22)

From bad to worse

When hunger gnaws our bellies
then to Lima we shall go,
but unless the Lord goes with us
our journey will bring us woe!

Pray for your peasants, Mary,
for heavy is our cross,
Pray that we follow Jesus,
counting everything else as loss.

After the astrologers had returned to their land, an angel appeared to Joseph and said, 'Arise, take the child and its mother and flee to Egypt. Remain there until I tell you that you can come back. Herod will do all in his power to kill the child.'

Then Joseph set out for Egypt in the middle of the night with the child and his mother. So it came about what God had prophesied through the prophets: 'Out of Egypt I called my son.'

(Matt. 2.13–15)

1. José and Maria took the child with them to Lima. They travelled seventeen hours in a lorry from Chontapampa along dusty roads filled with pot-holes; the vehicle was full to bursting – entire families migrating with all their belongings.
2. What a sad sight!
1. Once in Lima their cousin Gregorio put them up in his house, a precarious dwelling in the shanty town of San Cristobal. One night the cousin took José

along to a meeting of Christians where the following passage from the Bible was read.

When my people were young, I loved them very much, and out of Egypt I called my son. I taught him to walk, I took him in my arms, but he did not recognize that I was helping him to develop. I was close to him without forcing him; I cherished him; I was like one who brings liberation from the yoke of the oppressor. I bowed down and gave him food to eat. How could you abandon me, my people? You make me bitterly angry, but I will not destroy you, for I am God and not a man. I am Yahweh, your God from Egypt, the only one who can save you, and I am in your midst.

They are killing you, my people! Woe! Where is your king?

Return to Yahweh your God. You will follow me; I will roar like a lion in the night. They will come from Egypt, trembling like doves. Your shoots will spring forth, my people, and you will again tend good pastures.

(after Hosea 11–14)

In the mountains we are fond of singing songs at Christmas dedicated to the child Emmanuel ('Manuelito' we call him). Nearly all the songs are of wonder that God should become poor like us. In Egypt he went from bad to worse, because he and his parents were exiles, driven by necessity from their home.

God wanted his son to share our life of poverty and suffering. When he travelled to Egypt he must have shared all the discomforts of travel that we all know so well, together with the hardship of taking up your roots and going to a new and strange city.

He didn't keep silent

Wake up, brother worker,
wake up from your dreams,
life for mountain farmers
is not what it seems.

Let us raise our voices
echo forth our shout,
justice must be ours again
let us never doubt!

It will stop, it will stop,
one day we'll stop the exploitation
when workers of field and factory
join arms to make revolution.

1. When Jesus was a little older, he went with his parents to Cajamarca City for the religious fiesta in honour of The Lord of Justice. There was a festival of song as part of the celebrations, and the main square was full of people. Jesus enjoyed the singing very much and stood up near the bands. One band presented a song called 'Wake up, brother worker' (printed above), but the priests and town authorities who had organized the fiesta were very annoyed. One of them shouted out,
4. 'Condor Beer aren't giving prizes for that sort of subversive rubbish!'
1. So the choirmaster spoke through the loudspeakers:
6. 'We haven't sung for a prize. We just want the people to hear our song.'

1. The organizers of the festival hurriedly brought the songs to an end, saying that it was time for the procession.

Jesus Blanco went off with the musicians. They told him that the song that caused the trouble had been composed by a worker who had been born in the Andes, and that the choir director himself was a farm-worker.

After the procession was over, Jesus went with them to the Bishop's House where a group of Christians were in a training course. Jesus listened carefully to everything, and sometimes put questions.

'Do you think that the fiesta should always be celebrated in exactly the same way as before, just because that's the way it's always been done?'

The training course teachers were very surprised at his sharpness and intuitions, and they finished up putting some questions to him. One of his replies was:

'I think that Our Lord of Justice isn't so very pleased at being carried in procession on a special stretcher covered in gold. I think that in these difficult times the stretcher of the Lord is the poor themselves.'

Talking points

▷ Do we understand the reply of Jesus? What do we think?

▷ Do the words and actions of Jesus Blanco in Cajamarca City have very much in common with the words and actions of Jesus Christ in Jerusalem at the age of twelve?

Let us recall p.127 of our book. Jesus understood well the prophets of Israel, and above all he acted according to the way they prophesied.

When the exiles were living away from their country, some of them missed their beautiful temple in Jerusalem, and would say things like,

'So God was with us all the time, and worked miracles for us!'

God ordered Ezekiel to be a prophet for the exiles and to teach the Israelites that God was with his people even when they were not in their country; that their exile had come about because of a situation of injustice for which many of them were guilty; that they should be converted again and begin a new path to their total freedom. They should understand that their real temple was the Lord himself,

and that they were the temple of the Lord.

When Jesus came, the former Yahweh of Armies had become a small child, one of them.

Listen, man, to what I have to say. Take this scroll and eat it. (It was filled on both sides with lamentations, sighs and cries of despair.)

Then go to the exiles from your people and tell them what I, the Lord, command you, whether they listen to you or not.

Behind me I heard thunder and roaring when the glory of the Lord rose from its place.

The spirit of God which had seized me took me away. I was shattered and very disturbed. I returned to the exiles. For seven whole days I sat there stiff and without moving.

(after Ezek. 3.1–15)

He too was a worker

1. And so Jesus Blanco returned with his parents to Lucmapampa, and lived obediently with them. His mother kept in her heart the memory of all these happenings, as Jesus grew like any other boy. Each day he grew stronger in body, and sharper in his mind. Everyone had a special affection for Jesus; it was obvious that God had a very special love for him also.

Jesus had to work hard, just like his parents and neighbours. The smallholding was barely sufficient to support them, even in a good year. So José used to fill in odd moments making doors and chairs and yokes and anything else made of wood. Jesus used to help, of course, and in time became as good as José; he learned to turn his hand to whatever work was needed to help the precarious family budget.

Jesus attended all the meetings of the village community. Whenever there was a problem or need he was there. He was always interested in understanding the reasons behind problems and difficult situations. He used to attend the training courses held at the parish and later at Diocesan House in Cajamarca. He used to carry his small transistor radio around with him, listening to the Andean folk music and also to the news programmes.

Jesus suffered when he saw how exploited the farm-workers were, both by the people of the cities and by the big multinational companies. When the group studied the Bible together, Jesus tried hard to apply what he read to his own people. He was worried by the lack of union and organization among the farm-workers.

But he went about things in a quiet way. In fact at times he was doubtful whether he would ever make a leader at all. However, his parish priest used to encourage him. 'We need you, Jesus.' Still, Jesus was silent, and finally replied, 'Not yet, Father.'

One day Jesus composed a song. He didn't want the others to know he had written it, but he gave it to the priest, and they all sang it at the next meeting.

The time has arrived
for sowing to begin
all the neighbours are here
and all of our kin.

The oxen are ready
to plough up our land
let's begin with a fiesta,
let's call in the band!

Then we'll scatter the seed
and cover it up
and we'll pray that the rain
will make it grow up.

Jesus often sang his own song as he worked, though on several occasions his mother heard him sing a different chorus line:

The time has arrived
for sowing to begin
I am that seed
which must die in the ground.

Maria wondered why he changed the words.

Jesus returned with his parents to Nazareth and was obedient to them; and his mother kept all these things in her heart. And Jesus increased in wisdom and in stature, and in favour with God and man.
(Luke 2.51f.)

Jesus went to his home town and began to teach. All those who heard him were very surprised.
'Where did this man get all this?' they asked one another. 'What is this wisdom given to him? How can he do such miracles? Is he not the carpenter, the son of Mary?'
(Mark 6.1–3)

Talking points

▷ Why do we often think that field-work is inferior in some way to other work?

▷ Why do we sometimes want our children to have a 'better' job?

▷ How are we helped by knowing that Jesus too was a worker like us?

We are your people, O Lord,
a people in search of your love.
All our manual work
is shared with you,
all our sweat and grief
is known by you.

Let's walk with the Lord

How could you leave me, my people? I am the Lord your God, the only one who can save you, and I am in your midst. I am like one who frees you from the yoke of oppression. You will follow me!
(after Hos. 11 and 13)

He too liked fiestas

There was a wedding in Cana of Galilee. The mother of Jesus was also there, and Jesus had been invited with his disciples. When the wine ran out, his mother said to him, 'They have no more wine!'

Jesus replied, 'You do not need to tell me what I have to do, mother, my time has not yet come.'

She said to the servants, 'Do whatever he tells you.'

There were six clay water pots in the house, each of them holding between eighty and a hundred and twenty litres. Jesus said to the servants:

'Fill them with water!'

They filled them to the brim. Then he said to them:

'Take a sample and bring it to the steward of the feast.'

This they did, and the man tasted the water. It had become wine. He called the bridegroom and said:

'People usually put the best wine on the table first, and then produce more ordinary

wine when the guests have already drunk a good deal. But you have kept the best wine to the end!'

Jesus did this in Cana of Galilee. It was the first miracle with which he showed his glory, and his disciples believed on him.

(after John 2.1–11)

Our God-of-the-poor is not a sad and long-faced God. He didn't come on earth to take away our innocent pleasures. Quite the opposite. Jesus is among us with the one purpose of taking us all to the great and final fiesta. Our God-of-the-poor is a happy God. He enjoyed, and continues to enjoy, parties and joyful get-togethers.

Of course, we'll have to work and struggle hard in order to be admitted to the Great Fiesta at the end of time. But we must have faith that it will come about. It is a question of following the way of the Lord, knowing that at the end we shall meet him, and there will be the great wedding feast that he has promised. Saint John, his disciple, told us about the Cana fiesta (on the opposite page) and it is he who also tells us about the wedding feast at the end of the world.

Then I saw a new heaven and a new earth; for the first heaven and the first earth had passed away, and the sea was no more. And I saw the holy city, new Jerusalem, coming down out of heaven from God, prepared as a bride adorned for her husband; and I heard a great voice from the throne, saying, 'Behold, the dwelling of God is with men. He will dwell with them, and they shall be his people, and God himself will be with them; he will wipe away every tear from their eyes, and death shall be no more, neither shall there be mourning nor crying nor pain any more, for the former things have passed away.'

(Rev. 21.1–4)

Come, come, come to the fiesta
come to dance and come to sing,
though we're poor it doesn't matter:
Share your food,
share everything.

Let's denounce the cruel oppression:
let no one be king and no one slave
sharing our lives and hearts and fortune
is the most Christian way to behave.

Let's walk with the Lord

Awake, awake,
put on your strength, O Zion;
put on your beautiful garments.
You who were once a slave,
loose the bonds from your neck.

How beautiful upon the mountains
are the feet of him who brings good tid-
ings,
who brings good news
and says to my people,
'Your God is king!'

Hearken, your watchmen raise their voices
and sing,
for they see
the Lord face to face.

The Lord comforts his people,
Yahweh goes before you.
All will see
how our God brings salvation!

(after Isa. 52.1·10)

UNIT 9

Jesus, with the Poor, on the Way to Liberation!

'I would like to knock at all the doors
and ask for anyone at all,
and then, weeping softly,
give pieces of fresh bread to everybody;
and snatch away the vineyards from the rich
with the two sacred hands
that with a stroke of light
flew unnailed from the cross.'

(César Vallejo, d. 1938, Peru's greatest modern poet)

Change your life-style!

Shego and Nico are brothers who have met up again after several years' separation. Shego is surprised to see that his brother has a better-than-average house in Santiago de Llapa.

'I see things are going well for you, Nico.'

'You could say that.'

'How do you manage to have such a fine house?'

'Look, brother, I'm earning good money nowadays because I've come to the conclusion that the majority of people, even the poorest, will buy any kind of rubbish as long as you give it good sales publicity. It's something I learned from seeing TV when I was in Lima.'

'So you make money without really working for it?'

'And why not? Why should we kill ourselves working unnecessarily?'

'I'm sorry to hear you speak like this, Nico. I believe we should all be doing our bit to improve the plight of the poor, instead of taking advantage of other people to get rich quick ourselves.'

'You're wrong, man. I don't want to waste my life being a do-gooder.'

'In that case, you're self-centred, Nico, and I'm ashamed to have a brother who lives off the misery of other people.'

Jesus says: 'He who does not accept the kingdom of God like a child will never enter it.'   *(Matt. 10.15)*

John came into the whole country by the Jordan, preaching the baptism of repentance for the forgiveness of sins. As it is written in the book of the words of Isaiah the prophet,

'The voice of one crying in the wilderness: Prepare the way of the Lord, and all the world will see the salvation our God brings.'

But when he saw many Pharisees come to be baptized, he said to them,

'You brood of vipers! Who warned you to flee from the wrath to come? Bear fruits that befit repentance. Even now the axe is laid to the root of the trees which do not bear fruit.'

And the people asked him:

'What shall we do?'

John replied, 'Those who have two ponchos are to share them with those who have none, and those who have food are to do likewise.'

Tax collectors also came to be baptized, and asked him what to do. John replied,

'Collect no more than is appointed you.'

Soldiers also asked him,

'And what shall we do?'

He said to them,

'Do not use violence or extortion, and be content with your wages.'

And John spoke much else to the people, until Herod had him shut up in prison.

(after Luke 3.3–18; Matt. 3.7–10)

Now after John was arrested, Jesus came into Galilee, preaching the gospel of God, and saying, 'The time is fulfilled and the kingdom of God is at hand; repent and believe in the good news.'

(Mark 1.14f.)

Talking points

▷   'What do we have to do to change our life-style?'

▷   'What things should we stop doing in our lives?'

Let's walk with the Lord

Come, my brothers, to the fiesta,
to the fiesta of Saint John;
all the harvest is safely gathered,
rain has fallen, sun has shone.

Our Saint John lights up our way,
inviting us to bear our load
along a straight and narrow path
to our sure and last abode.

And the people of Israel said to one another: 'The way of Yahweh is not just.' Then Yahweh said to them: 'Do you say that my ways are not just? Be converted, turn away from all your sins, or you will end in disaster. Get yourselves a new heart and a new spirit. Why will you die, my people? See, I have no pleasure in the death of anyone, no matter who. So repent, and you will be saved.'

(after Ezek. 18.29–32)

He too takes risks

In the village of Naranjo a serious problem has arisen: During the rainy season the irrigation ditches have been destroyed by the heavy rains, and so the people can no longer irrigate their fields. Although the villagers have organized themselves to reconstruct the ditches, the town authorities stop them doing this because they wish to use the water for other purposes more to their benefit. They have threatened the farm-workers with imprisonment if they resist, and these are in a fairly desperate state of mind . . .

'They treat us as if we were criminals.'

'And call us rebels.'

'What can we do?'

Seeing what things were like, Jesus Estela offers his help.

'Look brothers, I haven't collaborated with you up to now, partly because my smallholding is irrigated directly by the stream, and not by the ditches. But I can see that you have justice on your side and I want to show solidarity by working with you to resolve the problem.'

'They can send us to prison for this, you know, and there's no reason why you should suffer, since you're not affected.'

'Just because there is danger of imprisonment I want to help, so that we can confront the town authorities united and undivided on this matter.'

Just as Jesus Estela joins up with his neighbours, taking risks with them, so Jesus Christ joined up with the sinful people of Israel, even though he was without sin, when John was baptizing at the River Jordan. He didn't need to join up, but he voluntarily shouldered their griefs and sufferings.

Then Jesus came from Galilee to the Jordan to John, to be baptized by him. John would have prevented him, saying, 'I need to be baptized by you, and do you come to me?'

But Jesus answered him, 'Do as I say, for it is fitting that we should do whatever is the will of God.'

Then John consented. And when Jesus was baptized, he went up immediately from the water, and behold, the heavens were opened, and he saw the Spirit of God descending like a dove, and alighting on him. And they heard a voice from heaven saying, 'This is my beloved Son, with whom I am well pleased.'

(Matt. 3.13–17)

In this passage of scripture the Spirit of God is represented as a dove; this is the sign of unity between God and his people.

Talking points

▷ Why did Jesus wish to be baptized?

▷ What do you think happened when it says that Jesus heard 'a voice from heaven'?

▷ Later on, Jesus asks two of his followers: 'Can you drink the cup that I am going to drink, and receive the baptism that I am going to receive?' What sort of baptism is he referring to here?

▷ What are we accepting, or letting ourselves in for, when we are baptized?

Let's walk with the Lord

Living with the poor
Christ redeemed us,
He is the door
that freed us.

Mary his mother
watched over him,
Jesus our brother
walks with us.

Behold my servant, whom I have upheld, my chosen, in whom my heart delights. I have put my spirit upon him, he will bring forth justice to the nations.

Who will believe us?

Yahweh is on our side.

This man grew up before God like a root out of dry ground; he spent his whole life in suffering.

It was our suffering that he took upon himself.

(after Isa. 42.1; 53.1–4)

Faithful to God and to the people!

In the village of Condorpampa the people are very excited because a new priest has come to live with them for a time.

'It's the first time somebody has taken an interest in us.'

'With his help we'll build a new church.'

'That's a good idea, man, and once we have a church of our own there'll be no limits to what our village can do!'

'And we can even all get together and make a road to connect up with the next village and so have a weekly market here in Condorpampa.'

But there's something wrong in all these ideas. It doesn't occur to anybody that the most important thing is a change of attitude, before all the proposed activities can begin; simply because everybody is really thinking of his personal benefit.

The owner of the village shop is interested in the profit he will make when the community buys the land from him.

The village elders are thinking that in time their village may become a District Capital, and so one of them would become a mayor.

Jesus also was tempted to think of his personal benefit. He could have brought about a false revolution by violence, as many false revolutionaries want to do today.

But he didn't give way to this and other temptations. In his baptism he had pledged himself to stand side by side with the poor and to work with them, and not to do everything by himself and for himself, 'lording it' over the masses of people he so loved (and loves).

Matthew tells us of Christ's temptations and how he overcame them:

Then Jesus was led up by the Spirit into the wilderness to be tempted by the devil. And he fasted forty days and forty nights, and afterwards he was hungry.
(Matt. 4.1f.)

The temptation of the easy way out:

And the devil came up to Jesus and said to him, 'If you are the Son of God, command these stones to become loaves of bread.' But he answered: 'It is written, "Man shall not live by bread alone, but by every word that proceeds from the mouth of God."'
(Matt. 4.3f.)

Jesus could have used his power to excite the people, but without uniting them for a greater purpose.

But in the wilderness Yahweh let the people hunger that he might make them know that man does not live by bread alone. Recall your ways!
(after Deut. 9.3)

The temptation of showing off:

Then the devil took Jesus to the holy city, and set him on the pinnacle of the temple, and said to him: 'If you are the Son of God, throw yourself down; for it is written, "God will command his angels to protect you."'

Jesus replied, 'Again it is written, "You shall not tempt the Lord your God."'
(Matt. 4.5–7)

Jesus could have done miracles just to get the people to follow him, but this wasn't the way he had chosen to lead his people to freedom.

You shall walk the way which Yahweh commanded you. Yahweh is a jealous God; do not tempt him as you tempted him in the wilderness. Keep his commandments, and you will be free.
(after Deut. 5.33; 6.15–18)

The temptation to lord it over them:

The devil showed him the glory of all the kingdoms of the world, and said to him, 'All these I will give you, if you will fall down and worship me.' Then Jesus said to him, 'Begone, Satan, for it is written, "You shall worship the Lord your God and him only shall you serve."'

Jesus could easily have imposed his revolution and forced it on everyone. But God is not interested in a revolution that ends in slavery.

Take heed lest you forget Yahweh, who brought you out of Egypt when you were a slave. Worship the Lord your God and serve him alone. *(after Deut. 6.12f.)*

Talking points

▷ Can we make mistakes when we genuinely wish to improve the position of the poor? Give examples of mistakes you have made.

▷ What should we do after we have made the mistakes?

▷ Where is the seller of sombreros (in the photo opposite) mistaken?

He had nowhere to lay his head

One day John was standing with two of his disciples; when he saw Jesus passing by, he said, 'Behold the lamb of God.'

The two disciples of John heard him say this and followed Jesus. Jesus turned and saw them following, and said to them, 'What do you seek?' They said to him, 'Master, where do you live?' He said to them, 'Come and see.'

So they went with him and saw where he lived, and spent the whole day with him, for it was already about four in the afternoon. One of the two, who had heard John speak and followed him, was Andrew, Simon Peter's brother. He first found his brother Simon and said to him, 'We have found the Messiah.'   (John 1.35–41)

Some months later a lawyer came up to Jesus and said to him,

'Master, I will follow you wherever you go.'

Jesus replied, 'Foxes have holes, and birds of the air have nests, but the Son of man has nowhere to lay his head.'

(Matt. 8.19f.)

Talking points

▷ Why didn't Jesus have a decent house to live in?

Naturally, when Jesus lived in Nazareth with his parents he lived in a house, but once he began his public work he had to be constantly travelling about with no fixed place to live in. He accepted the hospitality of his followers, though sometimes he must have had to sleep in the open air, or go without a meal, as has happened to all of us when we have had to travel.

The disciples of Jesus had to imitate his way of life, or else leave him.

A pilgrim, or a pathfinder, can't just settle down to living in one house all the time, because he has to be prepared to take his message from place to place.

The same sort of thing happens with us. For example the Salvatierra family spend a part of the year in Naranjo, planting and harvesting maize, camote, fruit, etc. Then they have to travel high up the mountains to Pino Alto to sow their potatoes. Sometimes one of them has to travel down to the Pacific coastlands to work in the sugar or cotton harvest as a peon.

Whenever anyone puts his life at the service of other people, he can't sit back and have a simple, domestic life like the majority. He has to put up with and accept joyfully a lot of sacrifice and insecurity and financial loss, for the good of the people who need him.

▷ Do you know of any professional person who acts in this way?

▷ Do you know any Christian leader who has deliberately sacrificed a comfortable way of life in order to live at the service of others?

The feet of the poor are bleeding
as they walk over stony paths
but Jesus is with them, leading
them on to a road that is straight.

Let's walk with the Lord

Go and preach, 'The kingdom of heaven is at hand. Take neither gold nor silver, nor food for the journey, but only the clothing and shoes that you wear, for the worker has a right to his food.'

(after Matt. 10.7–10)

181

Jesus announces the good news

The whole zone of Pedregal is excited about the latest news from the El Dorado mine, where the miners have declared a strike. Asuncion Vasquez, a retired miner, reads the miners' declaration:

'The mining company has not paid our wages for ten months. They do not give even the minimum safety precautions in the shafts. The medical facilities are completely inadequate. Finally, the own- ers of the mines show not the least interest in our conditions of work, or in the living conditions of our families.'

'How true it all is', says Asuncion to his nephew. 'That mine has been the cause of very much suffering for all of us.'

'But why do people carry on working in the mine if conditions are so bad there?'

'Because the poor have to work some- where.'

182

'And won't they suffer even more by going on strike?'

'They certainly will. But for me it is still very good news, because at last the miners and their families have got together to fight against the injustices. I am very happy to see this happening, and I'm going over to the mine to offer my help.'

Talking points

▷ Why does Asuncion Vasquez consider the strike 'good news'?

▷ What other good news have we received recently?

▷ How can we find out what is good news for the farm-workers?

▷ What is the most important single item of God's good news?

In the language of the New Testament (Greek) the word for 'good news' is 'evangelion' (Spanish: 'evangelio'). When Jesus began his public work he wanted to make quite clear what he understood as 'good news':

Jesus came to Nazareth, where he had been brought up; and he went to the synagogue, as he usually did, on the sabbath day. And he stood up to read. He was given the book of the prophet Isaiah. He opened it and found the place where it is written,
'The Spirit of the Lord is upon me, because he has anointed me to preach good news to the poor. He has sent me to proclaim release to the captives, and recovery of sight to the blind, to set at liberty those who are oppressed, and to proclaim a year of grace from the Lord.'
Then he closed the book, and gave it to the attendant and sat down. Because all eyes were on him, he began to speak and said,
'Today this scripture has fulfilled in your hearing.'

(Luke 4.16–21)

Our bishops have told us that God sent Jesus to free us from all kinds of slavery. Sin subjects us to ignorance, hunger, wretchedness and oppression. In other words we must free ourselves from the injustice and hatred that spring from human selfishness.

So Jesus has come to free us not only from sin, but also from all the evil that is the result of sin.

To our church at last arriving,
Long the journey, hard the striving,
But you teach us to be free,
And your path we now can see.
O Father, Son, Spirit,
We give you our hearts.

Let's walk with the Lord

'They will know that I am Yahweh when I break the yoke and free them from their oppressors. They shall dwell in safety, and no one will make them afraid. I will make abundant crops to grow, so that they shall never suffer hunger again, and no one will despise them. Then they will know that I, Yahweh, am with them, and that they are my people.' That is the word of Yahweh.

(after Ezek. 34.27–30)

'Blessed are you who are poor'

(if they treat you as they treated the good prophets)

Agapito Nunez has never wanted to join the others in the weekly meetings in the village church. Eladio Chumpitaz tries to persuade him to go, but Agapito replies:

'No, Eladio. The priests were always on the side of the bosses and the landowners, who would wine them and dine them and put them in their pockets. Afterwards they would say: "Be patient, my children. If you are suffering now, it is because God wants it that way. You'll be happy and blessed in the other life." And of course the bosses were delighted with all this talk; it kept the Indians in their place, nice and tranquil. No thanks, I don't want any truck with all that bunkum.'

'I quite agree with you, Agapito. It was just as you've described, for a long time and in a lot of places. That was the religion of the exploiters. But it isn't the religion of Jesus. Just the opposite. Jesus told the poor they had to make efforts to change things, just as all the prophets had told them before Jesus. When we are struggling to bring about a better society it's then that we are happy and blessed, as the gospel says. Even if they persecute us and set their dogs on us. Weren't you happy when they took you prisoner for taking part in the miners' strike?'

Let's walk with the Lord

I thank you, Father, Lord of heaven and earth, because you have hidden these things from the wise and understanding and revealed them to babes; yes, Father, for that was your gracious will. No one knows the Son but the Father, and no one knows the Father but the Son and any one to whom the Son chooses to reveal him.

(after Matt. 11.25–27)

'Woe to you who are rich'

Blessed are you poor, for yours is the kingdom of God.

Blessed are you that hunger now, for you shall be satisfied.

Blessed are you when men hate you, and when they exclude you and revile you, and treat you as criminals; for so their fathers did to the prophets.

But woe to you that are rich, for you have received your consolation.

Woe to you that are full now, for you shall hunger.

Woe to you that laugh now, for you shall mourn and weep.

Woe to you when all people speak well of you; for so their fathers did to the prophets.

(Luke 6.20–26)

Happy are we,
the poor of the earth,
for ours is the kingdom of God.

Happy the humble,
the sorely oppressed,
for they will inherit the land.

Happy are those
in search of the right,
for it will be theirs to the full.

Happy are those
who thirst after life,
for theirs is the kingdom of God.

The poor stay close to Jesus

When the irrigation ditches were washed away in Naranjo during the rainy season, the house of Amalia Huayac (a widow with five children) was also destroyed. The community of Naranjo have agreed to work together to build her another house to live in, and Jesus Estela has been encouraging the people to rally round. But when the agreed day comes several of them have excuses:

'I'm sorry, brother, I know we agreed to help Amalia, but I really have to prepare my field for sowing beans; it's urgent.'

'Sorry Jesus, but I'm in the middle of putting up a corral so that my sheep don't escape.'

Jesus Estela is annoyed and angry:

'Some people give more importance to plants and animals than to their fellow human beings. Poor Amalia and her children are sleeping in the open air! There must be somebody willing to help.

Jesus then goes to the very poorest people of the village.

'Of course we'll help. We're poor ourselves, so we can understand what she's going through at this moment.'

'Look, Jesus, I'm a cripple, but at least I can join in by cooking a meal for the volunteer helpers.'

Even old grandfather Timoteo Ledesma offers to cut straw to make the adobe bricks!

And so the house was built.

Talking points

▷   Have you had experiences like this?

▷   Why are so many reluctant to help their neighbour in need?

▷   Is there anything we can do about those who are reluctant?

▷   Does the photo opposite mean anything to you?

When the better-off and more important people saw how Jesus spoke and acted, they didn't want anything to do with him. So Jesus told this story:

A man once gave a great banquet and invited many; and at the time for the banquet he sent his servant to say to those who had been invited, 'Come; for all is now ready.'

But they all began to make excuses. The first said, 'I have bought a field and have to go out to see it; please accept my apologies.'

Another said, 'I have bought five yoke of oxen and am going to try them out; please accept my apologies.'

And another said, 'I have married a wife, and so I cannot come.'

The servant came and reported this to his master. Then the man was angry and said to his servant,

'Go quickly out into the streets and lanes of the city and bring in the poor and maimed and blind and lame. For I tell you, none of those who were invited shall taste my banquet.'   *(Luke 14.16–24)*

Jesus was followed by crowds of town and country workers, fishers, tradesmen, sick people – all of them humble folk. They were all 'special folk' for Jesus.

Talking points

▷   Where is Jesus in your village or community?

▷   How can we be sure that we are one of his 'special folk'?

Peasants are we,
poor and oppressed;
sad is our life,
with never a rest.

Enlighten our night,
help us to cope,
tell us good news,
strengthen our hope.

Jesus we'll follow,
he is our Way;
we shall press forward
through night into day.

Let's walk with the Lord

Thus says Yahweh, the liberator of the people, to the one who is despised by all the world, the slave of tyrants:

'The important people will prostrate themselves before you, because Yahweh has fulfilled his word. Yahweh protects you; in times of crisis he will help you. They will not suffer hunger or thirst, because he who has pity on them will lead them, and by springs of water he will guide them.'   *(after Isa. 49.7–10)*

Jesus trusts in us

One day Jesus left the house where he'd been staying, and went to the lakeside. So many people gathered round him that he had to climb up into a boat to be heard. All the people remained on the beach, while Jesus spoke to them about a lot of things, using vivid examples to bring home his message. In doing this he fulfilled the ancient prophecy: 'I shall speak to them by means of examples, and I will tell them things that have been kept secret since the foundation of the world.'

·*(after Matt. 13.1–3, 34f.)*

The poor had gone to hear Jesus. He told them that the kingdom of God was theirs in a special way, that he wished to accompany them in their path to free- dom, and for this reason it was important that they realize their own value. He put to them examples like the following:

The kingdom of heaven is like a grain of mustard seed which a man took and sowed in his field; it is the smallest of all seeds, but when it has grown it is the greatest of shrubs and becomes a tree, so that the birds of the air come and make nests in its branches. *(Matt. 13.31f.)*

Jesus tells us that the poor are like the grain of mustard seed, the seed of free- dom, and that this seed has to grow and grow until everybody concludes that the best way is to join up with the poor and not against them.

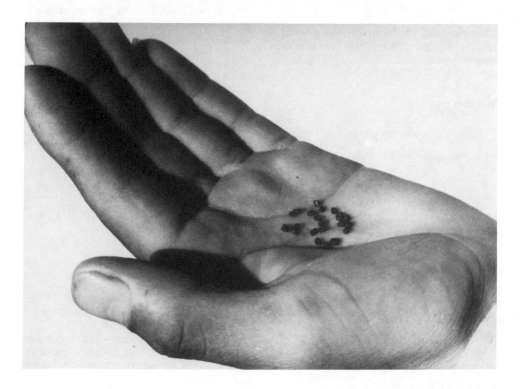

Talking point

▷   Do we have as much trust in our capabilities as Jesus has?

Only the poor can bring freedom

Jesus also gave them this example:

The kingdom of heaven is like leaven which a woman took and hid in three measures of meal, till it was all leavened.
(Matt. 13.33)

Jesus tells us that only he, only we with him, can bring about the authentic revolution that will really change the world. If a revolution does not include as its authors the poor, then it will end up as a new form of injustice and exploitation. Only the poor can bring freedom. But we poor need to be completely filled and inspired by the Holy Spirit of the Lord if a total freedom is going to come about. We don't always realize it at the time, but when we are acting for the freedom of our brothers the Lord is there.

Jesus, the Great Poor Man, is also the Great Liberator. He liberates us and makes us liberators in our turn . . . as we walk towards a total liberation promised by him.

Talking point

▷ What do these promises of Jesus demand from us?

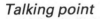

They come from afar,
and sit round the fire,
find warmth in its glow,
that warmth is from God.

The peoples must fight,
again and again,
to see that this fire,
does not lose its flame.

The first weak spark,
grows powerful and bright,
the strength of the poor
is united might.

Let's walk with the Lord

Rejoice, you who were a people without a
future,
capable of nothing.
My people, exult with joy,
you who had lost all hope.
Be ready,
for you will conquer the whole earth.
I will be like a husband to you.
I will free you,
for I love you for ever.
We shall never part.
However hard they try,
they will never conquer you.
You will be like a fertile mother.
Your children shall tread my paths
and will see liberation.

(after Isaiah 54)

189

The last shall be first

At that time the disciples came to Jesus, saying, 'Who is the greatest in the kingdom of heaven?' And calling to him a child, he put it in their midst and said, 'Truly I say to you, unless you turn and become like children, you will never enter the kingdom of heaven. Whoever humbles himself like this child, he is the greatest in the kingdom of heaven.

What do you think? If a man has a hundred sheep and one of them goes astray, does he not leave the ninety-nine on the hills and go in search of the one that went astray.

So it is not the will of my Father who is in heaven that one of these little ones should perish.'   (Matt. 18.1–6, 12–14)

Talking points

▷   What are we looking for when we want to improve our world?

▷   Are we always faithful to our fellow workers?

Let's walk with the Lord

I, the Lord, the first, and with the last, I am He. My people, do not fear. You were as helpless as a worm. But I will make you into a flail with which to thresh the enemy,

and I will make them vanish like the dust carried away by the wind. You will be my light, and my liberation to the ends of the earth.   (after Isa. 41.4–16; 49.6)

190

Let's be real revolutionaries!

You are the salt of the earth. But if the salt loses its savour, how can things be salted? The salt is useless, and has to be thrown away and trampled underfoot.

You are the light of the world. A city set on a hill cannot remain hidden. Nor do people kindle a light and put it under a bushel; they put it on a lampstand so that it lights everyone in the house. So let your light shine before men, that they may see your good works and glorify your Father in heaven. *(after Matt. 5.13–16)*

Talking point

▷   When do we cease to be real revolutionaries?

This is our body
to make the New Man,
this is our blood
to make the New People.

Our lives must be given
to make the New Path,
removing for ever
the old path of selfishness.

With veins that are tense
and nerves that are fire,
from our flesh and blood
the New Christ is born.

Love is blood-stained wool,
making up a skein
of exquisite happiness
and excruciating pain.

Who is my neighbour?

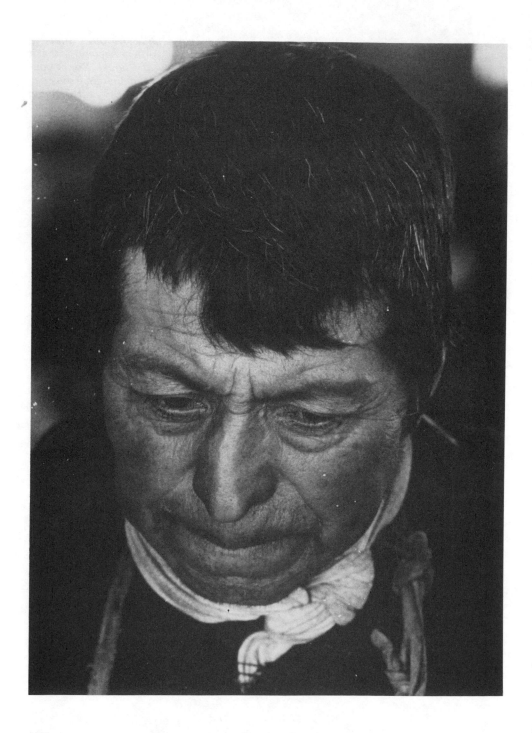

A man from the village of Condorpampa was walking down to Chontapampa with his only cow when he fell victim to a couple of cattle-rustlers, who stole his cow and left him half dead by the roadside.

By chance a priest was passing by that way, but on seeing the man he passed by on the other side.

The same thing happened when a catechist was walking down the same mountain path: he too passed by on the other side.

But the third man to use that path was a traveller from Lima; he saw the wounded man and took pity on him. He did his best to cure his wounds with alcohol and oil, then tied him on to his mule and took him to the nearest house. He even gave some food and money to the owners of the house so that they shouldn't be out of pocket.

Talking points

▷ Who do you think was neighbour to the victim of the cattle-rustlers? Clearly the one who 'took pity'. And Jesus tells us: *'Go and do likewise'* (read Luke 10. 25–37).

▷ Has anything similar ever happened in your village? Who tend to act rather like the priest and the catechist in the story?

▷ Which of the characters in the story are you reminded of by the illustrations of the face and the hands on these two pages?

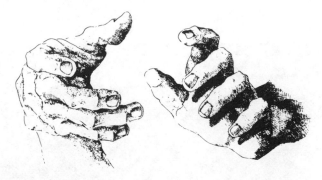

He is with us all the time,
and we do not recognize him.
He is with us all the time,
his name is Christ the Lord

His name is Christ the Lord and he is hungry
he clamours through the mouths of starving Asians,
and many who can see him, cross the pathway:
imagining there'll be more such occasions.

His name is Christ the Lord and he is thirsty,

he thirsts for justice in the world's affairs,
but many who can see him, cross the pathway:
perhaps because they're busy with their prayers.

Let's walk with the Lord

He has showed you, O man, what is good; and what does the Lord require of you but to do justice and to love kindness, and to walk humbly with your God?

(Micah 6.8)

193

We must look after the sick

Tomasa Chavez, from the village of Las Lagunas, is thirty-five, and has eight children. One day she feels very ill; her body aches so much that she has to lie down in bed. Later on her neighbour Paula arrives.

'How is Tomasa, then?'

'Bad.'

'What's wrong with her?'

'We don't know, but she seems to have sharp pains in her stomach.'

'Are you going to take her to the doctor in Chontapampa?'

'No we're not. That old drunkard will only write out a prescription for a lot of expensive medicines, and we haven't got that sort of money.'

'So what are you going to do?'

'We're giving her medicinal herbs, but if she gets worse we'll have to call the "witch-doctor" of Santa Cruz.'

'But they say he's gone to Chiclayo.'

'What a pity; well, we'll have to keep on giving her herb teas and soups until he comes back.'

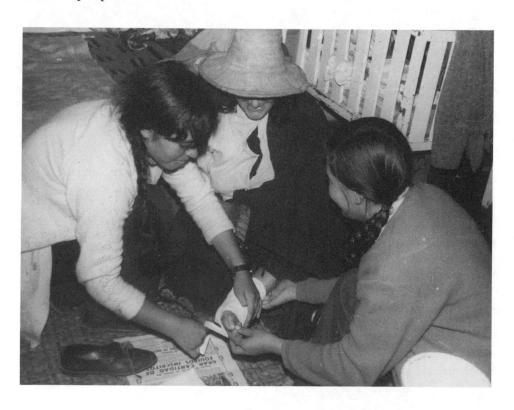

Talking points

▷ What health and medicinal facilities are there in your region?

▷ Why are the government health posts so often worse than useless?

▷ Why are the herbs and folk remedies often better than 'modern' medicine?

▷ What are the good and bad points about 'witch doctors'?

▷ Why can they often cure ailments that the doctors and hospitals fail to cure?

At the time of Jesus, in Palestine, there were many ill people, and Jesus was very concerned about them. Almost every day he looked out for them, had pity on them, and cured those who had faith in him. He only refused to cure when the people were looking for entertainment.

Jesus went with Jairus through a great crowd which pressed round him. And there was a woman who had had a flow of blood for twelve years, and had suffered much under many physicians, and had spent all that she had, and was no better but rather grew worse. She had heard of Jesus and came up behind him in the crowd and touched his garment, for she thought, 'If I touch even his garments, I shall be made well.' And immediately the haemorrhage ceased, and she felt in her body that she was healed of her disease. And Jesus, perceiving in himself that power had gone out of him, immediately turned about in the crowd and asked, 'Who touched my garments?'

His disciples replied, 'You see the crowd pressing about you, and yet you ask, "Who touched my garments?"' And he looked around to see who had done it. But the woman, knowing what had been done to her, came in fear and trembling and told him the whole truth. Jesus said to her, 'Daughter, your faith has made you well; go in peace, and be healed of your disease.'   (Mark 5.24–34)

His name is Christ the Lord and he is suffering,
he longs to be made whole and shed his worry,
and many who can see him, cross the pathway:
perhaps they're late for Mass and have to hurry.

Let's walk with the Lord

Jesus healed many of disease and gave many blind their sight. He told them, 'Go and tell John what you have seen and heard: the blind receive their sight, the lame walk, lepers are cleansed and the deaf hear, the dead are raised up, the poor have good news preached to them.'   (Luke 7.21–23)

The bereaved must be helped

After two weeks in bed with severe stomach pains Tomasa Chavez dies, leaving a husband (Francisco) and eight children. Francisco is very upset for all sorts of reasons.

'What terrible bad luck! Last year I bought a pair of oxen after a lot of hard saving, and now I'll have to kill one of them to pay all the expenses of the funeral and the wake. If I don't do that the neighbours will say I'm mean and didn't love my wife.'

'How many nights will the wake last, Dad?'

'At least two, my son, otherwise the people will be saying we're burying your mother while her body is still warm, and that we couldn't get rid of her quickly enough. We must make a good job of burying her.'

196

Talking points

▷ What is the cost of a 'wake' in your village?

▷ Are all these expenses really necessary?

▷ Do the mourning neighbours help the bereaved family to meet the costs?

Jesus liked to be with bereaved families, but he didn't just go along to weep, eat and drink:

Now Jesus loved Martha and her sister and Lazarus. He said to his disciples, 'Our friend Lazarus has died. Let us go and see him.'

When he arrived, Jesus found that Lazarus had already been buried for four days. When Martha heard that Jesus was coming she went to meet him and said:

'If you had been here, my brother would not have died. But even now I know that God will grant all that you ask him.'

Jesus said, 'Your brother will rise again.'

Martha replied, 'I know that he will rise again at the resurrection on the last day.'

Jesus said, 'I am the resurrection and the life. He who believes in me will live though he die, and he who lives and believes in me will never die. Do you believe that?'

She replied, 'Yes, Lord.'

When Jesus saw that Martha was weeping and that the Jews who had come were also weeping, he was deeply moved. He asked,

'Where have you laid him?'

They replied, 'Come and see.'

Jesus wept. The Jews said, 'See how he loved him.'

Jesus raised his eyes to heaven and cried, 'Father, I thank you that you have heard me. I say this for the sake of those standing by, that they may believe that you sent me.'

And after this he cried out with a loud voice,

'Lazarus, come forth!'

And the dead man came out.

(after John 11.5—44)

▷ We cannot bring the dead back to life as Jesus did; but what can we do to help the bereaved?

Someone's suffering, Lord, Kumbaya.
Someone's happy, Lord, Kumbaya.
Someone's crying, Lord, Kumbaya.
Someone's dying, Lord, Kumbaya.
O Lord, Kumbaya.

Let's walk with the Lord

Blessed be the God and Father of our Lord Jesus Christ, the Father of mercies and God of all comfort, who comforts us in all our affliction, so that we may be able to comfort those who are in any affliction, with the comfort with which we ourselves are comforted by God.

(II Cor. 1.2f.)

The whole man must be cured

Segundo is giving his opinion at the weekly meeting of Christians in Loma.

'The most important thing is to pray to God to forgive us our sins.'

'Well it's more than just that,' answered Artemio. 'I think the most essential thing is to help other people when they are in need. For example, there are a lot of sick people in our village. What is the point of speaking to them of the after-life if we don't help them to be healthy and happy in this life?'

'But that is just where salvation comes in, salvation from our sins.'

'No, Segundo. Jesus said that he had come to bring freedom to the oppressed, healing for the lame, the deaf, the blind . . .'

Talking point

▷ Who is right, Segundo or Artemio?

Let us see what Jesus says in the following gospel passage:

Jesus returned to Capernaum, and it became known that he was at home. Many people gathered together, so that there was no longer room for them, not even about the door, and he preached the message of God to them.

Then four people came, bringing someone who was paralysed. And because they could not bring him near because of the crowd, they removed the roof above Jesus, and let down the pallet on which the paralysed man lay. When Jesus saw their faith, he said to the paralysed man, 'My son, your sins are forgiven you.'

Now some lawyers were sitting there. They thought to themselves: 'What is this man saying? He has blasphemed God. Who can forgive sins but God alone?'

Jesus immediately knew what they were thinking and said, 'What are you thinking about? Is it easier to say to this paralysed man, "Your sins are forgiven" or "Arise, take up your bed and walk?" But that you may know that the Son of man has power on earth to forgive sins – he said to the paralysed man – "Arise, take up your bed and walk!"' (Mark 2.1–11)

Talking points

▷ What is Jesus teaching us here?

▷ Can we really follow Jesus in the path of liberation if there is sin (selfishness) in our heart?

▷ Can God cleanse our heart if we don't make a real effort to help those who don't have enough to live a human life?

Yes, I will arise
and go home to my Father.

Mercy, O Lord,
in your goodness have mercy,
wash me of guilt
and cleanse me of sin.

Mercy, O Lord,
for I know I'm a sinner,
all my misdeeds
were against your true love.

Let's walk with the Lord

Build up, build up, prepare the way, remove every obstruction from my people's way! I am enthroned on high, but I am with those who are of a contrite and humble spirit. Because of your wickedness I was angry for a moment, and struck you and left you, because you continued to go astray. But I have not forgotten you. Yes I will heal you. (after Isa. 57.14–18)

The dangers of 'hand-outs'

In the community of Condorpampa the people have organized themselves to make a road. For many years they had talked about this project, and how useful it would be for everybody. But the work had never been undertaken until Oscar Campos managed to get a consignment of free food (dried milk, soya, wheat) for those who were going to do the work. With the help of the free food the construction goes ahead fast, and everybody is pleased.

'Well, we've got a community we can be proud of now!'

'Long live Oscar Campos!'

'We'll have to elect him senior village elder.'

'You're right. With Oscar Campos leading us we'll make fantastic progress.'

But Oscar Campos is sad. He realizes that if it hadn't been for the free food, the road would never have been constructed. The people of Condorpampa only do communal work when there are 'hand-outs'.

And that means for Oscar that there has been no real progress in the community. People have taken advantage of the free food, that is all.

Oscar goes into hiding, partly because he has no desire at all to be elected 'elder'.

Jesus went to the other side of the Sea of Galilee. But a great crowd followed him because they saw the signs that he had done on the sick.

Jesus went up into the hills and sat down with his disciples. Now when he raised his eyes and saw that a great crowd had come to him, he said to Philip,

'Where are we to buy bread that these people can eat?'

Philip replied, 'Two hundred denarii would not be enough to buy even a little piece for everyone.'

Andrew said, 'There is a boy there who has five small loaves and two fishes, but what are they among so many?'

Jesus said, 'Make the people sit down.'

So they sat down, in number about five thousand.

Then Jesus took bread, gave thanks and distributed it to those who were sitting down; and also the fishes, as much as they wanted.

When they were full, Jesus said to his disciples,

'Gather up the fragments that remain, that none of them may be lost.'

And they filled twelve baskets.

Now when the people saw the signs that Jesus had done, they said, 'This is truly the prophet who is to come into the world.'

Now when Jesus saw that they wanted to come and seize him to make him king, he went into the hills by himself.

(John 6.1–15)

Talking points

▷ Why did Jesus disappear when the people wanted to make him king?

▷ Can you remember anything similar to the case of Condorpampa?

▷ Would you describe the road-construction in Condorpampa as a 'success'?

▷ Why is Oscar Campos sad?

▷ What must be done so that a village or community can make *real* progress?

They've petitioned me to sell you
a God that is easy to buy:
a mere insurance agent
or a bearded man in the sky.

And the only God I can give you
is a God who knew suffering and pain:
who invites you to freedom from bondage
and who gave you both body and brain.

Let's walk with the Lord

Observe all the commands I give you today, so that you can take possession of the land which I have promised to your fathers. Remember the way which Yahweh your God led you forty years in the wilderness. I wanted to test you, humble you and learn whether you would keep my commandments or not. I let you suffer hunger to show you that man does not live by bread alone but by all that comes from the mouth of God. *(after Deut. 8.1–3)*

Freedom is for everybody, but . . .

The weather is fine, and in the village of Pampa Verde, Candelario Perez and his family want to take advantage of it to plant their maize. They know the importance of choosing the seed, preparing the soil well and finally ensuring that the seed falls into the furrows.

'Hey up! Hurry along there; we want to finish the job today. Careful where you sow the seed, Felipe.'

'Why, isn't this soil here good, Dad?'

'No boy, when it's too near the trees there's too much shade.'

'We've got some yellow-coloured stony soil over there.'

'Yes, I know, and it's bad for maize as well.'

'And this couch-grass?'

'It's a complete nuisance, and will kill the young plants.'

A sower went out to sow. And when he sowed, some seed fell by the wayside, and birds came and ate it up. Other seed fell on stony ground, where there was not much soil. And it grew up quickly, because it could not strike root. But when the sun rose, it was scorched, and because it had no roots it withered away. Other seed fell upon the thorns, and the thorns grew up and choked it. Yet other fell on good ground and brought forth a good crop, some a hundredfold, some sixty-fold and some thirty-fold. He who has ears to hear, let him hear.   *(Matt. 13.3–9)*

Talking point

▷ How do you understand this story of Jesus?

Hear then the parable of the sower. When any one hears the word of the kingdom and does not understand it, the evil one comes and snatches away what is sown in his heart; this is what is sown on the path. The seed that is sown on stony ground is the one who hears the word and immediately receives it with joy; yet he has no root in himself to give permanence, so that when tribulation or persecution arise over the world, he comes to grief. The seed that fell among the thorns is the one who hears the word, but worldly cares and the deceit of riches chokes the word, and it brings forth no fruit.

But the seed that fell on good ground is he who hears the word and understands it and so brings forth a good harvest. Like the seed, they bring forth, some a hundredfold, some sixty-fold, some thirty-fold. He who has ears to hear, let him hear.
                                    (Matt. 13.18–23)

Jesus has come to free all people. Those of us who are poor and oppressed need to be free. The rich and the powerful also; they are slaves of their selfishness and of the situation created by their selfishness. Jesus tells us that he wishes to sow the seed of the good news in all men's hearts.

▷ How do you understand the story of Jesus now?

Let's walk with the Lord

Hear, my people, I hope you will understand me.
Do not trust in strange gods.
I am the Lord your God who freed you from Egypt; open your mouth and I will fill you.
But my people did not want me.
If my people had followed my way,
their enemies would soon have been put to shame.
You would already be eating the greatest delicacies.
                                    (after Ps. 81)

Through the cornfields let us go,
nurturing our future bread,
bread that brings both strength and
  health
with which body and soul are fed.
Forward, brothers, forward!
God our Father feeds us!

There are Some Who Oppose

The police commissioner and his gendarmes arrived again . . . and confronted Don Goyo . . . The commissioner began shouting at him: 'So you're the one who agitates the people, you're the rabble-rouser.' Don Goyo replies: 'All we wished to do was to form our syndicate, nothing more.' The commissioner let loose a string of oaths and bad language, and finally made a gesture to the most sadistic of the gendarmes as he said, 'You'll learn what I think of syndicates in a few moments.'

(*Lazaro*, novel by Peruvian author Ciro Alegria)

Those who despise the farm-worker

A new group of three nuns has arrived at the parish of Santiago de Llapa, and they are very keen that the farm-workers should form part of the Parish Council.

'But Sisters, how can you possibly think of including farm-workers?' replied one of the townspeople.

'Because they form the greater part of the population in this Province, and therefore they ought to be represented.'

'No, you just don't understand, Sister. The farming people are almost all illiterate; they don't understand things like Parish Councils. One could not possibly imagine one of them sitting next to a doctor, or a teacher or one of the ladies of our Town Guild. They hardly ever wash themselves, so you can imagine how anti-social that would make things.'

'But you know, Our Lord was always with the poor.'

'Oh, these people from the mountains aren't poor at all. They pretend to be poor, they put on an act, but they are always getting drunk and spending money on things like fireworks, and so on. No, Sisters, I'm afraid a great deal of education has to be done before the farm-workers will be able to join things like Parish Councils!'

Talking points

▷ What do you think to be the real reason why the man above opposes the participating of farm-workers in the Parish Council?

▷ A lot of people despise the farm-workers. Who are they? How do they show their feelings?

▷ What should we do when we come across this sort of hostility?

Jesus never despised anybody. He was ready to deal with every sort and class. He had to be true to his mission, received from his Father: to sow the good news in the hearts of everybody.

'I am born, and have come into the world, to say where the truth is. All who are on the side of the truth hear my good news,'
(after John 18.37)

At the time of Jesus there were many people opposed to the truth, just as there are today. For example: the hypocrite calls himself 'broad-minded'; the exploiter calls himself 'a damned hard worker'; the sinner calls himself 'a good sort'; the snob calls himself 'a cultivated man'.

But Jesus was on the side of the truth, and he called people by their real names. He didn't do this to insult them, but rather to help them know the truth about themselves. If a person believes he is 'good soil' when in reality he is as hard as a rock, or as prickly as a bed of thorns, then the good news of Jesus cannot bear a harvest. But if a person is 'bad soil' and recognizes the fact, then he can change, and can become good and fertile soil.

Jesus saw Levi sitting in his tax office and said to him, 'Follow me!' And Levi got up and followed him.
Now Jesus ate in Levi's house, and many tax collectors were also at table with Jesus; for there were many who followed him. Now when the lawyers and Pharisees saw that he was eating with them, they said to the disciples: 'Why does your master eat and drink with all these sinful people?'
When Jesus heard that he said to them, 'Those who are well have no need of a physician but those who are sick; I came not to call the righteous but sinners.'
(after Mark 2.14–17)

Townsfolk call us drunkards,
treat us like a joke,
yet without our custom
they would soon go broke.
Pray for your peasants, Mary,
heavy is our cross,
Pray that we follow Jesus
counting everything else as loss.

Let's walk with the Lord

Thus says Yahweh, 'Let not the wise man glory in his wisdom, let not the mighty man glory in his might, let not the rich man glory in his riches; but let him who glories glory in this, that I am the Lord who practises steadfast love, justice and righteousness in the earth; for in these things I delight.'
(after Jer. 9.22f.)

Using religion for wrong purposes

The Guild of St James, in the city of Santiago de Llapa, has always been made up of the most important citizens. It is a prestige organization, taking orders from nobody.

This year there is quite a problem because a group of teachers and students have by-passed the Guild in the organization of the annual fiesta; they now wish to spend the five hundred dollars profit from the bull-fights on a new roof for the city jail.

They argue that the fiesta is fundamentally a religious event, and that it is a very religious virtue to want to help the poor; and who more poor than the population of the city jail, who live in sub-human conditions?

The Guild members are furious.

'How is it possible that a bunch of students decide how they are going to spend the money left over from the fiesta?'

'They are just a lot of upstarts!'

'The prisoners are where they are because they deserve to be there, and I don't think we are here to give them a luxury hotel!'

Talking points

▷ What do you think of the Guild's attitude?

▷ Who controls the economy of the fiesta in your region?

▷ Do they render accounts to the others?

The Pharisees were very much against Jesus. They believed themselves to be 'good sorts'. They were proud because they knew the scriptures by heart. But the most important thing of all they did not know: that God is on the side of the poor and oppressed, and desires their freedom and happiness. The Pharisees were on the side of the rich and powerful; they liked to be looked up to.

When they heard Jesus say that people could not serve God and money, they mocked him, because they were lovers of money. (after Luke 16.13f.)

One sabbath, the day of rest, Jesus was going through the cornfields, and as they made their way the disciples began to pluck ears of grain. The Pharisees said to him, 'Look, why are your disciples doing what is not lawful on the sabbath?' Jesus said to them, 'Have you never read what David did, when he was in need and hungry, he and those who were with him? He entered the house of God and ate the consecrated bread which no one but the priests were allowed to eat, and gave it to those who were with him.'

He also said to them, 'The day of rest was made for man and not man for the day of rest. Therefore the Son of man is also Lord of the day of rest.' (Mark 2.23–28)

God ordered a day of rest above all so that the poor and the humble would not be exploited.

'You shall not do any work, so that your slaves can rest as well as you. Do not forget that you yourselves were slaves in Egypt and that I brought you up from there.' (after Deut. 5.15f.)

But the Pharisees used the law about the Saturday rest to enslave the humble.

The next day Jesus asked the Pharisees: 'What may a man do on the day of rest? Good or evil? Save life or kill?'
But they continued to keep silent. Jesus saw that they were angry and became very sad, because they did not want to understand. Then he spoke to a man with a paralysed hand: 'Stretch out your hand!'
He stretched it out, and his hand became whole. Then the Pharisees went away and began to conspire with the supporters of Herod's plans to kill Jesus. (after Mark 3.4–6)

They've told me that I must tell you
that God is a great dictator
with a rifle over his shoulder
and he'll get us sooner or later!

But if you make friends with the poor,
and not with the crème de la crème,
you'll find that the rich have depicted a God
that is not God at all, but them!

Let's walk with the Lord

Yahweh, you threaten them, but they will not see it. One day, to their shame, they will be forced to see that you care for your people. Yahweh, other lords have ruled us, but we acknowledge you alone as Lord. (after Isa. 26.11–13)

Those who want to keep their power

On a moon-less night in Las Lagunas, the darkness is suddenly lit up by a strong light: it is the house of Encarnacion Llamoctanta in flames. There is no way of saving it, and within minutes all the family's possessions have been destroyed. The news reaches Jesus Flores of Loma, and he hurries over to see his friend.

'What happened, then, Encarnacion?'

'It was deliberately done. We found a kerosene container which they must have used to spray the straw roof.'

'But who can it have been?'

'That is obvious; Venancio Chavez is behind it all.'

'But he is one of the richest men in the Province!'

'That's right. But he's always been bribing officials of the Ministry of Agriculture, so that his land is not affected by the Agrarian Reform, and so far he has kept all his land to himself. When he could see that we knew his game he got afraid, and he's taken his revenge on me because I'm one of the leaders. He has friends in high positions in Lima, so I wouldn't mind betting he'll never lose a law-suit.'

Talking points

▷ Have you ever known of a powerful person taking revenge on farm-workers?

▷ Is Venancio having revenge, or is it a threat?

▷ Can Encarnacion do anything at all to defend himself from such threats?

▷ We farm-workers are not as obedient and submissive as we used to be. Why?

Among the groups who held power at the time of Jesus were the Herodians, who were the friends and relations of Herod Antipas, governor of Galilee. They supported Herod for their own advantage.

When they saw that Jesus was on the side of the poor, and was stirring their consciences, they began to fear they were going to lose their power, so they united with the Pharisees, another group equally afraid of losing their privileges.

Then the Pharisees and the supporters of Herod began to take counsel to see how they could kill Jesus. (Mark 3.6)

Then the leaders sent some of the Pharisees and supporters of the Herodians to Jesus to provoke him to say something over which they could accuse him.
(Mark 12.13)

And they gathered together for a discussion. 'What do we do now? If we let him go on in this way, everyone will believe in him and the Romans will come and destroy our holy place and us. It is better for us that just one man should die.' And that very day they took counsel to kill him.
(after John 11.47–51)

Let's walk with the Lord

He has stretched out his mighty arm,
and scattered the poor with all their
  plans.
He has brought down mighty kings from
  their thrones
and lifted up the lowly . . .

Hear, you rulers of the people. You should know what is right, you who hate the good and love the evil. You tear the skin from my people. You exploit and devour them, and when their flesh is consumed you break their bones, crush them and throw them in a cauldron. One day you will call on me, but I will not answer you.
(after Micah 3.1–4)

'There was once a rich man'

There was once a rich man who wore fine and elegant clothing and was always giving sumptuous parties.

And there was a poor man called Lazarus who was covered with sores and sat on the ground at the rich man's gate. He would try to still his hunger by eating the scraps which fell from the rich man's table. Even the rich man's dogs came and licked his sores.

One day the poor man died, and the angels took him to Abraham's paradise. The rich man also died. When he came to the place of torment, he saw afar off Abraham, and Lazarus with him. Then he cried out,

'Tell Lazarus to come and cool my tongue, for I am terribly tormented with this fire.'

But Abraham said to him,

'My son, remember that things went well for you in your life and badly for Lazarus. Now he is comforted and you are suffering. Besides, between us and you there is a great abyss.'

Then the rich man said,

'At least send Lazarus to speak to my friends so that they do not come to this place of torment.'

But Abraham said,

'They have Moses and the prophets; should they not hear them? If they pay them no attention, they will not believe even if one rose from the dead.'

(after Luke 16.19–31)

Talking points

▷ Have you ever known persons like the rich man of this story?

▷ Why do rich persons act like this?

▷ How does God react to their attitude, according to this story?

By telling this story Jesus wanted to leave no doubt about the dangers of riches.

Blessed are you poor, for yours is the
    kingdom of God.
Blessed are you who weep now, for you will
    laugh.
But woe to you rich, for you have already
    had your delights.
Woe to you who laugh now, for you will
    weep for sorrow.

(after Luke 6.20–25)

No one can serve two masters. Either he will hate the one and love the other, or be faithful to one and despise the other. You cannot serve God and money at the same time. (Luke 16.13)

When Abraham speaks in the story, it is God himself speaking when he says:

'Between us there is a great abyss.'

Why do you think God says, 'between us and you (the rich)'?

Because God is on the side of the poor, beside the poor; better still, God made himself poor, is poor.

He who was in divine form took on human form, became one of many; and after he had lived like just one more slave, he humbled himself further and was willing to die 'the cruel death' of the cross.

(after Phil. 2.6–8)

'Between us and you there is a great abyss', says our Poor God. How indeed could there be, in the same place, the slave and the slave-owner who enslaves him? In the kingdom of God, where there is complete liberation, there will be no room for exploiters and oppressors. Somebody might object: 'I'm rich, but I don't exploit anybody.' Jesus leaves no room for doubt: he condemns the rich man in the story because he allows the poor man to stay in his state of abject poverty, thus showing that his heart is closed to the poor man.

▷ What ought we to do, so that one day there will be no oppressors, no exploiters?

Calumny and detraction

A new teacher, Romulo Santisteban, has come to the village school of Lucmapampa. He is very enthusiastic and wants to improve the school facilities. He begins by persuading three farm-workers whose land borders with that of the school to donate a small piece of land each so that a playing-field for the children can be made.

At the beginning everybody is pleased with the idea. But later on the PTA refuses to collaborate, and criticisms like the following are heard:

'The school has done well enough without a sports field for twenty years; why do we want one now?'

'That new teacher must be a communist, wanting us to give away our land free!'

'At least the previous teacher never bothered us with new ideas and suchlike.'

In the end the playing field remained only a dream.

Later on another problem arose, when the roof of the school began to leak. But by this time the teacher was so anxious to avoid further confrontation with the parents that he allowed the roof to leak.

'We'll have to get this teacher replaced; he doesn't do a thing.'

'He's a lazy good-for-nothing, and always has been.'

And so it seems that nothing can ever be good news for the PTA of Lucmapampa.

Talking points

▷ Does it also happen in your village that attempts to do good are given bad motives by people who are malicious gossips?

▷ Look up in a dictionary the meanings of the two words 'calumny' and 'detraction' and then ask yourselves how many persons you have damaged with them.

John the Baptist was in prison; his followers told him all that Jesus was doing. He sent two of them to ask Jesus whether he was really the expected liberator or whether they were to wait for someone else. They came to Jesus and asked him. While they were there Jesus healed many sick people. His answer was:

'Go and tell John all that you have seen and heard. Tell him how the blind see, the lame walk, lepers are cleansed, the deaf hear, the dead return to life and the poor have the good news of liberation told to them. And tell him, too, "Blessed is he who is not offended by me!"'

Then Jesus began to speak to the people about John.

'What did you expect when you went into the wilderness? A reed shaken by the wind? A man in fine clothing? You know that those who wear fine clothing and live in luxury have their homes in royal palaces. So what did you expect? A prophet? Yes, John is indeed the one of whom scripture says "I send my messenger before you to prepare your way."'

When they heard that they all recognized, even the tax-collectors, that God is just. But the Pharisees and lawyers rejected God's plans. Then Jesus said to them:

'With what shall I compare this kind of people? They are like children sitting in the market place, where games are played, and their friends call out, "We have played flutes for you and you have not danced, we have sung sad songs for you and you have not wept. For John the Baptist came, who neither eats nor drinks, and you said he was possessed. And here am I, eating and drinking, and you say I am a glutton and a drunkard, a friend of sinners and the lowest of the low. But I tell you one thing: those who know who God is have understood what I am doing.'

(after Luke 7.18–35)

Talking points

▷ What does Jesus teach us by his behaviour?

▷ What does the above story in fact mean?

It's not easy to pursue
what is right, what is true;
it's not easy to fight on
when the others lose their heart.

How quickly we forget
our neighbour's sorrow;
how blind we are to see
beyond tomorrow.

Let's walk with the Lord

I hear the people talking, 'Let's show him, let's show him, this prophet who brings us disaster.' Even those who used to greet me now say, 'Perhaps he will be deceived, and then we can deal with him.' But the Lord is with me and my enemies will fall. Sing to the Lord, for he saves the life of the poor.

(after Jer. 20. 10–13)

Those who don't want to share

Abelardo Julca is a good sort who is held in esteem by his fellow-villagers in Pino Alto. He is a weaver of sombreros, and has established a fairly good retail business. Every week he pays a few dollars in advance to his neighbours who also make sombreros, then he buys the finished products at a low price and takes them into Santiago de Llapa on market days, where he usually makes a handsome profit.

Abelardo is held in good esteem, because people see him as a man who supports his own village: if there is a quota to pay he pays promptly, and if a communal job has to be done at the school or the irrigation canal he sends his peons to work in his name. But now a group of villagers plan to set up a Co-operative for the manufacture and sale of the sombreros which nearly everybody makes; they hope in this way to improve their earnings. They invite Abelardo to participate, but he refuses because his profits will be less than before, and he wants all his sons to study at the University of Trujillo.

Talking points

▷ Have you ever thought of a plan similar to that of the sombrero Co-operative?

▷ What difficulties did you encounter?

▷ What do you think of Abelardo's attitude?

▷ How can the owner of a lorry help a farm-worker?

As Jesus was setting out on a journey, a man ran up to him and asked him, 'Good teacher, what must I do to inherit eternal life?'

Jesus said to him, 'Why do you call me good? No one is good but God alone. You know the commandments: do not commit adultery, do not kill, do not steal, do not lie, do not cheat, honour your father and mother.'

The man said, 'Master, I have done all that from my youth.'

Then Jesus looked on him affectionately and said, 'You are lacking one thing. Go, sell all you have and give to the poor, and then you will have treasure in heaven. And then come and follow me, even if it costs you your life.'

But when the man heard that, he became troubled and went away sadly, for he was very rich. And Jesus looked on him and said to his disciples: 'How hard it is for the rich to enter the kingdom of God.'

The disciples were terrified at what Jesus said to them; but he said to them once again,

'My children, how hard it is for those who put their trust in riches to enter the kingdom of God. It is easier for a camel to go through the eye of a needle than for a rich man to enter the kingdom of God.'

(after Mark 10.17–25)

When Jesus said to the rich man 'do not cheat', he was reminding him of God's commandment:

You shall not exploit your poor worker. Pay him his daily wages, for he is in need and requires the wages to live. Otherwise, he will cry out to Yahweh against you.

(after Deut. 24.14f.)

It seems that the man had even kept that commandment as well as the others.

And yet he did not enter the kingdom of God because his heart was closed to the poor; he had no desire to work and struggle for the freedom and happiness of the many poor and oppressed of his time; he did not want to follow the way of Jesus. The kingdom of God already begins when we begin walking towards freedom. Those who are unwilling to take risks do not liberate themselves and so do not liberate others.

▷ Do you risk anything for the freedom of your fellow-men?

▷ How and in what way?

We know that you'll come,
we know you'll come soon,
and you'll be sharing your bread with the poor.

The thirst of all those without you,
their sorrows and their griefs,
we offer with this bread and wine,
O Lord.

Let's walk with the Lord

If you give the hungry what you have set aside for yourself, if you satisfy their desire of the needy, then your light will shine in the darkness. Yahweh will lead you at all times; in the wilderness he will still your hunger, and you will always be full of strength like a young man. You will raise up the people from the ruins and all will say to you, 'You have given us a new house.' *(after Isa. 58.9–12)*

The opposition is strong!

Arnulfo Perez, the elderly churchwarden of Pampa Verde, is very bitter against those who want to change the way of celebrating the annual fiesta, and so he tells his friends that come what may the fiesta must be done in the traditional way.

'Just fancy,' says Don Arnulfo, 'they are talking about "the priestly mission of the baptized" and other such empty phrases. They even tell me I can't make a little money on the side selling candles and holy pictures, as I've always done.'

'Well, we're all on your side,' says Jorge Manosalva, owner of a large Volvo lorry. 'I've just made the first down-payment on my vehicle, and I too need all the trade I can get at this year's fiesta.'

'I'm certainly going to put up my marquee and sell beer, just as I've always done,' adds Artemio Becerra, 'and I bet you the farm-workers will come along and get drunk as they've always done, in spite of the new-fangled ideas.'

Talking points

▷ Why are Arnulfo and his cronies opposed to the changes?

▷ What can be done to improve things in the teeth of such great opposition?

▷ Why do most poor people tend to support Don Arnulfo on occasions like this?

John said to them all, 'I baptize with water, but one is coming who will baptize with the Holy Spirit and with fire. He is mightier than I, and I am not worthy to loose the strings of his sandals. He has his winnowing fork in his hand to separate the wheat from the chaff. He will gather the wheat into his granary but the chaff he will burn with unquenchable fire.'

John gave the people many other warnings. He also attacked the ruler Herod because of Herodias, his brother's wife, whom he had taken as his own wife, and because of the many evil things that he had done. But instead of listening to him, Herod committed another even greater crime: he put John in prison.

(after Luke 3.16–20)

Herod wanted to kill John but he was afraid of the people, because they all regarded John as a man who spoke in the name of God. *(after Matt. 14.5)*

Jesus had said that John was the greatest of the prophets, a prophet with great power. But Herod also was powerful, though in a different kind of way.

Herodias hated John and wanted to kill him, but she could not. She found an opportunity when Herod gave a banquet for his leaders on his birthday and all the most important people came. Herod ordered John's head to be cut off.

(read Mark 6. 14–28)

We have already seen how the Phariseees and the Herodians opposed Jesus, because of their vested interests. Behind them were their chiefs, the Sanhedrin and King Herod himself.

One day some Pharisees came to Jesus and told him, 'Go away from here, for Herod wants to kill you.'

Jesus replied, 'Go and tell that old fox, "See, today and tomorrow I drive out evil spirits and heal the sick, and the day after I will have reached my goal. But I continue on my way today, tomorrow and the day after, for a prophet cannot perish outside Jerusalem.' *(after Luke 13.31–33)*

They've told me that I must tell you
that God is the cruellest of kings,
and that we are no more than his puppets
while he plays around with the strings!

But if you make friends with the poor
and not with the crème de la crème,
you'll find that the rich have depicted a
  God
that is not God at all, but them!

Let's walk with the Lord

See, I send you like sheep among wolves. Beware. They will bring you before tribunals and scourge you. They will even bring you before rulers and kings for my sake. But do not fear those who can only kill the body. *(after Matt. 10.16–18)*

219

'I came not to bring peace'

Ambrosio Maita has been appointed Justice of the Peace for his region of Colpa. He has every intention of acting honestly and uprightly and impartially.

One day a case is presented where his own brother is chief litigant, and it is obvious that his brother is in the wrong.

'Ambrosio, I know that you will come down in my favour, because you are my own brother.'

'Santiago, I have sworn solemnly to uphold justice, and therefore I cannot come down in your favour.'

'But you are my blood brother!'

'I am also a Justice of the Peace and have to do what is right.'

'In that case you are no longer my brother!'

See, I send you like sheep among wolves. Beware. They will bring you before tribunals and scourge you. They will even bring you before rulers and kings for my sake.

The day will come when people betray their own brothers; parents will even betray their children, and their children will rise up against them. You will be hated by all for my name's sake.

(after Matt. 10.16–22)

Talking points

▷ Have you ever had to choose between favouring your family and friends and doing what you know to be right and just?

▷ What other situations do you know that cause conflict and don't allow you to live in peace?

The pupil is not higher than his master. The pupil should be content to be like his master. If I, who am head of my household, am called leader of the demons, what will they say of my people? But do not be anxious about that. What I say to you in secret, cry out from the rooftops!

Do not fear those who can kill the body; they cannot kill our spirit. Do not be afraid. My father cares for you and watches over your life to the tiniest detail. If you acknowledge me publicly, I will acknowledge you before my Father.   (after Matt. 10.24–33)

Fear not, little flock. God is your Father and he will give you the kingdom. I have come to cast fire on the earth and how I wish it were already kindled! I have a very difficult task to perform, and how I wish it were all over!

Do you think I came to bring peace on earth? No, I tell you, I came to bring divisions!   (after Luke 12.32–51)

▷ How do you understand these words of Jesus?

▷ How should we apply them to our life as farm-workers?

Let's walk with the Lord

When they heard all that, many of those who followed Jesus said,

'What he says is very difficult; who can accept it?'

Jesus said to them,

'Does this offend you? How will you feel when you see me die an evil death? Yet this is the only way by which I can enter my Father's glory.'

And Jesus asked the Twelve, 'Will you too forsake me?'

Peter replied, 'Lord, to whom shall we go? You have the words of life. You are the liberator.'   (after John 6.60–69)

The Lord is on his way
a brand new world to make,
he calls the poor to help him
the blood-stained thrones to break.

The Lord is lighting up
a world grown soft with sin,
he shines his light in all our hearts
and asks to enter in.

Wanted: Persons of Determination

Youth ends when enthusiasm dies. To face life with inertia is cowardice. It is not sufficient in life to think of an ideal; we must make every effort to achieve its realization . . . the value of thought is measured by the social action it engenders.

(José Carlos Mariátegui,
Temas de Nuestra America)

Ready to give our lives

In the community of Condorpampa the road construction works have advanced well with the help of the free food handouts obtained by Oscar Campos for the workers. But now there are other problems. The road has to be cut into the side of a deep ravine and the work is much harder. As well as that, the distribution of the free food has become a real headache . . . some have received more than others, some have sold their rations to a local shop where they are being re-sold at twice the price, and so on. Everybody is disillusioned.

Gradually the workers abandon the construction work, and the community ends up by being divided into small groups and factions that quarrel among themselves.

Oscar Campos feels very hurt by the whole situation. One day his wife says to him:

'Oscar, why don't you just give up working for the good of the community? The people are very ungrateful, and it's just not worth the effort.'

'No, Cleodomira, come what may I must keep up the struggle.'

'Well, I think you're a fool to give up your life for these people.'

Talking points

▷ Are there any community projects that have remained incomplete in your region?

▷ Why did they remain incomplete?

They they asked Jesus, 'What shall we do to perform the works that God wants of us?'

Jesus replied, 'What God wants of you is that you should believe on him whom he has sent.'

'I am the bread of life. Your forefathers ate manna in the wilderness and they died; but what I am talking about is the bread which comes down from heaven. He who eats of that will not die. I myself am this bread which has come down from heaven; he who eats of this bread will live for ever. The bread that I shall give is my own body for the life of the world.'

When they heard all that, many of those who followed Jesus said,

'What he says is very difficult; who can accept it?'

Jesus said to them,

'Does this offend you? How will you feel when you see me die an evil death? Yet this is the only way by which I can enter my Father's glory.'

And Jesus asked the Twelve, 'Will you too forsake me?'

Peter replied, 'Lord, to whom shall we go? You have the words of life. You are the liberator.'

(after John 6.60–69)

▷ Why do Peter and the other apostles not abandon Jesus?

▷ What does Oscar Campos need in order to continue with determination?

The poor of the world are thirsty
for justice and for peace,
their journey is unending
till hate and oppression cease.

The Lord of Heaven is thirsty
for justice and for peace
his battle is unending
till hate and oppression cease.

Let's walk with the Lord

If anyone comes to me and prefers his father, his mother, his wife, his children, his brothers, indeed his own life, he cannot be my disciple.

Anyone who will not risk his own life cannot be my disciple.

(after Luke 14.26f.)

Doors close and windows open

The failure of the road construction in Condorpampa underlines the divisions that exist between the villagers. Oscar Campos begins to think, and comes to the conclusion that the village has never really been a community at all; everybody has tended always to seek his own well-being, often at the expense of others.

Oscar also concludes that the new road would probably increase rather than lessen the exploitation and individualism in the village. It is better to leave the road half-finished and use the energy to form a group of persons who can reflect on their situation.

When Oscar first mentions the idea of a reflection group of this sort, they take no notice of him.

Talking points

▷ Have you ever felt as frustrated as Oscar Campos because of the lack of response of your community?

▷ What can be done in such a situation?

In the photograph we see a young man similar to Oscar Campos, making an effort to unite the people. It is absolutely necessary that the people share a common faith in God and in themselves.

▷ How can this be achieved?

At the beginning of his public life Jesus was sorely tempted, and realized that his mission was going to be difficult.

Later things went better and many people began to follow Jesus. But very quickly he concluded that most of them were following him for reasons of self-interest. He also realized that the leaders of the people were never going to be converted. Since Jesus was unwilling to change his goal and programme, he had to accept that he would be persecuted.

This was an uncomfortable realization, especially for the apostles, as we note in the following passage:

Then Jesus began to teach them that the Son of man must suffer many things and be rejected by the elders and high priests and lawyers. And he spoke very decisively about that.
But Peter took him aside and began to rebuke him. However, Jesus turned round, looked at the disciples and said to Peter, 'Get behind me, Satan! You do not think like God, but like men.' Then Jesus called his disciples and the people together, and said, 'If anyone will follow me he must forget himself and follow me, even if it costs him his life!'

(after Mark 8.31–35)

We shall walk in darkness
if the sun is absent,
we shall walk in solitude
if our God is absent.

God is true companion
and he leaves us never,
if he walks beside us
we shall walk for ever.

Let's walk with the Lord

Return to our God, who is always ready to forgive. Yahweh says this: 'My thoughts are not your thoughts and my ways are not your ways. Just as the heaven is higher than the earth, so my ways are beyond your ways and my thoughts beyond your thoughts.' *(after Isa. 55.7–9)*

Man's inhumanity to man

Emilio Vasquez has woven two sombreros and walks down to the Sunday market to sell them. When he is about to enter the town of Santiago de Llapa a young man called Cesar Hoyos calls out to him:

'Bring your sombreros over here for the municipal certificate!'

'What's that all about?'

'If you want to sell your sombreros in the town market you have to have a certificate signed by me.'

'How much does it cost?'

'Ten cents per sombrero.'

'That's a lot of money; I'm a poor man.'

'Sorry, but that's not my problem.'

'Will you accept five cents?'

'Ten cents each sombrero or you don't enter the market.'

Emilio finished up paying the twenty cents and walks on to the market. The young man Cesar is very pleased with himself because the official municipal rate is in fact only five cents per sombrero; the rest he pockets for himself.

Talking points

▷ Do you know people who take advantage of their job or position to steal from the poor?

▷ How is the municipal tax system operated in your area?

▷ Is it just?

▷ If not, how can it be changed?

Zacchaeus was a tax-collector, and at the time of Christ this was the most despised of professions. The tax-collectors worked for a foreign government (the Romans), and most of them took advantage of their position to enrich themselves at the cost of their fellow-Jews. No self-respecting Jew would be seen in the company of a tax-collector.

Then Jesus came to Jericho, where Zacchaeus lived. Zacchaeus wanted to see Jesus. But he could not, because there were many people, and Zacchaeus was not very tall. So he ran ahead and climbed a tree to see Jesus, near to where he would pass by.

When Jesus came to the place, he looked up and said to him, 'Zaccaeus, come down quickly, because today I have to stay at your house.'

Thereupon Zacchaeus came down quickly and welcomed Jesus with joy.

The prophet was going to do what no important Jew would ever do: enter a tax-collector's house! No wonder he was criticized!

Zacchaeus came up to the Lord and said, 'See, Lord, I am giving half of my possessions to the poor, and if I have cheated anyone, I shall restore it to him fourfold.'

Jesus said to him, 'Today salvation has come to this house.'   (after Luke 19.1–9)

Jesus, who came to bring salvation to all people, can change the hearts of the least likely persons.

▷ Why is Zacchaeus converted?

▷ What must Cesar Hoyos do if he wishes to live as a Christian?

Let's walk with the Lord

I thank you, Lord, with my whole heart.
When I called on you, you answered me.
They sing of the ways of the Lord,
because the glory of the Lord is great.
Although the Lord is so great,
he accepts the lowly.
The Lord will bring things to a good end for me.
Lord, your love is eternal.
Do not leave uncompleted,
what you have begun.
(after Ps. 138)

Give us a heart big for love,
Give us a heart strong and just,
New people struggling in hope
workers with aspect uncouth,
new people casting off chains
pilgrims in search of the truth.

Families in solidarity

It is a January night, moonless and damp. The Chuquimango family have gone to bed early after a heavy day's work. But Juan wakes up; he has heard shouts:

'Ayayay! Neighbours, help me! My cow has been stolen!'

Juan wakes his wife Gumercinda:

'Wake up, there's been a robbery.'

'Where?'

'I believe it is Rogelio Mego who is shouting. Listen . . .' (*shouts continue*)

'Yes, it is Rogelio. I'm going over to help him.'

Juan gets up, lights the candle and goes running over to his neighbour's house. Already several other neighbours have done the same, and the candle flames light up the darkness. They divide into groups to look for the cow or the thieves. Rogelio is desperate; he is a poor man who made a great effort last year to buy his cow. If the animal is not found there will be no milk for the calf tomorrow and no cheese to sell at next week's market. The search is in vain. Juan returns tired and angry to his house.

'Damn the whole lot of them; why do they have to steal from a poor guy like Rogelio? If we steal among our own, how can we ever expect to improve our community! We'll have to organize ourselves against these petty thieves, and give them what they deserve.'

Gumercinda looks at Juan in his angry tiredness. She says nothing, but she is thinking:

'Yes, I wish there were no thieves and cattle-rustlers . . . but how can we stop them while there is so much unemployment and hunger in the country? As long as we don't get better living conditions for all farm-workers, what Juan is proposing is a waste of time.'

Jesus went on and came to a village; and a woman named Martha received him into her house. Martha had a sister called Mary, who sat at Jesus' feet to hear what he said. Martha had her hands full with work. She went to Jesus and said:

'Lord, do you not care that my sister has left me to do all the work? Tell her to help me.'

But Jesus replied, 'Martha, Martha, you worry and fret about too many things. Only one thing is needed. Mary has chosen the best, and no one will take it from her.'
(after Luke 10.38–42)

Perhaps we find it difficult to understand what Jesus is saying. Martha and Mary, as well as their brother, were good people, and good friends of Jesus. In fact John tells us that 'Jesus loved greatly Martha, her sister and Lazarus', and that Lazarus was a good friend of Jesus and his disciples: 'our friend Lazarus' Jesus calls him when speaking of his death (read John 11. 1–44).

Martha was a woman who concerned herself greatly with attending to other people. She was a great worker, and worked for others. But there was a danger in her temperament: she didn't go to the root causes of a problem.

In our smallholdings, if we don't pull out the weeds with all the root we shall only see the weeds grow again. The same with injustice and poverty. If we don't try to find the root causes, all our hospitality to others, and our kindness, will not solve the real problem. Jesus wanted the entire Bethany family to understand fully what he had said on another occasion:

Devote yourself entirely to the kingdom of God and what is necessary for that, and you will also get all these things.
(after Matt. 6.33)

Talking points

▷ How are things in your own family? What are you doing to help the problem cases of your own village?

▷ Is there much thieving in your area? What can be done about it?

A man and his wife
must live out their life
in the sort of unity
that results in solidarity
with God's poor.

Farm-workers unite
to struggle day and night
for God's poor!

Let's walk with the Lord

Jesus said to Martha, 'I am the resurrection and the life. He who believes in me will never die. Do you believe that?'
She said, 'Yes Lord, I believe that you are the Christ, the Son of God, who will come into the world.' *(after John 11.25–27)*

Women who are not afraid

One day a Pharisee called Simon invited Jesus to eat in his house. Simon was curious to know this Jesus who worked wonders but was just a poor carpenter from a poor northern village. Simon took no trouble in offering Jesus the customary courtesies offered to all guests.

Here in the Andes it is our custom to invite a guest or a traveller to 'sit down and rest'. At the time of Jesus, in Palestine, it was the custom to offer water to wash the feet, as well as a kiss of welcome.

During the meal in Simon's house, a woman with a reputation as a whore came in and gave Jesus a kiss, and then proceeded to wash his feet with her tears, finally pouring over him a costly perfume.

Seeing this, Simon was scandalized, and said to himself: 'If this man were a prophet he'd know what sort of a woman is touching him.'

Jesus knew what Simon was thinking, and that he was a hard-hearted man. He also knew that the woman had a heart full of love.

Afterwards he said to the woman: 'Your sins are forgiven; your faith has saved you; go in peace.'   (after Luke 7.36–50)

Talking points

▷   Can a whore have a heart full of love for God and her neighbour?

Luke mentions several women who accompanied Jesus during his lifetime and remained faithful until his death on the cross.

And Jesus went through many cities and villages, preaching and proclaiming the good news of the kingdom of God. The twelve apostles accompanied him. So too did some women whom he had healed of evil spirits and illness, including Mary called Magdalene from whom he had cast out seven evil spirits, and also Joanna the wife of Chuza, one of Herod's stewards, Susanna, and many others, who helped him with their possessions.

(Luke 8.1–3)

Mary Magdalene decides to follow Jesus whatever the consequences. We have seen how we tend to give little importance to the role of women in our Andean rural society. We don't allow our women to participate in the decision-making in the community. The society in which Jesus lived was very similar, but he managed to encourage at least a few women to free themselves from the prejudice of their time and place.

▷   What is stopping women in the Andes from being as determined and as decisive as Mary Magdalen?

Let's walk with the Lord

The Lord is my light and my salvation,
whom then shall I fear?
The Lord protects my life,
of whom shall I be afraid.
My heart told me,
'Seek the Lord to be with him.'
And I am seeking you, Lord,
to be with you.
I am solitary and unprotected,
do not leave me alone!
You are my God, my saviour,
Lord, show me your way.
Have trust in the Lord,
be bold, do not lose courage!
Yes, have trust in the Lord!

(after Ps. 27)

I'm just a poor country-woman
who never stepped inside a school,
how I'd love to learn a few simple things
so that men wouldn't think me a fool!

And if I do learn,
I won't sit and cluck,
I'll tell all my friends,
and share my good luck.

Men who leave everything behind

The first persons to follow Jesus were Simon Peter and his brother Andrew, James and his brother John. They were all fishermen.

They lived in a small town on the shores of the Lake of Galilee; the lake was very big, almost a small sea.

The lake was good for fishing, and these four men earned their living by fishing from it. It was hard work, and often dangerous, since the fishermen used to have to row out to the centre of the lake in small boats, and there let down their nets into the water. When the nets were full, all of them had to lift them up into the boat, a difficult job when the nets were very full.

Sometimes their lives were in danger, since if the wind blew strong the waves grew in size and strength, and threatened to fill and sink the boats.

The fishermen were simple hard-working people, very much like the farm-workers in some ways: their hands were rough from the manual work, and they appreciated greatly coming home to a warm kitchen fire after a difficult or damp day.

Jesus went along the shore of the Sea of Galilee and there he saw two brothers. One was Simon, also called Peter, and the other was Andrew. They were fishermen and were casting their nets out. Jesus said to them,

'Follow me. I will make you fishers of men.'

So they both immediately left their nets and went with him.

(after Matt. 4.18–22)

Who were these first friends of Jesus?

Peter was married. He had a violent temperament, acting first and thinking afterwards.

James and his brother John were known as 'the sons of thunder', which must mean that they had very strong characters. James was always ready to have a discussion or a quarrel with anyone.

John shared his brother's temperament, but was younger. He was a bit of a dreamer and the favourite friend of Jesus; he was the only one of the twelve to accompany Jesus right up to the moment of his death.

Andrew we don't know very much about, but we can notice from the Gospels that he never seems to have accompanied the other three when Jesus called them aside.

Talking points

▷ Today in the northern Andes there are many farm-workers who are assuming leadership at village level in the Catholic church; this seems to be the only way the church can fulfil the mission of the Gospel.

▷ How do other people react to these farm-worker catechists in your area?

Lord, be my friend,
you take me by the hand,
you lead me on the way,
you bring me to the Father.

'Follow me', you tell me,
'leave everything behind,
look not back in sadness,
and happiness you'll find.'

Let's walk with the Lord

I am the good shepherd. The good shepherd gives his life for the sheep. The one who works for wages, and is neither a shepherd nor the owner of the sheep, runs away when the wolf comes and abandons the sheep, so that the wolf falls on them and scatters them. I am the good shepherd, and give my life for the sheep.

(after John 10.11–15)

235

'Here I am – send me!'

The priest had visited the village of Pino Alto several times. Gradually he has managed to form a small Christian group. But now the priest wants the group to work together more independently, without relying so completely on him. And so he chooses the most active persons and calls them:

'Francisco, Avelino, Rosa and Guzman, I want you to be responsible for the growth of this Christian community.'

'What does that mean, Father?'

'We don't know how to speak in public very well!' (and several other protests)

'Look friends, I know you all to be persons who have a real love for your village. You, Rosa, know how to encourage the parents to use the first aid box. Francisco, I believe that the love and union in your family is an example for the other villagers. Guzman, you are already one of the elders of the village, and you have performed your duties well. Avelino, you know how to write a document or a letter. These qualities that you all show of being good neighbours are the most important qualities needed for Christian leadership.

Talking points

▷ Do you know any farm-workers with a religious responsibility?

▷ How are they fulfilling their tasks?

Jesus went up the mountain and called to him those whom he wanted, and they came to him. And he chose twelve to be with him and whom he could send out, to preach and to drive out demons with power.

These are the twelve; Simon, whom he also called Peter; James and his brother John, the sons of Zebedee, whom he called Boanerges, which means Sons of Thunder, Andrew, Philip, Bartholomew, Matthew, Thomas, James the son of Alphaeus, Thaddaeus, Simon the Canaanite and Judas Iscariot, who later betrayed him.   *(Mark 3.13–19)*

In our world today, just as in the world of Jesus, there is a great deal to do. It is the duty of the whole Christian community to preach the good news of Jesus.

Jesus said, 'The harvest is plentiful but the labourers are few. Pray therefore to the Lord of the harvest to send labourers into the harvest.'   *(Matt. 9.37f.)*

To receive a responsibility of leadership in a Christian community, two things are needed:

the will and decision of the person concerned

the acceptance by the community and the authorities of the church.

We shall announce your kingdom, O Lord:

A kingdom of justice and peace,
A kingdom of life and truth,
A kingdom that requires great struggle,
A kingdom that is not part of the 'system',
A kingdom that has already begun,
A kingdom that will have no end.

We shall announce your kingdom, O Lord!

Let's walk with the Lord

I heard the voice of the Lord, who said to me, 'Whom shall I send, and who will go for us?' Then I replied, 'Here am I, send me.'   *(Isa. 6.8)*

237

We must not turn back

Avelino Huaman, from Pino Alto, has offered to help all those people who want to avail themselves of the government's offer to assist the poor to obtain their birth certificates. Several times the families in question have gone to see Avelino, on dates fixed by him beforehand, but Avelino has not been around.

Today is the last opportunity, because the Mayor of Santiago de Llapa wants all the petitions to be in the council offices before the last day of the month, which is tomorrow.

The people turn up at an early hour, anxious to regularize their position by obtaining their certificates, but Avelino fails to appear because he has gone to visit his brother in the next valley.

As a result of his absence, more than one hundred families miss the final inscription date. They are annoyed with Avelino, and Francisco Atalaya says to him:

'Avelino, how could you think of leaving all those people in the lurch?'

'I wanted to see my brother. I have a right to do what I like with my time!'

'In that case you are not fit to be a leader of this or any other community because you're not true to your word.'

Avelino then got annoyed with Francisco, and after that incident gave up working for the community.

Jesus said, 'What do you think? A man with two sons called the first and said, "Go and work in my vineyard." "I don't want to," the son retorted, but later he changed his mind and went. Then the father called the second son and gave him the same task. "I'm going," he said, but he didn't go. Which of the two did what his father wanted?' (after Matt. 21.28–31)

Jesus also said, 'No one who puts his hand to the plough and then looks back is fit for the kingdom of God.' (Luke 9.62)

Talking points

▷ When Jesus gives the example of the plough, what kind of work is he referring to?

▷ Which of the two sons in the parable looks like the man in the photograph?

The first friends of Jesus left their families and their jobs to follow him. Sometimes they must have felt regrets about their decision.

'Anyone who is ready to leave house or brothers or sisters or father or mother or wife and children or fields for my sake and the good news will receive a hundredfold in this world – houses, brothers, sisters, mother, children and fields – though with persecution, and in the world to come eternal life.' (after Mark 10.28–30)

▷ Is it true that God rewards us when we line up on his side?

▷ How have you experienced this 'hundredfold'?

With a strong desire to serve you
we entreat your saving cure,
may our life be always clean, Lord,
and our love be always pure.

If you walk beside us always,
then our steps will never fail,
we shall risk all dangers for you:
hunger, shipwreck, torture, jail.

Let's walk with the Lord

No one has heard that another God than you has done so much for those who trusted in him. You go before them, so that they do what is right, and always remember your ways. (after Isa. 64.2–4)

We go forward in spite of everything

The newly appointed Christian leaders of Pino Alto organize weekly prayer meetings. As well as that they do their daily work with a new spirit of enthusiasm; they are beginning to be aware of the wonder of being a Christian.

Rosa Hoyos continues her work with the first aid box; Francisco Atalaya is

succeeding in getting the people to build themselves a new church; while Guzman Perez is trying to persuade the villagers to set up their own Co-operative for the production and sale of sombreros.

But problems soon arise. Rosa's husband says with annoyance one day:

'Your trouble is that you're into a thousand and one things, and you're neglecting your own children, to say nothing of me. Why don't you leave the first aid box to somebody else?'

Francisco gets worried when he realizes how much he has neglected his own smallholding while he has been busy with building the church. Guzman, for his part, has found himself running into bitter opposition over the sombrero business, especially from those with vested interests in the sombreros of Pino Alto.

Because of all these problems, people start to drop off in their attendance at the weekly prayer meetings.

Talking points

▷ What sort of problems did you encounter when you began to work for others?

▷ How could those problems be resolved satisfactorily?

▷ Do you think it important to share responsibilities, and not be indispensable?

Jesus begins by personally announcing the kingdom of God. Later he attracts certain followers by his message and example; later still he sends out those followers with a simple message.

The message is such that it doesn't need people with lots of schooling to announce it. The disciples learned the message and the way to put it over with simple agricultural examples from Christ himself.

The message is: Recognize that God has come to visit his people; believe in God's mercy, and begin a new life as the children of God that you are.

Jesus charged his disciples to proclaim the kingdom of God and heal the sick. He said to them: 'Take nothing with you on the way, neither a staff nor a purse, nor bread nor money. Take only one poncho, not two. And remain in the house you enter until you travel on. If they will not receive you, leave that place and cast its dust from off your feet as a protest.' Then they went out and travelled from village to village, to proclaim the gospel everywhere and heal the sick. (after Luke 9.1–6)

Let's walk with the Lord

Though some may tell you it's useless
that nothing will change at all,
keep up your faith and courage,
remember your Christian call.

Though your steps appear to be senseless
and your path appear without end,
you are making a road for others
and your name will be blessed by men.

The seventy-two disciples returned full of joy and said,

'Lord, in your name we even cast out demons!'

Jesus said,

'I saw Satan fall like lightning from heaven. Know that I have given you power over all the forces of the enemy, and no one will be able to do you harm.' (after Luke 10.17–20)

Evaluation helps us to advance

When the priest makes his next visit to Pino Alto he learns of the changed situation. He meets with the three leaders for reflection. They conclude that they are in need of greater support, knowledge and courage, and ask for a training-course to meet these needs.

The priest welcomes their suggestion, and asks them to come along to the course with all their problems and difficulties, but also with faith.

The four-day course takes place in the parish house in Santiago de Llapa, and there are other Christian leaders from other villages. They exchange experiences, successes and failures; there is plenty of time to analyse what they have done in the light of the gospel, and celebrate the eucharist together. Perhaps what most impresses the leaders from Pino Alto is their discovery that Christ went through the same sort of difficulties that they have experienced.

The three leaders return to Pino Alto with great enthusiasm. They know that they have learned something.

Talking points

▷ Have you ever attended a training-course?

▷ What were the good points and the bad points of the course?

▷ Do you feel the need of on-going formation like this? How can this be organized?

Jesus devoted a lot of time to the formation of his friends. He shared with them both the successes and the failures of their ministry. For instance, he was very contented when they returned from a mission one day and told him what they had done:

'I thank you, Father, Lord of heaven and earth, that you have hidden these things from the wise and learned, but have revealed them to these little ones.

Blessed are those who see what you see, for I say to you that prophets and kings have longed to see them and could not.'
(after Luke 10.21–24)

He was also concerned that they should not become over-tired:

'Come apart and rest awhile.'
(Mark 6.31)

Many things he explained to them apart, so that they should understand things better. They put questions to him also:

Then the disciples went to Jesus when they were alone, and asked him.
(Matt. 17.19)

We learn by doing, by acting, and then by evaluating what we have done, so that we realize our talents and our limitations.

Come, Holy Spirit
fill us with your love,
you can give us courage
and freedom from above.

Guide us, Holy Spirit
into ways of peace,
give us perseverance
till our life shall cease.

Let's walk with the Lord

O God, search me out,
know my heart,
test me and see my thoughts.
See whether I am going on an evil way,
and lead me to your eternal life.
(after Ps. 139)

Correcting faults helps us to advance

The Christian community of Pino Alto made great progress after the training-course, but later on a different series of problems arises.

Since Francisco Atalaya can read better than the other two leaders, he considers himself more important and begins to dominate the prayer meeting on Sunday evenings.

Apart from this, it had been agreed to give two instruction sessions to all those parents wishing to have their babies baptized, but Guzman has allowed his cousin to have his child baptized without any instruction at all, and in addition he and his cousin got drunk at the party held after the baptism.

Rosa feels disheartened by all this, especially when she hears that people are offering money to Guzman to baptize their children without having to listen to the instructions. But one Sunday evening she brings up all these problems during the prayer meeting; it is a difficult and embarrassing meeting, but gradually the farm-workers help Francisco and Guzman to see the deficiency and recognize that they must change their attitudes. At the end of the meeting everybody feels that they have learned a great deal, and that the same errors will not be repeated in the community.

Talking points

▷ Have you ever found yourself in a situation similar to that of Francisco or Guzman?

▷ Do you find it easy to recognize your own faults and correct them?

▷ What do you think of Rosa's attitude?

The mother of James and John came up with her sons and prostrated herself before Jesus like someone wanting to ask a favour. Jesus said to her, 'What do you want?'

She replied, 'In your kingdom, let one of my sons sit on your right hand and the other on your left.'

But Jesus retorted:

'You do not know what you ask. Sitting at my right hand and at my left is not mine to give, but is for those whom my Father has chosen.'

When the other disciples heard that, they were angry with the two brothers. But Jesus called them to him and said,

'You know that the rulers of the nations rule over them with a firm hand, and the mighty ones exercise authority over them. But among you it is not to be like that. Whoever wants to be great among you shall be as a servant, and whoever wants to be first shall be the slave of all.'
(after Matt. 20.20–27)

Several times Jesus corrected his disciples for failing to understand his message, or failing to put his teaching into practice:

'How little you understand, and how hard you find it to believe!' (after Luke 24.25)

▷ Who should call attention to our faults?

We are all sinners,
and confess our guilt,
we have often gone away
from the path of love.

We shall go on fighting
against our failures,
asking you in your goodness
to make our lives
and loving pure.

Let's walk with the Lord

Yahweh, you know that the ways of men and women are not in their power, that it is not up to them where their footsteps go.
Judge us, Yahweh, but with moderation. Do not be angry, in case we all perish.
(after Jer. 10.23f.)

Praying helps us to advance

At the weekly meeting of Christians in Pino Alto, the farm-workers are discussing the topic of prayer. All are agreed that prayer is necessary, but Salatiel Rojas insists that 'saying more prayers' is what is most important.

'We must say a lot of prayers so that God will not punish us,' says Salatiel.

'So you think that it is a great number of prayers that will save us?' asks Rosa.

'Obviously; my brother-in-law, for example, always leads the people in his village to pray the rosary together.'

'I don't agree,' says Guzman Perez.

'Prayer for me is like a beautiful conversation between friends or lovers.'

'But don't forget,' says Rosa, 'that lovers don't talk all that much. When you are in love you don't need to talk so often.'

'Why don't we read in the Bible about what Jesus said concerning prayer? He is the one who ought to put us right in all this,' says Francisco Atalaya.

They look for and find this text:

When you pray, do not use many words, as the Gentiles do, who think that they will be heard for their much talking. (Matt. 6.7)

Talking points

▷   How do you pray?

▷   How do the two girls in the photograph pray?

▷   Is it a good idea for special people to do our praying for us?

Often Jesus used to go away to be alone with God his Father.

Early in the morning, when it was still dark, Jesus got up and went into a lonely place. There he prayed.   *(Mark 1.35)*

When he had finished his prayers, his disciples asked him, 'Teach us how to pray.'   *(Luke 11.1)*

Then Jesus taught his friends the Our Father.

Jesus wants his friends to talk with God, and to know him well. Only in this way can we make any progress in our path of liberation. We need to know how to love in the way that God loves.

Love your enemies, do good without ex-pecting anything in return. So you will be sons of the Most High, who is gracious to the ungrateful and the sinners. Be merci-ful, as your Father is merciful.
(Luke 6.35f.)

If you, who are evil, know how to give your children good things, how much more will your Father in heaven send the Holy Spirit to those who ask him for it.   (Luke 11.13)

When we pray the Lord's Prayer we are asking for liberation to come quickly, and we pledge ourselves to bring that about. Only the person who becomes a peace-maker can say the words 'Our Father' and understand what they mean.

Let's walk with the Lord

Our Father in heaven,
hallowed be your name,
your kingdom come,
your will be done
on earth as in heaven.
Give us today our daily bread.
Forgive us our debts,
as we forgive our debtors,
and free us from evil.
(Luke 11.2–4)

Hear my prayer, O Father,
even though I'm poor,
Hear my prayer, O Father,
open wide your door.

UNIT 12

Jesus Struggles and Triumphs: The Path is Open!

'Nucanquis purinanchis,
nyannyun puscananchis'

'The strong man who weeps with the weak man – he
who suffers with us – will live'

(ancient Quechua song)

They decide to do away with him

Recall what Jesus had said when Peter, at a very critical time, had recognized him as the *Christ* (special envoy) of God:

The Son of man must suffer many things. The elders in the Jewish council, the leading priests and the lawyers will condemn me. Now we are going up to Jerusalem, where everything that the prophets wrote about the Son of man will happen. Mark well what I say to you: soon they will hand me over to the enemy. They will mock me and abuse me; they will spit on me, scourge me and finally kill me. But on the third day I shall rise from the dead.

If anyone would follow me he must forget himself and follow me always, even if its costs him his life.

(after Luke 9.22–24; 18.31–34)

Jesus Flores Huaman is a poor farm-worker from the village of Loma. By means of weekly prayer meetings and reflections on their situation he has managed to unite the villagers considerably.

The authorities dislike him intensely . . . because he tells the villagers not to allow themselves to be deceived and not to exploit others, not to give bribes to the authorities, and to work together to achieve justice for their brothers.

Recently, thanks to Jesus Flores, the villagers have made a new bridge. But somebody is displeased: Alfonso Medina, who wanted the bridge to be built nearer his house so that he could set up a small business there; he is very angry and goes to Santiago de Llapa to speak with his cousin the mayor.

Another person who is angry with Jesus Flores is the parish priest, who is not at all happy with the idea of farm-workers being catechists.

There comes a moment when all the authorities of the town come to an agreement: Jesus Flores must be done away with, because his activities are a threat to others.

Talking points

▷ Can you relate a similar incident where people in authority have opposed the good actions of a farm-worker?

▷ Who are the people who show their opposition? What are their real motives?

Many Jews believed in Jesus when they saw what he did. But some of them went to the Pharisees and made a report. Then the high priests and the Pharisees called a session of the council and asked,

'What shall we do? This man performs so many miracles. If we allow him to go on, everybody will become his enthusiastic supporter. Then the Roman authorities will intervene and destroy our temple and our people.'

Caiaphas, the chief priest, said,

'Do you not understand? Do you not see that it is better for us if only one person dies, than if the whole people is destroyed?' *(after John 11.45–47)*

It is not the poor, ordinary people who decide that Jesus must die, but rather the rich and the powerful, those who govern the country. In Palestine the Governor was a representative of the Roman Empire, backed up with a strong military presence. This Roman Governor used to appoint the High Priest, who was the highest authority of the Jewish State, together with his Supreme Junta (the Sanhedrin). The Supreme Junta was made up of the high priests, the heads of the richest families, and middle-class people like the scribes and pharisees. All these people decide that Jesus must die.

▷ Why do the political, military and religious authorities unite against Jesus?

▷ What could the poor of Palestine have done against this alliance of the rich?

We are a people walking through life crying 'Come, Lord, come!'
We are a people searching in this life for total freedom.

We poor are waiting for the dawn of a day of justice and peace.
We poor have put our trust in you, Christ our Liberator.

Let's walk with the Lord

Lord, our God, the leaders of the people are allied against you and your anointed. Hear now, Lord, how they threaten us! Now give your servants the strength to proclaim your message boldly and resolutely. *(after Acts 4.24–30)*

In triumph to the town

A few weeks later the fiesta in honour of the Miraculous Cross is being celebrated in the town of Santiago de Llapa. The farm-workers put on their best ponchos and sombreros and make their way merrily to the fiesta; musicians and dancers also accompany them.

Jesus Flores goes with a group of friends from Loma. They are all in the best of moods, and as they wend their way they sing a song composed by one of them:

Neighbours of Loma village:
cynics have been defeated
because with Jesus Flores
our bridge has been completed!

Talking points

▷ Has there ever been an example in your village where the farm-workers have achieved an objective of common interest and have celebrated a fiesta afterwards as a result?

▷ Sometimes we have gone to the town with great enthusiasm in order to resolve one of our village problems. What has been the result?

They were near to Jerusalem, and two disciples went ahead and brought an ass and her colt, as Jesus had bidden them. Then they put their ponchos on them, and Jesus sat down. Many people spread their ponchos to cover the streets. The crowd which went before Jesus kept shouting, 'Hail to the son of King David! Blessed is he who comes in the name of the Lord! Glory to God!'

When Jesus entered Jerusalem the whole state was in an uproar.

'Who is this man?' many people asked. And the crowd which went with Jesus cried, 'This is the prophet Jesus from Nazareth in Galilee.' (after Matt. 21.1–11)

▷ Why do the ordinary people show such happiness as they accompany Jesus into Jerusalem?

▷ Why does Jesus enter on a donkey, instead of on a pedigree horse?

The prophet Zechariah had announced the liberation of a humbled people. But first, he said, there would have to be a strong sign. Zechariah speaks of a mysterious shepherd who will achieve this liberation after having been rejected and killed, before the people will recognize him as their Liberator. The prophecy of Zechariah is fulfilled in Jesus:

Yet a remnant will return. I will encamp at my house as a guard against robbers, and the oppressors shall not return, for now I know his mercy. (Zech. 9.7f.)

Let's walk with the Lord

I sing to the God of the people
because he came to deliver us;
we are strong because we are poor
and for the Christ he has promised to give
  us.

Rejoice and sing, my people, for your king comes to you. He is just, victorious and humble, riding on an ass. He does away with chariots and war-horses. He establishes his peace among the nations. This is the word of God. (Zech. 9.9f.)

Jesus gets very angry

Jesus Flores and his friends arrive at the town, and go straight to the church where the parish priest is celebrating Mass. The members of the Guild of the Holy Cross are there. In the church porchway there is a crowd of people selling things – some are selling candles to burn in church, and they are making a fat profit from the sale; others are selling holy water, others display for sale cakes and buns, while others are even selling strongly alcoholic drinks usually kept for a later hour.

Jesus Flores becomes embittered at the sight of it all, and begins to kick the stalls to one side, away from the porch. There is fierce resistance and shouting.

Inside the church the parish priest hurriedly finishes the Mass, and together with the Guild members walks to the back of the building to discover the cause of the disturbance.

'What is happening here?' he asks angrily.

'Father, this church is God's house, but with all this buying and selling that you and the Guild members permit, it has become a den of thieves.'

Then Jesus went into the temple and threw out those who bought and sold. He overturned the tables of the moneylenders and the stalls of those who sold doves. Then he said to them:

'God says in holy scripture, My house shall be a house of prayer, but you have made it a den of thieves.'   (Matt. 21.12f.)

Jesus was fulfilling what Yahweh had predicted he would do:

Hear the word of Yahweh, all you people who come in through these doors to worship Yahweh:

'Mend your ways and then I will dwell with you in this place. Do not trust in the lying words, "The temple of Yahweh, the temple of Yahweh is here." For only when you truly do right, when you do not oppress the stranger, the widow and the orphan, will I dwell among you.

But you put your trust in lying words which do not help you. Yes, you steal, kill, commit adultery, swear false oaths, and then you come and appear before me!

Is this house, then, which bears my name, a den of thieves?

I am not blind. You did not listen to me when I spoke constantly to you. And when I called you, you gave me no reply. I will destroy this temple, and I will cast you off from before my face.'   (after Jer. 7.1–15)

Talking points

▷   Why did Jesus become so angry?

▷   Do you know of people who make money out of religion?

▷   What state of heart must we have in order to go to church?

He has stretched out his mighty arm
and scattered the proud with all their plans.
He has brought down mighty kings from their thrones
and lifted up the lowly.

Let's walk with the Lord

Will you not see the light,
you who do evil,
who swallow up my people as though they were bread,
who do not call on Yahweh.
You seek to bring to nothing the plans of the poor,
but Yahweh remains his refuge.
(Ps. 14.4, 6)

A meal of dedication

There is a lot of quarrelling and brawling in the town of Santiago de Llapa, so Jesus Flores and his friends retire to a secluded house, and have a meal. Jesus feels that this is a kind of farewell meal for himself, and he is in a thoughtful mood. The atmosphere at the meal is one of great affection and union. Jesus Flores says to his friends:

'We have worked together for our community, and that must continue. We must have as a goal the freedom of all people, and a more just life for those who are especially poor. Each one of you must dedicate himself to this worthy aim. Don't put your personal gain before that of your people.

Only in this way can we show our faith in God our Father, because we are then treating other men as our brothers.'

Talking point

▷ We eat every day. But sometimes we have a meal that marks a special occasion, for example when a friend or relation is going on a long journey. Can you recall such a meal? What was the atmosphere?

It was shortly before the feast of un-leavened bread when the passover lambs had to be slaughtered. When the time had come, Jesus sat at table with the twelve. Jesus said to them,

'I have greatly desired to celebrate this passover meal with you before my death. For I say to you, I shall not celebrate this meal again until it has its true meaning in God's world.'

Then he took bread, thanked God, broke it in pieces and gave it to them with the words, 'This is my body which is sacrificed for you. Do this in remembrance of me.'

Likewise he took the cup after the meal and said, 'This cup is the new covenant sealed with my blood, which is shed for you.'   *(after Luke 22.7–20)*

Why was Jesus so anxious to celebrate that paschal meal? For the Jews, the paschal meal or supper was very important. God himself had commanded them to celebrate it each year.

So they shall recall all their lives the day on which they came up out of Egypt.
(Deut. 16.3)

In the Last Supper, Jesus wanted to celebrate the New Liberation, that he had come to bring us. The following day he was to die on the cross; afterwards he would rise to life, thus leaving open the way of total liberation. But Jesus wanted to have this Last Supper with his friends before all this happened. He commanded us to repeat his action: 'Do this in memory of me.' The eucharist is our Paschal Supper. The word 'eucharist' means 'giving thanks' to God our Father.

Jesus knew that the time had come for him to leave this world and go to the Father. He had always loved those who had listened to him on earth, and he loved them to the end.   *(John 13.1)*

In the passover meal the Jews used to eat the paschal lamb, remembering the blood of the lamb that had saved them from death in Egypt. Now Jesus is the paschal lamb: his blood shed on the cross is our salvation.

They also ate bread without leaven, very ordinary bread which reminded them of the privations and the hurry that accompanied the journey out of Egypt. Now Jesus himself is our bread, our food that accompanies us in the journey towards our liberation. The Jews also remembered the alliance that God had made with their ancestors on Mount Sinai; now the new alliance between God and his people is sealed with the blood of Christ on the cross. When celebrating their paschal meal, the Jews renewed their covenant with God: the command-ments of the Law. Now, Jesus speaks to us of the new commandment which is necessary to observe if we wish to be truly free.

Christ has given his body and blood
for the liberation of us all.

He is also daily sustenance
so that we might live like brothers.

We are mighty with his body
with his blood we'll change our world.

Let's walk with the Lord

This is my commandment, that you should love one another as I have loved you. Greater love has no one than this, to lay down his life for his friends.
(John 15.12f.)

He let them take him

Meanwhile, the churchwardens, urged on by the parish priest, look for Jesus Flores. They are lucky: one of his friends is ready to tell them where to find him, if they give him a few dollars. He knew that Jesus and his friends would be just outside the town, resting in a farm.

It is dark at the farm, and Jesus Flores is worried and sad, because he is afraid of what is going to happen. So he goes on a little further than the others and prays.

'Thank you, God, for having helped me to live for others. Help me now to be true to my dedication, even though it costs me my life.'

Jesus Flores is afraid and continues praying, until he finds peace in his heart. At that moment the traitor-friend arrives, and points out Jesus to the municipal police who are with him; he embraces Jesus (as he had arranged to do, so that the police would know which man was Jesus), and Jesus is taken away prisoner.

After the meal Jesus set out with his disciples and went into a garden. Judas, who was to betray him, knew this place well. So he went there, accompanied by some of the temple guards and soldiers who had been sent by the leading priests and Pharisees.

Jesus was well aware of what would happen to him. He went up to them and asked, 'Who are you looking for?' They replied, 'Jesus of Nazareth.' Jesus replied, 'I am he.'

When Jesus said, 'I am he', they drew back and fell to the ground.

Simon Peter, who had a sword, went up and cut off the right ear of the high priest's servant. But Jesus said to him, 'Put up your sword. The Father has destined this cup of suffering for me. Must I not then drink it?'

Then they arrested Jesus, fettered him and took him away. (after John 18.1–12)

It seems that Judas was one of the guerillas who joined up with Jesus hoping that he would lead an armed resistance against the Roman armies. Perhaps Judas was disillusioned with Jesus, and his methods for changing society.

But Jesus allowed himself to be captured. He had not come to defeat oppression with force of arms. He had come to free the poor not just of Israel, but of the entire world. He had also come to help the rich change their attitudes.

All in all, it seems that the cross was the only way.

When Jesus says 'I am', he is reminding us that he is God who has come to save and free us. In the Bible Yahweh repeats many times 'I am', meaning that he alone can save, and that nobody will impede him.

'I am the only saviour.' (Hos. 13.4)

Talking points

▷ Have you ever known a man to betray his friends?

▷ What has been the reaction of the ordinary people?

Let's walk with the Lord

'I am the good shepherd and give my life for my sheep. No one can take my life, for I give it freely. I have the power to give it up and to take it again. So I act as my Father ordains.' *(after John 10.11–18)*

Condemned

In the Parish House Jesus Flores is asked why he had caused such a scandal on the steps of the church. Jesus does not reply, so they take him to the town authorities. The town authorities are at a banquet, and don't want to be disturbed.

'Look,' says the mayor, 'this is a poor devil who has got himself into a fix. Why don't we just fine him and let him go?'

But the churchwardens are displeased with this, and begin shouting and causing a general disturbance, saying finally:

'If you release this man, then you are not fulfilling your duty; Flores is guilty of causing a public scandal, and we'll denounce him to the Prefect.'

The town authorities are frightened. They try to wash their hands of the business and then send Jesus Flores to jail.

They took Jesus to the house of the high priest. But they could not find any fault in him, to condemn him to death. Finally the high priest asked Jesus whether he was the saviour promised by God. When Jesus said, 'Yes,' they all cried out, 'He is guilty and deserves to die.'

In the meantime Peter denied Jesus. 'I do not know this man,' he said in the courtyard of the house where the high priest lived.   (after Mark 14.53–72)

Early in the morning they brought Jesus to the Roman governor, Pilate. The leading Jews accused Jesus of causing an uproar among the people and claiming that he was king.

Jesus said to Pilate, 'Yes, I am a king, but my kingdom is not like other kingdoms.'

Pilate was not bothered, because he was convinced that Jesus could not endanger the mighty Roman empire. He wanted to set him free.

But the leading citizens brought further charges against Jesus. Jesus said nothing. Pilate did not know what to make of him. Finally he thought of a way out and said to the assembled crowd:

'There is a custom to release a prisoner at Passover. Who shall I set free, Barabbas the robber, or Jesus called Christ?'

The people allowed themselves to be convinced by their leaders and they all shouted:

'Free Barabbas! Let Jesus die! Crucify him!'

Pilate asked, 'Why, what evil has he done?'

The leading priests cried, 'If you set him free you are not Caesar's friend. Crucify him, crucify him!'

Then Pilate washed his hands and said, 'I am innocent of the death of this innocent man.'

Because he was anxious to keep in the people's good books, he condemned Jesus to crucifixion.

(after John 18.28–19.16)

Talking points

▷ Why was Jesus condemned to death? Who do you think are guilty of his death?

▷ What do you think of Pilate's action of washing his hands? And Peter's denial?

▷ For the great mass of poor and sick who followed Jesus, was he a just man or a man fit only to be killed?

Let's walk with the Lord

Who believes what Yahweh does? This man grew up before God like a root in dry soil. He was despised and avoided by people, hated, and taken account of by no one.   (after Isa. 53.1–3)

Tortured

During the week of the fiesta, the jail of Santiago de Llapa is full of drunks and brawlers. When the police throw Jesus into the prison yard there are guffaws of laughter; they throw him so roughly that he has fallen into a puddle of filthy water. One of the guards kicks him in the stomach and shouts abuse at him.

The kick in the stomach makes Jesus vomit; he cannot get up; so they give him another kick in the face. There on the ground, covered in mud and vomit, Jesus Flores thinks of the way Christ was treated on Good Friday, and of the millions of poor wretches along the corridors of history who have received similar treatment from men who 'obey the orders of superiors'. When he receives yet another blow, in the chest, Jesus Flores loses consciousness. Anyone looking at him without knowing his story would take him for just one more town drunk, one more casualty of the town's annual celebrations.

When Jesus replied to the high priest, one of the temple guards standing by hit him in the face and said, 'How dare you talk to the high priest like that?' Jesus replied, 'If I have spoken falsely, then prove it. But if I am in the right you should not strike me.'
(after John 18.22f.)

The chief priests, the Jewish authorities and the teachers of the law joined the high priest in condemning Jesus to death. Some began to spit on him. They blindfolded his eyes, buffeted him on the ears and asked him, 'Who was that?' Then they took him to the guard, who again struck him in the face.

(after Mark 14.63–65)

Pilate had Jesus led away and scourged. The soldiers made a crown of thorns and set it on Jesus. They dressed him in a red cloak, stood before him and said, 'Long live the king of the Jews!' Then they struck him in the face.

(after John 19.1–3)

Talking points

▷ Who were those who beat and tortured Jesus?

▷ Do you know of persons who have been tortured for defending the poor?

Pilate was the man who could have done more than any other to prevent the torture and death of Christ, even though he appears in the Gospels as a man anxious to be fair. He was the representative of a foreign and oppressive colonial power, and his first priority was not to 'rock the boat', or do anything that would put his job or position in jeopardy. He had Jesus tortured so that the people would see what a powerless and ridiculous 'king' Jesus really was, but the chief priests replied:

'Our only king is Caesar!'

After this he was handed over to be crucified; Pilate humiliated Jesus and the Jews.

Some 'important' people are not bothered by being puppets or satellites of others. Some even allow their country to become a mere colony of another, as long as they can maintain their high standard of living and have security for the future. They become capable of anything, in order to keep their *status quo*.

But how can we explain that ordinary people and soldiers, who have come from poor families themselves, ill-treat their own kind? They are the victims of deception; they have been caught up in the system of exploitation, and have 'forgotten' their origins. As long as they continue to receive their salaries they continue to silence their consciences.

It is a very sad fact that so many poor people are ready to betray their own class and even their own kin. It is yet another instance of the sin of selfishness. We who are poor can also be self-centred and egoistical: it is not just a sin of the rich. Jesus came to free us from selfishness as well!

Because he fought for us
they had to end his life,
they cut his head clean off
and killed his dearest wife.

This song refers to the torture and death of Tupac Amaru II, a descendant of the royal Incas, who led a massive uprising against Spanish colonial rule in the Andes, in the 1780s, a revolt that was almost successful in restoring the 'Indo-americans' to the power they had lost in 1532.

Let's walk with the Lord

He was a man of sorrows, acquainted with grief, a man before whom one veils the face, abhorrent. But truly he has borne our griefs and our sorrows have oppressed him.   (Isa. 53.3f.)

A criminal's death

The following day the guards throw out all the prisoners into the street, Jesus Flores among them. Because of the ill-treatment he has received, Jesus falls down into the gutter. The people return-ing home from the fiesta, especially the younger set who have spent all their money and are still looking for entertainment, make fun of him.

'Look at the peasant who thought he could lead us to victory!'

Some of them kick his prostrate body. At that moment his mother arrives with a few women friends.

'Leave my son alone! He's a good man!'

'Get away and shut up, you old gossip!'

And they continue to rain blows on him, and somebody even takes out a machete and hits him with it. Jesus does not defend himself; apart from his mother and a few friends, everybody is hostile to him, or at least sadistically enjoying the spectacle. When Jesus Flores dies, somebody in the crowd quotes the local phrase:

'The annual fiesta is only complete when somebody is killed!'

Pilate set free the man they wanted, the one who had been imprisoned for murder and rebellion, and gave Jesus to them.

When they took Jesus out to be crucified, they forced a man who was coming in from the fields to bear the cross behind him. A great crowd of people followed him. Jesus saw them and said.

'Do not weep for me but for yourselves and your children. If people cut down a tree that is still green, what will happen to dead wood?'

Two criminals were taken with Jesus to the place of execution. When they came to the place called 'The place of the skull' they nailed them all to the cross. And Jesus said, 'Father, forgive them, for they do not know what they are doing.'

The people stood by and mocked. The leaders also mocked Jesus. 'He helped others. Now let him help himself if he really is the son of God.'

One of the criminals crucified with him abused him. 'If you really are the promised saviour, help yourself and us.'

But the other criminal rebuked him. 'We both have the punishment we deserve. But this man has done nothing wrong. Think of me, Jesus, when you come into your kingdom.'

Jesus replied, 'I promise you that today you will be with me in paradise.'

By now it was midday, and darkness came over the whole land until three o'clock.   (after Luke 23.24–44)

Jesus' mother and some women were standing near the cross on which he was hanging. When Jesus saw his mother and beside her the disciple whom he loved, he said to her, 'Now he is your son.' And to the disciple he said, 'Now she is your mother.'   (after John 19.25–27)

About three o'clock Jesus cried aloud, 'My God, my God, why have you forsaken me?'   (after Matt. 27.46)

Then he cried out again, 'Father, into your hands I commend my spirit. It is finished.' Then his head fell sideways, and he was dead.   (after Luke 23.46; John 19.30)

At that moment the curtain of the temple was torn apart.

But the Roman officer who was supervising the crucifixion praised God and said, 'This man was certainly innocent.'

The people, too, who had come simply for the spectacle, went away deeply affected. All who knew Jesus, especially the women who had come with him from Galilee, stood further away and had seen it all.   (after Luke 23.45–48)

He died for us

The death of Jesus on the cross must seem nonsense to those who only seek their own advantage.

But we poor, who stake our lives on liberation, find that it is God's power.

(after I Cor. 1.17–25; Luke 17.33)

Let us accompany our crucified Lord

When we celebrate Holy Week, the sight of the cross is a sorrowful sight for us farm-workers. We are accustomed to kiss the cross, and kneel before it in homage and remembrance. In our crucified Lord is fulfilled the prophecy made in the Book of Isaiah a long time before.

God:
Look at my servant; he does everything well, and things get better and better. Many people were dismayed at him because he seemed so inhuman and his form was no longer that of a man. Many people will open their mouths in amazement when they see something never seen before.

The ordinary people:
Who could believe it? Yahweh is on our side. This man grew up before God like a root from dry ground. He had no form, nor did he seem attractive. People turned up their noses at him, treated him like refuse. He suffered all his life and no one wanted to be with him. He was so abhorred that none of us had anything to do with him.

'God's punishment!', we said. But truly he has borne our griefs. In our error we took him to be guilty, our sins pierced him. He suffered the punishment that brings us peace, and through his wounds we are healed. We went astray like lost sheep, each his own way. But Yahweh put all our misdeeds on him.

He was ill-treated, and he collapsed. He did not open his mouth like a lamb being taken for sacrifice. He was wrongly imprisoned and no one defended him at his trial. Who cared what happened to him? They removed him from the scene. They killed him for the crimes of his people. They buried him with criminals although he had never done anyone wrong.

Yahweh wanted to grind him down with suffering, and he gave his life as a sacrifice for sin. Therefore he will see many descendants and live long, and Yahweh's plan will succeed through his hand. After much suffering he will see the light and share in abundance.

God:
My servant is the one righteous man. He alone brings justice to the humble people, for he took all their sins on himself. Therefore I will give him countless descendants. He will conquer the mighty and do with them as he wills. For he has given his life over to death and is regarded as a criminal, when in reality he has taken the sins of the many on himself.

(after Isa. 52.13–53.12)

But he triumphs!

The first anniversary of the death of Jesus Flores has come around. His family has observed the traditional one-year's mourning, and they are now preparing to bring the official mourning to an end.

Everything for the customary anniversary celebration has been arranged. On one of the walls of the house there is a black cloth with a white cross woven on it. Behind the black cloth, but not visible, is a red cloth.

From the kitchen comes the strong aroma of eucalyptus wood burning; for several hours Tomasa Cubas and her neighbours have been cooking in preparation for the fiesta. The house fills up; people pray the rosary, and then . . .

'Take away the black cloth! Take it away!'

'Now we can see the red cloth; red is for life!'

'Dance and sing!'

'Let us rejoice!'

Somebody comments, 'We can be happy celebrating this anniversary, because we are continuing the work that Jesus Flores began. He is with us in spirit in all our struggles and enterprises.'

Talking points

▷ Why do we celebrate the end of the official mourning?

▷ How do we understand the resurrection of Jesus?

▷ Is resurrection just something for an after-life, or does it begin in some way here and now?

Every good thing in life
every triumph of love over hatred,
of justice over injustice,
of equality and fraternity over
    exploitation,
of unity over disunity,
is one more demonstration of the
    Resurrection of Jesus in our life.

Early on the Sunday morning, just as the sun was rising, Mary Magdalene and other women came to the tomb. They were wondering who would roll the stone away from the entrance.

But when they arrived, they saw that the stone had already been rolled away. They went into the tomb and saw a young man in a long white robe sitting there.

He said to them, 'Do not be afraid. You are looking for Jesus of Nazareth, who was nailed to the cross. God has raised him up. This is the place where he lay. Now go and tell his disciples and Peter, "He has gone before you into Galilee. There you will see him, as he told you."'

(after Mark 16.2–7)

Jesus Christ has risen from the dead,
Jesus is our hope, our path, our love,
for he has conquered;
he has defeated pain and death!

Let's walk with the Lord

I know that my redeemer lives. I will see God out of my own flesh. My heart yearns for him. I will see him, I myself. You who wanted to condemn me must know that there is justice at last.

(after Job 19.25–29)

269

The way is open

One day soon after the fiesta of Santiago de Llapa had finished, Artemio Cotrina and Felipe Guevara were walking towards the village of Loma. They were discouraged because it seemed that everything they had been doing with Jesus Flores had ended in failure.

As they were walking, an unknown man joined them and began conversing. He asked them why they were so sad:

'You mean you don't know about what happened to our friend and companion Jesus Flores? He was a man who inspired a new confidence in us all, and just when we all thought things were really going to change in our favour, he was killed.'

The unknown stranger replied:

'Why are you so gloomy? Don't you understand that we really can change the world if we are determined enough, and if we are prepared to sacrifice our personal comfort? The example of your friend Jesus Flores has been given you not to mope and mourn, but to rejoice and go forward.'

Let us recall what happened with the two disciples who were returning sadly to their village after the death of Jesus Christ. Jesus himself joined them on their walk, but they had no idea who it was. When Jesus asked them why they were so long-faced, they replied:

'Jesus of Nazareth was a prophet. He showed his power to God and the whole people in words and deeds. Some days ago the leading priests and the government condemned him to death and nailed him to the cross. And we had hoped that he would be the one to free the people of Israel. Today is the third day since this has happened.'

Jesus said to them, 'How dim you are! How hard you find it to believe what the prophets said beforehand. The promised saviour must suffer all this before entering his glory.'

Jesus explained to them the sayings that related to him, from Moses and the prophets throughout scripture. When they arrived at the village Jesus acted as though he wanted to go on. But they restrained him and said, 'Stay with us. It's almost evening and soon it will be dark.'

So Jesus went in and stayed with them. When they sat at table he took bread, broke it into pieces and gave it to them. At that moment their eyes were opened and they recognized him, but he disappeared.

They immediately returned to Jerusalem where they found the eleven apostles and the other followers of Jesus gathered together. They exclaimed to them, 'The Lord is truly risen. Simon has seen him.' *(after Luke 25.19–34)*

Talking points

▷ We too are sometimes sad and disillusioned, and we have to remind ourselves that Christ came to free us; we ask ourselves how it is that the rich and powerful seem always to win out in the end. Why do we have to struggle and suffer so much?

▷ Sometimes we come to know Christians who don't seem to have or share our preoccupations; they sing exuberantly in their chapels about the wonderful after-life, and they don't seem to be at all worried about things here and now. Can they be right? What do you think?

Jesus tells us that everything done and said by Moses and the prophets – the struggle of a humble people for their freedom – was good. Jesus came to continue that story. He reminded us that the story is incomplete and impossible without suffering and death. To free ourselves we have to kill our selfishness; if we do not, then the exploitation will continue. This is also the story of the life of Christ: dying to himself and rising again. He has opened for us the path that guarantees the victory over our struggles and sufferings. The glory of heaven will be the end of the path, the total freedom.

Christ our elder brother,
from our Father sent,
is our strong deliverer
from discouragement.

Let's walk with the Lord

Jesus has pioneered a new way to life for us. He has opened it up to us with his own body. Let us hold fast to that hope, for God who has given the promise will stand by his word. *(after Heb. 10.19–23)*

A New People is Born

'I do not want a fatherland divided,
that bleeds from seven knives of steel,
I want the people's light shining from on high,
from the newly constructed house.
Everyone is welcome in my fatherland!
The rich were always foreigners:
let them go; nobody is obliged to stay;
I shall remain to sing with the workers
in this new history and geography . . .'

(Pablo Neruda, Chilean poet, 1904–1973)

From darkness to light

There is no light ... you can't see a thing ... everything is dark ... travellers fall or lose their way ... people are sad.

The children cannot study at school ... their parents cannot work ... only the thieves are pleased, and those who live dishonest lives ...

The rich and the powerful laugh at the sufferings of the poor ... some are hungry ... the harvest fails ... contagious sickness kills off children ... the drought has affected many this year ... the widows will be specially hard hit ... young girls are not sent to school and remain illiterate ... There is darkness everywhere!

Talking points

▷ Have you felt this absence of 'light' when things go bad for you?

▷ What sort of darkness is shown in the photograph?

On a certain occasion when the people of Israel were being badly treated by their leaders, the prophet Isaiah said these words:

The people of Israel will wander aimlessly, oppressed and hungry, and they will be reduced to despair because they are hungry, and they will curse their king and their God.

They will raise up their eyes to heaven, and then they will look to the earth, and they will find only the deepest misery to terrify them; they will see nothing but night.

But immediately afterwards he announces to them the liberation of the Lord:

The people that walked in darkness have seen a great light, and its brightness has shone on those who lived in the land of the shadow. You, Lord, have filled them with joy and they rejoice in your presence like those who rejoice at the harvest.

(after Isa. 8.21–9.2)

The Risen Christ is our Light. Uniting ourselves to Christ means not accepting passively the injustices of life, the exploitation and the man-made suffering. It means, rather, arming ourselves for a fight against these evils.

One day this fight will be won, when the Light inflicts a final defeat on the Darkness.

Meanwhile:

Count it all joy, my brothers, when you meet various trials, for you know that the testing of your faith produces steadfastness. And let steadfastness have its full effect, that you may be perfect and complete, lacking in nothing. (James 1.2–4)

People of God who suffer,
who thirst for justice and peace,
never should give up marching
till the final battles cease.

One day we shall see him
face to face in glory,
and then we shall see the meaning
of life's strange and noble story.

Let's walk with the Lord

Come, let us go up to the house of the Lord, that he may show us his ways. My people, come, let us walk in the light of the Lord.

(after Isa. 2.3–5)

Freed from sin

In Pino Alto, Juan Malaver's family is a total disaster. Juan himself drinks too much alcohol, and no longer thinks of anybody except himself. He shouts at his wife Ana and beats her, as well as his daughter Filomena.

His eldest son Jorge can't take any more, and migrates to Lima.

Anybody who goes to the Malaver house is at once aware that there is a great neglect and very little love. Ana is silent and sullen, Filomena very shy. Nobody talks during meal-times, and when Juan wants more food he shouts for it, often swearing. It is not surprising, therefore, that Ana falls ill with worry and grief. She is lying in her bed, and Filomena has run away to her uncle's house because she is so afraid of her father.

Alone in the kitchen, the fire unlit, and nobody looking after him, Juan is eating a plate of cold food. He comes to his senses, and realizes what a fool he has been. It is entirely his fault that his family is such a complete disaster.

He feels tremendously sorry, and asks forgiveness of his wife.

Three months later, what a difference! The house is cheerful, Ana is singing, Filomena smiles, and there is a welcome for any passer-by.

Talking points

▷   When we commit a sin, are other people always affected, or just ourselves?

▷   How many people were affected by Juan Malaver's sin?

▷   How can sins be put right?

When Juan Malaver fell into disgrace, he began to think. His disgrace was for him a kind of death, because his whole family was ruined.

As Christians, we too have taken part in death – in the death of Christ at our baptism – and when we think of that it should be sufficient so that:

We should no longer continue to serve sin as a master, because the one who died for us is already free from sin.

If we have died in Christ, we trust that we shall also live with him, because we know that Christ risen from the dead dies no more; death has no more power over him. Through death Christ has taken sin upon himself and conquered it once for all. Now he lives his true life for God.

So consider yourselves to be dead to sin, but alive to God and one with Christ our Lord.   *(Rom. 6.6–11)*

Yes, I will arise
and return to my Father!

Be merciful to me, O God
because of your constant love.
Because of your great mercy
wipe away my sins!

Let's walk with the Lord

I will put my law within them and write it on their hearts. They will all know me, from the greatest to the least, for I forgive them their guilt and think no more of their sins.
                                    (Jer. 31.33f.)

277

United in community

In Pino Alto a very united group has developed. They have built a 'community house' in the village, used during the day by the newly-formed Co-operative of sombrero makers, as well as by some of their wives who weave ponchos and dresses.

'We used to work each person in his own house, but now it is much better working together, and chatting while we work.'

'I agree: it is much better now; and besides, we are getting a better price for our sombreros now than before. Each one earns according to his need and according to the work he has done, and not by sponging and exploiting as before.'

On Sundays they meet to pray, and since they all know one another, they laugh and joke, and trust one another, and even the women and children pray in their own words and give their opinions about the Bible readings.

'In this atmosphere of joy and unity we know that the Lord is among us.'

Talking points

▷ Do you know a group of Catholics who live in this way?

▷ What are the obstacles in forming small groups like this?

▷ How was the group formed in the first place?

After experiencing the death of Christ, and the sense of disaster and failure that followed, two disciples met the Risen Jesus. They were so greatly affected by this meeting that they went running back to Jerusalem to tell their friends all about it:

There they met the eleven apostles gathered with their friends. They told them what had happened on the way and how they recognized Jesus again when he broke the bread.

While they were talking about these things, there was Jesus in their midst. He greeted them and said, 'Peace, my friends.'

They were very frightened and thought that they were seeing a ghost. But Jesus asked them, 'Why are you afraid? Why do you doubt? Look at my hands and my feet.

It is I. Touch me and see. No ghost has flesh and bones like those you can feel.'

When he had said that to them he showed them his hands and feet. They still did not believe him for sheer joy and fright, so he went on to say, 'Have you anything to eat?' So they gave him some baked fish, which he took and ate.

(after Luke 24.33–43)

Jesus wants his followers to be united in community. In this way it will be much easier for them to fulfil the prayer Christ made for them at the Last Supper:

'I pray that they may be of one heart and one soul, that they may be one in fellowship with us, as you, Father, are in me and I in you. In this way the world will believe that you have sent me.'

(after John 17.21–23)

The Lord has come to bring us peace,
the Lord has come to live among us.
We are brothers and sisters
with his life and his love.
We are brothers and sisters with one
   heart.

Let's walk with the Lord

I will unite them. You shall be my people and I will be your God. I will give you one heart and one life to share together. I will not forsake you, and I will delight in doing you good.   *(after Jer. 32.37–41)*

'There is the Lord!'

Now on the first day of the week Mary Magdalene came to the tomb early, while it was still dark, and saw that the stone had been taken away from the tomb.

She stood weeping outside the tomb, and as she wept she stooped to look into the tomb; and she saw two angels in white, sitting where the body of Jesus had lain, one at the head and one at the feet. They said to her, 'Woman, why are you weeping?' She said to them, 'Because they have taken away my Lord, and I do not know where they have laid him.'

Saying this, she turned round and saw Jesus standing, but she did not know that it was Jesus. Jesus said to her, 'Woman, why are you weeping? Whom do you seek?'

Supposing him to be the gardener, she said to him, 'Sir, if you have carried him away, tell me where you have laid him and I will take him away.'

Jesus said to her, 'Mary.'

She turned and said to him in Hebrew, 'Rabboni' (which means 'teacher').

Jesus said to her, 'Do not hold me, for I have not yet ascended to the Father; but go to my brethren and say to them, I am ascending to my Father and your Father, to my God and your God.'

Mary Magdalene went and said to the disciples, 'I have seen the Lord'; and she told them that he had said these things to her.
(John 20.11–18)

Talking points

▷ The evangelists tell us of how different persons were convinced that Jesus had risen. Look up other passages (at the end of the four Gospels) and describe to your companions in the group how it was in the cases of John, Peter, and Thomas.

▷ Are you really convinced of the presence of Jesus in your life?

▷ If you are, tell us how you became convinced.

Christ continues to be with us at the present time. He can reveal himself in many different ways. We can find him in:

The bread and wine of the Mass: 'This is my body, this is my blood.'
(after Luke 22.19f.)

A meeting of brothers and sisters: 'Where two or three are gathered in my name, there am I in their midst.
(after Matt. 18.20)

The poor: 'Whatever you did for the least of these my brothers, you did it for me.'
(after Matt. 25.40)

The Word of God: 'In former times God spoke to our ancestors through the prophets, but now he has spoken to us in his Son.'
(after Heb. 1.1)

▷   What other signs of Christ's presence can you find among us?

Resucito, resucito, resucito, Alleluia!

Rejoice, brothers,
for if today we love each other
it is because he is risen.

If we die with him
we live with him
we sing with him Alleluia!'

Let's walk with the Lord

*'Have I been so long with you and you still
do not know me? He who has seen me has
seen my Father. Why do you say, then,
"Show us the Father?" Do you not believe
that I am in my Father and he in me?'*
(John 14.9f.)

'Without love I am nothing'

Oscar Campos, of Condorpampa, has just visited Fulgencio Chuquilin, of Pedregal, to invite him to a training-course at the parish of Chontapampa.

'Another training-course? What for?' asks Fulgencio.

'To see how progress is being made in the Christian groups, and to learn from one another?'

'I've been to several training-courses, and I've learnt quite a bit, and so my village has benefitted considerably. But I don't think I need any more training.'

'But you don't have a Christian group meeting on a regular basis.'

'The people here aren't interested. I made them construct a new chapel in the cemetery, and I made them work on the new road, even though it took a lot of hard work. But the people are so ignorant; the only way is to force them to do things. Persuasion doesn't work here.'

Oscar returns to Condorpampa, not very convinced of what Fulgencio has told him. He knows that Fulgencio has more cattle than his neighbours, and he benefitted financially from the construction of the road in the village.

All in all, Oscar thinks, Fulgencio has a long way to go in his Christian formation.

Talking points

▷ What are the good points and the bad points in Fulgencio's way of doing things?

▷ What Christian values does Fulgencio lack?

▷ Why is it so important to form a Christian prayer group in each village?

▷ So that a group can function well, is it sufficient to elect a committee?

▷ If it is not sufficient, what more must be done?

The foundation of all Christian activity must be love. Fulgencio doesn't yet realize this. Jesus tells us:

I give you this new commandment, to love one another. Love one another as I have loved you. All will know you as my disciples if you love one another.

(John 13.34)

▷ Is the election of a committee enough?

You can do anything with love. If you love, you never treat another badly. Therefore love is the fulfilling of all the commandments. *(after Rom. 13.8–10)*

Let's walk with the Lord

Faith, hope and love,
and the greatest of all is love.

If we can flatten out the Andes
but we beat our wives and kids,
So what, Lord, so what?

If we overturn the government
but with hatred in our hearts,
in vain, Lord, in vain.

*God is love,
and he who lives in love,
lives in God and God in him.
We love God,
because he first loved us.
But if someone says,
'I love God',
and at the same time hates his brother,
he is a liar.*

(after I John 4.7–20)

'Don't stand staring up at heaven!'

In the community house of Pino Alto the work of making sombreros and ponchos has come to a halt, because Guzman Perez has recently announced that he is going on a journey to Lima.

'My brother has died, and my sister-in-law wants me to take over the small business that they ran together until he died.'

'So you are going to desert us, Guzman?'

'Now we are really sunk.'

'It's just one more punishment from God. The harvest has already been spoiled by heavy rains, and now you are abandoning us.'

'Look, brothers,' answers Guzman, 'the harvest was only spoiled for those who didn't take the ordinary precautions against bad weather. You can't wait for things to fall from heaven. Besides that, my going to Lima will merely mean that you will all have to take your full share of responsibility in the sombrero Co-operative that we started together. No Christian should be indispensable, you know.'

Talking points

▷ Have you ever heard farm-workers talking about 'punishment from God' when it was really their own fault?'

▷ What does God expect from us in these instances?

After his resurrection, Jesus appeared several times to his disciples. Then he said farewell to them, because they had become convinced that he was alive.

The disciples gathered with Jesus asked him, 'Lord, is now the time when you will bring liberation to the people of Israel?'

Jesus replied, 'It is not your concern when and in what way the Father will do these things. But when the Spirit comes upon you, you will receive power and go out to tell of me, in Jerusalem, in Judaea and Samaria, and to the uttermost ends of the earth.'

When he had said this, and when they were still looking on, Jesus was taken up into heaven and a cloud came to conceal him, so that they saw him no more. As they kept looking in his direction, two men clothed in white appeared to them and said, 'Men of Galilee, why do you stand there looking up into heaven? This same Jesus will come again.'

(after Acts 1.6–11)

'There is much to do, brothers!' said our great Peruvian poet, Cesar Vallejo.

The angel, speaking on behalf of Our Lord, says the same thing. Meanwhile we have to get down to the real work of Christ: the liberation of our brothers and sisters.

Love is not a question
of looking up to heaven.
Love is being active
mass-transforming leaven.

Love is blood-stained wool
making up a skein
of exquisite happiness
and excruciating pain.

Let's walk with the Lord

Truly I say to you, he who believes in me will do the works that I do. And he will do even greater things than this because I go to the Father.

Whatever you ask in my name I will do, that the Son may bear witness to the glory of the Father. (John 14.12f.)

God's Spirit gives us community life

At the Last Supper, Jesus had said to his disciples:

'I tell you plainly, it is better for you that I go away. For unless I go away the one who is to help you and encourage you will not come. But if I go away, I will send him to you.' *(after John 16.7)*

The disciples received the responsibility of continuing the task of Jesus, to take the good news to all people, but especially to the poor and the oppressed. But they did not have the strength to carry out that task. They needed to receive the life and strength of the Spirit of God. Jesus also had needed the Spirit. Before going to the Father, Jesus told his friends to await the arrival of this same Holy Spirit.

Then they returned to Jerusalem and went into the upper room of the house where they were staying. The apostles gathered together in prayer regularly, with the brothers of Jesus, Mary, his mother, and the other women. *(after Acts 1.12–14)*

In Lucma Walter Oyarce says:

'We need to finish off the school building, but the people won't collaborate. Each one of them is busy doing his own thing. But, even though we are few in number, we are determined to finish what we have begun.'

When Pentecost came all the believers were gathered together in one place. Sud-denly there was a great noise from heaven which resounded throughout the house in which they were. Then unexpectedly tongues of fire appeared to them, like flames, and they were all filled with the Holy Spirit and began to speak in other languages. *(after Acts 2.1–4)*

Peter was no longer afraid to speak in public. He told the people that God, by sending the Spirit, was fulfilling the prophecy of Joel, made at a time when the people were being very harshly treated:

Rejoice in Yahweh. My people will never be put to shame. I will pour out my spirit on all flesh, and your sons and daughters will speak as I bid them. *(after Joel 2.19–3.1)*

And so, strengthened by the Holy Spirit, that small band of men and women went announcing the Good News of Jesus from one place to another, to the 'end of the earth'. And they prayed over the new believers so that they in their turn might receive the strength and life of the Holy Spirit.

In the community tasks, when we feel tired or discouraged, there are usually those who encourage us to carry on. A community which tries to improve its situation is like the community of early Christians, the first to receive the Holy Spirit. It is not the Spirit himself who does the work, but he gives us life and strength so that we can do it.

Talking points

▷ Have you experienced living in an active and enthusiastic community? Relate your experience.

▷ What is the problem in the photograph?

Holy Spirit, come to us
come to every nation.
All our hopes depend on you
for our liberation.

We are but peasants
poor and oppressed,
but we'll overcome
if you are our guest.

Light up our darkness,
banish our fears,
give us the joy
that was promised for years.

Let's walk with the Lord

If the world hates you, remember that it hated me before you. They persecuted me and so they will also persecute you. When the Spirit of truth comes, which helps and encourages, whom I will send from my Father, he will speak on my behalf. And you too shall speak on my behalf.

(after John 15.18–27)

287

. . . and gives life to us personally

Anselmo Vasquez, of Las Lagunas, is a lifeless sort of man. He never wants to do anything more than the minimum necessary to survive. His presence is like that of a thick, cold, damp cloud. To meet him on a mountain path is an unpleasant experience:

'Hello, Don Anselmo!'

'Hello.'

'What's up? You're looking pretty sad today.'

'And why not? What is there to be happy about?'

People quickly leave Anselmo's company, which they find so unhelpful.

To meet Juan Lopez, from San Jacinto,

is quite the opposite experience. Juan is an active and contagiously enthusiastic man.

'Hello, Don Juan!'

'Hello there; how are you? Good to see you in these parts!'

'It's good to see you too.'

'I tell you what. I'm trying to persuade all the parents to make a voluntary collection for the new school roof.'

'You're always doing something like that, Juan.'

Talking points

▷ What sort of person are you: like Anselmo? or like Juan?

To be in contact with a man like Juan is like being in contact with the Spirit of God . . . he who gives life, who animates us to do good.

Paul had not known Jesus personally. He came to Jerusalem after Christ's death, and decided to persecute the first Christians and destroy their community.

But the Risen Christ appeared to Paul in a way that changed his life completely:

When he was on the road and already near to Damascus, a light suddenly shone from the sky. Then Saul fell to the ground and heard a voice which said to him,

'Saul, Saul, why are you persecuting me?'

Then Saul asked,

'Who are you, Lord?'

'I am Jesus whom you are persecuting all the time. Get up and go into the city and there they will tell you what to do.'

When Paul got up he remained blind until he was baptized in Damascus and had his eyes opened again.
(after Acts 9.3–19)

This meeting between Paul and Christ was an experience that gave Paul life and was to animate him for the whole of the rest of his life. For this reason Paul, in a letter, says this about what it means to be Christian:

The Lord is the Spirit. Now where the Spirit of the Lord is, there is freedom.

So because our face is no longer covered with a veil, we are a mirror which reflects the splendour of the Lord; so we ourselves increasingly become like Christ, for we partake increasingly in his glory. That is brought about by the Lord, who is the Spirit.
(after II Cor. 3.17f.)

Let us follow Jesus
for he is our Way,
he will reveal himself
on the last day.

He is all beauty,
wonder, truth, grace,
one day we shall see him
face to face.

Let's walk with the Lord

The Spirit which you have received is not a spirit of slavery, but the spirit which makes you children of God. And this spirit makes us say, 'Our Father'. The spirit helps us in our weakness.
(after Rom. 8. 14–17)

A church of persons

One day several farm-workers from different neighbouring villages meet in Chonta pampa. While they are conversing, Walter Oyarce, an elder of Lucma, says:

'Yes, we do need a meeting-place. In our village we've decided to build a church, and everybody is helping in some way. I believe that to be the most important communal work, because the church is the house of God. Besides, a village is always going to be better if it has its own church.'

'Well, of course,' answers Teodosio Cruzado.

But Oscar Campos insists on giving the matter more thought.

'Well, I believe it is very useful to have a place where we can meet for prayers and for listening to God's word. But I don't think it is the most important thing of all.'

'Then what is more important?' asks Teodosio.

'That we ourselves become the temple of God.'

'What's that? What do you mean?'

Talking points

▷ How many buildings were constructed by Jesus?

▷ Why did Jesus want to found a church?

▷ Did Jesus build his church with stones or with men and women?

You are like a building, built on the foundation laid by the apostles and prophets, and Jesus Christ himself is the corner stone.

You are no longer strangers in a land which is not your home, but you are like all those who belong to God. You are members of the family of God.

In Christ the whole building has its foundations and grows up to be a holy temple to the Lord. So you, united with Christ, must unite with one another, in order to become through his Spirit a house of God. (after Eph. 2.11–22)

If it is true that the church is formed of men and women who have their daily problems, then their meeting place, whether it is a large cathedral or a humble village chapel, ought to be at the service of all the needs of the community where it is situated. An example of this is the church of Diego Ferre, a shanty town on the coast, which has a large hall which is available for any kind of meeting or activity that benefits the people of the shanty town.

290

Talking points

▷ Some people say that we farm-workers are 'lacking in respect' when we speak out in church. What do you think?

▷ When you meet in the town church, or in your village chapel, do you mention your day-to-day problems and needs, or do you try to forget them?

O dear church, my sacred home,
holy family formed by God,
born years ago in Egypt's land
and through the Red Sea walked dry-shod.

Christ now calls and liberates us,
Christ unites us with his love.
Not just Jews, but all the poor
are called to glory in heaven above.

Let's walk with the Lord

Come to the Lord like a living stone. Men have rejected him, but for God he is a chosen stone of great value. You too must be like living stones for God to use in order to make a spiritual temple.

(after I Peter 2.4f.)

United as one . . .

Christ is like a body with many members, and though these members are many, they form a single body. So whether we are Jews, Greeks, slaves or free, we have become a single body by being baptized by the one spirit. And we have all drunk of the one spirit.

A body is not made up of a single member, but of many. You are the body of Christ, and each one of you is a member of this body. (after I Cor. 12.12–27)

In the time of Jesus, the people were divided into Jews and Greeks, slaves and freemen. There was a lot of hatred between these groups, and unity between them was impossible.

Talking points

▷ In our world of farm-workers, which are the antagonistic groups that cannot unite?

▷ How can they unite?

▷ Which groups cannot unite?

▷ Within a group not all the members are equal. Each one has his talents. How can we use the talents of each one without falling into division?

... and nourished from the same root ... we can advance!

Every Christian should be a member of a Christian group, but this is not enough. We also need a personal relationship with Jesus. To help us understand this, Jesus has left us the example of the vine and the grapes:

I am the true vine, and my father is the husbandman. He cuts off each of my branches which does not bring forth fruit; but he prunes and cares for the branches which do bear fruit so that they may bear even more.

You are already pure through the teaching which I have given you. Remain united with me as I remain united with you. A branch cannot bear fruit of itself; so too you cannot bear fruit unless you remain united with me.

I am the vine and you are the branches. Anyone who remains united with me and I with him, bears much fruit; without me you can do nothing.

Anyone who does not remain united with me will be uprooted and will wither like those branches which are gathered up and burnt in the fire.

(after John 15.1–6)

Talking points

▷ What does this comparison mean?

▷ How is your personal relationship with Jesus?

▷ Tell the group an example of how you have felt the presence of Jesus in your life.

Let us bless our loving Lord
who in faith unites us,
and who feeds us with his love
against the foe that fights us.

Let us live one single life
as the Lord commands us,
let us make a juster world
as poverty demands us.

The People with Jesus Christ Marching towards Freedom

When Christians
dare to give an
integral revolutionary witness
then the Latin American revolution
will be invincible

(Ernesto 'Che' Guevara)

Those of the way

The parish of Chontapampa has exceptionally difficult communications; many villages are in very isolated valleys. For this reason the parish priest decides to call together representatives of all those villages where there are Christian communities, so that they can know each other better, exchange experiences and become aware that they are not alone in their problems.

On the day of the meeting, farmworkers arrive from Pino Alto, Loma, Condorpampa, Las Lagunas, Pampa Verde, Lucma and other villages. Some villages are unrepresented, because they do not have active groups; these are: Pedregal, Lucmapampa and Colpa. Look at previous chapters of this book to see the activities of those villages that have active Christian groups.

For each parish to become a living community, it must be made up of small groups who share their faith and all that they have.

Talking points

▷ Is there a Christian group in your village?

▷ What does your group do?

▷ Who directs your group?

After Pentecost, the apostles threw themselves into the task of preaching the good news of Jesus in Jerusalem. Soon very many people listened and were converted. And so the group began to grow. Since they knew that they were in the way of liberation and salvation in Christ, they began to be known as 'those of the way' (see Acts 9.1–2).

Almost immediately there were clashes with the authorities, and many dispersed to other regions.

Now those who had to flee from Jerusalem taught the message of salvation wherever they went.

One of these, Philip, came to a village of Samaria and there taught about Christ. People came together and all listened to him attentively. (after Acts 8.4–6)

The new groups began to grow. One of the most important men converted to the way was Paul, who dedicated all the rest of his life to extending the good news of Christ.

Paul began his work in the community of Antioch, where he had been sent. They laid hands on him and his companions and sent them off. (after Acts 13.1–3)

After a few years there was a good number of communities. Most of the members were persons of humble status.

Consider yourselves, brothers. Whom has God called? Hardly one of you is educated or a powerful, well-to-do person. Rather, God has sought out those who are weak, those whom the world regards as simple. He has chosen the simple and those of no account. (after I Cor. 1.26–28)

The apostles felt the need to maintain unity among all these communities. On one occasion there was an important dispute, and this was resolved by a meeting of all the Christian communities in Jerusalem.

Brothers and sisters together
members of one church,
mindful that we shall discover
whatever we set out to search.

The church is on the march:
a new world is our goal,
a world where love and peace will reign
and people can become free and whole.

Let's walk with the Lord

Come let us go up to the mountain of the Lord. He will tell us his ways and we shall go where he bids us. For the words of the Lord went out from Jerusalem. Every people walks in the name of its gods, but we shall walk always in the name of the Lord our God. (after Micah 4.1–3)

Those who don't accompany us

The next day, at the meeting in Chonta-pampa, Oscar Campos explains that the problem in his village of Condorpampa is that a lot of Catholics don't show any interest in the prayer-group.

'They call us Protestants, and say they don't believe in prayer-meetings.'

Several other representatives say that the same problem exists in their villages. And so the question arises:

Should we try to find other ways of being more united with the old-fashioned Catholics?

There is a lot of discussion about this. The majority is in favour of unity, saying that it is important that Catholics should not be in two groups.

The priest then intervenes:

'Brothers, we should always do everything we can to promote unity. But we must not be blind. Those Catholics who are only interested in baptizing their children and going to a few religious fiestas each year are in fact lending their support to those who oppress the farm-

workers. They don't always realize this, of course. But the truth is that they don't want to go to prayer-meetings, because it means too much effort.'

Talking points

▷ Are there differences of opinion among the Catholics of your area?

▷ Are we at all guilty for the divisions?

▷ Can we heal the divisions?

▷ How can you convince the farm-worker in the photograph (on the opposite page)?

Recall that in Unit 5 we saw that we live in an unjust and divided society. The divisions between Catholics have their roots in the divisions that exist in our society. We cannot make common cause with a Catholic (however good he may appear to be) who by his actions is supporting those who exploit the farm-workers. It is a sad fact that many say they are Catholics, but they have no sympathy with the poor.

Beware of false prophets. They look like harmless sheep, but they are really dangerous wolves. You will know them by what they do. (Matt. 7.15f.)

All those who are against the poor, are also against Christ. Unfortunately, there have always been people in the church opposed or indifferent to the poor. Not only among the rich and powerful, but also among those who are more or less humble themselves.

For example, at the time of the second Archbishop of Lima, St Toribio, the rich Spaniards were very displeased with the Archbishop for championing the cause of the poor and especially the Indians.

On one occasion the Spanish Viceroy imprisoned the brother-in-law of the saintly Archbishop and wrote as follows to the King of Spain:

'I have not yet seen the Archbishop of Lima, because he is simply never here. He spends all his time with the Indians, and even eats with them in their own houses. Everybody considers this conduct totally unworthy of this archbishopric.'

And today Archbishop Toribio is a saint of the church!

Let's walk with the Lord

Today when you hear my words
do not harden your hearts
as your fathers did in the wilderness,
when they rejected me
although they saw my works.
The people rebelled against me,
and I thought,
'They are a confused and misguided
*   people,*
who do not understand my way.'
(after Ps. 95.8–10)

'Happy are those who suffer persecution'

Encarnacion Llamoctanta, of Las Lagunas, is talking about the failure of the attempt to unite their smallholdings in his village.

'I'm sure that one of the reasons has been that Don Venancio Chavez (who owns 800 hectares of land) has gone around telling people that we were practising communism. He threatened us; he even had my house burned to the ground. There's nothing we can do about him.'

'And I'd like to know what part Don Venancio played in the death of Jesus Flores,' says Rosa Hoyos.

'Well, he was obviously behind it all', intervenes Oscar Campos, 'but he would never be able to do anything like it again: we are too well organized now.'

At that moment the priest breaks in to read them part of a document from Christians in Paraguay, written in 1970:

'In one province the police wanted to destroy a farm-workers' organization. Their method was to pick out one of the leaders and to imprison him, so as to intimidate the rest. What can be done in this case? It seems that an elderly catechist managed to make contact with 150 farm-workers disposed to go to prison themselves. In complete silence they walked to the city jail and presented themselves to the Governor of the jail. 'Where is your leader?' asked the Governor. 'We are all leaders,' they answered. The group spokesman explained that to touch one of their number was to touch everybody, and therefore they should all have been imprisoned. When they were refused entry to the jail, they sat down in the street and began singing at full voice. Nobody moved – even when they were threatened by armed police – until night, when they decided to walk home. Their fear of imprisonment had disappeared and their spirit of solidarity had been strengthened!'

Talking points

▷ How does the example of the farm-workers of Paraguay help us to avoid the kind of failure described above by Encarnacion?

Jesus says:

No servant is greater than his master. Because they persecuted me, they will also persecute you. *(John 15.20)*

Take heed! People will hand you over to the authorities and have you publicly beaten. For my sake they will drag you before rulers and those in high places. In this way you will be able to speak about me before them. But it will not be you who speak, but the spirit of your Father will speak in you. *(after Matt. 10.17–20)*

To be persecuted is a part of our Christian inheritance, and sometimes it is even necessary in order to purge our communities of errors. But we must not expect a speedy or automatic improving of the situation. The same country of Paraguay is now even worse in the 1980s than it was a decade ago.

Let us heap up
the dry trunks of grief
that are the dried-up lives
of yesterday,
and from their ashes
a new great heat will return
during the dark night
that is the eve of
freedom.

Not machine-guns
nor the fear of death
nor the mafias of power
will be able to hold back
what was once a flame
of struggle and love.
Let us nurture the fire
that the people kindled.

(poem by Juan Damian)

Let's walk with the Lord

Secure justice for me, O God; plead my cause against this merciless people. For you are my God and my guardian; why do you forsake me? Why must I go around oppressed by my enemies.

Send me your light and your truth, that they may show me the way to where you are.

Then I will be grateful to you. Why should I hang my head?

I have set my hope on the Lord, he is my God and my redeemer.

(after Ps. 43)

The path of liberation is narrow

It seems that Encarnacion Llamoctanta has not understood very well the example from Paraguay mentioned in the last chapter, because he says:

'So we can't do anything about guys like Venancio Chavez; we just have to put up with them and wait for God to reward our patience at the end of time.'

'No way, man,' replies Oscar Campos. 'the farm-workers of Paraguay didn't just put up with things with patience; they showed bravery and confronted the injustice.'

'That's right,' says Francisco Atalaya, 'they were like the farm-worker who doesn't let himself be trampled on when he goes to a shop or an office in town. He knows how to stand up like a man, instead of cringing like a dog.'

'It is always necessary to use a certain amount of force in order to obtain our total freedom,' the priest intervenes. 'Unfortunately those who have power often abuse it, so we have to employ a certain counter-force in order to confront persons like Venancio Chavez. If 150 farm-workers walk to the police-station, even though they are unarmed, that constitutes a show of force.'

Talking points

▷   What difficulties have you found in the path to freedom?

▷   Have you tended to overcome the difficulties, or to look for an easy way out?

The church insists that people have to take the means necessary to oppose injustice. If they refuse to do this, nobody will believe in their Christianity. When the bishops of the world met in Rome in 1971 they said:

'The Christian message is love and justice. If we do not bring about a greater equality in the world, we shall lose all credibility . . . ' (*Justice in the World*, II, 57)

It is easier not to oppose injustice, and to say: 'That's life, and we can't change it.'

But Christ does not offer us this broad and easy path, only a narrow path of love for our fellow human-beings.

Enter by the narrow gate. The gate which leads to corruption is broad and the street easy. Many go by it. But the gate which leads to life is narrow and the way hard. Only a few find it.

(Matt. 7.13f.)

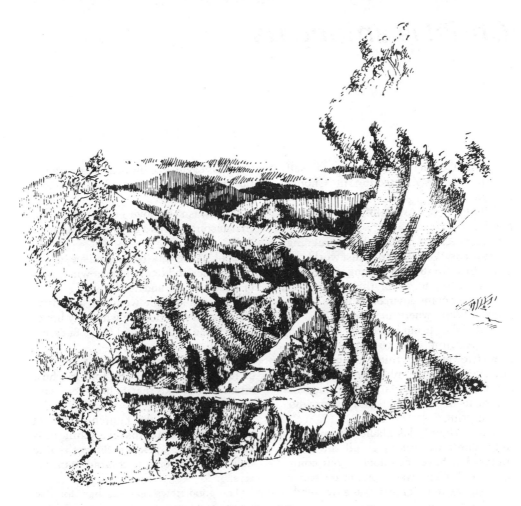

▷   Why does the Lord give us this example of the narrow way?

Hard is the fight
to sustain to the end,
to struggle for right,
the poor to defend,
on the side of the people.

Easy to talk,
to chatter and boast,
harder to strive,
to live through the dark
to the new day's dawning.

Let's walk with the Lord

Thus says the Lord, your protector, the
Holy One: 'I am your God and teach you
what is needful; I show you the way you
are to go.'

(Isa. 48.17)

Christis among us

Artemio Cotrina is not his usual self during the prayer-meeting in Chonta pampa.

'What's up, Artemio?' says Jesus Estela.

'It just seems to me that things are going badly for us. We live in an unjust world, we Catholics are divided among ourselves, and if we try to do anything the town authorities come down on us like a ton of bricks. Well, where is Christ? Has he abandoned us to our bad luck?'

'But Artemio, don't you remember that every time we do anything for our brother, however poor or humble, we are doing it for Christ? Christ is always present among us in our brothers and sisters who are suffering.'

'That's right,' adds Eladio Chumpitaz. 'Why don't we reckon up all the good things that have been done in our communities? When I was in prison and some of you came to visit me, it was a tremendous pleasure for me.'

'In Las Lagunas some of us are joining up our smallholdings so as to be able to feed our families better.'

'And wasn't it love of his neighbour that inspired Jesus Flores to do what he did?'

'Look at the way Teresa Quispe helped her brother and her nephews when they became orphans and homeless.'

'And some people were marvellous in the way they helped me when my house was burned to the ground,' says Encarnacion

'Last week I went to visit Ana, the wife of Juan Malaver, and she told me how much a visit like that helped her,' says Rosa Hoyos.

Arnulfo Perez, the churchwarden of Pampe Verde, thinks that everything he is learning at the weekly meetings is like sight being restored to a blind man. He says:

'The good news of Jesus has done so much good for me!'

Talking points

▷ It would be good to look again at all the examples we have studied together in this book, and ask ourselves where is Christ in our day-to-day lives as farm-workers.

▷ Can you add any more examples from your own life?

It is good for us to realize that in all these things we have been doing, Christ has been present.

'I was hungry and you gave me food;
I was thirsty and you gave me drink;
I was a stranger and you took me in;

I was naked and you gave me clothing;
I was sick and you cared for me;
I was in prison and you visited me.'
'Lord, when did we see you like this?'
'I tell you, what you have done for the least
of my brothers you have done for me.'
(after Matt. 25.35—40)

He is with us all the time,
and we do not recognize him,
he is with us all the time:
his name is Christ the Lord.
His name is Christ the Lord and he is
    thirsty,
he thirsts for justice in the world's affairs,
but many who can see him cross the
    pathway
perhaps because they're busy with their
    prayers!
His name is Christ the Lord and he is
    hungry
he clamours through the mouths of starv-
    ing Asians,
and many who can see him, cross the
    pathway:
imagining there'll be more such occa-
    sions.

Let's walk with the Lord

*When I was embittered, I was stupid and
ignorant; I was like a dumb beast before
you. But now I am always with you, for you
hold me fast and lead me as you will. You
take me by the hand to a glorious future.*
                            (after Ps. 73.21–24)

Love demands dedication

▷   Who can help him?

'There's one thing I don't understand,' says Artemio Cotrina.

'What's that?' asks Oscar Campos.

'Look, brother, if I visit a sick man or give clothes to a needy woman, the town authorities aren't going to persecute me. So why don't we just limit ourselves to good works like these, so as to have a quiet life?'

'No, Artemio, it's not enough just to help isolated cases of need. We have to go to the root cause as well, and that is what so annoys the authorities and those with power, because that way we uncover the injustice in the world.'

'I agree,' says Eladio Chumpitaz; 'as in my case: why was I in jail? Because of the injustice of the powerful!'

'And so when there is an individual problem, we have to look for the roots of that problem in our society,' affirms Oscar.

'Christian liberation is not just limited to either individual or social problems,' says the priest; 'it includes them both.' 'To change our unjust society we have to get into politics, otherwise our love of neighbour will be incomplete,' says Jesus Estela.

Talking points

▷ Have you ever heard of the word 'politics'?

▷ What do you understand by the word? Which people are involved in 'doing politics'?

▷ Which of our actions are merely individual, and which become political?

▷ Why does Jesus Estela say that our love of neighbour will be incomplete if we do not 'get into politics'?

A Chinese proverb says: If you want a hungry man to stay hungry, give him a fish; if you wish to take away his hunger, teach him how to fish.

Love for the poor is not just a question of almsgiving, but involves helping the poor to free themselves from their poverty. This means changing society.

To create a new society, a classless society without divisions, a society where professional people put their skills at the service of the majority, a more just society, we have to know how to act politically.

Give us a heart big for love,
give us a heart strong and just.
New people struggling in hope,
workers with aspect uncouth,
new people casting off chains,
pilgrims in search of the truth.

Let's walk with the Lord

He had shown you, man, what is good and what God wants of you: to be just and loving and to follow God with a firm resolve. *(after Micah 6.8)*

Injustice should be denounced

In some places the farm-workers have their own local newspapers, invariably mimeographed and very modest in appearance. These weekly or monthly broadsheets serve a valuable purpose in the more isolated regions of the Andes, especially as vehicles of information. The best-known of these newspapers is *Despertar* from Bambamarca, and the following letter and editorial are taken from its issue of 4 April 1976.

Dear Friends,

I am very sorry to have to report that things are going very badly in our village, all because of the many injustices being committed daily. I know that people don't like these bad things being revealed about them, especially by a group that calls itself Christian as ours does. We have been accused of slander and lies and receive insults every day.

But then we should not really be surprised: whenever a person or a group tries to find out the root causes of why things are unjust, we will always be hated by those who are really guilty, and who would like to see us dead. The same happened to Jesus; he died for being a fighter.

But I am not going to get discouraged. I have decided to carry on my work as village correspondent of *Despertar*, and to send in reports of injustice whenever I have the facts, whatever the consequences and whatever the danger to myself.

Edilberto Vasquez

EDITORIAL

This letter from one of our regular correspondents has made us all think of our own dedication, or lack of it.

When we have meetings with our correspondents we always insist on the obligation to make public the scandals and crimes that cause poverty and suffering. We defend the rights of our correspondents, and denounce those who act only through self-interest. The present situation is difficult, and we have to meet it united as one, so that the justice that Christ desires for us all may be brought about.

The Director

Talking points

▷ What media can you count on in your area as vehicles for the denunciation of injustice?

▷ How do those people who are denounced react?

▷ Relate those cases you remember.

When Peru was still a Spanish colony, when the natives of the land were being harshly treated by their colonizers, a humble friar set himself the task of denouncing the abuses. His name was Bartolomé de las Casas, and this is part of a letter he wrote to a priest who lived at the court of Carlos I of Spain:

'The last sixty-one years have witnessed untold abuse and ill treatment of the natives; for the forty years of his reign the Spanish king has done nothing, and the situation has been allowed by him to deteriorate.'

Friar Bartolomé thinks that the natives have no obligation to work gratis for the Kings of Spain; he later asks:

'Can't somebody there in the court make the king aware of the true position? Can't they see that not the smallest amount of gold-dust can be taken to Spain with a good conscience, because of the thousands of innocent people who suffer so much as a consequence?'

I was hungry
and you said 'population explosion';
I was without work
and you read me your manifesto;
I was homeless
and you built dehumanizing miners' huts;
I was naked, desperate
and you fought for your power-position.
I am tired . . . no more can I endure.
O God: give me strength to change at least a little bit of the world!

Let's walk with the Lord

Get ready and go for me. Set out and tell them all I command you. Fear me more than them!

They will fight you, but not conquer, for I am with you to free you, says God.

(after Jeremiah 1.17–19)

Let us unite in the struggle for justice

In their weekly meeting, the farm workers of Chontapampa have been discussing the letter and editorial in *DESPERTAR*, quoted in the previous chapter. They are impressed by the phrase 'united as one'.

'Just like the time when all of us from Chontapampa marched together to demand non-payment of taxes,' says Francisco Atalaya.

'That's correct,' says Oscar Campos; 'but the sad thing was that we never continued what we had begun so well: it was just a one-off campaign. It was a pity that we didn't organize ourselves as a result of that small victory.'

'But how are we going to form a big organization like that if we are still struggling with our small group and the weekly prayer-meeting?', asks Jesus Estela.

'Well, we need this experience, too,' says Eladio Chumpitaz. 'I remember that I belonged to a trade union when I lived a few years in Lima. We had to learn the hard way to fight against fear . . . fear of losing your job, fear of the bosses, fear of the police, and so on. It's not easy, but it's all part of the process.'

'And we've seen the case of the farm-workers of Paraguay: instead of being afraid of going to prison, they ended up offering to go to prison "united as one". That's what we need.'

Talking points

▷ In your region, what kinds of communal organizations exist?

▷ How do they function?

▷ Can their organization be improved? How?

'While there are certain organizations that come into being in order to deceive and manipulate the workers, there are other kinds of organization that result from a direct initiative of the workers themselves . . . ' (*Mother and Teacher*, a letter written to the church by Pope John XXIII, 144).

'Sometimes these organizations are not considered Christian, because some people consider Christians to be the allies of bosses and exploiters. But genuinely Christian farm-workers know that Christianity is the enemy of every type of exploitation. These Christians feel the duty to make the spirit of Christ penetrate these secular organizations' (read *The Progress of Peoples*, by Pope Paul VI, 81).

They invent great institutions,
they praise our organizations,
but they don't want our opinions
and they abuse our delegations.

They talk of revolution,
they want to change the bosses,
but when the harvest fails again
it's us who'll bear the losses!

Let's walk with the Lord

Rejoice, my people, for your king is coming to you. He will do away with the battle-fields and bring peace to the peoples. And those who are in prison will return to you, my people, full of hope. You will be the place of refuge for your children and like the hero's sword. They will be victorious.
(after Zech. 9.9–17)

Towards a society without privileges

A group of Christians from Chontapampa are reflecting about the new society of the future . . .

'I think it will have to be very, very different,' says Jesus Estela.

'I'll tell you all what happened to me. We have a literacy programme for adults, and the teacher asked young Pancho Escobar to give him a hand. Well, Pancho said to me: "Of all the cheek! The Ministry pays that teacher 500 dollars a month, and he wasn't going to give me a cent. So I said to him: "How much are the bosses in their Lima offices getting?!"'

'That's how things are,' answers Oscar Campos. 'It seems to me that we live in a society where those who work and suffer most are those who earn least. It shouldn't be like that.'

'And those who study in universities and places like that use their fine education just to make a big packet of money, and have no interest in helping those of us who produce the food of the country by the sweat of our brows.'

▷ Does the policeman in the shopping centre do *his* shopping there?

Talking points

▷ In our present society, we farm-workers serve the interests of the rich. Where does the guard in front of the shop in the photograph come from? Can he afford to buy in that shop?

▷ What sort of professionals do we need to help us in the Andes?

▷ Why aren't there any universities in the mountain regions?

▷ In some areas certain farm-workers have been prepared as health-workers or literacy promoters, etc. Why are these programmes nearly always a failure?

China is a very large country. It has more population than any other country. Thirty years ago it had about 500 million people, and 350 millions of them had no access to medical facilities. The other 150 millions only had access if they had money. All the doctors lived in the cities, and wanted to earn big salaries.

Then came the revolution, and everything changed.

Nowadays in China, the doctors are more in the rural areas in the cities. They do not earn as much as before, but they have less to do because all the people have received education in preventative as well as in curative medicine, and in the use of traditional herbs. Some of them receive a special training and become what are known as barefoot doctors.

▷ Could we ever have an experience like that of the barefoot doctors in our country? Would the project work well in our mountainous regions?

Let's walk with the Lord

A time is coming, says God, when I will change the fortunes of my people. I am with them to redeem them.

Give us a heart big for love,
give us a heart strong and just.

New people struggling in hope,
workers with aspect uncouth.
New people casting off chains,
pilgrims in search of the truth.

All those who devour you will be destroyed. All your oppressors will be driven away. All those who treat you with contempt will be despised. I will make your tribe strong again. You will constantly meet before me. Your leaders will come from your ranks. Who is ready to risk his life? (after Jer. 30.3–21)

. . . where everybody will have enough to eat

'If there were no privileges in society, nobody would have more or less than others,' says Rosa Hoyos.

'That's true enough.'

'Wouldn't it be wonderful! Imagine what it would be like if everybody had enough to eat all the time!'

'Yes, it would be wonderful. But how could such a change be made? We all have smallholdings, and whatever we do we can't make them any bigger.'

'But Peru is a big country, and if it were all governed for everybody's benefit, surely then it would be possible for everybody to eat.'

'Perhaps you are right . . .'

'Maybe . . .'

When Jesus saw the multitude it grieved him, for they came to him like sheep without a shepherd. So he spoke to them for a long time. When it was evening, his disciples came to Jesus and said,

'It is already late, and this is a lonely place. So send the people into the villages and the houses round about so that they may buy something to eat.'

'Why?' replied Jesus. 'Give them something to eat.'   *(after Mark 6.34–37)*

Then Jesus multiplied the bread.

Talking points

▷   What can we do to increase the amount of food?

But Jesus isn't just content to give ordinary food to the people. He was concerned about other sorts of hunger as well. For this reason he said:

I am the bread of life. He who eats of this bread will live for ever.

(after John 6.48–51)

▷   How do you understand this saying of Jesus?

▷   What are these 'other sorts of hunger'?

▷   How do you imagine a society without any kind of hunger at all?

The prophet Isaiah said this:

When there are no longer exploited people in your house, when you no longer threaten anyone or point a finger at them, when you give the hungry the food that you yourself would have liked, and those *in want what they need, then your light will shine in the darkness. My people will construct new houses on the broken-down walls and build on the foundations of the past.*

(after Isa. 58.1–12)

I search through the world
for a moment of friendship,
with a good glass of wine
and a crisp hunk of bread.

Let's walk with the Lord

Free me from the power of my enemies,
rescue me from the attack of the strangers:
their words are lies and their promise
  deception.
Our granaries should be full of all manner
  of food;
we should all have flocks and our beasts of
burden should be heavily laden;
no one should fall on us and rob us of what
  is ours.
Happy are the people who have this,
happy the people who have the Lord as
  their God! (after Ps. 144)

. . . and where everybody can make real progress

Oscar Campos is worried about the new stretch of road he is helping to make near Condorpampa, and he tells his neighbours about his worries:

'Look, brothers, I got all worked up and sentimental about that new road because I saw it as a means of progress for our villages. But let me tell you something: I've seen what has happened in Pedregal, where the road has been widened for cars. A huge signboard says 'Peru Progresses'. But what kind of progress has it been? At the beginning the road was widened in order to transport minerals from the El Dorado mines. But now the lorries of Nestlé are going into the area and buying up all the milk, and taking it down to Lima. Before they went in you could buy cheese in Pedregal, but not now. Before, you could always buy a bottle of fresh milk, but now Don Venancio Chavez has put up a beer shop instead. It doesn't sound like progress to me: I call it a new exploitation!'

Talking points

▷ Our society is always talking about the virtues of 'progress' . . . five-lane highways in Lima, canned food, plastic, etc. Who benefits from this kind of 'progress'?

▷ What sort of progress can you see in the photograph?

▷ Why have roads been constructed in your area? Who are those who have most benefitted from them?

Pope Paul VI said that real progress is when every man and every woman can share in its fruits. When we don't have enough to live on, there is a lack of progress. When the rich and the powerful continue to exploit us, and take the fruit of our toil, there is no progress.

When abject poverty is abolished and we have what we need for life, when we can defend ourselves against the catastrophes of nature, when we can study and work according to our capacities, then there is progress.

When our dignity is respected, when money does not remain the centre of life, when we work for the common good and work for peace, then there is even more progress.

When we give importance to God and the values of the Spirit, then there is even more progress.

When we have faith and try hard to bring about that complete liberation that Jesus desires for us all, then there is very much more progress (read *The Progress of Peoples*, 14 and 21).

▷ When can we say there is real progress in the rural areas?

▷ What needs changing in our rural areas?

Peasant farmer of the Andes,
who devours all your harvest?
Join hands with the city workers
and the future will be yours.

The wholesalers are rich
and know how to entice:
You sell them your crops
at an unjust price.

Let's walk with the Lord

I know well what I intend for you. I want to bring you peace and not unhappiness; I want you to have a hopeful future, says God. Do not believe the false prophets among you. Do not succumb to their persuasions, the fruits of their art.
(after Jer. 29.8–14)

The danger of installing ourselves

During a meeting of Christian communities in Chontapampa, Arnulfo Perez from Pampa Verde speaks:

'Brothers, it is a great pleasure for me to be here today, because I can see that we are from many different communities. In my village we are also making great progress and we are now planning to build a tower for our church.'

'It's my opinion,' says Oscar Campos, 'that brother Perez and his community ought to think a bit more about that tower. If the Christians of Pampa Verde think only of improving the looks of their church building, then they are forgetting a lot of things. To build a tower, with their problems, is like sitting back and folding your arms and thinking life is over. A Christian should always be on the march, just like Jesus who had nowhere to lay his head at night.'

Talking points

▷ All the communities represented at the meeting in Chontapampa are poor communities, and have a lot of problems, such as the departure of Guzman Perez for Lima, or the failure of the communal land project in Las Lagunas.

▷ What are the problems in your community?

▷ What do you think of the opinions of Arnulfo and Oscar?

The danger of installing ourselves, of making ourselves comfortable, is the danger of misunderstanding Christian doctrine. José Dammert, Bishop of Cajamarca, writes:

'It is true that stone temples should be respected by the faithful, but they should never become the most important thing.'

The ancient Jews used to venerate their temple in Jerusalem, but the prophets criticized their attitude:

Do not trust in words like 'Look at the temple, it's the temple of the Lord!' Rather, behave better, act justly and stop the oppression. (after Jer. 7.4–7)

▷ Is it important to finish the towers of the cathedral?

'The Christian message is that material stones cannot be everything. We cannot believe that in a time of great poverty the will of God is to build church towers. The first temple of God is our eighbour. He needs our respect, attention and love more than temples of stone. It is sad when persons calling themselves "very Catholic" only take into account the material appearance of a church building, while despising and ill-treating their brothers in Christ' (José Dammert, *Christian Temples*, 1973).

Let's walk with the Lord

Lord, show me your way that I may follow your truth: fill my heart with reverence for your word. O my God, the proud rise up against me, people who want to know nothing of you. But you, Lord, are good. Give me power so that my enemies are ashamed. You have helped me and comforted me. (after Ps. 86.11–17)

Pulling out selfishness by the roots

While they are talking about Arnulfo Perez's project to build a church tower in Pampa Verde, Francisco Atalaya raises his hand for silence:

'Brothers, I agree with what Oscar has said about the danger of installing ourselves, but I believe we have a more serious problem in my village of Pino Alto, and I freely recognize that I am as guilty as the next man. It is that we all want to lord it over our neighbours, and have power over others. It all comes from the selfishness that destroys everything in the end.'

'I agree with you completely, brother Francisco,' says Eladio Chumpitaz. 'If the roots of exploitation and injustice are in our society it's because they are fed by the selfishness in the heart of every man.'

Then Oscar Campos says, 'It's so easy to see other people's faults, so hard to see our own. We are capable of being Christian leaders in the village community, but in our own families we can be tyrants and despots.'

'I believe that selfishness is like the weeds that grow so easily in our fields; we have to work hard to root them out,' says Jesus Estela.

Talking points

▷ It would be a good exercise to look through previous chapters at all the cases of selfishness in order to reflect about them once again. Here are some of the examples:

Juan Malaver, the bully of his family (16)

The people of Condorpampa (193)

Fulgencio Chuquilin, the authoritarian village elder (69)

Venancio Chavez, the capitalist (80)

▷ Why is the house in the photograph in an untidy condition?

▷ What would happen if we managed to change society without changing persons?

▷ By changing persons, can we change society?

We shall not better our country without a different and renewed society. But above all we need new men and women who live according to the gospel, and are really free and responsible (Medellin, *Justice*).

We know that Christ has freed us from sin, but we must continue fighting for this freedom within ourselves, so that one day we can say with St Paul:

I have died to sin. I am nailed with Christ to the cross.

Therefore I live, yet no longer I, but Christ lives in me. As long as I live in this world, I do so trusting in the Son of God who loves me and gave his life for me.

(after Gal. 2.19f.)

We must risk our lives,
so that everyone strives
to say goodbye
to the old 'I'.

Joining hand in hand
throughout the land
growing wheat
that all may eat.

This is our body
for a new humanity.
This is our blood,
for a new people.

Let's walk with the Lord

Sometimes I speak to a people and promise to build it up and plant it. But they reply: 'There is no point in that! We do as we please, each according to his own ideas.' And then I lose interest in doing the good I promised them.' *(after Jer. 18.9–12)*

God is our strength

Francisco Atalaya and Oscar Campos are talking together during a few free moments in the Chontapampa training-course.

'When I'm here taking part in these meetings with you all, I get a lot of encouragement for my farm work,' says Franciso.

'But we get so easily discouraged,' says Oscar. 'I feel really marvellous when I'm here, but I know that when I get back to Condorpampa things will be very different.'

'You're right there. It's like when we have a long day's walk, and we need to rest now and again to regain our strength.'

'I'll have to try praying more.'

'My Uncle Humberto Morocho told me once that when he is walking in silence over the mountains, and the wind blows gently, it is as if God were talking to him. I think he is right: we have a lot of possibilities of talking with God in our kind of work.'

Talking points

▷ At times when you have to wait for someone and have nothing to do, do you get bored?

▷ What do you do when you are alone? Do you pray as a family?

We already know the story of Elijah, the prophet who acted very politically (and very violently as well). He was a man who used to pray a lot: he looked for God in solitude, and God made himself known to him. When the people turned against him, God used to give him strength to carry on his struggle for the people's liberation: 'Get up and eat, or the path will be too difficult for you'.

Moses also was a man of prayer: 'And Yahweh was talking with God face to face, just as a man talks to his neighbour.' One day Moses said to Yahweh, 'If you don't come in person, we shan't leave this place.'

The Lord answered him: 'I'll do as you ask me, because you are my friend.'

Moses used to pray a lot with the people; but he also longed to know God: 'Please, let me see your glory.'

God allowed Moses to see him, and Moses returned very excited (read Ex. 33).

Jesus himself used to find strength from praying. When his death was very near, he said to his disciples:

'Could you not stay awake with me even one hour? Stay awake and pray, so that you do not fall into temptation; the spirit is willing, but the flesh is weak.'

(after Matt. 26.40f.)

Let's walk with the Lord

When the sun arises
give us courage, Lord.
Alleluia, Christ is saviour,
he delivers us with his light and love.
We must not cease working
while the sun is high.

Till the sun has set, Lord,
we will work with you.

When a woman brings a child into the world she suffers pain. But when the child is born she forgets the pain and is only happy that a man or woman has come into the world.

I have told you this so that you may have peace. The world will treat you harshly. But do not lose courage. I have already overcome the world.   (after John 16.21–33)

Praise the Lord!

It is the final evening of the training-course in Chontapampa. For several days now the farm-workers have been listening to talks, discussing interesting points, conversing among themselves. All the participants feel they have learned a lot. Better still, they feel enthusiastic to return to their communities and work with a better will.

To conclude the training-course there is a celebration and fiesta, as is customary. Because of their high spirits, they raise the roof during the Sung Mass, they listen more attentively than ever to the Word of God, and together they receive the Body and Blood of the Lord. Then they prepare a large bonfire, and sit down to an excellent supper, braised guinea-pigs being the special dish. There is no drunkenness, since alcohol only gives a false joy.

For everybody present it really is a day of the Lord. Everybody is united, equal and full of joy. It is like a seed of the new society about which they have spoken so much, where everybody is free and at the service of others.

Talking points

▷ Why are the farm-workers of Chontapampa so happy?

▷ Earlier in the book we told of the happiness of the farm-workers going to the Sunday market, and during their fiestas. Do you think those occasions can also be described as days of the Lord?

God wanted his people to have a day of rest, a Lord's Day. He wanted it for two reasons:
> so that they could recuperate their strength after working;
> and to celebrate their freedom.

We too, the New People of God, need to rest, relax and celebrate the freedom that Jesus Christ brings us.

The Lord's Day gives us strength to carry on the way to total freedom. It is then that we most closely fulfil the words of St Paul:

Encourage one another with psalms and hymns as the spirit moves you. Sing and give thanks to the Lord with all your heart. Thank God the Father at all times for all things in the name of our Lord Jesus Christ. *(Eph. 5.19f.)*

▷ When are the right moments for us farm-workers to celebrate the Day of the Lord?

Let us march together:
He is our salvation.
Let us sing together:
He is our liberation.

Humbly we adore him:
He is our Creator.
Humbly we extol him:
there is no God greater!

Let's walk with the Lord

You will draw water with joy from the wells of salvation and at the same time you will say, 'Give thanks to the Lord and call upon his name. Tell all his greatness and his mighty acts. The whole earth shall learn of them. Shout with joy, my people, for all the goodness your God has shown you.'
(after Isa. 12.3–6)

325

Deliverance will come!

In Central Peru, the farm-workers often tell a story about 'Inkarri', a story that reminds us of the ideal society we all dream of. The story runs like this:

Inkarri was the child of the Sun and of a poor woman; he shared the sufferings of Andean farm-workers: his feet were often bleeding from long walks through the mountains, but the blood was merely mingling with Mother Earth, his real mother.

At a later time there is a struggle; Inkarri dies, killed by Spanish conquista- dores or by his own brother. But his head still exists and his body is still growing. One day Inkarri will come back: 'When the world turns over, Inkarri will return and will take power to himself as in former times. Then all men, Christians and non-Christians alike, will be as one.'

The history of Inkarri tells of a harsh reality: that Peru is divided. One part wants 'progress' and economic domina- tion, while the other is faithful to the ancient Peruvian society where every- body felt themselves to be children of the Sun and of Mother Earth.

Talking points

▷ It would be an interesting exercise to make a note of all the chapters in this book where mention is made of the two opposing societies that make up present-day Peru.

▷ Are there ways of overcoming this division, creating a new, just and authentic society?

Here is part of St John's vision of our final end, taken from the Book of Revelation:

They will be his people and he himself, God with them, will be their God. He will wipe the tears from their eyes, and there will be neither death nor sorrow, nor tears nor tribulation, for all that is past. He who sits on the throne has said: 'Now I am making all things new.'

(after Rev. 21.3–5)

And St Paul says:

It was his purpose to unite everything in heaven and on earth under Christ as head. May the God of our Lord Jesus Christ give you wisdom to recognize him and his plans.

May he open your eyes to see the destiny to which you are called.

For you will know what a rich and glori- ous gift God prepares for his people, and how overwhelmingly great is the power with which he works in us believers.

(after Eph. 1.9–23)

Let's walk with the Lord

Behold, I am coming soon,
bringing recompense to repay everyone
for what he has done.
I am the first and the last,
the beginnng and the end.
Amen, Come Lord Jesus!
                    (after Rev. 22.12.20)

And You . . .
Have You Made Your
Decision Yet?

'. . . to fight for everybody and to fight so that the individual may be a man, that all the wealthy may be men, so that the entire world may become a man.'

(Cesar Vallejo, Peruvian poet)

Life is struggling . . . and hoping!

Artemio Cotrina is climbing up the mountain side to his house in Loma, and when he gets there he looks back at the view.

It is a warm May day; the valley is visible below. In some of the farmsteads he can see women gathering in the maize cobs, throwing the outer leaves into a cloth to give to the cow or pig afterwards as feed. In other farmsteads the villagers are already ploughing up the land for the potato seed. There are groups of peons, or hired labourers, helping out where the farmstead is bigger. Here and there he can see the sun shining brilliantly on the tiny streams of water to the fields. Without water, life in the Andes would come to an end.

Artemio breathes deeply the fresh mountain air and thinks: 'Such is the life of the mountain farmsteads. There's a time to sow and a time to harvest. After life comes death and then life again. The sun and the water are like a mother and father to the plants.'

As Christian farm-workers we see similarities between our work and our faith. We sow the Word of God in order to harvest men and women who are new persons, freed by Christ, and who will dedicate themselves to bringing into being a new and liberated society. This work is not easy: it is like preparing the soil with our primitive tools . . . In the same way the Holy Spirit gives life and animation to every Christian just as the water and the sun make plants grow.

Artemio is like many other Christian leaders: he grows impatient because the exploitation, the abject poverty, the selfishness continue, and the long-promised total liberation does not arrive.

Artemio forgets something he knows very well. In order to obtain a good harvest we farm-workers have to work hard, even when the seed is sown, at irrigating, weeding, fighting against diseases and plagues. If we do our job well, then we can leave the rest to God.

The new world of God is like a seed which a farmer sows. He goes home, and continues his daily round, working and sleeping. Meanwhile the seed germinates and grows without his bothering about it. The earth makes plants grow and bring forth fruit of their own accord. First come the shoots, then the ears appear, and then they fill with grain. As soon as the corn is ripe, the farmer begins the reaping; then is the harvest. *(after Mark 4.26–29)*

Christ tells us that deliverance will certainly come; although there are people who want to spoil the harvest, the harvest for the kingdom of God is not going to fail.

With the Lord's help, one day we shall overcome our enemies. We must wait for that day by continuing to work and struggle hard that it may arrive as soon as possible.

Talking point

▷ What are the most urgent tasks we must undertake?

Let us bring to the Lord the gifts of his love,
Let us bring bread and wine for the sacrifice.
Open arms that sow with fear
Tired arms that reap with joy.

The pain and joy of farming folk,
our weariness, our lack of rest.

Let's walk with the Lord

Trust in the Lord and do good, live in your land and remain faithful to him.
Love the Lord with all your heart, and he will give you your heart's desire.
Put the future in the Lord's hand, trust in him and he will come to help you.
(after Ps. 37)

Do your sowing well!

In the village of Naranjo work goes ahead to remake the irrigation canal destroyed during the rainy season.

Jesus Estela is working with the others when he is swept away and killed by an avalanche. The relations, neighbours and several Christian leaders arrive for the 'wake'. Under the direction of Oscar Campos, from Condorpampa, they all agree to share the costs of the wake and the funeral. They don't want a repetition of what has so often happened in the past.

'It is not right for people to have to bankrupt themselves when a relation has died, as occurred when Don Francisco buried his wife Tomasa.'

'Yes, it is better that all the mourners help out on these occasions.'

'I believe we ought to petition for damages from the authorities of the province. They were opposed to us repairing the canal, and never raised a finger to help us, and now one of our companions has died.'

'In memory of Jesus Estela we must finish off the job of the new canal. His death must be for us an added reason for working hard.'

Talking points

▷ We often say that the death of a person is a tragedy for his friends and relations. Do you think that Estela's death has only been a tragedy in Naranjo?

▷ How can we improve our wakes so that they become a real help to everybody present?

We can compare the death of a Christian to the seed that falls into the ground:

Unless a grain of wheat falls into the ground and dies, it remains alone. But if it dies in the earth it brings forth much fruit.
(John 12.24)

It is not only by our death that we sow the seeds of liberation, but also when we work and struggle; what matters is that we work and struggle well.

Do not worry! Everyone will reap what they have sown. Those who have only sown selfishness will reap death. Those who sow the spirit of God will be given fruit which does not decay.   (after Gal. 6.7f.)

Complete freedom will be the fruit of our efforts, our work and our deaths as well. All this is united to the life and death of Christ. The triumph of Christ assures our final triumph also.

Death is destroyed! Victory is complete! Death, where is your victory? Death, where is your power? We thank God that he gives us victory through Jesus Christ.
(after I Cor. 15.54–57)

▷ What can we do at this time to be able to say that we are doing well with our spiritual sowing?

The worker has come back home,
dragging his tools behind him,
his poncho and his sombrero
smell of earth, wherever you find him.
Up-mountain or down-mountain,
wherever there's work he'll be found.

Let's walk with the Lord

So the glory of my Father will be seen when you bring forth rich fruit. I love you because my Father loves you.
Abide in this love, as I have loved you. I have said this that you may fill me with joy and your joy may be full.
(after John 15.1–17)

Your baptism compels you

For a time the death of Jesus Estela leaves the community of Naranjo paralysed. Nobody has the heart to work. Then one of the village leaders, Anselmo Zuniga, a young man, brings the neighbours together.

'Look, brothers, the death of our companion Jesus leaves us with a debt to pay.

'We must finish the canal and name it "Jesus Estela". We will invite the farm-workers from the neighbouring villages to work with us, since they too will share the benefits of the canal.'

And so it happened. The work advanced quickly, and with enthusiasm. Among those who offer their work are Artemio Cotrina, Eladio Chumpitaz and Oscar Campos; during a moment of rest the three of them are looking at the canal and the avalanche that killed Jesus Estela.

'It's just like a baptism, brothers,' says Eladio. 'A death that brings forth new life. Look how united the people are now, how the villagers of Naranjo have lost their fear of the provincial authorities, how we have come along to help out.'

Talking points

▷   What is it that makes Eladio think of baptism?

▷   How can baptism be like a death?

One day the disciples James and John said to Jesus:

'We would like you to give us seats on your right hand and on your left when you come into your kingdom.'

Jesus said, 'You do not know what you are asking. Can you drink the cup of suffering that I must drink? Can you be baptized with the baptism that I face?'

They said, 'We can.'

Jesus said, 'You will indeed drink the cup that I drink and be baptized with the baptism that I face. But it is not for me to give places on the right hand and on the left. God will choose who is to sit there.'

(after Mark 10.37–40)

▷ What is the meaning of baptism according to the words of Jesus?

Baptism is a serious dedication. One who is baptized has to be ready to fight for the freedom of his poor and oppressed brothers. If necessary he will have to give his life, as did Jesus. It will then be a baptism of blood.

▷ If baptism is such a serious matter, is it a good thing to practise infant baptism? Would it not be better to wait till they are old enough to understand?

Eladio, Artemio and Oscar talk about this last point, but finally they remember what Jesus had said:

'Suffer the children to come to me and do not forbid them, for theirs is the kingdom of heaven.' *(Mark 10.14)*

Oscar Campos says, 'Jesus is saying here that liberation is also for them; in fact for Jesus children come first.'

▷ What must we do so that people can understand the serious nature of baptism?

The Lord has called them,
and now he consecrates them
by light and water.

Brothers and sisters, remember
that baptism requires of us all
a strong dedication of service
to the suffering, the sick and the poor.

Let's walk with the Lord

Now give your servants the power to preach your message boldly and resolutely. Help us to heal the sick and do other wonderful things in the name of your holy Son Jesus. *(after Acts 4.29f.)*

Let your children share the good news with you

Artemio Cotrina from Loma is returning with the determination to try to set up a programme of prepared baptisms in the next village of Quinua, where there is no Christian group. As can be imagined he meets with opposition. Florencio Rojas says that he has no time for such new-fangled fancies.

Angela Flores, who is going to be godmother to her nephew, says that it has always been regarded as a sin for the parents to attend the baptism of their child. Nevertheless, Artemio manages to convince Eleuterio Flores and his wife Rosa Maria that they should attend.

'Look, friends, it is we parents who have the chief responsibility of bringing up these children, and giving them a Christian education.'

'I understand now, Don Artemio. And what's more I've heard from my cousins that since this sort of baptism started in Loma that people get on together a lot better in the village. And they tell me that they don't just pick anybody to be godparent, nor are there useless expenditures as there used to be when we had to go to town for baptisms.'

Talking points

▷ In your village are there still persons who react like Angela?

▷ Why does the church demand that the parents be present at baptism?

▷ Why does Artemio go to so much trouble to prepare the parents for a baptism?

At a time of baptism all the relations and friends turn up. Often it is the only opportunity to converse with the parents. It may not be easy, but we have to do all in our power to help people understand at least this basic truth:

To be baptized is to begin to follow the way of Jesus. If you are not going to dedicate your life to struggle against wretchedness and squalor and exploitation, better not to be baptized. If you are not ready to offer your life – even your death – for your companions, better not to be baptized. Baptism unites us with Christ, puts us on his way, and in his struggle against evil:

When we were baptized we were buried with him. But just as he was raised from the dead by the marvellous power of God the Father, so now we too can lead a new life. Do not give even the smallest part of your body over to sin, so that it cannot be used as a weapon against the good. Rather, put yourselves at God's disposal, as those who have come out of death to new life. (after Rom. 6.1–23)

▷ When we baptize a child, how can we be sure he is going to always follow the way of Jesus? Only if we, the parents, are determined.

In baptism we answer the following questions:

Do you promise to give your children a good example of a Christian life?
Do you promise to teach them the word of God?

▷ Taking the photographs into account, how can we put these promises into practice?

Let's walk with the Lord

Take heed of the commandments which I gave all the people. And I will send them the prophets who will turn the hearts of the parents towards their children and the hearts of the children towards their parents. (after Mal. 3.22f.)

Let your whole family serve the community

Florencio Rojas is listening to a pre-baptismal talk given by Artemio Cotrina in Quinua, but he is obviously antagonistic; Artemio is speaking about the obligation of parents and godparents to educate their children. At last Florencio can contain himself no longer:

'Look, Don-whatever-your-name-is, I don't send my children to school because the teacher in this village is a complete disaster. I'm a poor man and my children can't be wasting their time at school. As for other people's children, that's their business!'

'I understand your problem, Don Florencio, but wouldn't it be a good idea for you to get together with the other parents and try to improve your school?'

'I'm not for time-wasting activities like that.'

'It may be time-wasting for you,' says Eleuterio Flores, 'but that's because all you can think of is your own smallholding. If you are going to be a godparent then you are taking on a responsibility for your godchild in the name of the whole community. As members of the same village, I think we ought to do something to make Quinua a better place for our children. Personally, I am very grateful that Don Artemio has taken the trouble to come along and help us with his Christian reflections. It is like seeing life in a new light. Thank you, Don Artemio.'

The disciples of Jesus were humble and poor. But sometimes they were tempted to become like the rich and powerful. For example, when James and John went to ask for the first places for themselves the other disciples were envious of them. So Jesus took the opportunity to speak about baptism, and said to them all:

'As you know, the rulers of the earth are tyrants over their people and those who have power let others feel it. But it is not to be so with you. If any one of you wants to be special, he must serve the others, and if anyone wants to be at your head he must be the slave of all. For even the Son of man did not come to be ministered to, but to minister, and to give his life as a ransom for all men.' *(after Mark 10.42–45)*

Talking points

▷ During the pre-baptismal talks, do we mention real day-to-day village problems?

▷ How do you think the pre-baptismal talks ought to be organized?

▷ During the baptism ceremony the parents and godparents have to answer this question:
Do you promise to educate your children to serve the community and to live like brothers and sisters with the others of the community? What do you think this question implies?

It is our solemn duty
these children to assist,
to understand the beauty
and truth of Christ's good news.

They now belong to Jesus,
each one for him a gem,
our weariness and struggles
will one day fall to them.

Let's walk with the Lord

All have the same concern, love and dedication. Do not act out of arrogance or laziness. None of you is to assert himself above the others, but is to think of them as more than himself. Do not pursue your own interests, but act for the benefit of others. Remember the standards that Jesus Christ has set. *(after Phil. 2.5–18)*

Godparents, too, are important

Several months ago Clothilde Becerra, from Colpa, gave birth to a son, and now she is thinking of baptizing him. What most concerns her is that the boy should manage to have a 'good' godparent. But she speaks to her husband:

'Artemio, we must get Casimiro baptized. Have you thought of a godfather yet? It must be somebody with money.'

'Of course. The other day I was with Venancio Chavez, and I took the opportunity to talk to him about the matter.'

'And what did he say? Did he accept?'

'He certainly did! I had to chat him up a bit, and I gave him a couple of bottles of alcohol while I was at it.'

'Good for you. Don Venancio has a big business, with lots of land, as well as a car and lorries.'

'That's why I spoke to him. He's the richest man in the area and is able to help all his godsons.'

'I'm glad of what you have done; it's much better than having a mere farmworker godfather in poncho and sombrero!'

Talking points

▷ What do you think of this case?

▷ When somebody chooses a rich godfather, does he always come up to expectations?

▷ Is there a situation of exploitation and blackmail in all this? What are the real obligations of godparents to godchildren in baptism?

▷ What is the ideal sort of person to be a godparent?

To think over these points we could do worse than read these words of St James:

My brothers, if you hold the faith of our Lord Jesus Christ, the Lord of glory, show no partiality. If a man with gold rings and in fine clothing comes into your assembly, and a poor man in shabby clothing also comes in, and you pay attention to the one who wears the fine clothing and say, 'Have a seat here, please,' while you say to the poor man, 'Stand there,' or 'Sit at my feet,' have you not made distinctions among yourselves, and become judges with evil thoughts?

Listen, my brothers, has not God chosen those who are poor in the world to be rich in faith and heirs of the kingdom which he has promised to those who love him? But you have dishonoured the poor man. Is it not the rich who oppress you, is it not they who blaspheme that honourable name by which you are called? (James 2.1–7)

We parents and godparents
assume responsibility
to bring Christ's truth to all men
and women in our vicinity.

Let's walk with the Lord

The Lord has said, 'This people only draws near to me with words; it honours me only with lips, but its heart is far from me. Its faith is only habit and parrot-like repetition.' (after Isa. 29.13)

You too receive the Holy Spirit

In the village of Quinua two young men are conversing, Feliberto Carranza and Pancho Escobar. Feliberto wants to go to Lima, because he thinks Quinua has absolutely nothing to offer him.

'The problem about our village is that we are totally ignored by the authorities and everything is dead. The farm-workers don't want to collaborate in any improvements. I'm tired of it all.'

'You're right in what you say about the authorities and about the villagers,' answers Pancho. 'But instead of deserting our village perhaps we ought to try to change things first; that is part of our Christian undertaking to serve the community before looking for own comfort.'

'I'm not worried about our village; but I am worried about myself living in a backwater without prospects.'

'Don't be so selfish, man. There's no real progress in keeping your talents and energies for yourself, but there is when you use them for your fellow villagers. With your capacities, you could easily become a Health Promoter. I am already thinking of becoming a volunteer literacy leader.'

Talking points

▷ In your village, do most of the young people migrate?

▷ A lot of our young people know a lot about farming, and even have farmland, but they don't want to stay in the Andes. Why not?

What Pancho says is true: our Christian undertaking is to serve the community and not look for our own comfort first. And this is even truer if we have received the sacrament of confirmation.

Formerly the bishop used to go to all the parishes to confirm small children. Nowadays young people and adults who already have a dedication to their communities may ask the bishop to confirm them when he next visits their region.

Why has there been this change? Because confirmation is to help us dedicate ourselves more seriously to our neighbour. This dedication is not just restricted to our village community, but to all the poor and oppressed of the world.

When the apostles learned that Samaria had received the word of God, they sent Peter and John there. They went and laid hands on them, so that they might receive the Holy Spirit.   *(after Acts 8.14–17)*

When the bishop says to us at confirmation, 'Receive the Holy Spirit', he commands us to be like Jesus.

The Spirit of the Lord is upon me, for he has anointed me and sent me to bring the good news to the poor, to proclaim liberation to the captives, new sight to the blind, to set the slaves free and to announce the Lord's day of grace.   *(after Luke 4.18f.)*

When we help our brother
to shake off his oppression,
then we're making headway
towards your great liberation.

One day we shall surely
see you as you are,
give us all your Spirit
for your kingdom seems so far.

Let's walk with the Lord

See, they say, 'Our bones are dried up, our hope is gone, it is all up with us.' So prophesy and say to them, 'My people, I am putting my spirit in you so that you live again, and I am bringing you to your land, and you shall know that I, Yahweh, have said it and performed it.'
(after Ezek. 37.11–14)

Your marriage is very important

Eladio Chumpitaz, the Christian leader of Lucma, is talking with the village teacher, Nelly, and one of the elders, Walter Oyarce. The latter has done a lot of campaigning to organize a visit by the mayor in order that civil weddings may take place.

'Don Walter, it seems to me a good idea that the mayor should come here, but I think we also ought to have a few meetings to prepare things,' says Eladio.

'Naturally, so that the ceremony will go as smoothly as possible.'

'Not just that,' says the teacher, 'but, more important, so that the young persons know what marriage implies and involves.'

'How right you are. In this village a lot of young people get married without having the least idea of what love and understanding are,' says Eladio.

'Like my cousin, Heriberto Oyarce, for instance. He got married a short while ago, with a lot of expensive food and musicians from the town, and I've heard recently that he and his wife Leoncia are already fighting.'

'All right, then,' says Nelly the teacher. 'I propose that Don Eladio and myself prepare a few talks and discussions for the young people of the village.'

'Very good, I completely agree.'

'And perhaps we could do something for those already married but who are going through a difficult time with their partners,' adds Eladio.

Talking points

▷   What are the problems when persons get married very young?

▷   What sort of preparation should couples have?

The Bible teaches us that marriage is very important in the eyes of God. It shows us in a very simple manner the affection and tenderness shown by God when he created Adam and Eve.

And so God said:
  'Let us make human beings in our own image.'
  So God created man and woman and gave them his blessing. First God created the man. Then he thought, 'It is not good for the man to be alone. I will give him a companion and helper.'
  Then God created the woman and made her like the man. When he saw her, the man said, 'She is flesh of my flesh.'
                    (after Gen. 1.26–31; 2.18–23)

At the beginning God commanded men and women to work in the world, and so to be like their creator. Later, when the people of Israel were awaiting their freedom, we see that God needed married couples to carry out the plan of freedom; a man and a woman struggling together to achieve liberation are like God himself.

We farm-workers will never achieve liberation if we do not give importance to our married life. When we sow the maize or potato seed, we first prepare the soil well; if not, the plants will be weak and will not produce a good crop. It is the same in marriage. If we do not prepare well – and continue to nurture afterwards – then our marriage will not produce very much happiness; it will be a failure.

To love is to share,
forgetting your pleasure,
finding in sacrifice
an immense treasure.

How fine it is to live for love;
how like the life of God above,
giving joy and happiness,
giving yourself: that is love!

Let's walk with the Lord

David said to Abigail, 'Praised be God who has sent me to you today. Praised be your wisdom, for you have prevented me from shedding blood. But thank God above all that you have restrained me from doing you harm.'   (after I Sam. 25.32–34)

Walking together is better

Between Heriberto Oyarce and Leoncia Cubas things are daily getting worse. Their harvest has been disastrous this year, and Heriberto tries to forget his sorrows with alcohol and prostitutes. Leoncia feels resentful, and begins an affair with a younger man. While he is with her one day a condor carries off one of their chickens from the corral. At that moment Heriberto arrives home.

'You stupid, evil, dirty slut!' he shouts at Leoncia, while the young man makes his escape.

'You drunkard, you lazy womanizer,' replies Leoncia in the same tone.

'The next time you do that I'll kill you.'

Heriberto pushes Leoncia into a corner of the house, where she sits crying. Heriberto then slams the door as he leaves for the nearest liquor store, where he can drown his sorrows and forget his sadness.

'Why, oh why, did I marry that woman?' Heriberto laments.

Talking points

▷ Do you know of cases like this?

▷ Do some marriages break up for other kinds of reasons? What sort of reasons?

▷ Who is usually to blame in these situations?

When Jesus began to make known his way of liberation, he went to a wedding and helped the couple (read John 2. 1–11). In this way he teaches us that marriage is very important in the project of liberation.

Later on, the Pharisees asked him:

'Is it lawful for a man to send his wife away for any reason?' Jesus replied, 'You know that in the beginning God made man and woman and said that the man would leave father and mother to be with his wife. The two are then one body. They are thus no longer two, but one. And what God has joined together, no one may put apart.'
(Matt. 19.3–6).

The Pharisees opposed the liberation of the poor. All enemies of the people want the woman to be inferior, and the man to do everything alone. They know that that is the surest way to keep us all in subjection. But God thinks the opposite. Man alone cannot walk along the path of freedom; neither can woman. God wants man and woman to be closely united. God is there with them, because God is love; a love so great that life itself is sacrificed for the freedom of the poor and oppressed.

Here is a profound mystery. I am referring to Christ and his church. Wives, be obedient to your husbands; in so doing you show that you are obedient to the Lord. Husbands, love your wives as Christ loved his church, giving his life for it to make it his people. *(after Eph. 5.21–26)*

▷ What can we do to improve our married life?

Let's walk with the Lord

Love is patient, love acts kindly,
is not jealous, is not proud;
love refuses to remember sins long past;
if our struggle is inspired with love,
   victory is sure.

Love is as strong as death. Its arrows are fiery lances, flames of Yahweh. Even the waters of the sea cannot quench love or drown it. If anyone should try this with all his might, he will only earn contempt.
(after Song of Songs 8.6f.)

Married couples working together

Oscar Campos from Condorpampa has invited Rosa Hoyos from Pino Alto to come to one of his village meetings to explain certain principles of first aid.

Afterwards several of them are talking:

'I didn't see your wife here today, Don Oscar.'

'No, she never comes along to our meetings.'

'It's the same with my husband. He says I'm always gadding about, deserting him and the home.'

'My wife says the same thing about me and the smallholding, and there seems no way that she'll understand otherwise. I'm quite sure Juan Chuquimango and his wife Gumercinda would be in agreement.'

'I don't know them.'

'They're good sorts, and they work together. But I really don't know how we could go about organizing meetings for married couples.'

'Perhaps the first step ought to be to bring the women together separately, women like Elvira Montenegro, and Ambrosia Vasquez, and then it would be easier to get the husbands along at another date.'

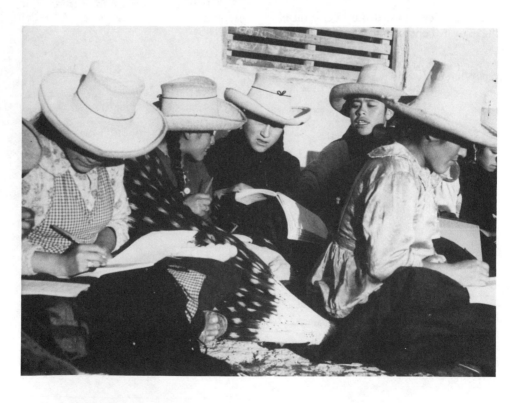

Talking points

▷ In your village, are there meetings for couples or for women?

▷ What do they do in these meetings?

▷ Where there are no such meetings, would it be worth while trying to begin them?

▷ What is the particular value in married couples' meetings?

In the journey towards liberation, a good couple of farm-workers can do a great deal. But if they unite with other married couples, they do an amazing amount.

Dedicated Christians must help each other to see the importance of a united couple and family. Many of us in the Andes are not married either civilly or religiously, though in the sight of God we have made a real intention to be united until death. But it would be a good thing for everybody to get married civilly, so that families can have more security, and so that the wife and children enjoy their legal rights. This way the husband will have taken his responsibilities even more seriously.

And the religious ceremony? When we husbands and wives have made, as Christians, a serious dedication to our communities, then we should seal that dedication before God and our neighbours. This way, Christ, by means of the sacrament of matrimony, will be more present in our life and our efforts.

Let's walk with the Lord

Yahweh, make this woman like Rachel and Leah, who both gave birth to the people of God. Because of her, may you prosper.
(after Ruth 11)

The priest assists us in our dedication

It is fiesta time in the village of Naranjo. The canal named 'Jesus Estela' has been finished and it is going to be inaugurated with a blessing. The priest from Chontapampa has been invited. Christian leaders from other villages are also present.

'You've completed a very important work with this canal,' the priest tells Oscar Campos and Eladio Chumpitaz.

'I believe it will be very useful to the communities,' says Oscar. 'Look, practically everybody is proud of having completed the job. Besides, most of them have smallholdings that will benefit directly from the irrigation water.

'Yes, and it has been the means of uniting the villagers as never before. Let's hope we'll maintain this unity so as to go on to other things that need doing in the community.'

The conversation is cut short when the chief village elder arrives and asks the priest to give the blessing.

'Excuse me, Don Jaime,' says the priest. 'The blessing is going to be given by the Christian leaders of the community, and not by me. This has been agreed on. They have accompanied this work

with their prayers, reflection and manual work. I will stand beside them.'

Talking points

▷ Why do the workers of Naranjo organize a fiesta to inaugurate the canal?

▷ Some people think that a blessing is only to mark the completion of a work. But for Christian leaders, is the blessing an ending, or a continuance of a new beginning?

▷ Can only a priest bless? Was it correct for lay Christian leaders to bless the canal?

In the Bible many men and women gave blessings. They blessed persons who had done some good for their people, rather than inanimate things. They also bless, or give thanks to, God.

And when the men and women of the Bible give blessings, they are renewing their own dedication to the service of their people, and their deliverance. The priest is here to help and encourage us to see life in the light of the good news, to understand what is for our good and what is for the good of the community. Obviously, he too blesses; he blesses us and God. The priest helps us to take responsibilities without waiting for him to always take the initiative.

▷ How is it in your community? Do you rely too much on the initiative of the priest?

▷ Why do we celebrate the 'pararaico' (fiesta in honour of a newly-built house) as in the photograph? How can we include a house-blessing in this ancient ceremony?

All hands together
to change the world.
All hands together
to till the land.
All hands together
to pull up the weeds.
All hands together
to share our joy.

Let's walk with the Lord

Jesus Christ gave his life for us. Thereby we know what love is. We too are obliged to give our lives for the brethren. If anyone sees his brother in need and closes his heart to him, how can the love of God be in him? (I John 3.16f.)

Our sick need us

In Pino Alto the old man Nashu is dying. The family have done everything possible to get medicine, but old Nashu does not get better. Now they want to call the priest to give him the last rites. But the towns of Chontapampa and Santiago de Llapa are far away. Rosa Hoyos hears of Nashu's plight and she goes to speak with Francisco Atalaya:

'Don Francisco, didn't we agree to take care of our sick and dying?'

'Yes, but we haven't done anything about it yet.'

'Exactly, but I believe we should. Old Nashu is dying, and Ana, Juan Malaver's wife is ill in bed.'

'I've also heard that there is illness in Teofilo Chuquimango's house in Condorpampa.'

'Well, it must be time to do something. We have a first aid box, but that is not enough. We must go and visit the sick and their families.'

'And not just to wail and mourn with the families, but to offer them some real comfort.'

Talking points

▷ What difficulties are there in the Andes for the sick and dying?

▷ What can the Christian leaders do in their visits to the sick?

▷ What have you done in your village?

▷ Do you have a first aid box? Who operates it? Why is it not enough?

Is any among you sick? Then call the elders of the community that they may pray for him in the name of the Lord. The prayer of faith will save the sick person, and if he has committed sins, they will be forgiven him.
(James 4.14f.)

An illness can unite us more with Christ. It unites the sick person with Christ because with the suffering the sick person can repent of his sins and think of Christ's cross; in that way he comes to know better the way of life. An illness also helps those of us who tend the sick person to be more united with each other and with Christ.

When we are with the sick person we can pray for him by placing a cross in his hands, saying: Brother, receive the cross on which Christ died for love of you. Offer your pain to God by means of Jesus Christ.

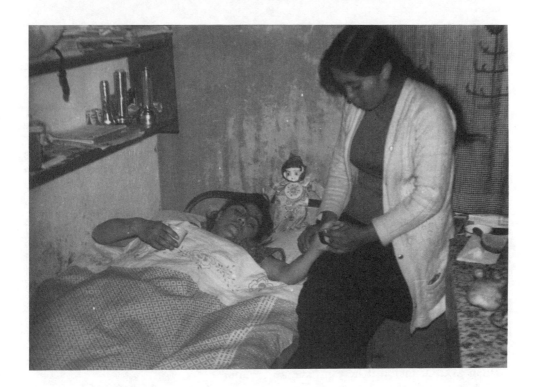

Our Christian dedication in the community should be shown by our active concern for the sick.

For example:

support the installation of a first aid box;

learn how to avoid different illnesses and help others to do the same, especially through hygiene and correct nutrition;

learn to use the natural herb medicines in our region;

learn how to pray for a sick person; when he is dying we cannot give him more medical help, but we can pray.

Let's walk with the Lord

You have laid much hard tribulation on me, but you will bring me to life again and I shall be comforted anew.

(after Ps. 71.20f.)

Making progress means forgiving one another

Even though Guzman Perez migrated to Lima, the Co-operative of sombrero-makers in Pino Alto continues to thrive. One day a member of the group, Juan, meets up with a friend, Asuncion, in Santiago de Llapa, and notices that he is wearing a new sombrero identical to those made in his Co-operative.

'Hello there, Asuncion! I see you've bought one of our sombreros!'

'That's right, Juan. But it was expensive: I paid thirty dollars for it last week.'

'Thirty dollars? That's impossible; Emilio Vasquez, our Co-op salesman, tells us that he sells them at only twenty-five dollars.'

'No, Juan. I paid thirty dollars.'

Juan asks Asuncion if he can have a closer look at the sombrero, and once he is convinced that it really is from his Co-operative, he returns to his associates with the sad news that Emilio has been cheating them all. The whole group meets, and confronted with the evidence, Emilio admits what he has done:

'Ah, brothers, how ashamed I feel. I met up with Don Abelardo Julca, who said I was a fool not to earn more, and I really did need the money.'

'That is what selfishness does to a man,' complains Francisco Atalaya.

Then the group punishes Emilio severely and throws him out. As a result of this, the poor man goes completely bankrupt and the Co-operative dissolves soon after.

Talking points

▷ What do you think of what Emilio did?

▷ Do you think the severe punishment of the group was justified?

▷ Can a group be saved and purified by throwing out members who commit errors?

God does not act in this way. Let us see:

The tax collectors and sinners all came to Jesus to hear him, so the Pharisees and lawyers criticized him:

'This man accepts sinners and eats with them.'

Then Jesus told them this parable:

'Which of you, having a hundred sheep and losing one, does not leave the ninety nine in a field and go out in search of the lost one until he finds it? And when he finds it, he joyfully puts it on his shoulders and, when he comes home, summons his friends and neighbours and says to them, 'Rejoice with me, for I have found my sheep which was lost.' *(Luke 15.1–7)*

God wants us to act like him. That is how we are children of God. Moreover, in the Lord's Prayer Jesus taught us to pray, 'Forgive us as our debts, as we have forgiven our debtors.'

Peter once asked Jesus, 'Lord, if my brother sins against me, how often shall I forgive him? Seven times?'

Jesus replied, 'I tell you, not seven times but seventy-seven times.' *(Matt. 18.21f.)*

By that Jesus meant to say that we must always forgive. And he went on to tell a parable about a man who would not forgive. He ended with the words:

So too will my heavenly Father do to you if each one of you does not forgive his brother from the heart. *(Matt. 18.35)*

A few weeks later, during the Sunday prayer-meeting, members of the Co-operative are thinking about these texts and decide they must stop being vengeful and forgive. So they make plans to speak with Emilio, ask his pardon for what they have done and have a celebration of their reconciliation.

In this way the group can start up once again. Forgiveness is a step from death to life.

▷ How can a rural community express its collective forgiveness?

We are all sinners,
we confess our guilt;
we have gone far away
from the path of love.

Have mercy upon us,
Father above;
we your dear children,
trust in your love.

Let's walk with the Lord

Love your enemies and do good to those who hate you. Pray for those who spite you and do evil to you, that you may be the children of your Father in heaven. He makes his sun rise on the just and the unjust. *(after Matt. 5.14)*

How God forgives us

The pardon given to Emilio Vasquez by the sombrero Co-operative helps him to put in order certain domestic problems between himself and his wife, Ambrosia.

Emilio had been stealing, but there had been a motive. One day he had discovered that Ambrosia was having an affair with his cousin Nicolas Cubas from Quinua. Ambrosia had defended herself:

'I need to buy things for the children, and if you are so useless you cannot earn more money then I have to do things my own way.'

It was then that Emilio gave in to the temptation to earn more money from the sale of sombreros, deceiving his associates.

When the associates forgave him, things began to change between Emilio and Ambrosia. Both began to realize the gravity of what they had done to each other. One day they were able to say:

'But Ambrosia, whatever made you act like that with my cousin?'

'I'm really sorry now. Nicolas is also very sorry and wants to ask your forgiveness. He wants to make things up. "When cousins fall out, the heavens shout," as the saying goes.'

'I forgive you, Ambrosia, and I must forgive my cousin Nicolas as well. I think I understand for the first time the words we pray every day: "Forgive us our trespasses, as we forgive those who trespass against us."'

Talking points

▷ True married love is when a husband and wife know how to forgive each other. Have you ever had experience of this forgiveness?

▷ Why is adultery worse between close relations?

Jesus Christ attaches great importance to forgiveness. If somebody has sinned it is as if he has died. If we forgive him, it is like giving him life. If nobody forgives him, then he shuts himself in on himself; he cannot have life. We are all sinners, but we are fond of condemning others. Jesus was not like this. We see him in the case of the woman taken in adultery.

He said:
'Let him among you who is without sin throw the first stone.'
And when her accusers had left, Jesus asked her:
'Woman, where are those who accused you? Has no one condemned you?'
'No, Lord, no one.'
'Then nor do I. Go your way and from henceforth sin no more.'
(after John 8.7–11)

Jesus gave an example we all know very well: that of the prodigal son who went to ask his father's forgiveness:

'Father, I have sinned against heaven and before you.'
But the father said to his servants.
'Go and get the best garment and put it on him. Let's eat and celebrate. For this my son was dead and is alive again.'
(after Luke 15.21–24)

Jesus left us something very precious: the sacrament of reconciliation.

If your brother has wronged you, then speak with him before two witnesses. If he listens, you have gained a brother. If he does not listen, then bring more witnesses. If he still does not listen, then tell the community. Truly I say to you, that what you bind on earth shall be bound in heaven, and what you loose on earth shall be loosed in heaven.'   *(Matt. 18.15–18)*

And the apostle James tells us:

Acknowledge your sins to one another and pray for one another, and you will be healed.   *(James 5.16)*

The group at Pino Alto celebrated with great joy the mutual reconciliation. Even the priest came from Chontapampa. Ambrosia, Emilio and Nicolas were all there. Everybody finished up by understanding the meaning of the sacrament of reconciliation, because they had just experienced it.

▷   How do we celebrate the sacrament of reconciliation (formerly known as confession)?

Let's walk with the Lord

My people said, 'Yahweh has forsaken me and the Lord has forgotten me.' Can a woman forget her child, a mother her own son? And even if you forget your children, I will not forget you.   *(after Isa. 49.14f.)*

Fraternal meetings are important

At the next Sunday meeting it is decided to celebrate the new beginning of the sombrero Co-operative. There is a lot of discussion about how to celebrate.

Salatiel thinks that everything that is being done and is going on in Pino Alto must be mentioned and celebrated.

For Rosa Hoyos the celebration is mostly to renew their Christian dedication, because she remembers how difficult things were at the beginning with the Christian leaders.

Emilio Vasquez is celebrating chiefly his reconciliation with his working companions, and his determination to work honestly in the future.

For Juan and Ana Malaver it is a celebration in thanksgiving for Ana's recovery from illness, as well as the new sympathy and understanding that has grown between them because of the illness.

'If we celebrate all our efforts and sacrifices we can give thanks for our modest achievements,' says Francisco Atalaya. 'And when we look at the life of Christ we realize once again that he is the one who is always giving us new life like this.'

Talking points

▷ Do you have Christian meetings in your village?

▷ What are the occasions when you meet together?

▷ Why is it difficult for farm-workers to speak as openly as they did in Pino Alto?

On one day of the week we assembled for the Lord's Supper. Paul spoke to those gathered together. But because he wanted to move on the next day, his talk lasted well into the night. Countless lamps were burning in the room on the upper floor where we were gathered. (after Acts 20.7–9)

It is not mere chance that the Christians mentioned by Luke met on the first day of the week. On this point the Christians had separated themselves from the Jews, replacing Saturday with Sunday as the holy day. It was on a Sunday that Jesus rose from the dead; so in this manner they could proclaim their faith. When Christians meet together, they are not satisfied with just reading texts from the Bible, but they try to discuss among themselves how to apply God's word to their daily lives and problems.

There is one important sign that expresses well our unity with Christ: it is 'the breaking of the bread', as mentioned in the above passage from the Acts of the Apostles.

▷ What does the 'breaking of the bread' mean?

Let's walk with the Lord

I pray for all who hear me and believe in the word of my disciples. I pray that they may all be one. As you are in me and I in you, so too they should be one in us. Then the world will believe that you have sent me.
(after John 17.20)

'Take and eat, this is my body . . .'

What is the 'breaking of the bread'? Francisco Atalaya explains:

'It is a simple meal with bread and wine during which we eat the body of the Lord.

We remember the freedom he has won for us, and we "communicate" with him as a pledge of our desire to share in his dedication to total freedom.'

When Absalon Mejia from Las Lagunas hears this, it reminds him of something that happened to him: he was unjustly accused of having burned the house of Encarnacion Llamoctanta, and of having stolen a pair of oxen from Venancio. Since Absalon had no money, he could not pay for a good lawyer to prove that he had not done these things. As a result Absalon was sentenced to two years imprisonment.

At the end of the two years, Absalon returned to his family. There was great happiness, and they celebrated Absalon's freedom with a special family meal.

Talking points

▷ Have you ever had a similar reason for having a special meal with your family or friends?

Such a meal is like the last supper of Jesus and his disciples.

Take and eat, for this is my body which is given for you. Take and drink, for this is my blood which is shed for you. Do this to remember me.
          (after Luke 22.17–19; I Cor. 11.24–26)

Jesus explains the meaning of this bread:

The bread which I give you is my flesh, and I give it for the life of the world.
          (after John 6.48–51)

Every day we have to eat, otherwise we should die.

If we do not eat the meal of Jesus, we shall not have God's life in us.

Since everybody who shares in the meal of Jesus shares the same bread, then there must be a special bond of friendship between them.

In his first letter to the Christian community in the city of Corinth, Paul complains that there is no union between the Christians:

Above all they have told me that there are divisions among you. When you come together you do not really celebrate the Lord's Supper.
          (after I Cor. 11.18–20)

Eating the body of the Lord in a united way, we can continue advancing along the way of freedom. If we are not united, then freedom is not possible. The Lord's body is the food that gives us all the strength we need to be able to advance in spite of difficulties and contradictions.

▷ How do *we* celebrate the Lord's supper?

We cannot walk ahead
without the Master's bread;
give us always that food,
your body and blood, O Lord.
Let us all eat of this bread,
the bread of unity;
the Lord has made us one in faith,
in hope and charity.

Let's walk with the Lord

Whenever you eat this bread and drink this cup, you proclaim the death of the Lord till he comes again. So anyone who behaves unworthily when he eats the bread of the Lord and drinks from his cup, is guilty of the body and blood of the Lord.
          (I Cor. 11.26f.)

The way continues . . .

At the meeting in Pino Alto, Francisco Atalaya says:

'As far as I can see, these things we have mentioned and many others besides are like what happens on a journey. For example we know that "many hands make light work" and that is why the sombrero Co-operative is making good progress; because they share the work and the profits.'

'And of course,' says Rosa Hoyos, 'it is important to be sure that we are journeying along the right way; sometimes we need somebody to tell us which turnings to take, and how to take good short cuts. That is life.'

'Since God is in everything we do, he is just like our pure mountain air that we breathe in during long journeys. And sometimes we have to rest a while so as to breathe better: perhaps that's a bit like our weekly meetings,' says Salatiel Rojas.

'But the way isn't always smooth,' says Juan Malaver. 'There are stones and mud and so on. What does that mean?'

'It means that God's kingdom hasn't come to us completely yet. The journey isn't over, the way continues.'

I am the Way, the Truth and the Life.
(John 14.6)

Talking points

▷   The majority of the cases in this book are taken from real-life experiences along the way towards freedom. Do what the villagers of Pino Alto have done: see Christ in your experiences along the way of life.

Come Holy Spirit, come, for we need you;
you are our strength, help us to heed you.

Help us follow Jesus – he is our way –
so come to glory on the final day.

Guide us at all times, with your light from above;
help us not to extinguish the fire of your love.

Let's walk with the Lord

Open up the way for the people!
Prepare the road! Prepare the road!
Make it clean, leave no stones on it!
Raise high the banner, that all may see it!
Say to my people, 'Look, your saviour comes.'
They will call you 'The holy people, the people whom the Lord has freed.'
(after Isa. 62.10–12)

Awake!

Yes, the new consciousness has arrived;
like a thief in the night . . . here it is in the pregnant
    silence,
in the prophetic darkness.

We feel it beating in the old body of the race,
as if the dried-up spring should suddenly burst with
    water.
The dead heart, the secret entrails, reinitiate the
    dynamism of a pendulum . . .

Come now, for the new consciousness has arrived.
New sap is throbbing through the old trunk.

               (Luis Valcarcel, in *Storm in the Andes*)

Awake!

Oscar Campos has climbed to the mountain tops early one morning. Now, when the first rays of light are bathing the valley below, he stops to look. And he thinks:

'There are the villagers of Pino Alto, Quinua, Loma and Condorpampa. Well below them, in a warmer part, is Naranjo. I can just about see the abandoned estate-house of San Jacinto. In the distance I can see the shining roofs of Chontapampa.

Higher up there is the road to Pedregal and El Dorado mine. On the other side is Santiago de Llapa.'

Oscar things about all these places . . . the struggles and difficulties they have known . . . their Christian groups . . . the death of Jesus Flores and Jesus Estela . . . the exploitation that continues . . . the evil life of Venancio Chavez and men like him.

Here and there the houses emit the smoke and the fresh perfume of eucalyptus that betoken the preparations for breakfast.

People are waking. Some open the gates of their corrals, to release the animals. Others walk spade in hand to begin the work of the day.

'Yes,' thinks Oscar, 'it is high time for us to awake. Not only from the daily routine of the farmstead. We must awake from our ignorance, from our sloth, from our fear. We must all awake and walk firmly and resolutely along the path that leads to our own freedom, that Jesus came to bring us!'

Wa – ake u – up! Wa – ake u – p!

And the cry of Oscar Campos echoed all round the valley.

Description of people and places in the imaginary province of San Andres

Colpa   Artemio Becerra and his wife Clothilde own a village shop outside which they organize a fiesta (48). Artemio is opposed to any changes in the fiesta of Pampa Verde for reasons of self-interest (218). He chooses Venancio Chavez to be godfather to his son (340f.).

Ambrosio Maita is justice of the peace and tries to act in a just manner (220).

Condorpampa   Oscar Campos is the principal catechist of the village. His family fail to understand his dedication (104f.). He feels the presence of Christ at the weekly meetings (138). He is involved with the scuffle with police over the Pastoral Centre in Chontapampa (84). He tries to construct a road to the village, but the attempt fails when there are no more free food hand-outs (200, 224). This is an important experience for him and he feels the burden of leadership (224). It compels him to reflect (226) and at a later meeting with other Christian leaders in Chontapampa he shares his worries with the others (316). He insists that the church is made up of people (290). He is one of the most active leaders at the meeting in Chontapampa (296–324). After this meeting he directs the celebration of the 'wake' for Jesus Estela (332) and later takes part in the work on the new 'Jesus Estela Canal' (334). He is present at the blessing of the canal (350). He invites Rosa Hoyos to visit his village to speak about a first aid box (348). He wants to organize meetings to help improve family life (348). He has the final words of the book (366).

Juan Chuquimango and his wife Gumercinda are a dedicated couple. We first meet them doing their daily work (12, 14). They give lodging to Pancho Escobar of Quinua (50). They are aware of their village's problems, such as theft (230f.), and they are keen on taking part in the meetings for married persons proposed by Oscar Campos (348).

Teofilo Chuquimango, brother of Juan, receives no medical attention for his wife Clemencia in Chontapampa (72).

Elvira and Lucha are two village women who have a hard life (20) and who would stand to benefit from a meeting for women (348).

Rogelio Mego has his cow stolen (230).

Las Lagunas   Encarnacion Llamoctanta is the Christian leader of this village. He is in favour of collectivizing the smallholdings (42); although this plan fails, he continues to publicize his opinions, and his house is burned down by Venancio Chavez as a result (210). Encarnacion is active at the meeting in Chontapampa (300ff.).

Santos Llamoctanta, brother of Encarnacion, suffers because of his son's irrelevant education at the Secondary School (76).

Venancio Chavez owns 800 hectares of land in the village and is the richest man in the zone. He has a large shop in Chontapampa (80). He exploits poor farm-workers like Benigno Rojas and others (38, 63, 112). He is opposed to the collectivizing of the land and orders the burning of Encarnacion Llamoctanta's house (210). He takes advantage of the new road to Pedregal to build a shop (316). He is probably involved in the death of Jesus Flores (300). Has several godsons who work for him (341f.).

Tomasa Chavez, poor sister of Venancio, falls ill (194) and dies (196).

Anselmo Vasquez is the village pessimist (288).

Absalon Mejia is imprisoned unjustly, accused of having set fire to the house of Encarnacion Llamoctanta. He leaves prison after two years and celebrates with his family (360).

Loma Jesus Flores is the Christian leader of the village. He is present during the troubles at the Pastoral Centre in Chontapampa (84). Tries to put heart into discouraged farm-workers (148) and organizes a written protest against the village authorities (132). This creates enemies, not just in Loma but also in the town of Santiago de Llapa (250). During the fiesta (252) Jesus clashes with traders at the church entrance (254) and after a farewell supper with friends he is betrayed (258) and sent to jail by the town authorities (260); there he is tortured (262), and on leaving jail he is killed (264f.). In spite of his death the activities initiated by him continue to thrive, all of which is remembered during the first anniversary celebration of his death (269).

Artemio Cotrina is another Christian leader of Loma. Accompanies Jesus Flores in his efforts (148, 198), but not in his death. Takes part in Christian leaders' meeting in Chontapampa (304ff.). In the village of Naranjo participates in communal work and blessing of the 'Jesus Estela Canal' (334, 350). Sees water as fundamental to life (330) and prepares baptisms in the village of Quinua (336f.).

Marcial Luna converses with Hugo Cruzado about the future of their sons (22); tells the story of the solar eclipse (36).

Pedro Ruiz is a person who keeps to himself (64).

Juana Mego is glad that women are allowed an active part in village meetings (148).

Lucma Nelly Vargas is the village school-teacher; her school interests her greatly (53); also preoccupied with problems of villagers (344).

Walter Oyarce is an elder of the village. Collaborates with school-teacher for the good of the village, and promotes civil weddings. (53, 75, 286, 344). Converses with Oscar Campos about building a church for the village (290).

Lucmapampa José Blanco and Maria Silva are young lovers; they wish to marry, but Maria is found to be pregnant (142); they discover this to be part of God's plan, and go to Chontapampa to get their birth certificates (152). In the chapters that follow the birth of their son is described. To escape an epidemic of whooping-cough they travel to Lima (165) where they live in a shanty town.

Romulo Santisteban is the new school-teacher, and everything he does is criticized by villagers (214).

Naranjo Jesus Estela is the Christian leader of the village. When the irrigation canal is destroyed by the rains he proposes its reconstruction (176f.). He is concerned with the house of Amalia Huayac, destroyed by the same disaster (186). Takes an active part in leaders' meeting in Chontapampa (296–324). Dies when an avalanche falls on construction workers (332). A 'solidarity wake' is celebrated (332) after which the new canal is given the name 'Jesus Estela' (334).

Alejo Salvatierra and his wife Maria are a couple from the village. They have just built themselves a new house (28); they say the life of a farm-worker is a hard life (32). They have to travel continually between their tiny but dispersed plots of land (181).

Amalia Huayac, a poor widow who loses her house in the rains. The poorest of her neighbours help her build a new house (186).

Pampa Verde Arnulfo Perez is the churchwarden. He is at a meeting of people who want to ring some changes in the celebration of the annual fiesta (58). He looks after the statue of Saint John and benefits financially from this (61). With Artemio Becerra and others he opposes the changes in the fiesta (218). He is present at the meeting in Chontapampa and begins to change his attitude, though his understanding of Christian dedication is still scanty (304, 318).

Clodomiro Paisig is Justice of the Peace of the village. In a dispute over boundaries, he pronounces in favour of the man who gives him a bribe (56).

Teodosio Cruzado is a village elder, taking his part in communal tasks (69).

Candelario Perez is a conscientous farm-worker (202).

Pedregal Fulgencio Chuquilin, strong-charactered village elder. In spite of having assisted at parish training-courses, he uses brute force to make people do communal tasks (66, 69, 282).

Asuncion Vasquez, former miner, rejoices at the news of the miners' strike in El Dorado (182).

Anaximandro Marin, young man who migrates to Lima (106).

Pancracio Quispe, cousin of Anaximandro, loses his house in a fire; his wife dies later. He is helped by his sister Teresa (46f.). Has witnessed the exploitation of the workers in Lima (106).

The shepherds of the village receive good news, and visit the new-born child in Chontapampa, taking him presents (156f.).

Pino Alto Francisco Atalaya is a Christian leader in this village. Has a good family (237), and is chosen as leader for this reason. Criticizes Avelino Huaman for his failure to keep his promise (238). Assumes responsibility for the construction of the village church and as a consequence his farm-work suffers (241). Is domineering (244) but assists at the Sunday prayer-meetings (246, 358, 362). Takes an active part in Chontapampa pastoral meeting (302). Together with Rosa Hoyos organizes help for the sick (352).

Rosa Hoyos is another Christian leader. Knows how to encourage parents (237). Husband gets annoyed because she spends much time with her first aid box (241). Asks for recognition of leaders' faults (244), actively present at Sunday meetings (246, 358, 362). Assists at Chontapampa pastoral meeting (296–324). Spends time visiting sick (304, 352). Goes to Condorpampa at invitation of Oscar Campos to talk about her first aid box, and they also talk about marriage preparation (348).

Guzman Perez is another Christian leader in the village. Is imprisoned for defending the Pastoral Centre in Chontapampa (84), knows how to animate neighbours for communal work (237), but then gets into trouble for having begun a sombrero Co-operative (241, 278), until he migrates to Lima (284). His failing as leader was not to prepare well for baptism, and getting drunk (244).

Avelino Huaman is chosen as Christian leader (237) but lets down the group and eventually leaves them altogether (238).

Juan Malaver is a villager who ill-treats his wife and children, but is converted (276). Celebrates his reconciliation at Sunday meeting (358).

Ana Lopez is wife to Juan Malaver. Complains of a hard life (18). Later falls ill (276) and Rosa Hoyos visits her (304).

Emilio Vasquez is an impoverished maker of sombreros (24), exploited by Abelardo Julca (63). Joins group of sombrero makers (286), later swindling the other members (354) because he needs money. The other sombrero makers finally pardon Emilio his lapse (355). His wife is unfaithful to him (356) but is later reconciled to Emilio.

Abelardo Julca buys and sells sombreros. He exploits (63) but is not such a bad person. He does not want to become a member of the sombrero Co-operative (216), and is the man responsible for persuading Emilio Vasquez to deceive his fellow members (354).

Salatiel Rojas is a devout man, but with immature ideas about prayer (246). As he participates more and more in the Sunday prayer group, he changes his ideas, and at the end he wants to 'celebrate' everything that has happened in his village (358).

Quinua   Roberta Villanueva is the school-teacher. She comes from Lima and is unhappy in her job (52).

Florencio Rojas quarrels with his wife Maria about the education of their children (54). He does not want to attend a pre-baptismal talk given by Artemio Cotrina (336). When he attends the talk he quarrels with Artemio (338).

Nicolas Cubas is a farm-worker. He arranges the civil wedding of his daughter Leoncia through bribery (74). He is a womanizer, and Ambrosia Huaman is one of his conquests.

Heriberto Oyarce is cousin to Walter Oyarce of Lucma. Has a shot-gun wedding with Leoncia Cubas (74). The marriage is a disaster (346f.).

Pancho Escobar is a youth of the village. When asked to help in a literacy programme he scorns the idea because the job will be unpaid (312), though later he changes his attitude and undertakes the work. He discusses this with Feliberto Carranza, who has decided to migrate (342).

Eleuterio Flores is cousin to Jesus Flores. Approves of pre-baptismal talks given by Artemio Cotrina (336ff.).

Angela Flores, sister of Eleuterio, has a few old-fashioned ideas about baptism (336).

San Andres de Chontapampa   Largest town of the region and capital of the province. A big meeting of farm-workers takes place (8). Dr Vargas neglects his work at the Health Centre (72), the Head Teacher has alienating ideas on education (76). On Sundays the farm-workers come to the town market (78), where there is much injustice (79). One of the principal shops belongs to Venancio Chavez, a good example of capitalism in practice (80). Alberto Gomez, another shopkeeper, advises Glicerio Longa to go in for 'holy resignation' (82f.). The town authorities prevent the parish house being converted into a pastoral centre for the farm-workers (84). The arrival of the bus from Lima is a cause of joy (86), but every Monday there are migrations to the coast (88f.). Those who migrate often return for the annual fiesta (90). Public transport is bad (92). The real activists in the parish are all farm-workers (94). Problems with the Co-operative (96f.). José and Maria Blanco from Lucmapampa are marginalized by the town when Maria is about to give birth (152); her son born in a corral (154), visited by shepherds (156f.), and by three professionals (160f.); the baptism takes place (158), followed by their removal to Lima because of an epidemic of whooping-cough (165). Later on an important meeting takes place in the town with representatives of most of the villages (296–324).

San Jacinto   Eladio Chumpitaz is the local Christian leader, and is also responsible for Lucma, where he talks about the problem of private smallholdings (41), and where he works for the benefit of married couples (344). In San Jacinto he explains what life was like in the past under the big landowners (115). Eladio is imprisoned for his role in the formation of a trade union (118), and speaks about the selfishness in the sharing out of land (122). In a conversation with Agapito Nunez, tries to convince the old man that real religion implies the liberation of the poor and humble (184). Takes active part in Chontapampa pastoral meeting (296–324) and thanks Christians for visiting him in prison (304). During the meeting he tells how he learned to struggle fearlessly against the big landowners (310). He is present at the blessing of the 'Jesus Estela' canal in Naranjo (350).

Agapito Nunez is an old man who recounts the struggles in the days when San Jacinto was a feudal estate (100f.). Does not believe religion can bring liberation (126.).

Juan Vasquez is a dynamic type (288f).

Santiago de Llapa   Second town of the province. Here occurs the death of Jesus Flores during the annual fiesta (252–65).

Hugo Fernandez is cousin to Artemio Cotrino and is a salesman for whom economic progress is everything (120).

Shego is another commercial traveller whose capitalistic ideas about life give sorrow to his brother, Nico (174).

The parish priest is one of those who are opposed to Jesus Flores (250, 254, 258).